THE SAVING LOVE
COLLECTION

Dawn Huskey

To order additional copies of this book, contact:
Xlibris
844-714-8691
www.Xlibris.com
Orders@Xlibris.com
836422

CONTENTS

LOVED TWICE

THE LOVE THAT SAVED ME

A BEST FRIEND'S LOVE

A SURPRISE LOVE

LOVE IN THE RAIN

THE SAVING LOVE COLLECTION

This collection of stories shows how love can save a person. Will they survive the attacks of the jealous and possessive? Will their relationships be intact when it is all said and done? They all discover how love works as they go through challenges. They feel immediate attraction when they finally find the love they have been searching for.

Please follow the lives of Michael and Marie in "My Dream to My Nightmare." They are haunted by possession and diverted identity.

Katie and Travis as they fight jealousy in "Love."

Sarah and Scott as they fight a stalker from the past in "Loved Twice."

Seth and Jamie as they battle the dark past in "The Love That Saved Me."

Dawn and Jason as they discover their friendship goes deeper in "A Best Friend's Love."

Tori and Ryan as the love they share is started by surprise in "A Surprise Love."

Sean and Ashlee as they rekindle a forgotten attraction in "Love in the Rain."

DEDICATION

To all those who believe love can change them. To the love of my life Michael Jason Huskey.

MY DREAM TO MY NIGHTMARE

Dawn Huskey

INTRODUCTION

My name is Michael, and my life is not what I wanted it to be. I was in high school when I met her. The love of my life and my very first and last girlfriend. We were married after graduating from high school. That was five years ago, but now my wife is missing, and I am going crazy. She has only been missing for two days now, and she is pregnant with our second child. My daughter is four, and she keeps asking for her mom. She looks like her a lot; and every time I look at her, I cry. I keep thinking about our nine-year life together and how much I miss her and can't wait until she is back in my arms again. I know the police are on the case, and they are doing all that they can to find her. I have to keep my mind on her. If I don't, I feel like I am going to lose her. So let me take you back to when we first met.

CHAPTER 1

The First Years

FEBRUARY 14, 2011

Michael's first year in high school and five months into it is when he sees her. He was carrying his lunch tray and did not realize he was staring at her so much that he bumped right into her and dumped what was left of his lunch on her. Shock and then realization crossed her face when her eyes locked on his. She immediately said "I am sorry" and started helping me clean up the tray. Michael said, "It is my fault. I could not stop looking at you. You are beautiful, and I want you in my life [in his mind, he said, *Oh my god, I can't believe I just said that out loud. What am I going to do now?*]." She smiled and said, "My name is Marie. You are sweet. Do you dump your tray on every girl you met?"

He smiled and said, "Only the beautiful one. My name is Michael." As he touched her hand, his heart skipped a beat. Michael couldn't stop smiling. "Can I walk you to your next class, Marie?"

"Sure, you can."

It was all over for him then. Michael declared that Marie would be my first and last girlfriend, and he knew from that point on that she would be his wife someday. No more searching, no more looking for the woman of his dreams. She is here finally. For the next five months, Michael proved it to her. She decided to give him her hand as my girlfriend a week after the tray incident. Once summer was upon them, and they were inseparable. If they were not together, they would be calling or texting each other. They met each other's parents, and their parents started hanging out together. Michael even started to call her parents mom and dad; she did the same to his parents as well.

Over their high school years, Michael was protective of her and would not let anyone put her down. She was even hospitalized in their tenth grade when her head hit the goal post in her soccer game. Michael would not leave her side the whole time in the hospital. She had a concussion and was in a coma for three days. Michael would pace for most of the time and pray that she would be okay. He wanted her to wake up and see him there. He wanted to feel her arms around his neck as he kissed her. He wanted to see her sweet smile and hear her voice again. Those three days felt like three years. Finally, she opened her eyes and smiled when her eyes landed on him. Three days after that, she came home and was able to go back to school; but she could not play soccer for another month after, which lasted past the season.

Some kids did not like their relationship. Others did. They have a unique relationship. He doesn't see many relationships like theirs around them. Their classmate would tease them. But they did not seem to care. Marie is white, and Michael is black. As Michael looks at her. Marie has beautiful long brown hair with waves that highlight her face. Her eyes are so full of life, and I drown in them every time I look at her. Her skin freckles when kissed by the sun. Her smile is enough to brighten up my mood when I feel down. Her smile also tells me things are going to be okay. She would call me her knight in shining armor.

Michael's skin is light like milk chocolate. His hair is in braids that just touch my shoulders. She would say that Michael's dimples make her smile, and my sport-like body is always hiding from her, (until our wedding night, but that part will come later), but she knew it's there. I also play soccer, and I run track. I am also a weightlifter. She would also say that she gets lost in Michael's deep-brown eyes. None of what kids are saying bothers him. The only opinions he care about are the ones from their best friends and family. Michael's friends and family love Marie. Michael knows her friends and family love him.

Her best friend's name is Rue, and they have been friends since birth basically. Michael's best friend's name is Ben. They have been friends since Michael moved into the neighborhood. Tenth grade, the group grew bigger by seven more people. They had become our best friends as well. We would hang out on the weekends; and as soon as summer hit, we all would become inseparable. Marie's brother Greg and his two brothers, Steven, and Nick, became a part of that group as well. Marie and her brother are close, and she could not leave her little brother behind. Michael's two little brothers got a long with Marie's brother very well.

During their eleventh grade, a new girl started at their school, and she seemed attracted to Michael. That did not sit well with Marie. This attraction created a little rift in their relationship. She did anything and everything she could just to stay near Michael. Every time Marie would see Michael coming up the hallway, she would also see her walking near him or next to him. When Marie was not within eyeshot of Michael, Emily would make her move. She flirted with him, but he ignored it. She would ask for Michael's number. He would not give it to her. Michael told her that he was off the market, but that did not faze her. She still came after him. Marie confronted her and warned her to stay away from him, but she did not listen. Emily would leave notes in his locker and stick around to see if he would read them. He would hand them to Marie, and Marie tore them up and put them in the trash.

One time, Emily followed Michael home and tried to allow herself in, but he barricaded her out with his brothers' help. Emily got desperate one morning and walked up to Michael and planted a kiss right on his lips in front of Marie. His hands were in his pockets, and he tried to pull away, but she wrapped her arms around his head so that he could not get away. When she released him, Marie knocked her flat on her butt. When Emily got up, she punched Marie back; and the fight began. Michael desperately pried Emily off Marie; and once Emily released Marie, He moved to Marie and held her and moved her away from Emily as Emily punched at his back, trying to get to Marie.

Finally, Ben was between him and Emily, pushing her all the way to the principal's office. Michael picked up Marie and rushed her to the nurse's office. Her eyes, nose, and mouth were bleeding. Her face was starting to swell. He was concerned about Marie's head because of her accident last year. Emily escaped with a black eye and a split lip.

Emily was suspended for two weeks, and Marie got two days. Emily's parents were concerned that Marie's parents were going to sue. They decided it was best to move Emily to an all-girls school. After a week, Marie's face had only little evidence that something had happened at all. Marie's head checked out to be okay! After that, people knew not to mess with me or Marie.

Their junior prom came around, and Michael was excited not to have to worry about asking anyone out because he had a date already. She took his breath away when he saw her as she walked down the steps in her purple short dress and her purple strappy shoes. Her dress came down to between her knee and her upper thigh. The skirt flared out a little. The dress also had crisscrossing straps on top of her chest, and it showed just a bit of cleavage. The dress had a little sparkle to it as light hit it. She was so beautiful in that dress. My eyes never left her the whole night. Michael thought to himself. Marie is mine, and I am hers. I can't believe that she is still mine to this day.

PRESENT DAY

These are the thoughts going through Michael's mind. Where is my wife? I am pacing again. I have not slept in two days. My parents and our friends are worried. They all have been at my house since I noticed she did not come back. I did not get a phone call yet demanding money. My wife just vanished. I pray that our three-month pregnancy is doing okay. Please, God, bring back my wife. Protect her until you can bring her back to me. Protect our baby inside of her. I will do anything to see her smile, to hear her laugh, to look in her beautiful eyes and drown in them once again.

Michael never thought of himself as an emotional person, but now it is hard to fight the emotions. It is hard to not be a puddle of a blabbering mess on the floor, but he just let it all go. Michael hits the floor and cries. Sobs came out like a swollen river. Savanna, Marie and Michael's four-year-old daughter came over to him and wraps her tiny arms around his neck, and he wraps his arms around her tiny body. He held her as both of us cried. In her tiny voice, she said,

"Daddy, Mommy and the baby will come home. God will bring them home. Just you wait and see."

May 30, 2014

Their senior prom night was another night that took my breath away. Marie's dress was floor length that had a split up her right leg that went up just past her knee. The top of the dress had spaghetti straps and scooped front that showed off a little more cleavage than her junior prom dress, and this dress was light blue. On the straps had sequence the length of the straps. That night, Michael had a plan that he prepared for all year. She had no idea that their parents and brothers were there. When Michael walked onstage, she thought he was going to announce our senior-class king and queen because he was the class president. She was shocked at the words that came out of his mouth.

"Marie please join me onstage." She made her way up. "I have loved you since first colliding with you. I knew right then that I wanted you in my life. What were the words you heard me say that day?"

As Marie stepped up to the microphone, she said, "You said that I was beautiful and that you wanted me in your life." As she was saying that Michael dropped to one knee and opened a box. She looked at him and smiled. "Marie, please be in my life forever. Please do me the pleasure of being my wife. Will you marry me?" Her tears were streaming down her cheeks, but they were not sad tears. They were tears of joy.

"Yes, Michael, I would love and be honored you as your wife." He slipped the ring on, and the audience cheered and clapped. Their family rushed up and joined them onstage. Michael stepped to the microphone again to make another presentation. "I now have the pleasure of announcing our senior-class king and queen. Please welcome onstage our 2014 queen Rue and her king Mike."

"Thank you, Michael [as Rue and Mike made their way up], and congratulations. You better treat my best friend right," Rue warned Michael. Our family left, and we finished enjoying our senior prom.

Marie's mind was going a mile a minute after the dance. I simply told her that everything was planned and ready for us. "What do you mean that everything is ready for us?"

"I started this when our senior year started and enlisted the help of our moms. It just so happened that your mom knew where you kept your dream wedding book, and she pulled some ideas from it and placed it back in your room just how you left it. June 6 is our graduation, and June 21 is our wedding. All we would have to do now is get the marriage license and shop for your dress." All Marie could do was stare with shock and excitement at Michael. "I wanted to be married before we go off to college so that we do not have to live with anyone else. We can start our college experience together, supporting each other. What do you think? I hope you are not mad! Please don't be mad at me."

"I am not mad. I am excited, and I cannot wait until I see what our mothers have done. I can't believe that my mother knew where my wedding book was. I have to admit that I started that book when we first met." Now I am in shock and excited because Marie felt the same way I did when we first met. "Wait a minute. You had this all planned out? How did you know I would have said yes? What would have happened if I said no?"

"I would have kept asking you until you said yes. I had plans for the second, the third, and if it was needed the fourth time. But thank you so much for saying yes the first time."

"I could never turn you down. I knew when we met that it was going to be forever with you. You are my world, and you are the one I live for. No matter what happens in the future, you will be the reason I live."

"Marie, you are the same for me. These past four years have been the most rewarding and the best years of my life, and I can't wait to see what the future holds for us."

June 6, 2014

Marie was named valedictorian of their class, and after she spoke, Michael had to speak. They were able to present the 2014 graduating class along with their principal to their superintendent. It felt good being up there with her and then watching each other receive their diplomas. After the ceremony, both families gathered together and celebrated. They also ironed out some details on the event happening two weeks from now.

June 21, 2014

The big day is finally here and Michael is nervous. He is hoping Marie likes everything that their moms did. At the church, Michael was staring out the window, enjoying the beauty of the day. He whispered to himself, *God, thank you for today. Thank you for the beautiful woman you placed in my life. Please let me care for her the way you want me to. Thank you for keeping her life here with us. Our lives are in your hands.*

Ben is by Michael's side, walking up the aisle to await his bride. The aisle is lined with flowers and flowing fabric that he knows Marie would like. There are purple and white candles beautifully placed in areas around the room. The wait felt like an eternity.

Finally, Rue comes down the aisle. She finds her spot in front, and the music starts Canon in D minor, Marie's favorite. The doors open, a minute goes by, and the first thing Michael sees is her dad. Then he turns, and latched on his side was the most beautiful sight that he ever imagined: Marie in a white strapless dress with beads and diamonds on the top. The skirt touched the floor and contoured her legs with patterns of beads and diamonds that match the top. In her hand, she held a simple light-purple-and-white bouquet. On her head, she had a simple veil that hung from the back of her head with a little hairclip made with the same kind of flowers in her bouquet.

She looked at their parents, and her smile was even bigger. Her smile was shining as she locked her eyes on me. She was stunning, and she was walking down the aisle to meet me to be my wife. My mom caught me with tears rolling down my cheeks and a smile as big as Marie's.

The pastor starts, and all I see is the beautiful woman standing in front of me, waiting to be released by her dad. Finally, Marie was released by her dad, and her beautiful hand filled mine. Her soft touch sent shivers up my spine. I listened contently, or so it seemed. My thoughts went to Marie standing here next to me, wanting to be mine forever. I cannot believe this was happening. My dream is coming true right before my eyes. When the pastor asks me, "Do you, Michael, take this woman?" I missed his cue. Marie had to nudge me back from my thoughts, and I finally said, "I do!"

Then when it was Marie's turn. She says, "I do."

Finally, the pastor says, "I now pronounce you husband and wife. You may kiss your bride."

Everyone cheers and claps. I lead my beautiful bride out the doors to greet everyone as they come out.

CHAPTER 2

Present Day

Michael is still sitting on the floor, holding his daughter; and his mother comes over to him and helps him up to his feet and guides him over to the couch. "Do you want me to take her?"

"No, Mom, it's okay. I want to hold her more. Plus, I think she has fallen asleep." It is taking all he has just to stay awake. Michael lays his head back, and five minutes later, he is asleep with his daughter still in his arms. Michael's mom covers him up and watches him sleep like she did when he was a child. Marie's mom, Michelle, comes out and sits with Sophia and asks, "What do we do now? Michael should not be alone right now. Watching him go through this pain has to be tough on you."

"Yes, it is. But not knowing where your daughter and our unborn grandchild is has to be tough on you."

Michelle grabs Sophia's hand and says, "We will get through this together."

THE DAY MARIE GOES MISSING
(THROUGH MARIE'S EYES)

I am outside enjoying a beautiful day. I wonder up the street, smiling at the beauty. Michael was at the house occupied with Savanna while I take a break. I don't have to work, but I help Michael with his assistant manager's job. When he comes home with work, Michael, and I do it together. I enjoy my time with Savanna. I cannot wait to see how Savanna will interact with her new sibling. This is the last thought I had before I was hit from behind by something really hard. I wake up and find myself in a cage in a basement by myself. I search my pockets frantically and find that my phone is not in my pocket but on the wall just out of reach. It lights up as Michael is calling me. His name and picture are on the screen, pinned up to torture me. I hear the door open and someone coming down the steps. The person stops short of the only light in the room. "Oh good, you are awake. I hope you are comfortable because you will be here for a while."

I plead with this shadow of a person, "Please let me go. I am pregnant, and I need my husband."

"That is so unfortunate because you made a big mistake years ago when you stopped me from enjoying my man. If I can't have him, no one can."

I now recognize the voice, "Emily!"

"You do remember me. Yes, that makes me proud." She steps into the light, and I see what the years has done to her. It seems the desire, stress, and planning aged her. "I plan on bumping into Michael and taking him as my own, and you can have my leftover, which is upstairs cooking dinner."

"Emily, please don't do this. I am carrying Michael's child."

"When that child is born, the child will become mine."

Marie thinks quickly to protect her unborn child. "If you take this child from me, Michael will know you have me, and he will come for me, and he will not be yours. He will be mine."

"Fine, I will have my own baby with him. On second thought, I would not want anything that came from you. The child can stay here with you hidden away from Michael. Now I have to go watch my future husband and figure out the right time to bump into him. Goodbye for now."

Marie starts to cry, thinking to herself, *What is going to happen to me? How are we going to get out of this? Oh, baby, Momma will figure out a way out of this.* A man walks down the steps with a dinner plate in his hand. "Miss, I will take care of you while she is gone. She is my wife. I wish she wasn't, but if I tell anyone you are here, she will kill me. I am like you. I am her slave chained to this house, and the only phone is on the wall where I can't reach. Luckily, for you, I am a doctor, and I can help with the baby."

"Sir, what is your name?"

"My name is Richard, and your name is?"

"Marie. It is nice to meet you."

He slides the plate to me under my cage through the hole. "I don't know how many times I can get down here to you to give you food and water without her finding out, but I will do my best."

"Thank you, Richard, for your care."

BACK TO THE PRESENT DAY (THROUGH MICHAEL'S EYES)

I wake up the next morning still on the couch and Savanna on my lap and sleeping away. My family is sleeping on the floor, in chairs, and couches. Police officers are on duty around the house, keeping watch over my family. I think to myself, *Is this the way life will be from now on?* I slowly sit up and move Savanna from his lap onto the now-empty spot I once was sitting, and I go into the kitchen and I grab something quick to eat and then head out front for some fresh air. I walk to the sidewalk to grab my paper and realizes the front page. "What a beautiful picture of her," I touch the picture of my wife.

Then, out of nowhere, a person slams right into him, knocking him down to the ground. "I am so sorry, sir. Let me help. Wait, Michael, is that you?"

"Yes, it is me. You should watch—" As he spins around, he notices who had run into him literally knocking him to the ground. "Emily! Hi."

"Hi, Michael, I did not know you live here."

"Marie and I have been here for almost two years now. When did you move in?"

"It has been a couple of weeks now. My husband and I love the neighborhood." She looked down at the paper Michael was holding. "You said Marie. Is she your wife now?"

"Yes, she is. We were married a couple of weeks after graduation."

Emily gasped. "I was looking at the paper this morning. Now I am putting two and two together. I am sorry to hear that about your wife. Does the police have any leads on where your wife is?"

"At this point, no. We are all holding on and hoping she is okay. Her daughter wants her mom back, and I am not sure how our unborn child is doing either."

Emily gasps again. "She is pregnant also! Listen, if you need anything, here is my number. I will be happy to help any way I can."

"Thank you, Emily. If you see anything, please don't hesitate to call the police line listed in the paper."

"Michael, before I go, can I get a picture of you? My husband won't believe if I told him who I ran into if I did not show him proof. He went to high school with you."

"Yes, sure, what is his name? Maybe I knew him?"

She takes out her phone and clicks a couple of pictures. His name is Richard Stevens."

"I remember Richard. How is he?"

"He is good. He is a doctor. I don't get to see him a lot, but he is mine."

"That is good to hear. I am glad you found someone. My daughter will be waking up right about now. I need to go make her breakfast. It was nice talking to you."

"Yes, Michael, likewise. I guess we will be seeing each other around the neighborhood sometimes. I hope you will have a chance to meet up with Richard soon also."

"Yes, that will be nice. Goodbye, Emily."

"Goodbye, Michael."

Emily ran back in the direction she came from; and when she was out of sight, she cheered at her success. She ran back to her car and raced back to show Marie just how successful she was. She downloads the pictures she took of Michael onto a computer and hangs them all around her Michael's room. Then she prints some for downstairs. Emily heads downstairs to Marie. "So, Marie, here is my plan. For as long as Michael stays nice with me, you get to live. The more interaction I get with Michael, the more I let Richard take care of you. But the first rejection I get from Michael, I will come back here to hurt you. For now, I want to torture you with images of us hanging together. I want to see your pain as I talk to, be with, and comfort Michael, the same pain I felt when I had to watch you two flirt, kiss, and hug each other. I want you to experience the pain I felt." Emily throws the pictures at Marie. Emily felt satisfaction in the pained look on Marie's face. Emily let out satisfied laugh and called up to Richard, "Take care of our guest, will you?"

"Yes, my lady."

At that moment I watch as my phone lights up again with Michael's picture and message. Before the screen goes black, I see the words "I love you." I smile and I hold my hands over my heart.

Meanwhile back at Michael's house. I am back in the house and I am welcomed by Savanna as she jumps into my arms. "Daddy, I am hungry."

"Really? I think I can hear that roar in your stomach. Oh yes, there it is again. What would you like me to make for you, my roaring princess?"

"I would like a bowl of Frosted Flakes please and a cup of chocolate milk."

"Okay, coming right up, sweetheart."

"Daddy!"

"Yes, dear!"

"I love you!"

"I love you more!"

"No, I love you more!"

Michael smiles and hugs his daughter as he takes her into the kitchen. While he is making her breakfast, He is thinking, *I need to take care of Savanna. I still need to provide for her and keep her safe. Marie would want me to take care of Savanna.* I decided that I still need to work. I need to provide for Savanna even though my heart is not into working. I have to do what is best for Savanna. My mom's footsteps interrupts my thought process as she walks into the kitchen and gives me a kiss on the cheek. "Good morning, sweetheart."

"Good morning, Mom. Mom, I've decided that I need to work so that I can still take care of Savanna because it is not going to do us any good if I just let myself go. I need to be strong for her. Please, can you guys watch her while I am at work and help her take her mind off this bad stuff?"

"Yes, darling, we will help you take care of her. Michelle and I have been talking about this, and I agree with you. You have a responsibility to your daughter, and right now, she needs you. We all will help you."

"Thank you, Mom." He wraps his arms around in a hug. Then he turns to Savanna. "How would you feel if Daddy goes to work today?"

"You will come back, right, Daddy? You promise to come back and not leave me after work?"

"Yes, Daddy promises that I will be right back after work. I will not leave you. Today and every day that Daddy goes to work, you will be with all four of your grandparents."

"I will be hanging with Grammy, Pop, Grandma, and Pop-Pop! Yay!"

"I am glad you like the idea. Daddy is going to go get ready for work. I will be down to give you your special hug and kiss, okay?"

"Okay, Daddy."

As I go upstairs, I sent a text to Marie just to say I love you.

Michael is glad he works as an engineer just up the street from the house. If anything happens, it will take him just ten minutes to run back. He really does not want to leave Savanna, but he knows he has to. Marie would have wanted it this way. She would take comfort in knowing that Savanna is the first thing on his mind and that she is being cared for the way she needs to be. Michael hopes she is being cared for as well wherever she is.

Back where Marie is being kept. Marie picks up the pictures just thrown at her and start to cry. She misses her family, and she longs for Michael's arms around her. The thoughts running through her mind, I close my eyes as I imagine our honeymoon and our first night together in our college apartment. I was studying business because I wanted to help Michael run one of his own. He studied engineering. He loves the detail that went into that. I imagine his arms around me and the way he makes me feel that I am the only one he sees. I look at his expression in the pictures. It is filled with pain and worry for me. I want to tell him that things will be okay, that I will be home soon some way somehow. I look up at my phone as it lights up again, and I see his picture come up on the screen. I know he is thinking about me and listening to my voice. I am hoping that somehow, they can track the phone to me, and I whispers, "I am here. Please find me."

As Michael was get ready for work, Michael promised himself that if Marie was not found anytime soon that he would record everything so that she would not miss a thing with Savanna. He picked up his phone. A thought ran through his mind, I have to hear her voice. He dialed her number. It rings, but her greeting answers, and he hears her voice. Michael leaves a message in hopes that she will be able to hear them. Then a thought—Michael breaks into a sprint down the steps to the charge officer. "Brian, can you track Marie's phone with just her phone number? Her phone remains active. When I called, it rang."

"Yes, we will be able to if the signal is not blocked by something." Brian typed the phone number into the computer, and the program is searching the different areas on the map. Then it stops at one place. Michael's heart skips a beat when it stops. Brian cues his mic and says, "Possible hostage location," and he reads the address into the microphone; and he springs into action. As he was leaving, he says to me, "I will let you know what we find." I decide one more day at home should do.

When Brian and his team get to the location, they find an old, abandoned building, and Brian's heart sinks. He did not want to go in and see her lying there. He led the charge in, and all they found was a signal generator that mirrored Marie's cell phone, sat there by Marie's captors. With that is a picture of Marie in a cage. Brian cursed and threw his hat to the ground. "Another dead end." A disappointed look on Brian's face when he got back to my house sends me a shiver of despair. Brian then hands me the picture, and my heart hits the floor. Marie was asleep with her head against the side of the cage.

⌒❖⌒

Emily started to hang around Michael a lot. She was a helpful asset to have as the case went on. Emily asked Michael if I wanted to go to dinner with her. "No, I am sorry, I can't. I have to be with my daughter, and I have her mother to find."

Emily was thrilled that he did reject her because she has an opportunity to inflict a little pain on Marie. When Emily got back to the house, she ran downstairs, opened the gate, and punched Marie in the face. Marie punched her back. Marie was able to knock her down just enough to get out. But Emily grabbed her and twisted her ankle. Her ankle broke under the pressure. Marie dropped to the ground. Emily got up and locked the cage back up. "That is for your husband rejecting me."

Emily walked back upstairs. Marie sat in pain, holding her ankle but laughing at the fact that Michael rejected her again. There were a couple more times that Emily came down to hurt Marie, and each time, Marie laughed in her face. "My husband will reject you every time." Marie watched as her phone lit up again with the words "Please stay with me. Fight for me." It was Michael's way of speaking to Marie's heart.

CHAPTER 3

Three Years Later

Michael and Brian are the only ones working on this case in between Michael's work hours and his time with Savanna. Each lead they will get ends up with a dead end. Emily has been really supportive for the past three years. She helps with the investigation all the while wallowing in her triumph. She is getting all the attention she needs from Michael. Emily enjoys the thrill of being rejected by Michael so that she can hurt Marie. Richard does the best he can when Marie is hurt. He wrapped her ankle when Emily broke it and gave her ice when Emily punched her face.

A couple of months into Marie's ordeal, the time has come for Michael's second child to be born; and while the events unfolded, Emily was enjoying a lunch with Michael and Brian, talking about the case and any leads they may have. Every time she got a chance, she would flirt with Michael, but he ignored her. That day, she was tired of being ignored and took out her frustrations on Marie. Marie just had her baby, so she was a little worn out. Emily took advantage of that and beat Marie so bad that she placed her in a coma for a day. Richard yelled at Emily, "Emily, she just had the baby. Stop, or you will kill her!"

"Richard, I make the demands around here, not you." Emily punched Richard and said, "Take care of that crying baby, or I will."

Marie's cage had bars that were big enough for Ricard to stick his hands in. He was able to check on Marie. He saw that she was in a coma, and his heart sank. He quickly made a bottle for the child and gave it to her to let her drink. Richard also wrapped the baby up in a clean blanket and said, "Your mommy will be okay. Welcome to the world, little one. I am Uncle Richard." Richard stayed next to the cage until Marie woke up. Richard was able to bandage Marie's wounds on her face. Richard had food service deliver to the house, but he could not say anything to the delivery boy. Emily had eyes and ears everywhere. Richard was able to buy clothing for the baby and all that they needed to survive. Marie named the baby Hannah, which was Michael's name for a girl if it was. Marie would tell her daughter all about her daddy and her sister. She would spend her days telling Hannah stories about their lives together, and Marie promised that they will see them soon.

"Guess what today is, Hannah."

"What is today, Mommy?"

"Today is your sister's birthday. She is seven today." Marie started to cry, and Hannah wrapped her tiny arms around her mom's neck. "We will see them soon, Hannah. We will see them soon."

Over the years, Emily has found a way to allow herself into Michael's house without him knowing, and she would watch him for hours. She would take pictures and, of course, torture Marie with them. Emily would see him naked and watch him sleep hugging Marie's pillow. She would also watch him interact with Savanna and dream that one day she will make her move. That night came, and Emily seized the opportunity to take him. Savanna was at a friend's sleepover, and he was all by himself in his bed. Emily readied herself and came out of hiding and into his bedroom. She immediately moved to his side and covered his mouth. "If you don't do what I want, they will die." She showed him the live video feed of Marie and his child. She watched as a look of shock and betrayal washed over his face. "You know where they are this whole time? Let them go, and I will do whatever you want. Let them go, and I can be yours." He pleaded for their lives. He wanted to take their place. He knew in the back of his mind that they were alive. "What do you want from me?"

"I want you to do to me what you did to Marie. I want what you gave to Marie." As she was saying it, she was tying Michael up and taking pictures while doing it. Emily striped off his pants, then striped off her clothes, and taped Michael's mouth shut. Michael closed his eyes so he could not see it was not Marie. Emily played, and his body reacted. Michael fought it, but his body reacted. He had streams of tears rolling down his cheeks. She did what she had to do, and he released. He wanted it to be Marie. Her face was all he saw. He could not open his eyes and see it was not Marie. Emily untied his hands and untapped his mouth. The whole time, she was taking pictures. "That was good for me. Was it good for you? So here is what you are going to do for me tomorrow night. You are going to meet me here at this place. You are going to wine and dine me and make love to me afterward without being tied up and mouth taped shut, and your Marie and child will live. The minute you reject me, they will die. I will leave you with this video feed. If you try to figure out where this is, they will die. I see anyone at this location, they will die. Do you hear me loud and clear?"

Michael nodded. Emily leaves and downloads the pictures to add to her wall and takes them down to see the pain on Marie's face. "You never told me how good he felt. Here are some more torture for you." Emily throws the pictures at Marie, and the pain of what they hold is now on Marie's face. "That's what I like to see. Thank you for the greatest man I will ever know. Oh, and before I forget, see that camera right there? He can see you now. Wave hi!" Tears stream down Marie's face, and she looks up at the camera and feels him watching. It is a good feeling. She studies the pictures and cries because she knew he was not into it. His eyes are closed, and his mouth was taped. The images Michael saw was probably her, and she held on to the thought that he did not want that. Thank god Hannah was sleeping. Marie looked up at the camera and motioned to it that she rejects the pictures; and she holds up the I-love-you sign, knowing that his eyes are watching. She has this new hope that she can at least tell him that no matter what she will love him.

Michael was watching the video. There is no sound, and he saw Emily give the pictures to Marie, and he saw the pain in her face. His heart broke, and he yelled at the phone, "Marie, no! I had no choice. She was going to kill you if I didn't." Then he watched as Emily left and watched as Marie rejected the pictures and held up her hand in the sign of I love you. Michael's heart skipped a beat. He held the phone close. He has a connection to his wife. He can finally see his child. Michael fell asleep holding the phone to his chest like he was holding Marie forever.

The next morning, Michael awoke and saw that his child is awake, and Marie is showing her pictures that Emily took of just him. Then she even had pictures of him and Savanna. Then he could see Marie pointing to the camera and telling her to wave at Daddy, and he sees her little hand go up and wave. It took all Michael had not to cry. Then Marie showed her how to make the I-love-you sign with her fingers, and she held it up to the camera. Michael is hoping that Marie can sense that he is watching. Then he could see Marie looking around for something. Then writing on the back of one of the pictures, Hannah and she showed to the camera. Michael smiled and said it was his name he picked for a girl. He could not wait until Savanna got home so that she can see her mom and sister. He held the phone in his arms until she got home.

When Savanna walked into the house, Michael held out his hands and kneeled to welcome her home with a hug. "I have missed you, my darling princess."

"Daddy, I have missed you too. Any new news on Mommy yet?"

Michael smiled and showed her the phone. Her face lit up when she saw her mom and could see that she has a sister. "Daddy, I have a sister!" Her face got even brighter that her wish came true and she has a sister. "Yes, you have a sister, and her name is Hannah."

"Wait, how do you know? Did you talk to mom?"

"No, she held up that picture with her name on it."

Savanna then started to cry as see looked at the video feed. In the middle of her sobs, she asks, "Can they see us?"

"No. It does not seem like they can, but I can guarantee you Hannah knows who we are."

"How do you know that?" "Your mom shows Hannah our pictures. She tells Hannah who we are."

"Okay, now are you going to show Brian this so that he can go get them?"

"Yes, he is on his way over now. Tonight, you have to go stay at your grandparents' house because I have to do something I don't want to do, but hopefully, it brings them home."

"Okay, Daddy!"

"Please go and put some fresh clothes in your suitcase."

"Can I take Mommy and Hannah with me?"

"Yes, you can, but when you hear Brian come in, please bring the phone back down."

"Okay, Daddy!"

Michael heard Savanna talking to the phone like she was talking to her mom. He wished that she did not have to pretend that she was talking to her mom. Ten minutes later, Brian walked in and Savanna was down the steps before Michael yelled to her. "Good job, little lady," Michael said in a cow boyish voice. Then Michael showed the video feed to Brian as Savanna went back upstairs. "Brian, I know who has them. She paid me a visit last night," and he showed Brian the cuts and bruises that the ties left behind.

"She was here last night?"

"Yes!"

"Then why did you not call me last night?"

"She would have killed my family if I called you. I also figured out that she has been in this house. I found her hiding place and boarded it up so she could not get back in and see you here."

"Michael, so you are telling me she has been here the whole time?"

"Yes, and so that she does not kill my family, I have to wine, dine, and make love to her tonight."

"Can we set a trap for her tonight?"

"Please, as long as it does not get my family killed." Michael gave the address to where all this is supposed to happen. "I will meet you at your office as soon as I drop my daughter off at my parents' house. I don't want her to know what happened to me last night. Oh, and one more thing, don't mention any of the plan to Emily because she is the one who has my family."

Brian's mouth drops, and then he curses and throws his hat again to the ground. Brian hands the phone back to Michael and runs out the door to his office to set a plan into motion. Emily does, in fact, call Brian and asks if there was any new leads. "No, Emily, we are still getting dead ends."

"I was just thinking. Do you think that Michael has anything to do with his wife's disappearance?"

The question stops Brian dead in his tracks. "Emily, why would you ask a question like that?"

"Because he is meeting me tonight for dinner, and I was just wondering if he did something to his wife for me." Brian heard the screw-up she just made, and now he knows exactly how to get her.

CHAPTER 4

The Takedown

Brian calls Michael and tells him the plan. "Brian, can you please do this before dinner? I really don't want to take her on a date."

"No. We have to make sure she knows she is getting away with it, and it has to be when you are in the act. Here is how it is going to go. You wine and dine her. Then you take her to the room where you start. As she thinks you are protecting your family, we will barge in and arrest you both in conspiracy to commit murder. I will get her to flip on you and get her to tell us the location of where you are hiding your family."

"I trust you that this works, and my family will be in my arms tonight!"

"Yes, that is the hoped-for outcome."

Michael is nervous, and he is shaking as he gets ready to give a woman who is not Marie what she wants. He keeps repeating in his head, *This is for my family, this is for my family, this is for my family.* Michael focuses on the way Marie would feel back in his arms. The way he will hold his daughter Hannah for the first time and hearing her call him daddy. He promises himself that he will never let them go. He can't wait to see Savanna's face when she sees her mom and her new sister. The joy that she and he have missed for so long. He can't wait to see a mother hold her child that she has not seen for three years. He yearns for this image; he yearns for the time he would get to spend with his family all together again. His tears won't stop flowing. The want of Marie by his side when he wakes up in the morning. The touch of her hands on him and the warmth of her smile when she sees him. He can't wait for all these. The three years will end tonight, and his family will be back in his arms, and the psycho Emily will be behind bars where she belongs.

Michael looks in the mirror. "Here goes nothing!" Out the door he goes. He drops Savanna off at his parents' house, not saying anything of what is happening. He doesn't want to get her hopes up. Then he meets Brian at the station. Brian gives Michael more details and gives Michael a note to slip to the front desk personnel. It reads, "Please give a key to the officers that ask what room I am in. Thanks, Michael." Michael is fitted with a listening device in his mouth so that Emily has no idea it is there.

Then the night begins when Michael steps down to the street and walks to the restaurant and hotel. He stands outside, waiting for Emily to walk up. His heart is pounding so hard that everyone around hears it or so he thinks. He spots Emily, and he puts on a show. "My Emily, you look beautiful tonight. Are you ready for a night you won't ever forget?"

"Yes, I am. Aren't you the gentleman tonight?"

As Michael loops his arm around Emily's arm. "Well then, follow me." Michael leads Emily in, and they were shown to his reserved table for the evening.

"You did all this for me?"

"Yes, just for you." Michael pulls out the chair for Emily.

She asks him, "Are you doing this because your family's lives are at stake?"

"NO, I am doing this because every girl needs to be wined and dined from time to time." The rest of the dinner was great.

They made small talk, and Emily talked about her dreams with him. Michael then asked, "Are you ready to go upstairs?"

"Yes, sir, I am." Michael walked her over to the front desk and checked in. As she was rummaging through her purse, he carefully passed the note to the desk clerk and mouthed, "Don't read it yet."

"Thank you, sir, and enjoy your stay." The desk clerk handed Michael his key to the room. They were in the elevator alone, and Michael started to kiss Emily sweetly, and Emily kissed him more deeply. When they separated, she said, "Wow, I so missed that. It is about time you kissed me back."

"You did not bring any ties, did you? You hurt me badly last night, and I did not like that."

"Oh, baby, I would never do that to you again. I promise."

He leaned over and kissed her again. Finally, the elevator opened; and they exited, still kissing each other. The whole entire time, Michael was pretending it was Marie and let himself go in her image. He kept reminding himself, *This is for my family, this is for my family, this is for my family.* Michael led Emily to the room and unlocked the door while still attached to Emily's lips.

Meanwhile, Brian and a team of officers came into the lobby, and the front desk clerk did what the note said and gave Brian the key. Michael and Emily were already undressed and kissing on the bed. Michael was caressing her whole body when Brian walked in and said, "Michael and Emily, you are under arrest for conspiracy to commit murder and kidnapping." Emily gasps and rushes to find her clothes.

"Michael, what are they talking about?"

Brian turned to Michael and asked, "Where is your wife and daughter? Where do you have them kept? They better not be dead because you will get life for it!"

Brian then asks Emily, "Do you know where he is keeping his family? Are you in on this? It looks like you two are free now to do whatever you want." As Brian is reading the Miranda rights to both, Michael is getting dressed. Brian handcuffs Emily, and his fellow officer is handcuffing Michael but enough to be loose on his wrists. The other officers collect their belongings and escort them downstairs.

While in the elevator, Emily could not keep her mouth shut. Brian had to keep reminding her to stay silent. Michael was sighing relief that it was over. As the officers escorted them through the front lobby, Michael mouthed a thank you to the front desk personnel and took note of his name. *Nice. Michael—like mine.* The clerk gave him a nod of you're welcome.

Emily was put into a separate cop car; and when the officer put Michael into another one, he released his hands. Brian came over and said to Michael, "Excellent performance."

"I did it for my family, and I just pretended she was Marie." He looked down at the phone when Brian handed it to him, and Michael felt relieved to see Marie rocking Hannah to sleep and staring up at the camera. With her free hand, she gave the sign of I love you. In that moment, Michael felt the deep connection and the love she has for him, and he prayed, *Thank you for keeping my family safe and protected when I could not be there. Please let her know I am right here with her. As I watch over her, touch her heart for me and let her know I will be there soon.* He watches his family sleep as they head to the police station in hopes that Emily turns on Michael and gives up the location of his family.

Another week goes by, and Emily will not give up the location. She keeps demanding to see Michael; and when Michael is ushered into the room, she cries. Brian turns the table on her. "If you don't give us the location of where Michael is keeping his family, you will never see Michael again. He will never be yours." That sent her over the edge, and she finally told the location of his family, and Brian led Michael into the room to say one last word to Emily. Brian uncuffed Michael's hands, and Michael leaned across the table and said, "I hate you. I never want to see you again." He walks out. Her sobs are heard all throughout the building, and Michael gets in the car with Brian to go get his family.

They arrive at the location, and the officers go in first. They find Richard chained to the house like a dog. They cut him loose, and he goes outside. Michael immediately recognizes Richard. He rushes to help him regain his footing. Michael could only say thank you for keeping my family safe. "You're welcome. I had to do it for you. You stood up for me when no one else would." Michael could hear officers saying clear, and he could not stand the wait any longer. Michael rushed in; and down the steps he went, grabbing a metal cutter on the way down.

He was the first one down the steps. At first, he could not see; but when his eyes adjusted, he saw the most beautiful sight ever. His beautiful Marie was standing, holding on to the cage around her; and in her sobs, she breathed out his name: Michael—the most beautiful sound a guy could ever hear. He ran to the cage door, cutting the object that secured it, and pulled it open. Marie jumped into his arms and sobbed even harder. Her wet cheeks buried deep into his neck, and the flood of kisses that came afterward was comforting and welcomed. Finally, the feeling of her in his arms melted his heart. All his worries, his loneliness, his yearning ended right there. The next sound heard in the room was "Daddy!" Michael bent down, still holding on to his wife, and scooped up his daughter for the first time. "Hi, Princess Hannah, it is finally nice to meet you. Let's say we get out of here, okay?" Marie could barely walk, so Michael lifted both up in his arms and carried them out into the sunlight.

Television cameras were everywhere. Marie had to shield her eyes from the sun. Michael carried them to the waiting ambulance. Michael got in and would not let go. The EMTs had to remind him that he needs to let go of at least his wife so that they can attend to her wounds. He held his daughter tight and did not let her go. He called his parents and asked them not to show the TV news cast to Savanna. He wanted to be there when Savanna sees her mom. His mom was crying; and in between her sobs, she said okay. She is upstairs taking a nap. Then he called her parents, and he put her on the phone the minute they answered, she said, "Hello, Mom and Dad." All he heard was cheering and crying all at once. She said, "Go over to Michael's parents please and don't tell Savanna yet."

When they got to the hospital, both Marie and Hannah were checked out. Hannah was a healthy little girl. Michael could tell that Marie took a beating. He saw all the scars and some of the recent bruises. Marie was a little weak and could hardly walk. Her ankle did not heal properly. The doctors had to rebreak and set it right. Marie held Michael's hand for that. Marie had signs of concussions. Richard was able to fill the doctors in on what Marie endured before she got there. But after all, this, Marie and Hannah were released and sent home with a wheelchair and instructions.

At 7:30 p.m., Michael wheeled both Marie and their daughter up to his parents' house and opened the door. Michael was the first one in and scooped up Savanna in a heartbeat as she shouted, "Daddy!" Marie heard her daughter's voice, and tears welled up in her eyes.

"Savanna, close your eyes tight for me. No peeking," her daddy asked. Meanwhile, Marie's mom said hello to Hannah by taking her off Marie's lap. Michael placed Savanna down in front of her mother and said, "Open your eyes." She did, and the room was silent, and all she could do was run into her mother's arms and sob.

In between her sobs, she manages to say, "This is the best day ever!" When she calmed down, her next question was "Where's my sister?" She turned around and saw her in their daddy's arms. She ran to her daddy, knocking them both onto the floor, and Hannah is heard saying, "Sanana." She wraps her tiny arms around her sister. Marie has streams of tears rolling down her cheeks as she is finally able to watch daddy and daughters together. Marie is getting hugs from parents and brothers.

Michael could not let go of his two beautiful daughters all the while keeping an eye on his wife. Tears of happiness are flowing. Michael finally lets go of the girls so that Savanna could show Hannah what she can do at Grandma's house. Michael scoops up Marie out of the chair and sits down on the couch with her on his lap. He hides his face in her neck. "I did something that I am ashamed of," he said as his voice was muffled in her neck.

Marie lifted his head so that his eyes could meet hers. "Michael, I know what you had to do, and I know you were forced into it. She tied you up and forced you. It is not your fault. I see the marks on your wrists to prove it."

"I had to make sure you stayed alive. I had to play along, but the night we caught her, I had to play along. I had to seduce her, or she would've killed you and Hannah. I was pretending to be with you so that I could do it. I am sorry. I had to do it!" Michael was holding her tight. "On the night she had me tied, my body reacted. I tried to fight it, but it reacted, and I released." Michael's sobs came harder.

Marie held him and told him, "I know, and I forgive you because it was not your fault. You had no control. She had the control, and you were saving me. When she pointed out the camera, I could feel you watching me, and I could feel your love for me, and no matter what you had to do to save us, nothing will ever make me leave you or love you less. I love you, Michael, and nothing could ever change that now."

Michael held her tighter and stayed buried in her neck longer. "I love you, Marie. I am feeling good now that you are back in my arms."

The grandparents helped the girls with ice cream and left Michael and Marie alone in the living room as they held each other. "So Emily messed me up a little in high school, and she had to come back and mess with this family again. Richard was the one who took care of us, and he was locked up in that house also. She threatened him that if he did not do what she said, she would kill him. The only time I saw her was when she would come down to throw those pictures at me and beat me. She enjoyed watching the pain across my face."

Michael looked at his wife with a sinking feeling, "Did she tell you why she was beating you?"

Marie did not want to answer that question. She asked, "Do I have to answer that question?"

Michael said, "Did she beat you because I kept rejecting her?" Marie's silence said it all. "Oh god, that was my fault. You were being hurt every time I turned Emily down. I had a feeling that something was up with her. She would hang out with Brian and me to help with the case. She would flirt with me and ask to go to dinner, and every time, I would ignore her and tell her no."

"Baby, this is not your fault. You did not know she had me. Every time she came to hurt me, I laughed in her face. I reminded her that you will always reject her."

Michael smiled at that. Then Michael talked more about his ordeal. "The night she tied me up, she told me she wanted what you had. She wanted me to give her what I gave you. Oh no, no, no, no! She made herself pregnant with my baby. She has a piece of me now." Michael started to shake and cry. "I am sorry, Marie. I am so sorry. I am so sorry." Michael repeated that over and over.

Marie held him closer and rubbed his back. She whispered, "We will be okay, we will be okay, we will never leave you." Marie reassured her husband. Marie asked Michael if he wanted to stay here tonight and go home in the morning. He said, "No. I want to be home with the girls in their beds and us in ours."

"Okay, take me home, you sexy man."

Michael smiled at that command. "No problem, ma'am!"

The girls finished their ice cream and said their goodbyes to their grandparents. Michael carried Marie out to the car while her dad carried her chair out to the trunk. They waved goodbye as they pulled out of the driveway.

CHAPTER 5

The Aftermath

Michael carried Marie up to the bedroom and placed her on her side of the bed. "I will be right back." He helped the girls get ready for bed.

Hannah was a little nervous. She was not used to being this far apart from her mom, and Marie heard her. "Hannah, come to mommy." Michael led his daughter to her. Michael picked her up and sat her on Marie's lap. "Hannah, I will be right here if you need anything. Don't be scared. Your daddy will not let anything happen to us anymore. I have an idea. Do you want your sister to sleep next to you tonight and you can try it tomorrow night?"

"Yes, sissy sleep with me." Savanna came in on that note and kissed her parents goodnight, and they both went to sleep in Hannah's bed. The girls were out the minute their heads hit the pillow.

Michael finally came back into the room, and Marie was crying. "What happened? Are you okay?" Marie had pulled the covers down and seen the blood on Michael's side of the bed. The small pools of dried blood that Michael did not realize was there. They are from the night his hands were tied behind his back and the ties were cutting into his skin. Michael dropped to his knees and said, "I did not know

43

how bad it was until now. I did not know they were there. I have not slept in this bed since it happened." Marie was holding her hand out to him. He picked her up, and she said, "I am sorry this happened to you. I was not here to protect you."

In between her sobs, he said, "She needs to pay for what she did to you." Michael placed Marie on the recliner. He took pictures just in case they are needed, and he stripped the bed and threw the sheets away. He got new sheets out of the closet, and Marie studied his expression. It was an expression of shame and regret. Then he looked at Marie. His expression changed. It was an expression of longing and wanting. Once the bed was clean, Michael placed Marie back on it. Her touch reassured him that she wanted him. She longed for him and that he did not need to feel ashamed anymore. They made a new memory in that bed that night.

Four Weeks Later

Michael would have a reoccurring nightmare once every two weeks. He was back on that night, and Emily was doing her thing. Marie sensed that Michael having a nightmare again, and she held him and whispered in his ear, "It's okay, baby. It's Marie. I am right here," and her voice soothed his body, and he softened.

Michael received the dreaded phone call. "Hi, Michael, it's Brian. I know you are not ready to hear this, but are you sitting down? Emily is pregnant, and the test came back. It is what you feared. It is yours." Michael stared at Marie and nodded as she was attending to Hannah. Marie's eyes filled with tears, but they did not spill over. She was able blink them away.

"Brian, what is the rules for expectant mothers in jail?"

"She will receive the proper care until she has the baby. Then the baby will go to the father if the father is willing. If there's no father, the baby will go to a parent or sibling of the incarcerated."

"Marie and I talked about this, and we decided the baby will come here. We will seek full custody of the child."

"Okay, I will get the paperwork rolling, and I am glad to hear you say that. A judge will most likely grant you full custody because, from what I gathered, her parents died in a car accident, and she has no other living relatives except for her husband, which has asked for a divorce and is moving way far away from her."

"Tell Richard to give us his address please when he does decide to move."

"I will. Are you and Marie available to sign papers tomorrow afternoon?"

"Yes, we are. What time?"

"How about two?"

"Yes, that works for us."

After the phone call with Brian, Michael's nightmare came every two days.

Michael and Marie show up in Brian's office at two, and he has so much more to tell them. "Emily is pleading not guilty to everything she is charged with. She is blaming this whole thing on Michael. Unfortunately, your battle with this chick is not over yet. Do you have a lawyer?"

"Yes, my dad is a lawyer. Let me call him right now." Marie pulls her phone from her pocket. Meanwhile, Michael asks about Emily's baby. "Emily is willing to fight you also for custody of the baby. She says that you told her to tie you up and you forced her to do it." Marie rejoined the conversation and caught most of it. "Wait a minute. Emily kept giving me pictures of Michael and Savanna.

There has to be so much more than what she gave me. She is obsessed with Michael."

"We looked all over that house and found nothing."

Marie shook her head no. "There has to be some secret room somewhere because I heard things in other places. Please, can we go back to that house and see if we could find it. If she was watching my husband, she has to have some record of it."

Brian was contemplating the thought. "Are you sure you want to go back there?"

"Yes, if it helps our case."

"Okay, we can go back there only as a witness. If you find something, you can't touch it. Understood?"

"Yes, understood!" Marie nodded.

Marie's dad arrives, and he greets them just as Marie grabs him and ushers him out with them. "Wait, where are we going?" Mitchel says with a shock of surprise.

"Dad, we are going to the location."

"What location? Oh, wait, that location." Mitchel follows with interest. Marie catches her dad up on what is going on, and his response was "Yes, I finally get to do something about this." Brian hands Mitchel the file on what they had on Emily so far.

They arrive to the location where Marie was held. Her heart started to pound, and Michael noticed right away she was uncomfortable. He was by her side, holding her as she went into the basement through the outside cellar door. The cage is still there, and she could tell that they must have cleaned a little in there. She was able to take in the full site of the basement, and she said, "The sounds would come from that wall right there." She leaned in closer, noticed something, and remembered the words Brian said back in his office; and she called after him. "Brian, I think I found something."

Brian rushed over and saw what looked like drag marks, and Brian leaned on the wall, and it moved. Brian finished opening it up, and lo and behold, Marie was right. It seems Emily would spend hours in here going through all the treasures she stored up. She had DVDs of Michael in the house. Pictures plastered to the walls and ceiling of Michael. Marie gasped as she walked in. Marie could not believe the images of Michael she had. Marie had her hand over her mouth. Then Brian found the proof they needed to turn this around on her. First, she did, in fact, record her encounter with Michael that night. It was playing over and over on the DVD player. Marie could see the pain in Michael's face, and she started to cry, and she screamed, "Turn it off!" Brian pulled the plug, and Marie turned into Michael and cried. Michael stood frozen as he took his wife in his arms.

Emily had mountains of footage of Marie and Hannah in the cage, as well as of him and Savanna. Brian called in the forensic team to collect the evidence, and Michael led his wife and father-in-law out of the room. Mitchel was on the phone calling his partner and making plans to prosecute and share this evidence with her lawyers. Marie could not stop crying. Michael held her close. "The pain you went through for me and Hannah is sickening. How could a person do that? I am sorry you had to go through that again the very next night." All Michael could do was hold his wife and rub her back. The forensic team went in and cleaned every piece of evidence out of the room.

Mitchel and his partners, along with the team, had the privilege of sifting through the videos and pictures. But Mitchel could not watch the videos that involved his daughter. His partner had to watch it, but he had to watch the one with his son-in-law to build the strong case against her. Then he went to work, making sure that the baby she is carrying does not pay for the mistakes the mother made.

A Couple of Months Later

Emily is now seven months pregnant, and she is thinking she is keeping the baby. The jury and the judge are ready to start hearing testimony. The first testimony comes from Marie, and she steps to the stand. Michael could not be in there when she testified because he is the next witness, and her testimony should not taint his. Meanwhile, Michael is outside, pacing. Marie told every truth she had, and she stuck to her story even when Emily's lawyer tried to pin it on Michael. Marie came back and challenged Emily's lawyer, saying, "Prove it!"

He immediately said, "No more questions."

Marie took her seat and heard her husband's name called next. She thought to herself, *Now the hard part.* Michael took his seat on the stand, and his eyes fell to his wife. With the look she had for him, it gave him confidence and strength. His father-in-law stepped up to the stand and asked Michael, "Describe the night you went through with Ms. Emily." Michael described what happened to him. When Emily's lawyer stepped to the stand, he seemed to not believe the story that Michael told him and simply said, "Let's watch the video." He insinuated that he saw something in the video that says something different. Michael watched Marie's face as she fully watched what happened to him, and he could see the tears welling up in her eyes. Marie kept her focus on Michael and telling herself, *I have to be strong for him. I have to fight these tears back for him.* She could see his tears rolling down his face. She mouthed to him, "I love you!" He smiled back at her. Finally, the video was done.

Emily's lawyer asked, "Did this act result in a baby?"

"Yes, sir, it did!"

"Was it your intention to have a baby with Ms. Emily?"

"No, sir, it was not!" "Whose intention was it?"

"It was Emily's intention. She forced herself on me."

Emily's lawyer seems to be trying to get Michael to admit that he wanted it to happen. "Mr. Michael, you did not invite Ms. Emily into your house?"

"No, I never invited her into the house." Emily's lawyer went to their table and pulled out a piece of paper and showed it to his father-in-law and then to the judge. "Mr. Michael, did you ever see this letter?"

Michael looked at the letter, and Marie could tell that he never saw that letter. "No, I have never seen this letter."

"Is that your handwriting?"

"No, it is not," Michael asked for a pad of paper and wrote some of the words he saw on the page; and sure enough, they didn't match up. Emily's lawyer was stunned.

Again, all he could say was "No further questions."

Michael took his seat next to Marie and breathed a sigh of relief. Marie's father called Richard to the stand. Richard took his seat and told everything that he went through. Brian was called and then a psychiatrist. The only question that was asked to the psychiatrist was by Mitchel, "Do you think that Ms. Emily has the ability to take care of the child she is carrying?"

The psychiatrist says, "In my professional opinion and my study of her, no, she is not capable to take care of the baby."

Emily's lawyer simply said, "I have no questions at this time."

Each of the lawyers had their last chance to persuade to jury to vote on their side. Then the jury went in to deliberate. The wait was not long, and Marie's dad said it was a good sign. The judge asked the jury, "Have you reached a verdict?"

"Yes, Your Honor." The jury member hands the piece of paper to the judge. Then he hands it back to him. "We the jury find the defendant guilty on the count of reckless endangerment. We the jury find the defendant guilty on the count of sexual assault on the first degree, and we the jury find the defendant guilty on the count of kidnapping of an adult and a minor."

The judge says, "I hereby sentence Emily thirty years to life, and when her baby is born, she is to hand the child over to the father."

As he banged his gavel on the stand, Emily started to shout, "Michael, please don't let them do this to me. I love you. Please come see me." She was carefully ushered out of the room. Michael held his wife, and their dad held both of them.

CHAPTER 6

The Birth

The day was upon Michael. He and Marie went to go pick up the new member of the family. As they wait, they could hear Emily say, "No, he is mine. Little Michael is mine."

The nurses reminded her, "Emily, you can't keep him here with you. You have to let him go." Finally, she let him go, and the nurse carried the baby boy out to Michael and Marie. Michael took him into his arms and asked Marie, "So, Mom, what is the name of your son?"

"His name is Michael Junior, my most favorite boy's name ever."

Michael hands him over to Marie. He also decided right then and there. He waited until Michael was loaded into his car seat, and she joined him up front. "Marie, I have been thinking about something. I am scared that she might get out one day and come after us. Are you satisfied with three kids, or do you want more?"

Marie looked at Michael, "Why do you ask that question?"

"I don't want her to hunt me down for another child and again take one from me, so I was thinking about getting snipped."

Marie smiled. "It's funny you should ask because Michael is not going to be the only baby in the house after five more months go by.

He will be joined by twins. Yes, you can go have that done because we will have five bundles of joy running around our house, and we are going to have to find a bigger house."

Michael was speechless and did not move for about five minutes. Then his face lights up and says, "Are you serious? We are pregnant?"

"Yes, we are pregnant!" They both laughed, and then Michael stopped and realized the second part of what she said. "Wait, there are two babies in there?"

"Yes, there are two babies in there. Can we go home please? We have two very excited kids at home who want to see their little brother." Michael put the car in gear and pulled out of the spot. He heads home where everyone is waiting to meet Michael. "Two babies—wow!"

Michael and Marie pull onto the driveway, and they can see everyone peeking out the window. Michael and Marie take Michael inside, and the first two to meet him were his sisters. Then Marie picks him up and says, "This is Michael Junior." Michael then takes him and passes him to his parents.

Sophia says, "He looks just like you, Michael."

Marie smiles. "That is why I named him Michael." Michael is now passed to her parents. Then he is passed to his uncles. Michael notices Richard and Michael, the desk clerk from the hotel, are in the house.

"Marie, come, it is time." Michael leads Marie to stand in front of their fireplace. "Please, can I have everyone sit wherever they can and listen? Today is a special day for me because this beautiful woman is here by my side, and she accepts this beautiful child lying in my arms as her own. Today, she signed the papers to be his mom, and in about an hour, it will be official. In the next hour, I want to honor some people who made this day happen. First and foremost, if it weren't for God, Marie and Hannah would not be here." Michael motioned for Hannah to come up. "Even though Brian is not currently here, he and his team never gave up in finding Marie and Hannah, which leads me to Richard. If it was not for him taking care of my family, they would not be here today. Here is a little token of our appreciation." Michael hands him an envelope with a thousand dollars in it.

"I know it is not nearly enough for taking care of my family in their time of need. Michael, the desk clerk at the hotel, your little act of duty saved my life, and you helped us take down my wife's captor." Michael hands him an envelope of a thousand dollars. "Our parents and brothers, your support and strength got me through the toughest time of my life. Marie and I are sending you on a cruise, leaving in a couple of weeks. You guys gave me the strength to keep going and fighting. Last but not least, my rock and my right-hand princess Savanna. The day you came to me and told me that they will be with us again gave me hope. You lit my path, and I am so proud of you."

Savanna smiles from ear to ear. "Daddy, someone had to do her job."

"And for that, you get to be the first to hold Michael, and you will also be the first to hold the twins."

Everyone in unison said, "Wait, what twins?"

Marie smiled. "We will be welcoming two more family members in about five months."

Everyone cheered and hugged. Then they moved to the kitchen and started to eat.

Michael was watching everyone. He thought this day would never come. Tears filled his eyes, and Marie comes to him and asks, "Are you okay?"

"Yes, these are tears of joy and the realization that this day is finally here, that our family is finally together under the same roof."

Marie reaches up and wipes his tears away and kisses him on his lips. "I would love it if you do more of that. I have missed that for three years. You have a lot to catch up on." Michael smiles down at his wife wrapped in his arms.

FIVE MONTHS LATER

The twins were born, and Michael got his procedure done. They are in the new house. Michael seems to be sleeping better with no nightmares bothering him. Marie got used to holding his hands when he slept. It helped him get past everything that happened this year. The twins are Tylor and his sister Taylor. Michael and the twins are giving them a run for their money, but Michael and Marie are enjoying every minute of it. Tomorrow one little girl is turning eight, and they have something planned for her mom.

The next morning, Savanna joined her dad in the living room and waited for Marie to come downstairs with Hannah in tow. Marie finally came down the steps with Hannah in her arms. The babies are still sleeping. "What are you two up to?"

"Mom, we have a surprise for you."

"But, Savanna, it is your birthday, so we should be surprising you."

"Mom, please sit on the couch. Hannah, please sit next to Mommy."

"Okay!"

Michael picked up Hannah and sat her down next to her mom as he kissed her on the forehead. Savanna retrieved a box of tissues. Marie commented, "Oh no, this can't be good."

Michael turned on their TV and started the video. The video started with Savanna saying, "While you were gone, we did not want you to miss a thing. So we recorded all the important moments." The slideshow started with Savanna and Michael getting messy and throwing glitter at each other and then the aftermath of the glitter fight. The next couple of slides showed some of Savanna's birthdays. A video popped up, and she said before her candles were blown out, "I wish for my mom and my baby brother or sister." The tears started to flow, and the tissue box was there. Another video pops up, and Savanna says, "Mommy, this is for you," and she smears icing all over Michael's face. Marie laughs.

Then another video comes on, and both Michael and Savanna are holding a cake that says, "Happy birthday to our new little one." Michael adds, "This was the due date of our baby, and I am hoping he or she is perfect. I wish I could be with you." More tears come streaming down. More slides of the two of them throwing water balloons at each other in the backyard. Then Savanna dumping ice water on her dad. Marie laughs. Then another video comes on with both Michael and Savanna singing happy birthday to Marie. Then another video of Michael toasting to their anniversary. "Marie, I will never forget this day. You made me the happiest man alive on that day." Slides come up of their wedding pictures. More tears stream down Marie's cheeks. More slides of parents' birthdays and anniversaries. For the finale, he said, "The day before you came home, your brother asked his girlfriend to marry him, and she said yes." The slides of him proposing and the smile on her face. Then Michael came on, and said these words: "No matter where you are, Marie, you are not going to miss important moments in our lives. We are all holding out hope that you will be able to watch this video. I love you, and I promise you that our daughter is being taken care of. I promise to find you. I promise to never give up and to have you in my arms again. In the meantime, you are in my dreams. We are dancing and holding each other. Until we meet again, my love, I am holding you in my heart."

The video ends, and the tears just keep flowing. Marie can't speak. She can't put into words the love she feels right now. Finally, she spoke, and she let them know that while she was caged, she could feel their love. She could feel Michael holding on to her. She held on to the images of her and Michael dancing at their wedding. "Those images are what kept me going and kept me alive." Marie stood up with Hannah in her arms and wrapped up her husband and Savanna up in her arms. "This is the best gift I could have ever asked for." They held each other for about five more minutes, and then one of the babies started to cry.

Michael let Marie spend time with her daughters, and he went up to tend to the one who was crying. He changed Taylor's diaper and dressed her to bring her down for breakfast. Then Tylor woke up and Michael put Taylor down in her crib and picked up Tylor. He changed him and put him down in his crib; and just on cue, Michael Junior cries, and Michael does the same thing. Then he came up with a clever way to bring them downstairs at the same time. He put Michael Junior in the front carry, and then he had each of the twins snuggled in his arms. He bounded downstairs. Marie turned around and laughed a little at the sight. Michael responded, "See, I got this."

He put each one in their highchairs. Michael fed Tylor. Marie fed Taylor, and Savanna fed Michael. Hannah is helping her mom feed Taylor while trying to eat themselves. Savanna wanted to do something as a family for her birthday, so she picked mini-golf, and Marie set up a surprise for her when she gets there. Her grandparents, her uncles, her soon-to-be aunt, and friends will be there, waiting for her; and when she gets to the first hole, they will yell surprise. That's what they exactly did. Savanna was a happy little girl. She had her family together, and that's all she really wanted. Her family together forever or so she thought.

The next day, Michael was getting ready for work with a smile on his face and newfound energy. Marie was watching him from the bed as she started to get up. "I love this about you. You are glowing."

Michael bounded over to Marie and just lifted her right off her feet. "I am just happy. All is right, and this is a beautiful day." In his mind, he is celebrating all the little moments in life. Being able to have Marie back in his arms and kissing each one of his kids before he leaves for work are wonderful things for Michael. Being able to come home at night and helping Savanna with her homework, feeding some of the kids, and helping Marie entertain the kids are what he loves coming home to. Michael let Marie freshen up, and he held out his hand to Marie as she took it. Michael lifted her up and carried her downstairs, staring into her eyes. Marie could only hold on. "Man, I could get used to this," she whispers in his ear.

He placed Marie at the kitchen table where he had made breakfast. "Please eat!" Then he bounded up the stairs and carried Savanna and Hannah down as well. Then the babies came down next. He kissed each and every one of his family members and said, "See you all tonight." Out the door he went. A half hour later, Michael's friend and boss calls Marie and asks if Michael was coming into work today. Marie's heart dropped, and she had a look of confusion on her face. "Yes, he left a half hour ago. He should be there by now." When she got off the phone with Michael's work, she immediately called Brian. "Brian, I just got a call from Michael's work. They are wondering where he is. I told them he should be there because he left the house on time. Brian, it is not like him to not show up for work."

The TV was on, tuned to the news. The news anchor says, "We have a couple of breaking stories right now. Emily broke out of prison this morning. If you have any information of her whereabouts, please call the police."

Marie started to panic, "Brian, she is out, and my husband is now missing."

"Marie, please tell me what Michael was wearing and driving today. I am also sending over police to watch the house and protecting you and the kids."

"Thank you, Brian." Marie told Brian what Michael was wearing that day. When she hung up the phone, she realized that Savanna was standing there crying. "Mommy, where's Daddy?"

Marie ran over to hold her daughter. "I don't know, sweetheart. Hopefully, he is just in another part of the building at his work."

Michael wakes up tied to a chair and not wearing any clothes. Emily is walking around him. His head feels so heavy and hurts. "What did you do to me?"

"You were in your car, and I hit you with my car. I got you out and saved your life."

"But why am I naked?"

"So that you can repay me."

"You are not going to get what you want from me."

"But I want you." She sits on his lap, taking it all in.

Michael fought it harder than he did before, but his body responded, and he released. Then he laughed. "What are you laughing about?"

"You are not getting a baby out of me again. I fixed it so that you can never get a baby from me again."

"Well, you will stay here until you give me one or give me back little Michael."

"No, you will not get either." Emily slapped him across the face. Michael's face feels like it was going to fall off. Michael blacked out.

Brian called Marie with the news that Michael's car was found, but there was no sign of him anywhere. "Marie, Michael was in an accident. It seems like a bad one, but he is not here." Marie sat down in a way that looked like she lost her balance. "Our parents are here keeping the kids occupied. I am coming there to deal with the car. Please get to work finding my husband."

"I am on it!"

"Thank you, Brian!" Marie grabbed her keys and told his parents that they found his car and she was going to take care of it. "Please, tell the kids."

"Don't worry about the kids. We got them."

Marie runs out and gets into her car, fighting back the tears so that she can drive. Marie gets to the accident scene, and she sees just how bad it is. Marie fights the tears back. The driver's door was smashed in, and the windshield is broken. The front of the car was unrecognizable. Marie laid her hand on what's left of the driver's door. The tears started to flow, and all she can say is "Michael, where are you?"

Emily is staring out the window with binoculars and laughing at Marie's dismay of the car. Michael was waking up again and heard Emily say Marie's name, and it perks him up a little. "Marie!" Emily notices Michael is awake. She walks over bragging about Marie's pain written all over her face. Emily pulls Michael over to the window and shows him Marie at his crippled car. Michael says nothing but takes in the sight as much as he can. Then Emily pulls him away. Michael thinks to himself, *Marie, I am right here. Please come find me.* "Well honey, I am going to go and find us something to eat. Please don't leave me again. Oh, wait, you can't go anywhere." Emily laughs.

When she leaves, Michael scoots himself over to the window with his feet being untied and barely sees as Marie takes care of the car, and he wills her to look around. When the scene was clean, he saw her leave. He yearns for her to return. He moves back over to where he was and starts feeling what hurts. He moves his arm, and he winces at the pain. His head is pounding and can feel blood running down his cheeks. He moves his stomach and winces in pain. He moves his hand and winces in pain.

Emily walks back in with food in her hand. Emily gives Michael scraps of what she was eating. Then she dumps a bit of water on Michael's mouth. Michael finally says, "Emily, if you are going to keep me here and want me to perform for you, you have to take care of my wounds and feed me more."

Emily slaps him again and says, "I will tell you what to do, not the other way around." Michael remembered what she did to Richard, and he now knows he does not have a chance to persuade her.

As Marie was leaving the accident site, she felt Michael with her. She felt his love, and she says to herself as she looked at nearby buildings, *Hang in there, baby. I will find you!* Marie follows Brian to his office, and they look at traffic cameras to see if they caught the accident. Marie spots Michael's car stopped at an intersection, and then it was not picked up again at the next. His car had to have been hit right where they found it. Then she thought if it was Emily, she could not have carried him that far away from the accident. She has to be held up in one of the buildings, and she shared her thoughts with Brian.

Brian went into action and set up a search team for the buildings around the accident. While out in search mode, the fingerprints came back from Michael's car, and a print belonging to Emily was found. Then Brian's team came across the building that had signs of someone being there. They slowly creep up the steps and then break the door down. The men fan out and search the building and found blood on the floor and a picture of Michael tied to a chair with his head slumped over and not wearing clothes. Brian's heart leaped out of his chest for Marie because he is going to show her this picture. He prepares to see the hurt and pain in her face. Brian gets back to the station and hands the picture to Marie. "It's happening all over again. I am sorry, Marie." Marie took the picture and immediately dropped it with a very serious, straight, angry look on her face and tears pooling in her eyes. Later, the blood is a definite match to Michael, proving that Marie was right and that Michael is hurt.

Emily knew she had to move and was glad she did because the police were in the rearview mirror entering the building she was just in. She and Michael are home free and was moving to a place where no one will know where they are.

THREE WEEKS GO BY

Marie is pacing, and every lead they get leads to a dead end. She thought to herself, *I guess this is how Michael felt when I was missing.* Marie thought of something, and she has a sinking feeling that she might be right. Marie told her parents she would be right back. She needed to drive to clear her head, but she went back to the house where Emily kept her. She left the car parked out on the road, and she walked the driveway back to the house. Her heart fluttered when she saw a car parked there. As she got close, she spotted Emily in the living room window. She carefully opened the door to the kitchen and slipped in without a sound.

As she got closer to the room, she saw Emily in. She saw Michael in the chair tied with no clothes on. Her heart sank. Marie took out her phone and dialed 911 and left it where she was. Emily was dancing naked in front of Michael. Marie could see he was not looking or was even awake. His head was slumped over, and she could see dried blood on his face and body. Tears started to fall. She looked around to see if there was anything to defend herself with, and she saw a metal pipe. Marie picked it up and stepped into the room where Emily was. "Emily, there you are. We have to talk."

Emily quickly picked up a gun and aimed it at Marie. When Michael heard Marie's voice, he lifted his head just barely. Marie slowly walked over to Michael. Emily lunged at her and said, "Don't you touch him! He is mine!"

"Emily, he is hurt bad. He needs help, or he is going to die. Put the gun down and let me help him please."

"Drop the pipe first, and maybe you can help him." Emily went on to say, "You had him long enough. It is my turn to have a baby with him. He is mine now, and you have to leave now." Emily heard the sirens, "What did you do? You called them again, didn't you? They will take me again and lock me away from Michael. I can't live without him."

Just then, Brian yelled through the window. "Emily, put the gun down!" Emily pulls the trigger on Marie and then pulls the trigger on herself just as the bullets start to fly. Marie hits the floor holding her shoulder but rushes to Michael's side. She frantically unties her husband and throws her coat over him. "Baby, please say something to me. You are safe now. I am here. Stay with me please. Don't leave."

"Marie, you found me!" His voice was barely a whisper. Marie held Michael on the floor until the EMTs were able to come in. When the EMTs picked him up out of Marie's arms, he seems to fade away.

Marie yells from the floor, "Michael! Stay here with me!" The EMTs put the paddles on him, and the line is flat. Marie puts a hand over her mouth as she hears them say clear, and she watches his body fly up and then down. Flatline. Marie is screaming his name, "Michael! Michael!"

The second time, "Clear!" The line starts to jump, and the EMTs rush him out to the ambulance. Back out to the road it goes. Marie stays frozen on the floor, staring at Emily's lifeless body. Then she buries her face in her hands. Brian runs in and sees Marie bleeding. He helps Marie to her feet and to the waiting ambulance. Marie has all color drained from her face. Marie is showing no emotion. Emily got Marie in the upper chest, which Marie forgot about, and she feels faint. The ambulance rushes Marie to the hospital. Marie blacks out from the blood loss.

CHAPTER 7

The Unknown

Marie wakes up an hour later and finds her mom by her side. Immediately, she asks, "Michael! Where's Michael? Mom please tell me, where's Michael?"

"Darling, he is in surgery. The doctors have not updated us yet."

"Mom, I want to go see him please. He has to know that I am here with him."

Marie starts to get up, but her mom stops her. "Marie, please wait until I get your doctor."

Marie's doctor comes in, and he says, "Now, Marie, you can't be up yet. You lost a lot of blood."

"Please, Doctor, I want to know about Michael!"

The doctor looked out the curtain and sees Michael's doctor walking toward Marie. "Hello, Marie, I am your husband's doctor. He is out of surgery. I don't know how he is doing this, but he is hanging on. The kind of trauma your husband is in should have killed him. But he is hanging on. His head was split open, and he had some internal bleeding. His whole left arm was shattered, and his right hand was badly broken. He lost a lot of blood. He has cuts and bruising all over his body, but he is stable. We will have you both in the same room in just a couple of minutes."

Marie looked at her mom and just started to cry. Her mom wraps her arms around Marie and says, "He is going to be okay. We are all going to be okay."

Moments later, Brian brings Marie her cell phone, keys, and jacket that Marie put on Michael. Brian asked, "How is he?"

Marie composed herself and said, "Thanks to us, he will be okay." Marie asked, "Emily?"

Brian said, "She did not make it."

Marie breathed a sigh of relief but felt some sorrow for her. The orderly came to move Marie to their room. Brian and her mom were in tow. Marie craned her neck as she got closer to the room. Michael was already there. He had so many more tubes coming out and in him than she did. "Michael, I am here, and I am not leaving." The orderly put Marie as close as he could to Michael and still allowed enough room to work on him. Her mom and Brian stayed a little while longer. The minute they left, Marie slipped out of her bed and into Michael's. "Thank you for staying. Thank you for fighting. I am here and not going anywhere. I love you!" After Marie said her words, she noticed that his heartbeat on the monitor increased a little and then settled back down to normal. Marie fell asleep listening to Michael's heart.

The next morning, she awoke to someone staring at her. She looked up and saw one of his eyes open. She shot up quick, and he smiled. She smiled. "I knew you heard me last night."

He lifted his right hand and soothed her hair. Marie got up and found a doctor. "He is awake."

The doctor looked at her with a crazy look on his face. The doctor followed her in and saw that Michael was awake. "Hello, Michael, welcome back. I am going to take this tube out of your throat. When I say breathe, breathe out for me. Okay ready?" Michael nods. "Now, breathe out."

Michael does and coughs and winces. The first words he says are "Hello beautiful," and he smiles. He then looks down at Marie's arm in a sling.

The doctor notices and said, "Your wife risks her life to save you and takes a bullet for you."

"Yes. I am the one who found you."

"Emily shot you?" Michael whispered.

"Yes, she did."

The doctor leaves Marie to tell Michael everything that he went through. "You died on me, baby. Please don't ever do that again."

"I will try not to."

Marie smiles and says, "I guess she likes the number three because she had you for three weeks and me for three years. They were three long torturing weeks."

Michael tells her, "I had to hang on for you. You told me not to leave you. I heard you speaking to me while you were at the accident site. I heard you say you will find me. I had to hang on because I knew you would find me."

Marie tells him, "I heard you also. You did tell me to come find you. I did find you. You also told me where you were, and I came right to you." Marie climbed back in bed with Michael and fell asleep. Michael wrapped his one good arm around her ever so carefully to not hurt her wound.

Marie could not leave Michael's side while in the hospital. The nightmares are back, and they are worse this time around. What helps is when Marie can curl up next to him as he falls asleep. Her head on his chest and the rhythm of his heart put him right to sleep.

She wakes up just in time to see the start of his nightmare, and her soothing touch with her whisper sometimes snaps him right out of it. Other times, it takes longer.

Michael was only in the hospital for about a week. Michael is still weak when Marie wheels him through the door of the house filled with people, but the sight of his children makes him smile. He noticed there was a scared look on Savanna's face that he did not recognize. "What's the matter, princess?"

"Daddy, I was scared that you weren't going to come back. I did not want to go through that again."

Michael smiles at her and says, "I came back because your mom found me, and do you know what else?"

"What?"

"You were my rock that kept me alive during the past few weeks. I had to keep you, your brothers, and sisters on my mind so that I could come back to you. You helped your mom save Daddy's life."

Savanna wrapped her arms around Michael's neck and cried like she never cried before. Michael took her onto his lap and let her cry while Marie was watching. She then walked over and wrapped both of them in her arms. Once Savanna settled herself, she kissed her daddy on the cheek and said, "Welcome home, Daddy."

"Thank you, princess." Michael greeted everyone, and Marie helped Michael slowly walk the steps to their bedroom so that Michael could lie down. He was slow moving, and everything hurt. Marie's mom carried Michael's chair upstairs and left the two of them alone. Marie helped Michael into bed; and before she could go, he wrapped his arm around her and just let it all go. He cried out his brokenness, his pain, and his shame. "Let it all go, darling. Cry. It's okay. Let it all go. I am not going anywhere. I know." She wraps herself around him. Then he drifted off to sleep, and Marie slipped away to return to the kids and their family.

A couple of hours later, Marie returned to the bedroom to lay down herself. Michael woke up and decided to tell her what happened to him. He had to talk about it to let him get through it. She wrapped herself around him as he spoke. The details hurt her hearing them. The torture he endured, the pain, the yearning, the agony he told her. The way Emily would get mad when he was too weak to perform for her. She would punch him, slap him, and kick him. There were other times where his body reacted, and he did not have the energy to fight it. He pleaded with her to help him or when she would not get what she wanted. It made her lash out at him even more. Marie's tears ran down her face as she listened. She wrapped herself tighter around him.

Michael opening up to her helped him cope with what happened. Being so open to Marie about what he was feeling and how he was feeling made their bond stronger. Michael is not used to being this vulnerable, this open; but now that he is open, he is grateful for someone who will listen to him and not judge him. Getting it out helped him with the nightmares. They became less and less. Michael would sometimes react when Marie would touch him a certain way but then would relax under her touch. Michael did not interact with Michael that much the first few days that he was home. But in time, Michael was getting the same attention that his siblings were getting from their dad.

It took a couple of weeks for Michael to fully regain his strength with the exception of his left arm. The doctors told him that it will be a long road to recovery for him. The one good thing is that Michael can return to work as long as he is only using his mind and not his left arm to work. Marie is his motivation, and she came alongside him and quietly supported him. Marie took care of the kids and him and made it look easy. Marie planned activities so that the family could spend time together. She watched with pride as Michael interacted with the kids, watching their faces light up and hearing their laugh when Michael would lift them a certain way. Seeing the look of joy on Michael's face when the kids attacked him and try to tickle him on the floor is an amazing reward for Marie. Michael loves being a father. It shows every day. That is all Marie can ask for.

Marie went up to the attic to retrieve something for the kids. She has not been up there since they moved in. She forgets the minute she realizes what she sees. There are pictures of Michael in the chair Marie found him in. There are pictures of Emily as she did what she did. On a TV played a new video of what Emily did to Michael those three weeks she had him. The pain in his eyes, the agony as Emily manipulated him, and the pain as Emily would tease him. Marie dropped to the floor with a gasp, and Michael heard it. Marie did not move. She was frozen when she heard Michael say. "What happened, babe? Are you okay?"

Michael moved slowly up the steps. Marie wanted to stop him, but she could not move in time. Michael found Marie on the floor paralyzed of the sight he was now focusing on. Marie is sobbing as she gets a determined, angry look on her face. She rips every picture off the wall and pushes stop on the TV. Emily was in the house creating what she loved the most, which is the look of pain on Marie's face, but she did not get to see it. She did not stick around long enough to see it. Marie finishes tearing down the pictures as Michael walked over to her and held her tight. "It's all over, Michael. It is finally over." Michael does not know what happened to Emily. Marie did not want to tell him until he was ready. "Michael, the night I found you, when Emily realized that she was going to lose you again was when she shot me and then turned the gun on herself. She killed herself for you."

"Then it is definitely over," Michael held Marie tighter and let out a sigh of relief.

The next day Brian came over to collect the evidence just in case a living relative comes seek justice for Emily. Brian did, in fact, find a living relative. "Emily has a brother, and he is coming to collect Emily's ashes."

Marie's heart skipped a beat. "Wait, she has a brother? I wonder if he helped her do all this."

"No, he lives in California and only realized of his sister when we called him. It turns out that Emily was adopted as an infant. Her mom was strung out on drugs when the state took her kids from her. Their dad was killed, and their mom turned to drugs to help soothe the pain."

Marie looked at Brian and said, "Brian, I don't want to meet this brother of hers. I can't take any more of her family."

Brian smiled a little and reassured her that he was not going to push the issue. "One more thing before I go, remember when I told you that Emily's parents died in a car accident?"

"Yes, did she have anything to do with it?" Michael asked.

"Yes, she did. She rigged the car so that the brakes would fail at a certain part of the road. We did not know this until we looked at the car again."

Marie asked, "What made you look at the car again?"

"The accident was ruled suspicious. We went to investigate more and that is when we found out Marie was taken, not knowing until now that Emily had Marie. We had to put Emily's suspicion on hold and help Michael with your disappearance."

"Thank you, Brian, for the information." Michael shook Brian's hand.

When Brian left, Marie sat at the kitchen table with her head in her hands. "Back on that day that Emily and I fought, never in a million years would I have thought that Emily would be capable of doing something like this. I just had a taste of it then."

Michael stood soaking it all in. "I wonder what made her so hung up on me."

Marie grabbed her laptop and said, "Let's do a little research on Emily." Marie typed in her name, and the search came up with a lot of stuff. As Marie scrolled, they came across a picture of Emily and her boyfriend. He looked like Michael's twin right down to his dimples. Marie read the article out loud that Emily and friends wrote in honor of her boyfriend.

In Honor of Trevor by Emily and Friends

I sit at my computer writing the words that will describe my best friend and the love of my life. Trevor was a part of me since we met in my backyard at six years of age. We have been together ever since. Today my heart is broken, and today I have to say goodbye to my best friend and the love of my life. Cancer took his life from me. He could not fight anymore. Now he is not fighting anymore. He is resting peacefully and healed. My heart, my body, and my soul will miss Trevor. He will be forever in my heart and never forgotten. Trevor, I will find you again. Wait for me. I will be there soon.

Your love,
Emily

She added a picture to the article of the two of them. Then the rest of his friends added their thoughts to the article as well. Both Marie and Michael sat back staring at Trevor's face and the way he looked like Michael, and they see why Emily would not let Michael go. Marie and Michael sit frozen for a couple more minutes before turning off the laptop.

Brian meets with Emily's brother. Brian explains what Emily was like and what she did. Eric could not believe what she was capable of, and he sat in shock as he listened. "I am sorry. I did not know I had a sister until you called me. How is the family that she attacked?"

"The family is healing now."

"That's good. Is there anything else you need from me?"

"No, I think we are good. If you have any questions, please don't hesitate to call."

"Thank you, Brian." Brian watched as Eric left his office. Brian could not help but feel sorry for the guy. He seemed lost and didn't know what to do next.

Michael is sitting with his family at the dinner table watching the interaction with one another. The moments in his life are special for him because they allow him to spend time with the most important people in his life. These moments were almost taken from him twice, but he fought for them. He is proud of the kind of family he has. He could not have asked for anything better. Michael looks into Marie's eyes and sees passion, love, and want for him. Sometimes he feels shame for what he has been through, but her look melts it away. The thought of not being able to look into her eyes scares him. Not being able to watch her interact with the kids and seeing her smile scares him. He never wants to go through that again.

His life is back to where he wants it, and that gives him pride. He knows that he will be around to see his kids graduate and see them get married. He will be around to walk each one of his daughters down the aisle. He will be around to teach his boys to shave and how to love their wives like he does Marie. He will be around to protect Marie and make her feel safe the way she made him feel. The connection is real between him and Marie. The bond between them is unbelievable.

Marie's instincts are nothing to mess with. She can sense when her family is in trouble. She is beautiful, and she is Michael's. Marie was looking at Michael as he was lost in thought; and she sees his pride, his love, and his want in his eyes. She smiles as she watches him dream his life. The warmth that she feels as Michael stares at her. She can't think of a better life than what she has right now. Marie gets up from her chair, walks over to Michael, and carefully sits on his lap and says, "This is where I belong." She slowly sweetly kisses him and holds him tight.

EPILOGUE

Michael and Marie's story shows just how much love can conquer anything, especially their kind of love. The trials that the family went through made their bond stronger. Their story shows to hold tight to the person who loves back. Michael and Marie show their kids just how important it is to honestly love someone. When they go through tough times, fight and keep fighting. When there is no more strength left, hold on a little longer. Hold on to the strength that God and family can only provide. No matter what the world says about the relationship chosen, stay strong and love anyway. Make love unique and deep with the one who promised. Your life will never be the same, and it will blow your mind. It certainly blew Michael's mind. Michael draws this conclusion that if we let someone deep enough into our hearts, there is a good chance we won't be disappointed. But if you hold them just out of reach, you will be disappointed. Enjoy your life because you only get one!

LOVE

CHAPTER 1

The Start of a New Chapter

Katie is twenty-three, a new college graduate who just moved into her apartment. Katie found an apartment because the commute to Delaware was killing her. The apartment was very close to her job that she has had for a year now. Katie flopped down onto the couch when a knock came on the door. Katie went to the door and opened it. Standing there is a man who looks about the same age as she with a good smile, and he is easy on the eyes. "Hello, I am Parker. I live right there." He pointed to the door right next to hers. "If you need anything, don't hesitate to knock."

"Thank you, Parker. I am Katie."

"It is nice to meet you, Katie." Parker shakes Katie's hand and excuses himself. Katie could not help but smile as she shuts the door. Her phone starts to ring, and Katie rushes to pick it up.

"Hello, Katie, are you all moved in yet? What is it like? Meet any cute neighbors yet?"

"Hello, best friend, yes, it is good so far, and I have a cute neighbor who might just be your type." Her best friend Alyssa lives in Maryland. They went through grade school and college together.

Parker smiles because he liked what he saw. Katie is a tall slender sporty girl, and she is his type. He looks forward to getting to know her. Parker is a musician for a local band and makes good money. He is seeing someone, but for Katie, he can make an exception.

Katie is thinking about Parker. He does have the looks. His body seems muscular, and his blond hair is wavy. He has deep-blue eyes that someone will get lost in. But Katie hopes that he does not fall in love with her because he is not her type. She likes the different color of skin in a man. She likes the deep-brown eyes, and she has her eyes set on Travis. He is a coworker of hers, and he is her partner in an advertising company. They have been working together for a year now. The chemistry is there between them, and she can tell he has his eyes set on her. She is planning on asking him to dinner, but she is a little scared of what he might say. Her moment will be at work tomorrow.

Katie walks into her shared office with Travis, and he is there with a smile. Katie's heart flutters at the sight. "You beat me today. What's up with—" Katie gives Travis a suspicious look when Travis interrupts her.

"I came in early to catch up on some work. Plus, I wanted to ask you a question."

The sincere look on his face makes her heart smile. "Okay."

"I have been wondering if you wanted to have dinner with me tonight."

Katie froze and then said, "You are asking me out on a date?" "Yes."

"I was going to ask you. So, yes, let's go." Travis smiles at the thought of Katie asking him. Katie's mind is now racing. *I can't believe he was thinking the same thing. Does he have feelings for me?*

For the rest of the day, it was hard to focus on work. She kept peeking at him, and she sometimes felt his eyes on her. The two of them sneak glances at each other all day. Travis smiles as he feels her eyes on him. He can't believe this is happening to him. Katie is a very beautiful girl, and he did not think she would say yes to go out with him. Her smile, her eyes, and the way she flirts with them make it hard to concentrate on work. It sure does make the day brighter and more enjoyable.

As the day came to a finish, Travis told Katie he will pick her up at seven. Travis watches her as she walks to her car. He can't believe she said yes. He is hoping that she has the same feelings for him. He is hoping she says yes tonight when he asks her the second question.

When Katie got home, Parker was standing at his mailbox, looking at his mail. "Hey, Katie, how are you?"

"Hello, Parker, I am good. How about you?"

"Katie, I was thinking, do you want to go out tonight?"

"I am sorry, Parker, I can't. I have a date tonight."

"Okay, no problem. Maybe another time."

"Maybe another time. Thank you, Parker, for the invite, though."

"You are welcome. Have a good night."

"Thank you." Katie walked into her apartment and changed.

At seven, her doorbell rang, and she opened the door. Travis was standing there with flowers and looking pretty hot. Travis was wearing a black suit with a light-purple shirt and different shades of purple tie. Travis smiled wide when his eyes fell on Katie. She is wearing a white sundress with little purple flowers on the neckline. "These are beautiful. Thank you!"

"You are welcome. Are you ready to go?"

"Yes, I am. Where are we going?" Katie asked with a smile.

"It is a surprise."

Katie closed the door to her apartment and left with Travis. She had a feeling that someone was watching her, but she shook the feeling away when she looked at Travis. Travis took Katie to the beach where he had a single table set up and covered plates with a bottle of wine. Travis remembered when Katie would talk about the kind of date she would like to have. "Wow, this is amazing. Travis, thank you."

"I knew you would love this. I remembered this when you talked about it." They sat down and started to eat and talk. Half into the evening, Travis asked his question, "Katie, I have been wanting to ask you a question for a while now. So here it goes. Katie, I would love it if you would be my girlfriend. I have feelings for you, and I can't keep hiding them."

Katie froze and sat in amazement. Then a smile came across her face, and she said yes. Travis stood up and scooped her up and gave her the sweetest kiss that he could ever give her. He hugged her and said, "Let's clean up and go for a walk."

"Sounds good to me."

Travis cleaned up dinner and put everything in his car. Then they walked the beach and talked some more. "Travis, before we get too far into our relationship, I want to let you know that I am the type of girl who wants to marry before I have sex. I want to make sure he is right for me, and I want to wait."

"I know you are that type of girl. That is why I wanted you as my girlfriend. I know that there will not be any pressure, and I want to wait also."

Katie looked at him and said, "Where did you come from?" She then stopped and planted a kiss right on his lips. Katie then asked, "How is this going to work at work? Are we going to get any work done?"

Travis smiled and said, "It's going to be hard, but we have been doing this working thing for a year now. When we are at work, we just have to stay focused on work."

"Okay, I think that might work. I just have to force myself not to stare at you the whole time."

Travis laughed and said, "I caught your eyes all day today."

Katie laughed. "I caught yours also."

Travis and Katie walked back to the car, and Travis took her home. At Katie's door, Travis gave her a long sweet good night kiss. The kiss left her speechless, and she smiled as she watched him walk away. Parker watched from the peephole in his door.

Parker is disappointed that Katie was kissing another guy tonight. Parker is putting a plan into motion to make Katie his. The next morning, Parker and Katie came out their doors at the same time. "Good morning, Katie. Do you want to go out tonight and have dinner with me?"

"Parker, I am sorry I can't. I don't think it will be a good idea because Travis is my boyfriend now. I don't want to ruin what Travis and I have."

"Oh, okay, I wish you best of luck and happiness."

"Thank you, Parker. Have a good day!"

"You too, Katie, thank you!" Parker watches as she walks away while thinking *Oh, Katie, you will regret turning me down. I can't wait until you are with me.* Parker fantasizes as he starts to think of Katie. He loves her smile and the way she says his name. He is also looking forward to seeing her exposed under him.

Katie is now more excited to go to work. She walked into her office and saw flowers on her desk. Travis is not there yet. She smiled and read the card. "Thank you for a wonderful night."

Travis walked in and saw the flowers and asked, "Who are the flowers from?"

"They are from you!"

"No, I did not send these flowers."

"Then why does the card say this?" Katie hands him the card, and he reads it.

Travis walked over to his desk and dialed the florist. "Hello, my name is Travis Andrews. Can you tell me who sent flowers to Katie McDaniel this morning?"

"I will place you on hold while I check for you." A couple of minutes later, she said, "Sorry, sir, those flowers were purchased with cash, and no name was used. We don't have cameras yet. I can't give you a description because I did not take the order."

"Thank you for the information." Travis turned to Katie and said the person paid by cash and they have no idea who the person was.

"Can I just pretend they are from you?"

Travis smiled and gave her a little kiss. For the rest of the day, they peeked at each other in between meetings and paperwork. Her lunches got even more interesting. Now she has a lunch date every day. Travis and Katie walked out of the office together.

Travis and Katie would spend time together after work either at Katie's or Travis's house. They would talk about their family life and some of their history. Katie explained to Travis that she is an only child, and it is just her and her mom. Her dad died when she was four. He was a soldier for the army. "I can remember only bits and pieces of him. My mom loves telling me stories about him. He had the biggest smile on his face when they placed me in his arms. It was love at first sight for him. He could not put me down. He would have held me forever if he could."

It was Travis's turn to tell Katie. "I have one brother, Kevin, and both of my parents died in a car accident. My dad was driving, and he lost control of the car on ice and ended up down an embankment. I was eighteen and became my brother's legal guardian. He was thirteen at the time. Now he is twenty and in college."

"Nice job, big brother."

"Yes, he followed in my footsteps, and when I became responsible of him, I became a role model of who our parents would want us to be. I know that they would be proud of both of us."

"Yes, they will be." Katie rubbed his back.

"Katie, you are the first person I opened up to about my parents. I have had two girlfriends before you and I became partners. I was not able to open up to them."

Katie looked at him with hope in her heart. "I feel honored. Always remember that you can talk to me about anything. I am a good listener."

"I am here for you also. I will protect you from anything. I know this might be a little early in the relationship, but I have to say it because this is how I feel." Travis takes Katie's hands into his and says, "I love you, and I have loved you since you became my partner."

Katie looked into Travis's eyes and saw the genuine truth to that statement, and she said, "I love you." They both stare into each other's eyes and kissed.

Travis decided to pick up Katie every morning for work. They spent every minute together, and they became closer. Parker was growing more and more jealous and angrier every time he sees Katie and Travis together. He figured out how to watch Katie whenever she was home. He was able to slip little video cameras into her walls and ceiling. They showed her bathroom and bedroom. They also showed her living room. Parker studied her schedule and took notes.

The one thing he could not figure out is why she was not bringing Travis into her bedroom so he could watch. One day, he will show her how. Meanwhile, he kept leaving her gifts at the office and her door. It is really starting to freak Katie out. When Travis brought her home one night, there was a note on her door saying, "He will never be good for you. I am more of a man than he is."

CHAPTER 2

The Fear

Katie is now freaked out. She does not feel safe in her apartment, but she is not leaving. She just has to take extra measures for her safety. Unfortunately, Travis is the partner who travels, and he will be out of town this week. Travis is worried about leaving Katie. "Please call me every time you leave the house and come home."

"Okay, I will. Go have fun and make me proud, partner. I will miss you, and I love you."

"I love you, and I will miss you terribly."

Parker will make his move. Parker made sure that he will be able to access her apartment. Two days after Travis left, he got in while she was sleeping. He blacked out his whole body and didn't make a sound. He went to her bed and covered her mouth with tape. Then he handcuffed her hands. She struggled and screamed muffled under the tape. She was crying for her life. He showed her a knife, put his finger over his mouth to tell her to be quiet, and then demonstrated what he would do if she did not listen. Then he let himself into her. It lasted for an hour. Then he left after uncuffing her. Then he reminded her what would happen if she said anything.

She was shaking uncontrollably when she dialed Travis's phone. The only thing she could say was help in a shaky, tear-filled voice. "Katie, I am on the next flight out. I will be there in two hours." When he hung up with Katie, he called the police and sent them to her apartment. When Travis landed, he raced to the hospital and made it in time to see Katie being wheeled back to her room. When she saw him, her tears started to fall. He went to her bedside and asked her, "What happened?"

In her tear-soaked voice, she said, "I was raped."

Travis climbed into the bed with her, wrapped his arms around her, and stayed there until her tears subsided and she fell asleep. Travis stayed with her the rest of the night.

The next morning, the doctor came in and explained the damage left behind. He also said that no DNA was left behind because he was wearing a condom. When the doctor left, Travis asked Katie, "Where did this happen?"

"In my apartment."

"That's it. You are not going back to your apartment. You are staying with me."

Katie agreed because, at this point, she did not want anything to do with her apartment. When Katie was released, Travis took her to his apartment and then went to her apartment to get some of her stuff. His heart sank when he saw the blood on her bed and the tape that was over her mouth. He quickly gathered her stuff and left her apartment. Katie took a couple of days off to recuperate. Travis slept on the couch to give Katie his bed. Katie would have nightmares, and Travis would run to her to soothe her.

While Katie was taking a nap, Travis went back to her apartment and cleaned it. He even replaced the whole bed for her. The blood went right through to the mattress. He had all the locks changed, and he noticed just how the man got into her apartment. Her sliding glass door to her balcony was open ever so slightly. He had the whole door replaced as well and installed a better locking system for it. Katie came home to her apartment after three weeks of being at Travis's. "Travis, thank you for doing all this for me. I love you for it, but you did not have to do it."

"I did have to do it. It will make me rest better knowing that all these improvements will keep you safe." Travis stayed with her at her apartment for two weeks. The first night she was alone, Travis had her keep him on the phone all night.

The next morning, Parker knocked on Katie's door. "Hello, Parker, how are you doing?"

"I am good. But I am here to find out how you are. I heard what happened."

"I am okay now."

"I am sorry I was not here that night, or I would have helped. I was at a concert."

"That's okay, Parker. I know if you were here, you would have helped and thank you. If you would excuse me, I have to get ready for work."

"You are welcome. Have a good day at work."

During the three weeks that she was at Travis's, the gifts stopped; but when she got home, they started again. She left them in the hallway and asked the maintenance man to get rid of them for her. Gifts would also come to her workplace as well, but Katie told the receptionist not to accept anything that comes anonymously and have them returned to the place it came from.

Travis did not like leaving Katie alone after dinner every night. Travis asked Katie, "I want to move in here. I feel uneasy leaving you every night. I will sleep on your nice, comfy couch."

"No, Travis, I can't let you do it and live on my couch. No matter how comfortable it is, I can't let you live like that."

"I will be okay. I am not sleeping right anymore, knowing that you are here by yourself."

Katie thought about it more and said, "Okay, but you are not sleeping on the couch. You are sleeping in the bed with me. It is comfier than my old bed and the couch thanks to you. I will even give you half of my closet."

"Okay, deal." Travis was in the apartment a week later. In a way, it made Katie sleep better also. As time went on, Travis and Katie got closer. Their love for each other grew deeper. They learned more about each other and their childhood.

For about three months, all gifts and letters stopped. Katie was back feeling her old self again. When Travis would leave on business, Katie went with him. Their boss realized they are stronger when they are together than apart. On one of their business trips, they went to Maryland and had time to visit her mom. Before they went into the house, Katie asked Travis not to mention what happened to her because her mom would flip out and demand that she moves back in with her. Travis met her for the very first time. "Travis, this is my mom, Katherine. Yes, she named me her nickname."

"It is nice to meet you, Mrs. McDaniel."

"Oh, please, call me mom. You are so handsome. Katie, you have great taste. I am proud of you."

"Thanks, Mom." Travis took the opportunity to ask Katherine a question when Katie went to the store to pick up some of her favorite ice cream. "I know guys are supposed to ask the father of the woman that he is with for her hand in marriage, but since Katie's father is not here, I would like the honor of taking your daughter's hand in marriage."

"The honor is all mine. I would love to have you as my son and let's just skip the in-law part." She smiled and gave him a hug. "Let me see the ring before she gets back since I am not going to be there when you purpose."

Travis smiled and asked, "How do you know I have it?" "A man like you who asks her parents has a ring all ready." Travis pulled it out his pocket and showed it to her. "Wow, Travis, she is going to love it." Travis had time to explain what he is going to do when he asks her.

When they got back home, Travis planned for the big question. He added one detail. Travis sent Katie's mom an online portal so that she would be part of the event. Travis took Katie on a scavenger hunt. She had to follow the clues that Travis left for her. The first one started at their workplace. "Follow your heart to find me. The first stop at the location of our first meeting as partners."

She went to their boss's office; and as she got to the door, her boss handed her the card that Travis left for her. "Now, Katie, please have fun. You and Travis belong together."

"Find a flower by our favorite fountain." There was a rose lying on the side of the fountain with another note. "Find a twin to the flower at our favorite park." On the bench sitting next to the entrance was another rose and a note. "There is a gift waiting for you at your favorite jewelry store." When she got to the store, the clerk handed her a box with a gold heart necklace with a note. "This is my heart given to you because you stole my heart the first day we met. Go to the last location where our first date was, and you will find me there." Katie put the necklace on and rushed to the beach and found him sitting at the table with a portal on it, and she saw her mom.

When she came closer, Travis rose; and then he dropped to one knee. "Katie, you are my life now. You are the reason I wake up, and you are the light in my life. Please do me the honor of being my wife. Please marry me?"

Her mom had tears in her eyes. Katie smiled and said, "Yes, I will be your wife." Her mom cheered as Katie kissed Travis. After the kiss, Katie said, "Hi, Mom! Did you know about this?"

"Yes, darling, he asked when you came to visit. He is a keeper, and I know your dad would have approved."

"Thanks, Mom. I love you."

"I love you too, sweetheart. Enjoy your night." She disconnected.

Katie could not let go of Travis's neck. Then Katie's heart sank. Tears started to come. "Baby, what's wrong?"

"I wanted to wait. I wanted my first time to be with you. Now my body is ruined for you."

"Baby, that was not your fault. Your body is perfect. I love you no matter what happened to you." Travis held her as she let it out. Her sobs hurt him to hear, but he did not let go until she had stopped. Katie and Travis walked back to the car.

She stared at her ring. It was a one-carat princess cut set in a silver band. "This is beautiful. Thank you, Travis."

He smiled at her and said, "Anything for you."

The next morning, there was a knock at the door, and Travis answered it. A police officer was there. "Hello, I am Officer Chris Smith. Is Ms. McDaniel home?"

"Yes, she is. Come on in and let me go get her for you."

Katie came out from the bedroom a moment later. "Hello, Ms. McDaniel. I have something that you might want to see."

Katie and Travis followed Officer Smith outside and stopped dead in their tracks when they spotted the big banner. The banner had a picture of her on the night of her rape. All the picture shows is her mouth taped and the man all in black over her with the words "I love you. Please come back to me. I miss you."

Officer Smith asked, "Do you have any idea who this guy is?"

"No, I don't. He did not speak to me, and his whole entire body was covered. There were no markings I could see—nothing."

Meanwhile, Travis ran over and started tearing the banner down. Katie asked Officer Smith, "How are you going to catch this guy if I can't describe who he is?"

"That is a good question, Ms. McDaniel."

The notes started to come. "Why are you with him? You are mine!" "I love you. Stop torturing me with him!" "You are beautiful! I want you again!" One morning, there was a picture of Travis attached to the door by a knife. There were no fingerprints or identifying marks on the paper. Travis thought, *Whoever this guy is, he is clever not to leave anything behind that can identify him. We have to catch him in the act, but how?* The police are stretched too thin to watch the apartment. Travis had no other choice than to hire a bodyguard. Travis rented the other apartment on the other side of Katie's for his new friend Paul. He has been protecting people for twenty years and has been damn good at his job. Paul is built and a fierce force not to be messed with.

CHAPTER 3

The Special Day

Katie and Travis were getting ready for their wedding coming up in just two weeks. It is a very low-key, intimate wedding. Alyssa is Katie's maid of honor, and Kevin is Travis's best man. When Alyssa met Kevin, it was love at first sight for her. Kevin has some of the same features as Travis, but his dimples are killing Alyssa. She melts every time she looks at Kevin. "Katie, you never told me his brother is so hot."

"This is the first time I have officially met him."

Both Kevin and Travis have light-brown skin and great muscle tone. They both are about six feet one inch, but the only difference is that Kevin has the dimples that almost every woman dreams about. Travis sports the braid look that sends Katie's heart fluttering, while Kevin sports the short-wave style. Alyssa is about a foot shorter than Kevin. He has long blond hair and the biggest blue eyes. Alyssa has good muscle tone as well. She loves to dance any kind of style from ballet to hip-hop. Kevin can't take his eyes off Alyssa either.

Finally, the big day has arrived. It was only the pastor, Travis, Katie, Katherine, Kevin, Alyssa, and Paul. They had the ceremony on the beach and a sit-down dinner at a restaurant overlooking the ocean. The honeymoon was on a cruise because Katie loves the ocean.

Katie was a little nervous on the first night. She had to keep reminding herself that it was Travis this time. She freely gave herself to Travis. It was beautiful and special. There were a couple of times she would close her eyes and quickly open them again to keep the memory away. Travis could sense that she was fighting the memory, and he would whisper in her ear, "It is perfect." Hearing his voice made her relax even more. They both were each other's first and only for the rest of their lives. They will cherish this forever. Travis is grateful that it is Katie he gets to share himself with. They spent two weeks on the cruise.

Travis surprised Katie with a gift of a house when they got home. It was a five-bedroom house that sat on five acres of land. It had a swimming pool in the back plus a mother-in-law suite next to the pool. When Katherine would visit, she would have a place to be. Paul had his suite also. He was in charge of setting up security. He put cameras everywhere, except for the bedrooms and the five bathrooms. There was a balcony in every bedroom and a huge eat-in kitchen. There were places for entertaining and a place for billiards.

Katie took Paul to get the last of her belongings from her apartment while Travis stayed to start unpacking boxes. Katie could not wait until she is able to relax with her husband at their new house. When Katie first met Travis, she never expected that he would be her husband.

Paul waited just on the inside of the door when he was hit from behind and then stabbed by something that knocked him out cold. The man was dressed in all black and without a sound put Katie to sleep. When Katie woke up, she was tied to a bed with no clothes on. She could see she was in an abandoned building of some sort. There were two cameras and pictures of her all over the place. She really started to panic when she saw the man coming over to her. He had a voice changer, and he was speaking to her. "You tried to leave me. I had to stop you. You are now mine. You can have all of me now. You are beautiful, and we are going to make sweet love together."

Paul came to and saw the police all around, and his heart just about stopped beating when Katie was not anywhere to be seen. The police was questioning him when Travis arrived, "Where is my wife? How is Paul? What did he do to him?"

Officer Smith answered the questions, "Travis, your wife was abducted. When we got here, Paul was lying on the floor drugged."

"Let me see Paul."

Travis walked over to Paul, and immediately Paul apologized that he could not get to Katie in time to save her. "Are you okay? It is not your fault. You were drugged. I should have been here also. The guy knew how to take you down."

"I am okay. We are going to get Katie back if it the last thing I do."

Officer Smith said to Travis, "There are no clues left behind." Officer Smith was pacing and yelling at his fellow officers. "I want answers. Find me answers. Now, people."

Then one of his officers came out of the bedroom and said, "Officer Smith, you need to see this!" Travis followed. They started to discover the cameras. There were five in the bedroom and three in the bathroom, and they traced the wire back to Parker's apartment. They immediately got a warrant signed by the judge and broke down the door to Parker's apartment. Travis followed but was warned by Officer Smith not to touch anything. That's where they found the videos of Katie in the shower, in the bed, and the night that she was raped. The officers started to take the evidence outside.

Officer Smith stayed in there until all of it was packed into evidence boxes. Travis was on his knees, frozen by what he saw. Officer Smith stepped out the door. Then the apartment exploded. Officer Smith screamed, "Travis!" Paul ran with Officer Smith, who found Travis and pulled him out.

Parker was laughing when he saw the video of the explosion on his phone. Then he showed it to Katie. "I have no more competition now for your love." Katie choked back tears but no luck. Her heart was broken. "Don't cry, sweetheart. I am here for you."

"You killed my husband. Get away from me. Don't touch me! I hate you! I hate you! I hate you!"

Parker punched Katie in the face. "Never say you hate me!"

"Who are you? If you are going to keep me here, stop hiding yourself from me!" Parker slowly started taking his black outfit off, and he showed himself to Katie. Katie gasped. "Parker! No, no, no! I hate you, Parker! Stay away from me."

Parker could not handle her saying she hates him. He got the tape and taped her mouth shut. Then he punched her and let himself into her again.

Paul and Officer Smith were working on Travis when the EMTs arrived. They took over. Travis was not that badly burned, but he did inhale a lot of smoke. He did get hit hard with some flying debris. His heart stopped, and he was not breathing. Meanwhile, Paul had to call Katherine, Alyssa, and Kevin. The EMTs were able to bring Travis back. They rushed him to the emergency room. Paul told Officer Smith that family members have been notified. Officer Smith then notified the news stations. Katherine turned on the car radio. Alyssa was driving because Katherine was crying too much. The radio announcer said, "We have breaking news at this hour. Police are looking for a missing twenty-three-year-old. Long brown hair, wearing a white T-shirt, blue jeans, and white sneakers, goes by the name of Katie Andrews. If anyone has information of her whereabouts, you are asked to call police."

Katherine and Alyssa made it to the hospital in just under two hours. They found Kevin in the waiting room, pacing. "I can't lose him. I can't lose my brother. I can't lose my only family I have left. I can't lose my new sister." Alyssa went over to Kevin and wrapped her arms around him. She held him until the doctor came out with an update about Travis. "Kevin Andrews, your brother is in a coma. He suffered blunt-force trauma to his head and face. He took in a lot of smoke. He also has burns on his arms, chest, and back. We have him stable for now. All we can do now is wait until he wakes up."

"Can we see him?"

"Are you all family?"

"Travis is her son-in-law, and she is my girlfriend." Alyssa smiled at Kevin and nodded. Kevin smiled back and nodded.

"Yes, you may go back to see him."

All three of them stayed by his bedside while communicating with Officer Smith about Katie. Paul joined them later that night. Paul went back and forth between the hospital and the search party. He did not give up on trying to find Katie. He feels responsible for all this, and he won't rest until Katie is found.

CHAPTER 4

Waiting and Watching

Three months have gone by. Travis is still in a coma. The doctors have been running some tests, and Travis has brain activity. His lungs are healing up nicely. The doctors can't figure out why he is not awake. Katherine gives him updates about Katie as she gets them from Officer Smith. "Travis, don't worry, they will find her. Hold on for her. She will be here soon."

Officer Smith is calling Katherine. "Hello, Katherine, this is Officer Smith. I am calling to let you know we have a break in the case. We may have found Katie. I am heading to the location where we suspect she is being held. I will call you as soon as I know."

"Thank you, Officer Smith. Please bring my daughter home." She hangs up the phone. "Do you hear that, Travis? They may have found Katie."

They arrive at the location. They sneak into the abandoned building. They slowly go in. They saw movement, and they froze. They listen. Parker is speaking to someone. They move closer. They see Katie lying flat on her back. They move closer. Parker has his back turned to them. "Parker, turn around and put your hands up." They hear a gunshot. They pull the trigger. Parker goes down. Officer

Smith rushes over to kick the gun away from Parker. He made sure that Parker stays alive to face trial. When his fellow officers handcuff Parker, Officer Smith is untying Katie. Parker hit her in the stomach. Katie is crying and shaking. Once Katie is loose, she throws her arms around Officer Smith and thanks him for finding her. The EMTs rush over to take care of Katie. Officer Smith asks if he could ride with Katie, and he gets into the ambulance. He dials her mom's number and hands the phone to Katie. "Mom!"

On the other end, all is heard is Katherine crying tears of joy. "Katie, it is nice to hear your voice!"

"Mom, I will see you shortly." She hangs up the phone and starts to cry.

Finally, Katie is at the emergency room. The doctors assess her injuries and send her up to surgery to fix the bullet wound. Katherine goes to Travis's room. "She is here. They found her. She will be here shortly."

Alyssa and Kevin join them in the room, along with Paul. An hour later, Katie is wheeled into the room next to Travis. She is still sleeping. She does not know that he survived. Her mom kisses her on the forehead and whispers in her ear, "Welcome home, sweetheart, welcome home." Then she slowly tilts her head toward Travis, so the first thing she sees is him. An hour later, she wakes up. She gasps, "Travis!" She slowly gets up.

Kevin and Katherine run to her side. "No, sweetheart, you can't get up."

"Please I must be with Travis."

Kevin lifts her up and places her in Travis's bed—wires, tubes, and all. "Travis, I am here. Please wake up. I love you."

Travis moves his head toward her voice, and he slowly opens his eyes. He focuses on her, and tears start to fall. He slowly moves her into a hug, and he does not let go. Katherine runs to get the doctor, and Alyssa is crying happy tears. Kevin goes over and kisses both Katie and Travis on the forehead.

The doctor comes in and says, "Wow, what a reunion. Travis, would you like the breathing tube out?" Travis nodded. "I need you to breathe out now," and the doctor pulls out the tube. He coughs and gags. His whispered his first words, "I am happy to see you." He stares at Katie. "Are you okay?"

"I am now that I am back in your arms and you are alive."

Travis can see the trauma Katie went through with the bruises and scarred cuts on her face. Travis wants to know what she went through, but he does not want to ask. Katie's doctor came in. He had a sad look on his face. "I would like to speak to Katie alone please."

Katie looked at the doctor and said, "No, they all can stay. They are family."

"Katie, you were three months pregnant, but when Parker shot you, he killed the baby. At this point, we don't know if it was Travis's or Parker's. We have to get you to surgery to remove the baby. We did not know that the baby was there until we looked at the ultrasound closely. I am sorry for your loss."

Kevin lifted his sister-in-law from his brother's bed and placed her back on her own. "Thank you, Kevin."

Travis is panicking. "She was shot." Now, Travis is mad. They wheeled her out to surgery. An hour later, they wheeled her back into the room, and she was sleeping. "We had a little complication. The baby was stuck in her uterus. It tore her uterus. She may or may not be able to have another baby. Time will tell. We took a sample from the baby and from Travis and Parker. We will get the results back within two hours. We have her sedated right now because of the pain she may feel when she wakes up."

"Thank you, Doctor," Katherine said to him as he left the room. Katherine cried for her daughter. She held her hand. Katherine is scared for Katie; she knows she always wanted children. Now there is a chance she may not be able to have kids. Katherine looked at Travis as he stared at his wife. Tears are in his eyes, and his heart is with Katie.

Two hours later, the doctor came back in again with a sorrowful face. "The baby was Travis's. I also believe that it is okay to bring Katie out of sedation."

The doctor administers the medication, and Katie wakes up. She winces a little and then a lot. The doctor then gives her pain medication, and that seems to subside the pain. The doctor leaves, and Kevin wheels Travis closer to Katie. Travis takes Katie's hand, and her mom takes the other. With sad eyes, Travis tells Katie, "The baby was ours." Katie stares paralyzed as tears run down her face. "The doctor said that there was a complication during surgery. There is a fifty-fifty chance we may not have kids." Katie lies in silence as tears run down her face. Her mom is holding her, and Travis is holding her hand. Her tears subside, and Katie asks Kevin if he could help her again. Kevin proudly picks up Katie and places her in Travis's bed. Kevin, Alyssa, and Katherine each give Katie and Travis kisses on the forehead. Then they leave them alone. Kevin left their room, and they were out in the parking lot. The emotions he felt overwhelmed him, and he broke down and cried. Alyssa holds him and cries with him.

When their tears subside, Kevin asks, "Are you serious about being my girlfriend?"

"Are you seriously asking me?"

"Yes, I am."

"I am your girlfriend."

"We are five hours away from each other. We can make it work," he said.

"Actually, we will only be five minutes away from each other starting next week. I found a dance studio that needs some help, and I accepted the offer. I will be moving in next week."

Kevin smiles and wraps her into his arms. "I will help you move." Then he kisses her sweetly on the lips. He watches as Alyssa and Katherine leave to go home. His heart has mixed emotions. He is happy he found Alyssa, and his brother is going to be okay, but he is also sad for his brother. His brother is strong, but he hates seeing him like he is now. His heart is breaking for his brother. Travis found his match, and they are going through heartache and pain. Kevin vows to help his brother any way he can.

Travis and Katie are talking about the ordeal. Travis asked, "How long have we been apart?"

Katie bit her bottom lip and said, "Three months."

"Three months!"

The shock of her answer made Travis shake. "I am sorry, baby. I was not there for you. I am sorry you were all alone for so many months."

As he was speaking, he touched her bruises and cuts on her face. He rubbed her back and held her closer. "I was numb after. I watched the explosion and I thought you were dead. I thought I lost you forever. I almost gave up, but something told me to fight. I dreamed of you. You were with me in my dreams, and when I saw Officer Smith coming for me, I saw hope but also a future without you in it. I did not want to go. I did not want to face the next years of my life without you. Then I woke up, and you are here with me, and I am here with you."

"I want to know what you went through. Please open up to me. I want to take some of the pain from you."

"I will talk to you, I promise. I am not ready to relive that yet." Katie started to fall asleep. Travis did not let go. Travis's thoughts were overwhelming, thinking about Katie and what she went through. He was not there for her. He could not protect her from the pain she went through. Holding her now is comforting, but he feels he does not deserve this and her.

He is feeling ashamed of himself when Paul walks up to him. "Travis, please don't blame yourself for this. It is my fault. I did not protect you and Katie properly."

"Paul, if it was not for you, I would not be here right now. You were attacked when Katie was taken because Parker was studying people around Katie. Please stay with us. Please don't worry. We are safe now."

Paul sits down on the small couch that is in the room and watches as Travis drifts off to sleep. Then he himself drifts off to sleep.

Travis and Paul wake up to the heart monitor beeping. Doctors and nurses had put Katie back in her bed and were working on her. Travis started to yell her name, "Katie, stay with me! Don't leave me!" Travis is struggling to get out of the bed, but Paul is holding him back so that they can work on her. They got her back, and now she is in a coma, and the doctors are running tests to know why.

Two hours later, the doctor comes back with some test results. "Katie sustained some trauma to her head and body. Some of those injuries are coming to the surface now. We are going to send her to surgery to fix her injuries."

As they wheeled her out, Travis said, "Katie, stay with me."

Two hours later, they brought her back in, but she was still sleeping. "Katie is still in a coma, but she is out of the woods. Now we wait until she wakes up." Throughout the day, nurses came in and checked on Katie. This time, Travis slowly went to Katie and slid into her bed with her. He held on to her tightly. He does not want to let go. With all the strength he had, he held her there with him, and he never wanted to let go.

Two weeks had gone by; and in those two weeks, Travis was released but he had not left yet. Katie is still in a coma with some brain activity. Paul goes back and forth to bring Travis whatever he needs. Alyssa and Kevin checked in a couple times a week, and Katherine called in on the portal four times a week. Travis was dozing one afternoon in the chair next to Katie's bed. Katie opened her eyes and was looking at Travis when Paul nudged him on the shoulder. Travis looked at Paul, and Paul pointed. Travis looked at Katie, and she was smiling at him. Travis sat straight up and gave her the sweetest kiss ever. "Hi, beautiful, I have missed you."

"I have missed you also."

"How are you?" Travis asked with loving eyes.

"I am okay. How do you feel?"

"I feel good now that you are awake." Katie then got a serious look on her face and asked, "Can we talk?"

"Yes, sweetheart." Travis asked Paul if he would excuse them, and he politely stepped outside.

"I would have asked him to stay, but I did not want him to feel bad."

"It's okay, Katie."

She started telling Travis everything what she went through. He would punch or kick her when she said the wrong thing. He would leave her alone for no more than two days; but when he came back, he would have food and water for her. It was good food, like he was pretending to be out on a date with her. He would also make her drink wine and then make love to her afterward, or so he called it. She would get sick, and he would clean her. She would run fevers; and he would bring her medicine, then leave for two days, and do it all over again. When she would describe certain things, Travis could hear the pain in her voice; and she would squeeze his hand.

Travis listened to every word and closed his eyes. Tears would run down his cheeks. When she was done describing her ordeal, she felt free but also scared. She was able to let some of it go. She was happy that she was able to open up to Travis and let him in. Travis climbed into bed with her and held her until her shaking stopped and she relaxed.

Chapter 5

The Healing

Two weeks later, Katie was released from the hospital and was able to enjoy their new home. When all this started, there were boxes and things everywhere. But when Katie and Travis walked into the house for the first time in four months, it was organized, and things were put into place. Pictures were hung on the walls, and all their clothes and personal items were put away. Alyssa and Kevin were standing there with smiles on their faces. Katie's face lit up. "Did you guys do all this?"

Alyssa excitedly said, "Yes, do you like? We can change it around and move things the way you want them. I did not want you to come home to boxes and the work after all you have been through."

Katie was still looking around. "It is perfect. Thank you so much, you two." Katie gave Alyssa and Kevin a hug. Alyssa then took their bags and led them upstairs to their bedroom and into the bathroom. "I made you guys a bath with relaxing bubbles. Both of you enjoy and relax in each other's arms, and when you are done, come downstairs. Dinner will be ready."

Katie asked Alyssa, "Aren't you supposed to be home at work right now?"

"I am home, but work won't start for me until tomorrow. I moved here to start my new job and to be closer to my boyfriend."

"Boyfriend? What boyfriend?"

"Kevin!"

Katie smiled and said, "Okay!" Then she looked at Travis. "Did you know about this?"

"Nope, not until now."

They both laughed; and once Alyssa had disappeared from the bathroom, they started to undress. Katie started to shake. Travis has not seen her naked since their honeymoon, and she was afraid of the scars all over her body. The fact that she is naked brings back memories. Travis realized her face and saw that she was trembling, "It's okay. It's me, Travis. I won't let anything happen to you. Come on, let me hold you."

Katie hesitated and then let Travis wrap his arms around her. He then kissed every scar and mark she had on her body. Travis made his wife feel beautiful as he rubbed her back, arms, legs, and body. He was not fazed by the marks on her body. He helped her into the tube and held her until she stopped shaking. Katie looked over her shoulder and said, "I am sorry I reacted that way. Thank you for what you did for me. I feel better."

"Katie, I don't want you to be scared in front of me. I am here for you and I will never go anywhere. Take the time you need to heal. I will be here by your side." Katie looked at Travis's scars from his burns. She ran her fingers over them and kissed what she could see. Travis feels better about his body as well. They soaked in the tub until the water got cold. They got dressed in comfortable clothes. Then they met Alyssa and Kevin downstairs.

"Alyssa, give me details on how this all happened. I have been so out of the loop, and I need a distraction," Katie asked over dinner.

"Well, if you have to know, I just want to say thank you for getting married to his brother. I could not stop looking at him." Alyssa was staring at Kevin the whole time. "Katie, I thought you were the luckiest woman alive until I met his brother."

Kevin stood up and said, "Okay, I was going to wait, but I can't anymore." Kevin got on one knee and asked, "Alyssa, I know that I have only known you for a couple of months now, but I have never been so sure until now that I have found my soulmate and the love of my life. Please will you be my wife?"

Katie gasped with delight, and Alyssa said, "Yes!"

Travis gave his little brother a high five as Alyssa was sharing the ring with Katie. Katie said to Alyssa, "Thank you again for doing all this. I don't know where I would be if I did not have you in my life. I love you, best friend and soon-to-be sister-in-law."

"I love you too, Katie, and I am glad you are okay," Alyssa said as she hugged Katie. "It is your turn to be my maid of honor."

"Yes, I will be honored."

Kevin and Alyssa left to give Travis and Katie some alone time. Katie walked through the whole house and opened drawers so that she could figure out where Alyssa put everything. Then Katie went to check out the pool house, the mother-in-law suite. Then she went to check on Paul. He was in the surveillance room. "Hi, Paul, I just wanted to see how you are doing. I have not been able to talk to you."

"I am doing okay, Mrs. Andrews."

"Please call me Katie. Mrs. Andrews is too formal for me. I also wanted to tell you that I don't blame you for any of this. I am okay now. Did Officer Smith say anything to you about how Parker did what he did? Did he also tell you that Parker is dead?"

"Katie, Parker had video cameras throughout your apartment, and he also made sure that he was able to get into your apartment.

Parker survived the wounds and is still in the hospital. Officer Smith said that Parker needed to pay for what he did, and death was too easy for him."

Katie sank into the chair by the door in shock when Travis joined them. "What's going on?" Katie filled Travis in on what Paul had just told her. A look of shock fell across Travis's face but only on the part that Parker is still alive. Travis and Katie walked to their bedroom and fell asleep in each other's arms.

The next morning, the advertising team was back in their office, getting to work. Their boss and coworkers came to their office and welcomed them back. "To one of my best advertising teams, welcome back and you have been missed. All I can say now is get to work," their boss said with a straight face then smiled. "Oh, and congratulations on your wedding."

"Thanks, boss." Travis smiled. An hour later, their boss came back in and said that he has a job for them in California, and they would have to leave tomorrow. They went home and started packing for a much-needed three-day trip.

When they were gone, something happened. Parker escaped the hospital, and now he is coming back with a vengeance. He is planning on how to get his girl back. He wants her man to pay for what he did.

Travis and Katie got the job done and had fun doing it. They were relaxing on the couch and turned on the TV. The news came on, and Katie's heart dropped to the floor. "Parker is on the loose, and I know he will be coming after me some way somehow." Katie starts to panic. She stands up and paces. She can't hold the tears back, and she starts to hyperventilate. Her heart is pounding, and then she faints. Travis is in midstride when she goes down, and he catches her before she hits the coffee table. "Katie!" Travis held her on the floor until she came to. "Katie, an ambulance is on its way. Are you okay?" Paul let the EMTs in, and they assessed Katie. There was no need to go to the hospital, but Travis had to keep an eye on her. Travis carried her up to bed.

A couple of weeks later, there has been no sign of Parker, but everyone is on high alert. The police are doing everything they can to find him. Katie has been jumpy and looking over her shoulder. She won't go anywhere without Travis and/or Paul.

A couple of weeks turned into a couple of months. The stress is getting to Katie, and she is not feeling right. She can't hold anything down, and she is feeling a little run-down. Travis went to work without her, and Paul stayed with Katie. Katie was napping on the couch. When she heard the gunshot, she sat straight up just in time to see Paul standing in front of her with his back turned toward her. Then he dropped to the floor. The next sight she saw was Parker. Her heart started pounding, and she got up to run, but Parker was there to push her down. Parker then picked her up, and she kicked and struggled against him. He put her in the bed and tied her up. He then left the room. A half hour later, he returned. "Now that we are alone, we can get down to business. If anyone interrupts us, the house will explode. If you try to escape, the house will explode. Just so you know, I did call the office to let Travis know if he did come home, he will kill both of us." He kneeled onto the bed and wrapped his arms around Katie. "Boy, have I missed you. We are not going to do anything right now. I am going downstairs to cook us something to eat. Oh, and that bodyguard of yours? He won't be bothering us anytime soon."

Parker went downstairs, spent an hour in the kitchen, and then came up. He ate and then tried feeding Katie. "Please eat, darling. You need to keep your strength up."

Katie spoke for the first time, "I can't eat. I can't keep anything down."

"Okay, you want to jump right to dessert." Parker took off her clothes and then his. He was about to go in when Katie heard a gunshot, and Parker fell to the floor. Katie saw Paul walk slowly to her bedside, and he covered her up. He had his phone in his hand and started untying Katie's hands but did not make it before Paul dropped to the floor. As Paul fell, his phone landed on Katie's lap, and he saw Travis's name across the screen. Then she heard her name coming from the phone. "Katie, what's going on? Paul, where are you? Someone please tell me what's going on."

"Travis, I am all right, but Paul is not. I can't help him because I am tied. The house is rigged to explode."

"Don't worry, I have help on the way." Travis did not hang up, and Katie can hear him talking to the bomb squad. She also heard a member of that squad say, "This is a sophisticated bomb. He has all doors and windows rigged." Travis then heard Katie get sick, "Oh, baby, we are working as fast as we can to get in there. Hang in there."

After an hour of inspecting the bomb, the team figured out how to disarm it; and within a half hour, it was disarmed, and Travis was upstairs untying Katie. The EMTs rushed in and started working on Paul. Travis heard them say, "He has a pulse. Let's move." Katie was frozen still covered in their bed, and she could not take her eyes off the lifeless body of Parker. Travis gave Katie some clean clothes and helped her get dressed so that she could leave the room. They went to the living room, and Officer Smith came to interview Katie. Then Katie ran to the bathroom because she felt sick. She then stepped out of the door and fainted. Travis ran to her side and called after the medics. They rushed Katie to the hospital.

Katie was sleeping when the doctor came in. "Katie will be fine. The stress combined with her being pregnant is what made her faint. You can take her home as soon as the paperwork is ready."

"Wait, Doctor, you said she is pregnant?"

"Yes, congratulations, you are going to be a dad."

Travis smiled and cried a little because he came close to losing her and the baby. Katie stirred and woke up. She saw the tears rolling down Travis's cheeks. "Baby, what happened?"

"I am fine. I am just happy. We are pregnant." Katie smiled and hugged him. The doctor released her, and they went to find out how Paul was doing. The doctor let them know that he will pull through. They went into his room and sat with him until he woke up. Katie hugged him and said, "I am safe and alive because of you. We will visit often. In the meantime, get better, okay?"

Katie and Travis arrived home. Katie saw the mess, and she became quiet. Her heart started pounding as she went over the events of the day in her head. Travis could tell she was deep in thought. Travis went over to her and took her by the hand. "I will clean this up. Go lay down, and I will be up soon."

"I can't go back into that room yet. I will be in another room." Katie left Travis and went upstairs. She walked by their room, just peeking inside. It is a mess also. There was blood on the floor, and the ropes were still on the bed. Katie ran to one of the other rooms and cried out the pain. Travis heard her and came by her side. He could not help but smile as he looked at her. He can't believe she is his and she is carrying his baby. He places a hand on her stomach and rubs. She settles down and looks at him with a smile, "I love you."

"I love you. I can't believe we have a little one growing inside this sexy belly of yours." He kissed her belly. Then he moved up to her lips. "I can't believe you are my wife. You make my heartbeat in wonder and joy. You make me happy and filled with love. You are my world. You are my life. I am proud to be yours." Katie takes him into her arms, and then she lets him in.

Alyssa and Katie were busy planning the wedding and having fun. Kevin and Travis are doing the guy thing. They are picking out their tux. Alyssa looked at Katie. "You look happy. What's going on?" "You are going to be an aunt and a godmother."

"Are you serious? I am honored," Alyssa said with a huge grin on her face.

The wedding day is beautiful. It was just as intimate as Katie's. Alyssa was glowing and the happiest that Katie has ever seen her. They are going to Hawaii for their honeymoon paid for by Katie and Travis.

CHAPTER 6

Moving On

Life is good now. The baby will be here in less than a month. Things are good at work. Because of the Andrews' team, the company has gained five more big clients. Paul is recovering nicely. Because of the bullet bouncing around in his body, he has to relearn how to use his right arm and leg. Alyssa and Kevin are expecting now. Kevin graduated and is now working at the same company as her and Travis. Alyssa also became the new owner of the dance studio she came to fix. The baby's room is purple and yellow. Katie and Travis decided not to find out the sex of the baby until it is born. Kevin and Alyssa are having a girl. They live down the street from them in a townhouse development.

Katie has about two weeks before the baby is here. She took maternity leave, and Kevin filled her spot at the company until she comes back. Kevin and Travis trade off driving to work. It was Kevin's turn to drive, and he pulled into the driveway, but Travis was not out waiting. He walked up to the door, and Katie answered, "Where is Travis?"

"You mean he is not out there waiting? He just walked out the door ten minutes ago."

"He was not outside waiting for me."

"Kevin, something happened to your brother. Where is he?" Katie ran to get her phone. She called Officer Smith, "Hi, this is Katie Andrews, and my husband is missing."

Katie is pacing, and the police is there, gathering as much information as possible, which is not much because he just vanished into thin air. Katie's cell phone rang with Travis's number on it. "Travis, are you okay?"

She heard a woman laughing on the other end of the phone, and Katie put it on speaker. "You took the love of my life from me. Now I will take the love of your life from you. Say goodbye, Travis."

"Katie, I love you."

Then she heard a gunshot, and the line went dead. Katie drops to the floor and screams out in pain. Kevin calls Alyssa and work. Then he calls Katherine. Katie then passes out. Kevin rushes to her side and then calls out for an ambulance. They get Katie to the hospital and take her right to C-section. Alyssa is with her when she wakes up.

"Katie, your baby is good and healthy, and the nurse will bring the baby in shortly."

Katie starts to cry, "Travis is not here to see his baby, and he is gone."

Alyssa wrapped her arms around her sister-in-law/best friend. The nurse walked in with Katie's baby. She placed the baby in Katie's arms, and Katie realized she has a boy. Katie says through tears, "Hello, Travis Luke Andrews Jr. Welcome to the world and family." Katherine finally arrived, and she held both her daughter and her grandson. They cried together. Katherine's heart breaks for her daughter and for her son-in-law.

Officer Smith went to the location that the call was made from. All he found was Travis's cell phone and a puddle of blood. There were no other clues. Travis's body was not there. Officer Smith visited Katie to give her the news. "Katie, we found the location of the phone call, but all we found was his cell phone and a puddle of blood. Travis was not there." Katie asked Officer Smith for Travis's phone. He hands it to her. She unlocked the phone and realized what was on the screen. There was a picture of Travis's body with a gunshot wound. Katie immediately handed it back to Officer Smith. "Where is my husband?"

Katie and Travis Jr. were released two days later. Katherine decided to stay with her daughter for at least a month to help her. Katie is being strong for little Travis. He looks so much like his dad. Katie's heart breaks for him. He will never see his dad. Katie promised to tell him about his dad. She will make videos of all his firsts: first steps, first words, first haircut, first homerun. Travis is going to miss all that. Travis would have been a great dad. The look in his eyes when he found out he would be a dad was priceless, and she would remember that always. She would remember the smile on his face when she said yes to dating him, then being his girlfriend, and then marrying him. Even though they did not get much time, it was the best time she could ask for. She thinks when they find Travis, that's when she will mourn; but until then, she will hold out hope that one day he will come home.

Four months later, Travis Jr. gained a cousin. Her name is Alexa Katie Andrews. Katie is holding her niece when Alyssa said, "She is not only your niece but your goddaughter also." Katie smiled. The next day, Katie goes back to work and is Kevin's partner. It feels weird to her because Travis used to sit across from her, and now someone that looks like him is sitting there. Sometimes it hurts when she looks at Kevin. She sees Travis looking back at her. Katie still has hope. One afternoon, Katie just started to cry as she was staring at Kevin. Kevin hugged his sister and told her, "We will find him."

"Thank you, Kevin."

TWO YEARS LATER

Katie is sitting at the kitchen table planning little Travis's birthday party. Alyssa and Katie decided to celebrate both Travis Jr.'s and Alexa's birthdays together in honor of Travis. These days are good. Little Travis is growing fast, and yes, his first word was *dadda*. His smile is Travis's, his features are Travis's, and his laugh is Travis's. Officer Smith is still on the hunt for Travis. He has been hitting dead ends lately. During the first year, Officer Smith got leads about the location of Parker's fiancé Rachal but missed her by minutes. She knows she is wanted for murder. Katie was in the store shopping for the party, and Travis Jr. was with Alyssa. Out of the corner of her eye, she sees Rachal. Katie runs over to Rachal and knocks her flat on her butt. "Where is my husband?" Katie then lands another punch onto Rachal and knocks her out cold. Katie then calls Officer Smith.

Officer Smith arrests Rachal and interrogates her. "Where is Travis?"

"I don't know who you are talking about." That is all she says when asked the question.

"You are Parker's girlfriend, aren't you?"

"Don't say his name. You are not good enough to say his name."

They have nothing to hold her on without a body. They only have forty-eight hours to hold her. Then she will be free. Officer Smith has forty-eight hours to get something that will lead him to Travis.

Katie is getting ready for the party. It has been two years exactly when her life changed. Now she gets to honor Travis by celebrating his son and his niece. Katherine did move in with Katie so that she could be there for her. Kevin and Alyssa arrived. Then Paul showed up. The party started. Katie stood up and said, "It's been two years for all of us. Our lives changed when we lost someone, someone who touched each one of our hearts. He will be here with us forever. We will see him in Kevin and Travis Jr. We even see him a little in Alexa. I will love him forever. To Travis, you will forever be in our hearts and never forgotten."

A voice came from the back, "I love you, Katie." Then they heard a big thud. Katie looks up in time to see Travis dropping to the floor in weakness. Katie screams, "Travis!"

Kevin was immediately on the phone with 911. Katherine called Officer Smith. Katie was by Travis's side. "Baby, stay with me please. You are here and safe." He reached up and touched her hair and face and whispered, "You are beautiful." Then he seems to drift into a coma. Five minutes later, the EMTs are there, working on him. They load him in the ambulance and rush him to the ER. Katie is with him holding his hand. Tears are running down her face. He is here with her now. Her heart can start beating again. They get to the ER and assess his injuries.

An hour later, the doctor came out to give Katie an update. "Hello, Katie, Travis's gunshot wound got infected. He has a 103-degree fever, and the infection is running his whole body. When he was shot two years ago, it was fixed, but as it healed, it collected bacteria because it was not covered properly. It looks like he has been fighting the infection since then. We are giving him fluids and very high doses of antibiotics. He is awake if you want to go see him."

"Yes, please." Katie's heart started pounding hard with anticipation. It seems that she can't get to his room fast enough. She finally walked through the door, and her eyes met his. His smile made her heart skip a beat. "You had to wait until my speech was over to make your entrance." She walked to his bedside. "It was a good speech. I had to make it special."

"Well you did. It was a hell of a good entrance. So you have a son. He is two today. He is Travis Luke Andrews Jr. You also have a niece, Alexa Katie Andrews. They are beautiful."

"I can't wait to meet them."

"Your son's first word was *dadda*. He knows his dad. I made sure of it."

Tears started streaming again. Travis wipes her tears. "I am here now. What kept me alive was the thought of holding you, seeing you, and kissing you. I kept going for you. I could not wait to hold our child. I kept your image in my head and held on."

"I held on to the hope that we would find you. I held out hope until I knew you lived or died. I did not mourn your loss until I was sure. After I heard the shot, I dropped to the floor. Then I passed out from stress. I had an emergency C-section because little Travis was in distress. He was born healthy."

Travis smiled. Katie climbed into bed with Travis and held each other tight. Katie finally was able to relax, and she fell asleep in his arms. Arms that she longed for. Arms that could hold her forever.

The next morning, the antibiotics are working. Travis's fever broke. He is looking better. Katie is still sleeping, and he soaks in the sight. He loves watching her sleep. She feels good back in his arms. Kevin came into Travis's room.

"Hey, big brother, how are you feeling?"

"Hey, little brother, I am feeling better. I hear you are a dad. How does it feel?"

"It feels amazing. She is beautiful, and I know she can't wait to meet her uncle."

The doctor came in and said, "Well, Travis, everything looks good. We are going to release you today and give you more antibiotics for the rest of the month."

"Thank you, Doctor."

Kevin drove them home. Travis and Katie walked through the door of their house and were greeted by Katherine and Alyssa. Katie picked up little Travis and asked him, "Do you want to see Daddy?"

He smiled and said yes. Katie took Travis over to his daddy; and for the first time, Travis held his son. The next thing he heard was "Daddy."

Katie broke down and cried. The sight was so beautiful. She longed for this. She could only imagine this. Now she sees it in front of her. Travis held his boy for five minutes longer and then passed him back to Katie and picked up his niece. He spent five minutes with her in his arms. "I have dreamed of this day every day I was gone. Now it's here, and I am home." Katie put little Travis down for a nap, and Alyssa followed with Alexa. Travis was sitting on the couch with Paul, Kevin, and Katherine sitting around him. Katie snuggled up against him, and Alyssa joined Kevin. Travis opened up to everyone what he went through. He did not expect to open up to everyone. The strength he feels is coming from the woman sitting next to him. It feels good to have her next to him. It feels good to see his brother and his family. It is now right, and Travis is where he belongs.

AFTERWORD

It's been a couple of years since the ordeal. A lot have changed. Travis and Katie are proud parents of three children. Little Travis has twin sisters, Kate and Ashley. Alexa has a little sister now named Erin. When Travis came home, Katherine decided to declare that both Travis and Kevin are her sons. She was the only parent figure in their lives. Kevin's children call her grandmom. Then tragedy struck when Katherine passed away. She suffered a heart attack that she could not recover from. Katie is coping with the help of her family. Travis, Katie, and Kevin now own the company they work for. The CEO and owner passed away, and he did not have a family. He had grown to love all three of them as his own, and he left it to them. Paul is married and still protects the family. They are expecting their first child. Katie can't believe that her life would lead her here. When she laid her eyes on Travis for the first time, she never thought that she would be here now. The way he looks at her, he sees their future in his eyes. She also sees passion and love. The way he holds her makes her feel safe and love. She gets to feel that for the rest of her life.

LOVED TWICE

CHAPTER 1

Facing the Lose

I am at the time of my life that I am forced to start over. Up to this point, my life was amazing. So let me take you back to where my amazing life started. Oh, let me introduce myself. I am Sarah, and it is just my dad, Kevin, and me. My mom and brother died during childbirth. It has been three years since my mom and brother had passed. I could not have gotten through this if I had not met the man of my dreams.

THREE YEARS AGO

Sarah is running down the hall of the hospital. She just found out her mom and brother passed away. Her cheeks are dripping with tears. She wants to get out of here and hide for a while. She can't deal with this, and her dad lets her go. This is her way of coping with what just happened. Sarah's thoughts haunt her. *My mom just fought to give birth to my brother, and she did not make it. Neither did my brother.* Sarah's mom hemorrhaged, and they could not stop the bleeding. Her brother's heart was damaged during the birth, and they could not bring him back. Her dad is on the floor with his head in his hands, sobbing. As she ran, she looked back; and then she ran right into Scott. He is like a brick wall. She hits him; and the next thing she knows, she is on the floor. "Miss, miss, are you okay?" Sarah looks up at him, and her breath stops. He helps her up, and he wraps his arms around her. "It is okay. Let it go. I will stay with you until you are okay." She has no idea what is going on, and she just lets it all go. Her sobs are loud, and she can't stop them from flowing. She feels comfort in his arms. He is a stranger to her, but he is holding her. She wraps her arms around him. They stand there for another couple of minutes. Her tears are just about over, and she looks up at him.

She finally asks, "Who are you?"

"Hello, ma'am, I am Scott, and I am a doctor here at the hospital. Today is my first day, and I never expected to run into someone so beautiful."

"I am sorry for running into you and crying on you. I am Sarah."

"I hope you weren't crying because you ran into me."

"No, I just lost my mom and my brother."

"Oh my god, I am sorry for your loss." My tears started again, and he pulled me in again. Scott pulls her over to a chair. He holds her again, "You can cry all you want to."

Half an hour later, her tears subsided, and she was able to composes herself. "Thank you for letting me cry on your shoulder. You don't even know me."

"It is my job to help people. If you need anyone to talk to, I am here for you. I know what you are going through. My dad passed because of cancer." Scott hands her his business card, and he adds his cell number on it.

"Thank you, Scott. I might take you up on your offer. When you feel up to it, I would like to take you to dinner. Since I let you cry on my shoulder, the least you can do is to have dinner with me."

For the first time that day, Sarah smiled. "I suppose I owe you that much. Do you pick up all the girls like this?"

"No, just the ones who cry on my shoulder," he says with a smile.

Sarah pulled her phone out of her pocket as she smiled and called his cell. "Now you have my number. Call me with the details, and I will let you know." They said their goodbyes, and Sarah went back to her dad.

Sarah could not help but think of Scott as she walked back to her dad. It has been a long time since she had arms around her. She did not let anyone touch her since she was thirteen. She is now twenty-one. Her parents or any of her friends could not touch her. Her past haunts her. She felt comforted when Scott hugged her, but it also made her uneasy. Scott is a very handsome light-brown man. When she ran into him, he felt like a rock. He has chiseled features, and his smile is bright. His arms felt strong. She could not believe he held her the way he did. She does not want him to do it again. How can she let him know that without telling him her past? His eyes feel honest and caring when he looked at her. She saw genuine concern when she told him about her mom. There is something about him, and she wants to get to know him. When she saw her dad on the floor, it brought her out of her head. She bent down and hugged him for the first time in eight years. The tears started again.

It hurt her heart seeing him that way. He was a strong man, but his world came crashing down. She was his life, and now he is lost without her. He looked at Sarah, and tears came harder. Sarah is an exact image of her mom. After an hour on the floor, Sarah peels her dad off the floor and drives both of them home. Her dad went right up to his bedroom without a word. Sarah's heart sank even more. Sarah has a long road ahead of her. Her dad needs her more than ever. Sarah started dinner and thought about Scott some more. Sarah took a plate to her dad. "Dad, please eat."

"I will, darling, thank you."

Sarah placed the plate on his bed and gave him a kiss on the cheek. "Dad, I am going to stay here with you until you are better. I don't want you to be alone."

"Sarah, you don't have to stay. I will be all right. You can go back to your apartment, darling."

"No, I am going to stay and take care of you. Besides, I can work from anywhere. That is one of the benefits of being a writer."

"Okay, on second thought, I will let you stay. I don't want to be alone."

Sarah could not sleep, and she felt inspired to write. She sat down at her computer, and the words just started to flow. It was 6:00 a.m. before she realized that she was writing all night. She wrote a sweet love story that started like the way she met Scott. She can't stop thinking about him. Even though she has been up all night, she feels energized; and she takes a shower to get ready for the day. By the time she goes downstairs, her dad was in the kitchen cooking breakfast. She enjoys eating with her dad. It is like old times, but one person is missing. After breakfast, she helps her dad clean up; and she goes upstairs. She emails her newly typed three chapters to her editor with excitement. Then her phone rings. She picks it up, thinking it is her editor. "Hello, Sarah, it's Scott. I hope I didn't wake you. I know it's early, but I could not stop thinking about you. How are you doing?"

His voice is so comforting, and she could hear his care for her in his voice. "I am doing okay. I actually did not sleep yet. I am a writer, and I was inspired. So I was up all night writing."

"Wow, that means the story you wrote will be epic."

"Thank you, Scott. I hope so. What's up? How are you?"

She could hear the smile in his voice when he said the next words, "I am a little sore from when you crashed into me yesterday. To make it up to me, I would like to take you out on that date we talked about tonight, say, at eight?"

With a smile on her face, she said, "Yes, that will be nice. But are you serious about the soreness? I am sorry."

"No, I was just kidding. I will see you then. Please, Sarah, get some rest."

"I will. Thank you, Scott."

They hang up, and Sarah takes a big yawn and curls up on her bed and falls asleep with a big grin on her face.

It was 2:00 p.m. when her eyes flutter open, and she looks at the bedside clock. *Oh, good, I have six hours to get ready.* Her stomach is in knots, and she is nervous about tonight. Her thoughts ran wild. *If he tries to hug me or kiss me, do I let him? He is so breathtaking. How can I resist his touch? The feel of his caring arms around me feels good, but I am scared to relive the memories.* She composes herself and goes downstairs to see where her dad is. He is on the couch watching TV. "Hi, Dad, I want to ask you something."

"Okay, go ahead."

"I know it has been rough for both of us, but I would like to know if you would be okay with me if I go out tonight."

"Baby, I don't want you to not live your life. Your mom would want you to continue to live and live to honor her. She wants you happy, and you make her proud."

"Thank you, Dad, I did meet someone yesterday. I actually ran into him, and he picked me up off the floor. Dad, he is hot." Her cheeks flush.

"That is great, Sarah." She sees a smile for the first time since yesterday. "I have to meet him."

"You will. He will be here at eight to pick me up."

"Okay!"

It was 8:00 p.m., and there was a knock on the door. Sarah's heart starts to pound, and her breath catches when she sees Scott. In that moment, she could see her future in his eyes and maybe even the freedom from her past. "Dad, this is Scott. Scott, this is my dad, Kevin."

"Pleased to meet you, sir. I am sorry for your loss."

"Thank you, Scott. What do you do for a living?"

"I am a doctor at the hospital. Yesterday was my first day."

"Nice! Now, on a more serious note, she is my only baby, and now she is all that I have left. Please take good care of her. I am counting on you to let nothing happen to her. Understand?"

"Yes, sir, I understand!"

"Okay, this is a start of a beautiful friendship. Thank you. Now go have fun."

"Dad, really, don't scare him away and behave yourself." Sarah gives him a sideways look as they head out the door.

"I found out a bit about you and your family, and I hope you don't mind, but I have an idea."

"What are you up to, Scott?" When Scott pulled into the familiar park, her heart smiled, and her eyes welled up with tears. "How did you find out?"

Scott has taken Sarah to the gazebo that her parents were married in at their favorite park. He says to Sarah, "I want to honor your mom with this night. My heart sank when you told me about your family, and I found someone who knew your mom and some details about their wedding. I hope you don't mind. I found out that your mom's best friend works for the hospital, and I talked to her."

Sarah's eyes lit up with joy. "I can't believe you did this. It is beautiful." Scott led her to the table he had set up on the gazebo. They talked and enjoyed each other's company. Scott cannot take his eyes off Sarah. He loves her smile and the way her eyes light up as she talks about her family. She is smart and strong. She has long beautiful brown hair with hints of red. She has the bluest eyes that anyone will get lost in. Sarah has long muscular legs and a petite body. He is falling head over heels in love with Sarah. He never knew he could ever feel this way about the first girl he went out with.

As the night went on, Sarah felt a deepening connection with Scott. He is right for her. Who would have thought that a man she just ran into yesterday would give her a memory like this? In a way, he brought her mom back to her. Scott asked her the next question with a shyness that made him look cute, "Sarah, this might be too early, but I would like to know if you would like to spend more time with me as my girlfriend?"

The question caught her off guard a little. She regains her composure and with a smile replies, "Yes, I would love that."

It is late, and Scott is driving Sarah home. When she got home, he walked her up to the door and leaned in to kiss her, but she pulled away with a scared look on her face. She said, "I can't. I am not ready for that yet. I am sorry." Scott could see fear in her eyes, and his heart leaped out of his chest. "It's not you. I am just not ready for that kind of touching."

"Sarah, it is okay. I will be here when you are ready. Don't worry, I am not going anywhere." He held her hand and kissed her on the hand. Then he smiled. "Please let me know when your mom's funeral is. I would like to be there for you."

"I will. Thank you, Scott. It was a wonderful night." He watched her go into the house. He could not help but feel her pain as she pulled away from him. A thought came to his mind. Something might have happened to her in her past that has her scared now. He promised to be there for her, and he hoped that she will trust him enough to open up to him.

The next morning, she called him and let him know when the funeral was, and they talked for an hour. "Scott, you are twenty-three years old and a doctor. How did you get that far already?"

"I am what you call a prodigy. I completed my four years of high school in two years, and I started my training when I was sixteen years old. I loved every minute of it. It challenged me, and I soak up information like a sponge."

"Wow, I wish I had a brain like yours. You sound amazing."

"Thank you, Sarah!"

Then Sarah asked him, "What was your dad like?"

"He was an amazing man. He taught me how to love by the way he loved my mom. He looked at her like she is his queen. They would dance with each other whenever their song came on. He did everything for her with no complaint. I had a great example in how I will treat my wife."

"Wow, he sounds amazing, and he sounds like my dad."

He asked her, "How are you doing?"

"I am okay. I have been helping my dad with arrangements. It is weird. I keep looking for my mom to walk into the kitchen. How did you do it when your dad passed?"

"I took it one day at a time. I also stayed strong for my mom, Lynn. She spent two weeks in her bedroom after he died. I took care of her. She is better now, and she is living her life in his memory."

In the conversation, they both learned that each other's grandparents are gone, and Scott has one aunt who lives in Atlanta, Georgia. Sarah's parents were the only children to their parents.

Sarah also learned that Scott's parents wanted another child, but his dad died before that could happen. "Well, Scott, I need to get off this phone so that I can go food shopping because my dad has no idea what to do in a store."

"Okay, darling, I will see you soon."

"Goodbye. Until then, Scott."

"Goodbye, Sarah." That reminded Scott that he needed to go to the store for some things that his mom forgot. He started to smile when he decided to go then on the off chance he would run into Sarah again.

Sarah is walking down the bread aisle, and she sees Scott walking toward her. She smiles so brightly. "Did you do this on purpose?"

"Yes, I did because I wanted to see you. But I did need some things also."

"I am glad you are here. I wanted to see you also."

Sarah glanced to the people behind Scott, and she started to breathe rapidly. Her eyes got big, and tears started to flow down her cheeks.

"Sarah, what is wrong? Tell me please!"

"Oh god, he is here. He is not supposed to be here. I don't want to see him."

Scott turned around and saw a man standing at the other end of the aisle looking at the buns. Sarah quickly turned and ran out of the store. Scott ran after her. "Sarah, did he hurt you? Please tell me. I am here for you." Panic is in her face, and she is breathing so hard that she is having trouble catching her breath, and she passes out. Scott catches her before her head hits the ground. "Sarah!" Scott sits on the ground, cradling Sarah in his arms. She comes to, and she quickly scrambles up to a sitting position just as the man comes out of the store, and he locks eyes with Sarah.

"Hello, Sarah, it is nice to see you. How are you?'"

"Get away from me" is all she can say. She starts to hyperventilate again. Scott grabs her and holds her tight to him. With her hands over her face, she lets Scott hold her. Scott picked her up off the ground and unlocked his car, and they got into the backseat so that he could continue to hold her, and she started to calm down.

"Sarah, what happened to you? Please let me in." She dried her tears; and as she still trembled, she let him into the darkness of the past. "I was thirteen years old when he raped me. He was fifteen years old. He raped me more than once. He threatened me. If I did not let him into me, he was going to kill me. After he had his way with me, he would hold me close to him and kiss me on the lips, my cheeks, and my neck as he held me. He did this to me ten times. I was not the only one he did this to. I was his brunette girl, and he had a red-haired and a blond-haired girl as well. My dad is the only one who knows and now you. That is why it is hard for me to be held and kissed by you. I am sorry."

"Baby, it's okay. I am never leaving you. You are safe now, and I will never let him hurt you again." In that moment, Sarah leaned up and kissed him. He could feel her pain, and he took it from her. He willed her pain onto him, and he kissed her back like he has never kissed anyone before. He slowly wrapped his arms around her, and she sank into him. She did not let go of his lips until she lost her breath. She sat trembling in his arms, and she allowed herself to start healing. She felt protected and safe in his arms.

Sarah stayed in his arms for an hour, sobbing softly. Scott felt her start to relax, and her trembling came to a stop. "Thank you for opening up to me. What happened to him, and how did you get him to stop?"

"His family moved to another county, and I have not seen him until today."

"Did he ever pay for what he did?"

"I don't know. I heard rumors that one of the other girls took him to court, but I don't know the results."

Scott sighed and said, "Do you want me with you as you finish your shopping?"

"Yes, please, I am glad you were here with me and I was able to tell you."

"I am glad I was here also. Now I am never leaving you. You are mine to protect."

Sarah smiled, and she gave him another kiss. With a smile, she says, "I can get used to this. I don't know why I let fear run my life."

"I understand why you were like that last night. You were hurt, and now you can start healing."

CHAPTER 2

The getting to Know You Stage

Over the course of the week, Sarah seemed to spend every waking minute with Scott. Since Sarah is a writer, she sat in Scott's office whenever he was at work. Scott really enjoyed her being there. The sight of her relaxed on his office couch, concentrating on her laptop, made him feel special. Whenever she was with Scott, she found inspiration for her book. For the first time in her life, she feels safe around someone not her father. Her future is getting clearer. She wants to spend the rest of her life with this man. She likes the fact that Scott only wants to kiss her. He does not want to push her into something that she is not comfortable with. Her heart is now filled with him, and she enjoys being in his arms now more than ever. She never thought she would let a man hold her again. She is happy it is Scott that gets to do it. She owes it all to the day she ran into him. A thought occurs to her: does her mom have anything to do with their meeting? After all, he does work at the same hospital even though they never met.

Scott picked up Sarah and her father and took them to the funeral. Scott insisted that he chauffeurs them around today. Sarah was able to meet his mom as well. She was a delight to be around, and she welcomed Sarah with open arms. Her love and compassion were seen in the way she helped Sarah and her dad. She now knows where Scott gets it from. Scott went up to the casket with Sarah. That was the moment he saw her mother. He gasps, "She is the one who hired me. I did meet her, and in that brief time of talking with her, I saw the love she had for her family and the passion she had for each one of her patients. I did not connect the two until now."

Sarah looked up at him with passion in her eyes, which made tears come faster and harder now. He hugged her closer. Sarah thought to herself, yes, she did have something to do with her meeting Scott. In a whisper, she leaned down and said, "Thank you, Mom, for this man."

Scott said to Sarah, "I owe this woman my life." As he gestured toward her mom, he said, "If it was not for her, I would not have had a life." Sarah looked at him, puzzled. "At one time, I was doubting myself. I did not think I could be a doctor because of the color of my skin. She came to my high school class, and she saw the doubt in my face, and she looked at me straight in my face. She then said, 'You can do what you want no matter what.' From that point on, I was inspired to be a doctor, and here I am today."

Sarah wrapped her arms around Scott. "I am happy I found you. I think my mom brought us together."

"I think she did also."

The funeral went so well her mom would have been proud. The church was packed with all the people whose lives she touched. She was a well-respected person. Before they closed the casket, her dad put her brother in the casket with her. As he wrapped him in his wife's arms, he said, "This is Trevor. May you rest well, my son, and enjoy your time with Mommy." He bent down and gave them both a kiss on the forehead and with the help of Sarah covered them up.

Sarah could not contain her tears any longer, and she let out the sobs that she held since the day they died. She dropped to the floor as the painful tears raked through her body. Scott walked up to her and picked her up in his arms and held her in his arms as he sat back down in his seat. Kevin loves how he takes care of his daughter; and he knows if Scott asks for her hand, he would gladly give it to him. It is a relief to see his daughter like this again. Allowing herself to be loved is a relief for him.

A week after the funeral, Sarah's life took a turn for the worse. She and Scott were walking back to his car after his shift at work. It was a long day for him, and he was so tired. Sarah would not let him drive. He looked so drained, and his energy level was depleted. When Scott reached for the handle of the passenger door, he collapsed. Sarah screamed, "Scott!" She ran to his side. He was still breathing, and she sprinted back to the hospital. She is screaming with panic, "Please help me. Dr. Scott just collapsed!" She ran back to Scott as he lay motionless, and the doctors ran to them. They lifted Scott onto the gurney and rushed him back to the hospital.

As doctors assess what is happening, Sarah is pacing in the waiting room. She calls her dad and his mom. A half hour later, they are by her side. "Not him, please, not him. I can't go through this again," Sarah said out loud.

An hour later, Sarah is back pacing again. She hates the wait, and her dad is asking her to sit. The doctor finally comes in. He sits with a grave face and faces Scott's mom with her hands in his. He asks if they can talk privately. "No, they are family. They can be here for this."

"Scott has leukemia, and he is going to need bone marrow transplant immediately."

Sarah jumps quickly and says, "Me. Test me please. I will give whatever I can to Scott."

Immediately the doctor says, "Okay, follow me." They got Sarah prepped for the testing. Sarah's heart is beating fast as she is thinking to herself, *Please let me be a match.*

As they sit and wait for the test results, the three of them are in Scott's room. He opened his eyes and asked, "What happened?"

Sarah let him know that he collapsed in the parking lot, and his mom told him why. Sarah also told him, "I am having my blood tested to see if I can give you my bone marrow."

"You would do that for me?"

And for the first time ever, she says, "Of course I would because I love you."

His face lit up, and his smile shone brighter than the sun. "I love you back."

At that moment, the doctor walked in with the news of her blood test and a huge smile on his face. "Scott, not only is Sarah a match but is also your perfect match." Scott's smile turned even brighter, and his tears started to fall. "We will perform the surgery in four days. Meanwhile we need to start collecting from Sarah."

Before she left the room to get prepared, Scott asked, "Sarah, please be my wife! I can't live without you."

Sarah looked at her dad, and her dad smiled and nodded. She smiled and said, "Yes!" She kissed him on the forehead and headed out the door for her first donation.

She came back in a bed, and she was asleep. The doctor asks that when she wakes up with pain to call him and let him know, and he will give her something. Scott climbed out of his bed and into hers. "Thank you, baby." He wrapped her in his arms.

She woke up a half hour later. She realized whose arms she was in, and she moved into him more. She winced in pain as she did, and it got worse. Scott asked, "Do you need painkillers?"

"Yes, please." Scott motioned to Kevin, and he went to go get the doctor. The doctor came in and gave Sarah some painkillers. When the doctor left, his mom came over to the bedside. "I think you are going to need this, son." She hands him her engagement ring from his dad. His eyes and smile widened, and he slipped the ring into Sarah's finger. She looks down with pride, and he says to her, "Thank you for saving my life."

She leans up and kisses him on the lips and says, "Anytime."

Scott fell asleep next to her, and she asked her dad, "Are you okay with this?"

"Yes, darling, I am, and I told him when you were out, I will be proud to have him as a son, and his mom will be proud to have you as a daughter. I am proud of you."

"Thank you, Dad! I love you."

"I love you too, sweetheart. Now rest." Sarah closed her eyes and drifted off to sleep.

Kevin and Lynn watched their children sleep. Lynn asked Kevin, "How are you doing?"

"It has been hard, but I know I have to stay strong for my daughter."

"You know it is okay for you to be human." He looks at her quizzically. "It is okay for you to let yourself grieve."

"I did. The day she died, I hid in my room for a while, and Sarah took care of me. The first time I saw her really cry was the day of the funeral. I knew from that point on that I have to be there for my baby girl and be strong for her."

"Make sure you take it a day at a time. I know what you are going through because my husband died of cancer a couple of years ago. If you need anyone to talk to, I am here for you."

"Thank you, Lynn. I could not ask for a better motherly influence for my daughter. I am happy she found Scott and you." Kevin and Lynn sat in silence and continued to watch their children sleep, and they dozed off themselves.

In the past four days, Sarah's body has been tortured by pain. She says it is worth it because it is saving her future husband. Now he is being prepped for surgery to transplant her bone marrow into him. She is hoping that this will work, and his leukemia is a thing of the past. He saved her from her past. Now, it is her turn to save him.

An hour later, he was wheeled back into the room, and he was still asleep. Sarah moves to sit in the chair beside him. She still feels pain, but it is not as bad as before. She watches him sleep. He looked so peaceful while sleeping. After an hour of watching him sleep, Sarah decided to write some more of her book. She has ten chapters already with ten more to go, and the words continue to flow right out of her. Her editor is loving every chapter she writes. As she was writing, Scott opened his eyes and stared at her. He can tell she was in deep thought, and she looked up at him and smiled. "Hello, handsome."

"Hello, beautiful."

"How are you feeling?"

"I am good now that I see you sitting there instead of a bed. Are you still in pain?"

"Just a little. It is tolerable."

"I am sorry, baby!"

"It's okay, Scott. You are worth it. If I have to do this again, I would not hesitate."

"Thank you, sweetheart."

"Anything for you, Scott, I promise. You saved me from my past. It is my turn to save you."

"Speaking of saving, can you do it again by saving me from boredom for the next two days by letting me read your books?"

"Yes, I can. In fact, I have both of them with me. It helps me when I write to have my book so that I can draw inspiration from it." She stood up and retrieved her first book and handed it to Scott. "There are only two so far. I am working on my third. They are sweet love stories." Scott started reading her first book.

They sat peacefully while she wrote her third book and he read her first book. Occasionally, she would look at him, and he would have tears running down his face. He would gasp at certain times and laugh at other times. It was two in the morning when both Scott and Sarah looked at each other. Scott finished her first book, and Sarah felt she finished writing her third book. "Wow, your book is amazing. I love the connection among the main characters. The end is so sweet. I love this story, and I love that it came from you."

"Just wait until you read my two book. Now my second book is not out yet, and you will be the first one to read it. It will come out in another week. Don't say anything to anyone that you read this book."

"I will not say anything. But for now, let's go to sleep. I will start reading this tomorrow or later on today. Then I will read your third book."

"Hey, no, it is not ready yet, and this version is not edited."

He gave her the biggest puppy-dog look ever. "Please!"

She took a deep breath and rolled her eyes and said, "Okay, I can't say no to you right now."

He smiled. "Now, I can't wait to read your words again."

She laughed at him; and just before she turned her computer off, she wrote the dedication for her third book, "This book is for the love of my life: my husband, Scott Harman." She smiled, saved her work, and closed her computer. She climbed into Scott's bed, and they fell asleep in each other's arms.

The sun was shining in Sarah's face when her eyes opened. It felt like four in the afternoon. But it was only eleven in the morning, and the nurse was in, taking blood from Scott. He was still sleeping. Sarah asked the nurse if that was for his test to see how well he reacted to her bone marrow. The nurse says yes. "When will we find out the results?"

"You will know before the end of the day today."

"Okay, thank you, ma'am."

"You're welcome." Sarah sat up, and her body was so sore from sleeping in the same position. She could tell that the painkillers have worn off, and she is feeling the pain now more than ever. She will not say anything to Scott. She does not want to see the look of concern on him because she will do this again if she has to. She went into the bathroom. She took a shower and thought about her wedding day. How in the world has it only been a couple of weeks since she met him, and he has already asked her? Was it in the heat of the moment, or is it because he really wanted her to be his wife?

When she came out of the bathroom, Scott was awake and reading her second book. "Good morning, handsome!"

"Good morning, beautiful! How did you sleep?"

"I slept good. How about you?"

"I did also."

Sarah then asked the question that had been bothering her all morning. "Scott, can I ask you a question?"

"Yes, you know you can ask me anything."

"Was your proposal at the heat of the moment, or are you truly ready to be my husband? I am sorry for asking this question. I really want to be your wife. I just want to make sure it is how you feel."

"Come over here please." He looked straight into her eyes as seriously as he could. Sarah went over to him, and he motioned her to sit on the bed. When she got there, he kissed her sweetly and then put his arms around her. "I love you. You are the love of my life, and I have never been so sure of anything until now. I truly want to be your husband. Please believe me. I am never letting you go." He said all that while looking straight into her eyes; and at that moment, she definitely saw her future and the compassion he has for her.

She kissed him and smiled. "Good answer."

He smiled at her. "Was that a test?"

"Yes, and you passed with flying colors."

He went back to reading her book. She sent the rest of her third book to her editor. "Oh, before I forget, the nurse was in and got your blood. They will have the results by the end of day today."

"Thank you for letting me know." Scott continued to read; and again, he was laughing at some parts, gasping at others, and crying at some.

As Scott finished her second book, his mom and her dad walked in for a visit. Then the doctor walked in with the results. They all held their breath. "Mr. Harman, we have some news for you. Your leukemia is in remission. But there is a 30 percent chance that it may come back, and if it does, it will be worse. You will be able to go home tomorrow after we run one more test."

Everyone breathed a sigh of relief. Sarah had tears of joy falling. All Scott could say while looking at her is "Thank you, thank you, thank you!" With tears in his eyes, he said, "You were right. This book is good. I love the way the characters interact with each other, and the love between them is so moving. Now, I am ready for the third one."

"You just heard your test results, and you are talking about my book in the next breath? I think you just became my biggest fan." She smiled and turned on her computer and handed it to him. The first line he read was the dedication, and his eyes fell on hers. "Thank you, sweetheart. You are the love of my life." He started in on the third book. He smiles on some parts and gasps at others. Occasionally, he would read a line and look up at her with a smile.

The next day Scott was released. On the way home, he read Sarah's book. He did not let her have her computer. He could not stop reading. It sounded familiar, and he loved how she incorporated their lives into it. The story was moving and inspirational. He could not believe that he gets to spend the rest of his life with the woman who wrote it. Before he read the last chapter of the book, he looked at Sarah, "Before I read this last chapter, can we make it official?"

"Make what official?"

"Your dedication to your husband."

"When would you like to do this?"

"This weekend."

She smiled and nodded.

CHAPTER 3

The Perfect Day

It was Monday. Scott and Sarah had a full day. First, they go for their marriage license and then ask their pastor if he could do a quick ceremony. After that was done, Sarah and her father pick out her wedding dress, and Scott and his mom go for his tux. Lynn asks her son, "Scott, are you sure you want to do this right now? You are only twenty-three, and Sarah is twenty-one. You both have life to live through still."

"Mom, I appreciate your worry, but I have never been so sure of this until I met Sarah. We can live our lives together. I have found my match, and I can't live anymore without her, without seeing her every day, and without feeling her arms around me every morning."

"That is what I thought you were going to say. I will be here for both of you, and, son, I am proud of you and the man you have become. Dad will be proud."

"Thanks, Mom!" he said with a smile, and he hugged her and kissed her on the cheek.

The rest of the week seemed to go by really slowly. Sarah spent most of her time in Scott's office as he worked. She worked with her editor via video chat. Her editor is stationed in New York, and Sarah lives in Pennsylvania.

On Friday morning, Sara was headed into the hospital when she felt arms around her. Then he spoke. Her heartbeat increased, and she started to panic. "Don't scream, or I will kill you." She felt the gun in her back, and she went with him to his vehicle. There was no one around it was early. "Please don't hurt me."

"Darling, I would not dream of it. But I heard you are getting married, and I wanted to give you a present." Brok took her to his van. It had dark-tinted windows, and it was parked where no one could see it. "You looked so beautiful when I saw you the other day, and I could not stop thinking about you. Thank you for not being one of the ones to turn on me back then." At that moment, she decided not to give him any more of her words or sounds. He laid her down in the back of the van. He tied her up and put tape on her mouth. He let himself into her.

When he was done, he held her again and kissed her repeatedly on the lips and neck; and this time, he added the breasts into his routine. That part is new for him. He held her for an hour. Then he said, "Now, I am going to let you go. If you tell anyone about this, I will kill your husband. Do you understand?"

Again, she did not make a sound. She did not even nod or move. He untied her hands and dressed her. He opened the door, and she ran back toward the hospital. She spotted Scott as he stopped and found her computer and purse on the ground. She could not scream his name. Her voice was lost, and she ran faster. As he looked up, she jumped into his arms and started to cry. "Baby, what happened?"

She whispered, "He found me, and he—"

"Did he hurt you?" Scott's heart started to beat faster, and he was breathing rapidly. "Baby, where is he?"

She pointed in the direction and did not see the van anymore. She was shaking, and tears would not stop flowing. Scott took her head into his hands and said, "Can I do a rape kit on you? I will do it with the help of a nurse. It will be just me and a nurse." Sarah nodded. He picked her computer and purse up, then scooped her up, and carried her into the hospital.

Scott found the closest nurse to help him. "Nurse Holly, I need your help." He laid Sarah down on the closest bed. "Holly, she is my fiancée, and she was just raped. I need you to be my witness and my help to do a kit on her."

They took Sarah to a private room and did the kit. Scott let Holly take it to the lab. "Sarah, we have to call the police. He has to be stopped."

"No, we can't. He told me he will kill you if I told anyone."

"I am calling the police. I can't let him do this to you again. I was not there for you, and I am sorry I was not there." He is holding her in his arms, and she is curled up on his lap, crying and shaking.

She says through her tears, "Okay."

"Hey, Sergeant, this is Dr. Scott Harman. I need you to come to the hospital. We have a problem."

"Okay, Scott, I am on my way." Sergeant Michaels was there within ten minutes. Scott was still holding Sarah, and she was asleep. "Scott, what happened?"

"She was attacked and raped by Brok Smith. We did a kit on her, and it is being stored in our lab. I want this guy behind bars so that she does not have to go through this again."

"How long ago did this happen?"

"Half hour ago."

"Did she describe the place or vehicle?"

"Yes, it was a blue club wagon with blacked-out windows."

"Did you do the kit yourself?"

"Yes, but I had a witness in here. It is Nurse Holly."

"Okay, good. Thank you for the information, and I will retrieve the kit and get on this right away."

"Thank you, Sergeant Michaels."

The next phone call Scott had to make was to her dad. "Kevin, I need you to come to the hospital."

"Sarah—is she okay?"

Scott took a deep breath and said, "She is okay, but she was hurt."

"I am on my way. I will be there in five minutes."

The next thing Scott heard was Sarah's computer ding as her editor was on the line. Scott opened her computer and responded to her editor. "Hello, Cheryl, Sarah is not feeling well today. She is resting."

Scott tilted the computer camera down at Sarah and back up again. "Hi, Scott, I understand. Please let her know that her third book is done and ready for printing. I just wanted her go ahead for the next step."

"Cheryl, you can go ahead with the next step? She will okay with it if she were awake."

"Thank you, Scott, and I hope she feels better soon."

"You're welcome, Cheryl. We will talk soon."

Kevin came into the room as Scott disconnected from Cheryl. "Oh, Scott, what happened to her?"

All Scott had to say was one name, and Kevin's heart sank. "Oh god, no! Did he—"

"Yes, he got to her. It happened before I got here."

Kevin leaned down and kissed his daughter on the forehead and stroked her head. "Oh, baby, please, let me help you this time." Scott told Kevin what has been done so far. "She did not want to do it at first because he threatened to kill me if she did."

"Are you still getting married tomorrow?"

"I don't—"

"Yes, we are! I am not letting him stop my day tomorrow," Sarah said while her eyes are still closed, interrupting Scott.

"Ok, sweetheart, we will still go through with it tomorrow." Sarah fell asleep again.

The director of the hospital, Christian, came in to see how she was doing. He gave Scott the rest of the day off so that he could take her home and stay with her. Kevin drove both of them home, and Scott stayed with Sarah as he placed her into her bed. She would not let go of him. She slept in his arms all night.

Sarah woke up before Scott, and she stared at him as he slept. Her first thought was, *I am going to be Mrs. Scott Harman by end of the day today. I can't believe this will happen today.* As he wakes up and smiles, the events of yesterday seem to melt away.

"Hi, beautiful, how are you feeling?"

"Hi, handsome, I am okay. I am ready to be your wife."

"I am ready to be your husband." He ran his hand through her hair and pulled her into a kiss. Then he realized, "Oh, wait, today is our wedding day. I should not be here right now. It's bad luck to see my beautiful bride before the wedding."

"I think that is only if she is in her wedding dress. I think you are safe right now."

"You think so?" he asks as he smiles and kisses her again. "Oh, before I forget, Cheryl called in on video chat and said your book was done and ready to be printed. I gave her the okay. I hope it was right," he said as he braced for impact.

Sarah laughed. "Yes, it is okay. You are allowed to make those kinds of decisions now. You are just hours away from officially being my husband."

He smiled. "Okay, Ms. Sarah Portman, are you ready to become Mrs. Sarah Harman?"

"Yes, I am. But you have to get out so that I can get ready to walk down that aisle to a sexy, handsome man."

"Yes, ma'am! I will see you in a couple of hours." He gets up and kisses her one final time and walks out of her room.

Kevin was making breakfast when Scott came out of her room. "Hey, Scott, how is our girl?"

"She is okay. It seems like she is putting what happened behind her and looking forward to the events of today."

"That sounds good. Are you ready for today?"

"Yes, I am so ready! I will see you later. Thank you again for standing with me."

"Of course, you are going to be my son, and I could not have chosen anyone better."

Scott left, and Sarah joined her dad in the kitchen. "How are you, sweetheart?"

"I am okay, Dad."

"Are you sure?"

"Yes, I am not going to let him ruin this day for me. For the first time, I have met my match. The man I want to be with the rest of my life. Nothing is going to take that away from me. It is not going to be like before. Scott saved me from that yesterday and from the past."

"Okay, I can't see you go through that again, not this time. I love you, Sarah, and it makes me happy seeing you happy."

"I love you too, Dad, and thank you for all you do." She wrapped her arms around her dad and kissed him on the cheek. He did the same to her. It feels good to finally be able to wrap his arms around his daughter. He loves to make sure she knows she is loved by her dad.

Lynn is there to pick up Sarah to get hair and nails done. Lynn is giddy and excited. She never had a daughter to do this with, and she can't wait to do this with Sarah for the rest of her life. "Lynn, I know this is the last minute, and Scott asked my dad if he could stand up with him. I want to know if you could stand up with me?"

"Yes, most definitely. I will be honored to do it." Sarah handed her a gift. It was a poem that Sarah wrote in a frame, nicely decorated with flowers and butterflies.

"Sarah, this is beautiful. Thank you. I love it."

Sarah smiled and said, "You are welcome."

They arrived at the salon and had a great morning together talking about their family and history. Lynn had a chance to talk about Scott's childhood, and the joy on her face is priceless as she talked about Scott.

Sarah got an updo with curls hanging from the top of her long bun. It looks like a bouquet of flowers. They put little diamonds throughout her hair. She got French acrylics on her fingernails and a French pedicure. Lynn decided to do the same thing as Sarah. Lynn and Sarah are now on the way to the church, and Sarah is getting nervous but excited. The thought of seeing Scott at the front of the church waiting for her is all she can think of. Sarah's dress is a white floor-length dress with white embossed flowers all through it with what the store calls stardust sparkling through it. The dress had spaghetti straps and a V-neck that showed just a hint of cleavage. Sarah did not want a veil because it took away from her hair. The sight of Scott is just ten minutes away, and the butterflies are fluttering in Sarah's stomach.

The moment has arrived, and Sarah's dad met her in the back of the church. Lynn went first, and slowly she walked up. The doors opened wide, and Sarah's breath caught, and her heart was beating fast. Her eyes locked on Scott, and his eyes filled with tears. He is smiling, and his smile is getting brighter the closer she gets. They finally reach the front, and Kevin kissed his daughter on the cheek and placed her hand in Scott's hand. He took his place next to Scott. The only other person at the church beside the pastor and the four of them is Scott's aunt Leslie. The pastor started, and Sarah could not stop looking into Scott's eyes. The eyes of love and protection. The eyes that she loves and can see her future in. The vows were said, and the rings were exchanged. The pastor says, "I now pronounce you man and wife. You may kiss your bride." Scott took one long look at Sarah and pulled her in and kissed her. Then he wrapped his arms around her and dipped her and kissed her again. Their parents and aunt clapped, and they walk out of the church together. They just decided to go out to dinner to celebrate.

Scott decided to keep the honeymoon destination a surprise until they get to the airport. They are going to Florida and staying in the same hotel and the same room as her mom and dad did while on their honeymoon in Disneyland and Universal Studios. This is the first time Sarah was there and was excited to go the first time with Scott. They boarded the plane, and they arrived in Florida three hours later. Scott had a limo pick them up from the airport. They will be there for two weeks. This will hopefully give Sarah an opportunity to forget about what happened the day before and focus on making new memories with Scott.

Scott checked in, and they were escorted up to their suite. As they stepped into the elevator, another couple boarded with them, and they could not keep their hands or lips off each other. Luckily for Sarah and Scott, the couple was rooming on the third floor. Any longer, they probably be undressed by the time Sarah and Scott reached their floor. Finally, they reached their floor, and their suite was the only one on that floor. The bellhop showed them how to swipe their room key and then press the button to the floor. That is the only way they can get to their room. The room is huge with an eat-in kitchen, a huge living room, and the bedroom and bathroom off to the left down a hallway. The suite was decorated with wedding bells and little bouquets. Scott said to Sarah, "The flowers are yours." Sarah's eyes are wide with surprise and delight.

That night Sarah and Scott connected in a way that no one would imagine. They felt beautiful, and the deep connection that they felt earlier went deeper. Finally, Sarah felt loved by a man she really wants to be with. She felt honored, beautiful, and cared for. She gets to feel this way for the rest of her life. Their life together has started, and it takes Sarah's breath away.

The next day, Sarah feels lighter than air, and it feels like she is on cloud nine. She wakes up and sees a beautiful sight next to her. Her husband was still fast asleep next to her. She sneaks out of bed and decides to make him breakfast hopefully before he wakes up. He thought of everything. There is a fully stocked kitchen in their suite. Of course, half of it is stocked with his favorite food: breakfast! She is whirling around the kitchen, lost in her delight, when Scott comes out of the room. He has the biggest grin on his face when she turns around and realizes he is standing there. "Good morning, Mr. Harman!"

"Good morning, Mrs. Harman! Are you making me breakfast?"

"Yes, I am, and it is your favorite." "You know me all so well!"

"I hope so! What would you like to drink, Mr. Harman?"

"Some apple juice please."

"Coming right up." Scott then retrieves the plates from the cabinet and sets the table. As he sets the table, Scott told Sarah why he picked this particular hotel and suite. Sarah stopped and looked at him in amazement. "How did you know?"

"I asked your dad, and he gave me all the details."

"You think of everything."

"Anything for my beautiful wife."

As they ate breakfast, Scott and Sarah decide how their weeks will go. They will spend two days exploring Disneyland and two days exploring Universal Studios. For today, they will spend the day at the beach. Scott is looking forward to seeing his wife in a bikini. He also set up a jet-ski trip and a boat ride to the Keys.

Meanwhile, at home, Kevin is getting not-so-good photos of Sarah from an anonymous source. He knows they are from Brok. They come with warnings: "If I don't see her here by tomorrow, she will regret marrying him." Another threat: "I want her in my bed forever." Kevin is turning every threat and warning over to Sergeant Michaels. "Thank god she is not here to see this. I know she is safe." Sergeant Michaels told Kevin that all evidence links Brok Smith to these threats and her attack. "He even knows how to be just one step ahead of us in every attempt to apprehend him. We are not going to give up on this until we have him in custody." Kevin got home and found two more pictures, and his heart skips a couple of beats. They are pictures of her and Scott in Florida. Kevin rushed back to Sergeant Michaels.

The two weeks seem to go by quickly; but it was relaxing, beautiful, and fun. While on honeymoon, Scott decided to have Sarah's things boxed up and moved to his apartment, which was much bigger than hers. He has a four-bedroom apartment with three full bathrooms, a den, living room, a large eat-in kitchen, and a game room. His building even has a pool on the roof. Sarah's stuff was delivered and put away before they got home. But when they got home, it did not look like that way. Sarah's clothes were all over the floor, spray paint was used everywhere with warnings, and some of Sarah's photos were destroyed. The refrigerator was open, and food was all over the floor. Wine glasses were broken, and some of the plates were shattered. The pictures that were sent to Kevin were scattered all over the apartment as well. Scott immediately grabbed their luggage and Sarah's hand and led them back out to his car. Then they saw Sarah's car. The tires were slashed, the word *whore* was spray-painted on it, and windows were smashed in. Scott opened the door, and Sarah got in. He went straight to his mom's house and called Sergeant Michaels. Then he called Kevin, and that's when Kevin told Scott about what he has been dealing with also.

"Sergeant Michaels, this has gone way too far. Do you have any ideas on where he is?"

"Scott, he is one step ahead of us every time. The minute we get close, he is gone."

"We have to catch him somehow some way."

"Scott, there is no *we*. The police will get him. Please stay out of it and let the police do their jobs."

Since Scott and Sarah are married, Sarah rides with Scott every day. She works from Scott's desk on her fourth book. She even answers his phone like his secretary. She sets up meetings and appointments for him. Scott likes the fact that she is there with him at work so that he knows she is safe, and she can still do what she loves. The hospital likes the fact that she is here also. They decided to hire her as Scott's secretary because he has never been on time or showed up for any of his meetings or appointments until now.

Sarah and Scott stay with his mom for another two weeks until repairs can be made to his apartment and better security installed. Scott even goes as far as adding better security to Kevin's and his mom's houses. Scott knows that Brok is studying them, and he decides to start changing his patterns. For about a month, Sarah and Scott did something different from the previous mornings before heading to work. They would use different entrances and modes of transportation and stop at different coffee shops before work. They don't leave the building when it comes to lunch. They order in or make it before they leave in the morning. It sucks they have to live like this, but it is keeping Sarah safe, and that is the most important thing on Scott's mind.

CHAPTER 4

The Shock

It has been five weeks since the last time Brok annoyed them. Things have gotten back to normal. But they still are not resting easy. He is still out there. One morning, on their way into work, Scott was hit from behind; and Sarah saw Brok running away with a bat in his hand. Scott hit the ground with a sickening thud. Blood started pooling out of his head, and Sarah screamed. Then she got sick. She then ran into the hospital and rushed people out. Scott lay motionless on the ground. Déjà vu has struck again. Nurses and doctors rushed out and attended to Scott as Sarah could not stop heaving. The rush of nausea kept hitting her when she would stand up; and the next thing she knew, she woke up on the ground as nurses came to her rescue. "Sarah, are you okay?" Nurse Holly was helping her up.

"I am okay, just feel a little lightheaded."

"Come on, let's check you out." "No, I want to stay with Scott."

"Let's check you out first. Then you can see Scott."

The test results of Sarah's checkup came back. Nurse Holly joined Sarah, Kevin, and Lynn in the waiting room with the news. "Sarah, your test shows that you are roughly seven weeks pregnant." Sarah smiled and then quickly started to cry. "Scott is going to be a father.

What if he never survives this? Any word on Scott? What if he is not here to see his child. Oh god, what if it is not Scott's child?" Sarah started to pace and panic.

Nurse Holly grabs Sarah's hands and says, "Scott will pull through this. He is in surgery now to repair the damage to his head. Please sit down. You pacing like this is not good for the baby."

"We are going to have a baby. I want to tell Scott."

Lynn and Kevin both hugged her with tears of joy and sadness.

Two hours went by, and finally, Scott's doctor came to give an update to Sarah. "He is in recovery and hanging in there. He sustained a very deep blow to the head. We were able to relieve the swelling and fix the damage. He is stable but in a coma. We will be wheeling him into a room in a couple of minutes."

"Thank you, Dr. Stevens," Sarah said as she gave him a hug. Finally, Sarah, Kevin, and Lynn are in Scott's room and around his bed. "Hello, handsome, I am here right here by your side. I am not going anywhere." Sarah grabbed his hand. Lynn grabs his other hand, and they sit. "Scott, I know I am probably going to have to tell you this again but hold on to these next words and fight your way back to us please. Your child needs you. You are going to be a father. Scott, please fight to come back to us." Tears started to flow down Sarah's cheeks.

Three days have gone by, and there still is no change in Scott's condition. Sarah is writing her story in the quiet room as she also watches Scott. Every now and then, Sarah would stare at Scott. Even though he is in this condition, she still draws inspiration from him. She would lean in and kiss him sometimes. She would also read to him some of the book she has written so far. Sarah got a little tired and laid her head down on his arm. She fell asleep. An hour later, she feels a hand on her head, and she sits straight up and sees his eyes locked on hers. He has a tube in his mouth, so he can't talk, but his eyes says it all. "Hello, handsome! I am going to let Holly know you are awake." She kisses him on the forehead. "I will be right back." He gives her a slight smile and a wink. She practically sprints out to the nurses' station. "Holly, he is awake."

"Okay, I will be right there."

Sarah sprints back to his room. He smiles when she returns. "I missed those eyes looking at me. I missed your smile. Thank you for coming back to me. I love you, sweetheart!" He smiles and winks at her again.

Holly and Dr. Stevens walked in. "Hello, Scott, how about we take that tube out?" Dr. Stevens says to him. Scott nodded. "One, two, three, now breath out."

Scott does and coughs a little. "Hello, beautiful!" These were his first words out of his mouth. "Baby, I heard you. We are pregnant. I heard you say fight for us. My child needs me. I am happy. I can't wait to meet our child."

Sarah has the biggest smile on her face that the Space Station can see it. Holly tells Sarah, "I will call your parents. Spend time with your man."

"Okay!"

Scott says, "I like your book so far."

"What else did you hear?" "I heard you love and miss me. I just did not hear how long I was out."

"You have been out for three days."

His eyes went big. "Do you know how I got this way?"

"Yes, Brok hit you with a bat and ran. He is still out there."

After the attack on Scott, Brok went into hiding again. Sarah and Scott have not heard from him. Five months go by, and Sarah is showing. Scott and Sarah go for their ultrasound to find out the sex of the baby. Her ob-gyn Megan puts the gel on her stomach and search for the baby, and the monitor lights up when the baby comes into view and the strong heartbeat sounds through the speakers. It is music to Scott's ears, and his grin is brighter than the sun. Megan smiles and says, "He is a healthy baby boy." Sarah smiles and says, "Scott Leonard Harman II is a healthy baby boy." She looks at Scott to get his approval of the name. Scott's smile of approval grows brighter. Scott is giddy about the revelation and calls his mom, Kevin, and Aunt Leslie.

Sarah is worried that Brok will show up at any moment and do whatever he wants to her. She has the life of her baby to worry about. On the back of her mind is that dread that the baby might be his. Sarah is deep in thought when Scott interrupts her. "What are you thinking about?"

"I am worried about the baby being Brok's. I have thought about it, and I would like to get the test done just to make sure it is yours and not his."

"Okay, we can do that."

When Sarah goes into work with Scott the next day, Sarah goes for a DNA test. They also take DNA from Scott. The hospital also has Brok's DNA from the kit they did. Now she waits, and she is on edge the whole time she has to wait. Then an email shows up in her work inbox. It was from an unknown sender and address with a subject line "My Baby." Sarah knew who would send it, and she opens it. There she saw a picture of her and Scott with a circle around her stomach. The words printed on it: "THIS IS MY BABY!" She pages Scott to call extension 207, which is his office. She tells him about the email. She is pacing when he comes through the door.

"Sweetheart, please stop stressing. It is not good for you or the baby. Please sit down!" Scott guides her to the couch in the room. She points to his computer on his desk and tells him to open her email. Sarah stands up again and starts to pace. "What if it is his? I can't tell him. Your name is going on the certificate, not his. I will deny him the opportunity to be a father. The test results come back tomorrow. Why can't they came back today? He keeps doing this to us. I don't know how much I can take."

"Baby, please sit down before something bad happens." Scott goes over to her and pulls her to sit down on his lap. "No matter what, I am the father." Scott places his hand on her stomach. Sarah closed her eyes and just melted in Scott's arms; and she let the stress, the worry, and the tension out with a cry like she never cried before.

The next day Holly brought the envelope with Sarah's answer. "Sarah, they came back." She hands Sarah the envelope. Sarah rips open the envelope quickly; and in the line for "Father is," her heart started to pound, and she raced out of the room and found Scott. She jumped into his arms. "The baby is yours. You are the dad!" She is laying kisses all over his face, and he.is kissing her when he can. Whoever was within earshot of the two of them cheered. When Sarah composed herself, she breathed a huge sigh of relief. Sarah wants so much to tell Brok that it is Scott's baby and leave them alone. She does not want to put herself at risk like that. She finds a way to backtrack the email and sends a reply. "You are wrong. This is Scott's baby. DNA results prove it. Now leave us alone."

Immediately, a reply pops up, "We will see about that." Sarah did not reply, but she forwarded it to Sergeant Michaels.

Sarah is now eight months pregnant, and the baby is strong and healthy. But the hospital wants to stay home now. Megan wants Sarah to stay off her feet. Scott did not like the idea, but he agreed with Megan. Sarah had a little scare a week ago, and it put little Scott at risk. Scott kissed Sarah goodbye and left for work. Of all days, this is his longest day. Sarah fell back to sleep, and the next thing she sees is Brok standing over her. "Hello, beautiful!" Sarah quickly jumps to her feet and backs away from him. "No, no, no, beautiful, I am not going to hurt you. I just wanted to see how you and our baby are doing."

"He is not your baby. He belongs to Scott."

"He is mine." Sarah sees the anger in his face, and he rushes over to her and throws her down on the floor. She feels a sharp pain in her back, and he is gone. Scott was there two minutes later because of the alert on his phone. The last thing she saw on Scott's face was panic as the world around her went black.

Sarah wakes up five hours later in the hospital. "Scott! Baby!" Her expression is grave. She also can't say that much because of the pain in her back. She winces a little when she sat up. Scott comes over to her; and with a calm face, he hands her little Scott. She smiles and cradles him into her arms. "Baby, he is perfect, healthy, and safe," Scott reassures his wife. Scott crawls into the bed with Sarah and just holds both of them in his arms.

Kevin and Lynn come back from getting coffee and appreciate the view. Lynn started to take pictures, and they relished in the precious moment. "Are you sure he is good?" Sarah asked her husband.

"Yes, he is good. I checked him over myself." Little Scott is a spitting image of his dad, and there is no denying now that he is Scott's son. Sarah's heart is full, and she is loving her life now more than ever. She just wished her mom was here to see this. Kevin might have read her mind because he said, "Your mom would be proud."

She responded jokingly, "Thank you, Grandpa!"

"No, I am Pop-Pop!"

"Okay, Pop-Pop." Sarah said with a smile.

Lynn said, "I will be, Grandmom." They all laugh and smile.

CHAPTER 5

The Memories and the Reality

PRESENT DAY

Walking down memory lane for Sarah is always a warming welcoming journey until the memory of the tragic day pops into her mind.

Two months ago, Scott's leukemia came back. It was bad—really bad. He has been fighting sickness, and they could not do any transplant this time because he would not survive until he got better. Sarah was doing her usual bone marrow routine. They have five days stored for when Scott gets better. She is on her way back from her last donation when she heard the heart monitors beeping and nurses and doctors running to Scott's room. She gets to the door but can't go any farther. Dr. Stevens and Nurse Holly are among those trying to bring him back. Sarah starts to yell Scott's name, "Scott! Please don't leave me. I love you!"

They worked on him for twenty minutes, but they could not bring him back. Sarah heard the worst thing she never thought she would hear from Dr. Stevens, "Time of death: 2101." Dr. Stevens looks at Sarah with such a grave look and watched Sarah drop to the floor with tears streaming down her wet cheeks. Lynn ran up the hall and stopped dead in her tracks when she saw Sarah, and she broke out in tears. Her sobs were loud. "Please, no, not my son!"

Sarah noticed Lynn standing there in shock, and she got up and wrapped her arms around Lynn. "I am sorry, Lynn. He is gone."

Dr. Stevens ushered them into the room for one last goodbye to Scott. Sarah hugs him and can't let go. "Scott, I will see you again, my love." This is the only thing Sarah can get out. She steps aside and lets Lynn say her goodbyes.

Kevin runs into the room. "Oh god, no!" He rushes over to hug his daughter. "Where is little Scott?" he asks his daughter.

"He is upstairs in the day care center."

"Should he be here?"

"Dad, will he understand this? He is only three."

"You can at least give him the opportunity to say his goodbye in his way."

Sarah agrees with her dad and leaves to go get little Scott. "Hi, Susan, I need my son for a bit."

"Okay, how is Scott?" Sarah looked at her with a grave face.

Susan gasps. "No, Sarah!"

All Sarah could do was nod and fight back the tears because of her son. "Mommy!" was the next thing Sarah heard, and Scott came from around the corner. With his smiling face in view, it got harder to fight back the tears. "Hey, little man, do you want to come with Mommy for a bit?"

"Yes, Mommy. Where are we going?"

"We are going to see Daddy."

"Okay, I want to show Daddy my new drawing of us," and he holds up a drawing of stick figures or his interoperation of them.

"Before we go, I have to tell you something." She sits down on the bench in the hallway and puts him on her lap. "Scott, remember when we told you about my mom and how she is in heaven watching over us?"

"Yes, Mommy. I will meet her someday. I can still talk to her but cannot see her."

"Yes, buddy. Your daddy is with her now." Tears started to flow as the realization crossed over his tiny face.

"Daddy is with her now? Will I be able to see him?"

"No, buddy, we can't see Daddy anymore, but we can still talk to him."

He starts to cry. "Can we see him now?"

"Yes, we can see him now just to say goodbye."

"Okay, Mommy! Let's say bye to Daddy."

Sarah arrives back into Scott's room. Lynn stands up and gives room for Sarah and little Scott. "Remember, buddy, he can't talk to us, but he can hear us."

"Hi, Daddy, Mommy says that you are going to see Mom-Mom now. I need to say goodbye for now. I will be a good boy for Mommy. I promise. I love you, Daddy."

Lynn cried harder with her hands on her head. Sarah held on to her son a little tighter. He has his dad's brain and understands a lot better than Sarah would have thought. Aunt Leslie finally arrived into the room and said her goodbyes. Lynn gave the doctor an okay to move Scott. The five of them stood in the empty room, paralyzed, not saying a word. Kevin broke the silence and pulled all of them into a hug.

Sarah is paralyzed when she gets home with little Scott in tow. Sarah got a call from the hospital about her bone marrow. "Hi, Sarah, I hate to ask this right now, but what would you like to do with your bone marrow?" Sarah breathes in sharply and then decides, "Holly, please give it to someone who needs it. It will not be fair to let it go to waste."

"Okay, thank you, Sarah."

The house feels empty without the giggles of Scott being egged on by his father. The memory of Scott tickling little Scott in the living room or the both of them making a cake for Sarah on her birthday. The memories are fresh; and everywhere she looks in the apartment, she sees memories of father and son doing something. The thoughts and memories are overwhelming, but she knows she has to stay strong for little Scott. Just like her dad was when her mom died. How does she move on from here? How can she look at little Scott's face and not choke up and sob? Then she heard Scott's voice echo in her mind, "She took it one day at a time and honored him by living her life. I love you, Sarah. Move on with your life if something happens to me. I want you to be happy. I don't want you wallowing in pain. These three years have been the best ever, and I owe it to you. You gave me these three years, and I am honored because of it. I love you, Sarah, and stay safe." All Sarah wanted to do is feel Scott holding her and wrap herself in him, but she has to get a little boy to bed. She then made it to little Scott's room; and just as she got there, she heard little Scott talking to his father. "Daddy, Mommy is hurting right now. I will be here for Mommy. Don't worry, I will take care of her."

Sarah had a little smile on her face when she entered the room. "What are you doing there, buddy?"

"Just talking to Daddy."

"Okay, are you ready to go to bed?" "Yes, Mommy, I am. Mommy, when I grow up, I want to be like Daddy. I want to be a doctor so that I can help people like Daddy did."

"You know what, buddy, Daddy would be proud of you, and I think you can do whatever you want."

"Okay, Mommy. Good night, Mommy. I love you!"

"I love you too!"

Sarah kissed him on the forehead and watched him fall asleep from the door. She then curled up in Scott's clothes and, hugging his pillow, cried herself to sleep. That night Sarah dreamed that Brok was back and she was running from him, but he caught her, but Scott was there and rescued her. Then he wrapped his arms around her. She then woke up. She thought to herself, *What? Now I am dreaming of him.* Then she remembered something. She has not seen or heard of Brok since he attacked her. He either went into hiding or died. Sarah looked over at her clock. It was 3:00 a.m. She cannot go back to sleep.

Sarah walks out to the living room. She turns on her computer and starts to write. She writes for an hour. Then she realized that she has family videos on her laptop. She clicks on her video library. She chooses one that has Scott and little Scott. She watches with tears in her eyes. She pauses the video on the smiling face of her husband. "Oh, Scott, how am I going to go through life without you? I miss your touch, your arms, and your kiss. I miss watching you sleep and play with our son. I will never forget our three years together. It was short, but it was the best time of my life." She turned off the video and went back to writing. Sarah gets lost in her story, and it relaxes her. She gets to leave her world and live in someone else's for a while. The next thing she knows, she is waking up to little Scott tugging on her shirt. "Mommy, I am hungry."

"Okay, little man, I will make you some breakfast."

Even though Sarah does not have to go to work, she goes anyway. It will give her something else to think about instead of Scott. She eats with little Scott and gets him ready. She heads out and takes her time getting to the hospital. She has some appointments to cancel and arrangements to prepare. She gets to work and takes Scott up to the day care center in the hospital. Even though she wants him near her, it will help keep his mind off his dad. As she heads to Scott's office, Holly comes up behind her. "Sarah, you should not be here today."

"Hi, Holly, I have to get some things done before I make the arrangements."

"Before I forget, I put Scott's things on his desk. We did not get them to you before you left yesterday."

"Thank you, Holly!" Sarah gets to Scott's desk and sees the bag with his things in it. She grabs the bag and sees his phone, pager, keys, wallet, pants, and a shirt. It also has his stethoscope in it. She opens it and gets hit with Scott's glorious smell. The smell of him mixed with his favorite Adidas body spray. She takes a big sniff in and savors every breath in. She grabs his cell phone and quickly closes the bag holding what is left in there.

She unlocks the phone and notices a video on the screen. She pushes play. It is Scott looking gray with bloodshot eyes and tears coming down his cheeks. "Hello, Sarah, they just took you to retrieve more bone marrow. I don't think I am going to make it to see you again. I have to let you know that you are the best thing that ever happened to me. The last three years have been the best. I am proud to be your husband and Scott's dad. Please take good care of yourself. Like I said before, please be happy and find love again. I can't bear it if you don't find love. My heart will always be with you and Scott. I love you, Sarah!" He blows a kiss at the phone, and then the video stops. Tears are streaming down her cheeks. Some thoughts go through her mind. *How did he know this was the end? This last thoughts and words here on the phone preserved for a lifetime. Thank you, Scott, for a wonderful life.* She closes his phone and turns it off. She puts his things and the phone in her bag and gets to work in canceling his appointments and meetings. Then she calls down the morgue to make arrangements with them.

A few minutes later, the director of the hospital comes into the office. "Hello, Sarah, do you have a few minutes to talk?"

"Yes, I do! What's up!"

"I know without Scott here, you are worried about your job, right?"

"Yes."

"Scott and I talked before he passed. I would like to know if you could become our hospital administrator. You will run two departments handling their events, billing, and meetings. Scott told me you are great at your job and will work really well with the hospital."

"He said that?"

"Yes."

"Okay, I will take the job. I have fun here and don't want to give it up."

"Nice, we love having you here. Since you came on for Scott, he has never missed a meeting or been late. I will have the paperwork sent up to you. You can keep this office it is the right fit for you."

"Thank you, Christian!"

"You are welcome!"

Sarah called the funeral home and made arrangements with them. Then she called the lawyer who drew up their wills and talked to him about the next steps she needs to take. By the time she was done all that she needed to do, it was lunchtime and she went out to get lunch. It is weird because this is the first time that she went out by herself.

She decided to walk. It was a sunny day, and she wanted to relish the memories this brings her. With her eyes closed, she takes a deep breath in; and she remembers Scott's smile on this kind of day. This made her smile, but her smile turned into a frown because she felt arms around her. She opened her eyes and saw Brok standing in front of her. "Hello, Sarah, I am sorry I have not been around for a long time. I am back now and heard the good news. Scott is gone now. We can be together and love each other."

"No, I never want to be with you. Let me go—now." Sarah is struggling to get free. Brok is pulling her into a secluded alley. He is also touching her everywhere while he is talking to her. "You look good. I want to take you now. I need you now."

The next thing, Sarah feels Brok let go of her. "The lady said no. Now, let her go." A voice from behind her sounds, and she turns around because it almost sounded like Scott's voice. She sees Brok lying on the ground, and she sees a familiar face. It is not Sergeant Michaels, but he looks like him. The man standing in front of her is hotter than Sergeant Michaels. "Are you okay, ma'am? Did he hurt you?"

Sarah looks down at Brok, and he is knocked out. "I am okay, but this man needs to be arrested by Sergeant Michaels."

"Sergeant Michaels—ah!" He holds up his finger and pulls out his phone. "Hello, big bro, I have someone that you may want to take off my hands. His name is—" He looks at Sarah, and she says, "Brok Smith."

"His name is Brok Smith." Sarah hears him say yes, and he hands her the phone. "My brother wants to talk to you."

"Hello, Sarah, is Graham serious he has Brok right there?"

"Yes, he does." When she said that, she hears the sirens growing louder.

"Those sirens are us. We are almost there. Quick, go with Graham before Brok wakes up." Sarah hands Graham back his phone. Graham grabs her hand and leads her out of there.

"So you are Sergeant Michaels's brother?"

"Yes, much younger brother. Hello, I am Graham Michaels."

"Hello, I am Sarah Harman."

"As in Mrs. Scott Harman?"

"Yes, did you know my husband?"

"Yes, he saved me a couple of times. Back in high school and again more recently."

"So you have known him for a long time?"

"Yes, for a long time. I am a freelance photographer, and I travel all over the world. That's why we probably have never met. So how is Scott nowadays?"

Sarah gave him a sad look and said sadly, "He is no longer with us. He passed yesterday."

"What! No! How?"

"Leukemia."

"Oh, Sarah, I am sorry. Was it long?"

"No, he had it three years ago, and then it came back two months ago. He lost his battle yesterday." Tears started to fall again down Sarah's cheeks.

Graham pulled the car over and wrapped his arms around Sarah. Sarah smells something familiar and lets Graham hold her. *The Adidas body spray—damn, he uses the same one as Scott's,* Sarah thought to herself. His arms are strong, and his goatee feels soft on her face. He is a perfect shade of peach, and his eyes are different shades of brown. His hair is copper-feathered back and split on the right side. He let her cry for a while before he pulled back out into traffic.

"Thank you," she said to him when she was ready.

"There is no need to thank me. It is my pleasure. So who is this Brok Smith?" "He has been a thorn in my side for a long time. Like you and Scott, we had history in high school. He attacked me about ten times. Then he found me again three years ago. He attacked me twice and put Scott in the hospital for three days. I am glad he is finally caught and out of my life. Where are we going, Graham?" "My brother asked if I can take you to the police station to give your statement."

"Okay, but can we stop for food? That was where I was headed."

"Yes, we can." They quickly went through a drive-thru window at a fast food place and grabbed something. They then went to the station. Sarah gave her statement and then heard Graham's version. She was thinking to herself while listening. This man comes out of nowhere to rescue her, and he knows Scott. Is Scott trying to hook her up or protecting her the best he can now? Graham is finished giving his statement. Sarah sees something in the corner of her eye, and it is Brok being led through the station by Sergeant Michaels. He is smiling at her as he walks by. Then just before he disappears from view, he blows a kiss toward her. Sarah rolls her eyes and goes back to listening Graham and the officer talk.

Graham and Sarah head back out to the car. "Sarah, where am I taking you?"

"I need to go back to the hospital. My son is there in day care, and I have some work to finish."

"Okay, I will take you back."

"Graham, this has been bugging me for a bit, but what were you doing that put you in the right place to rescue me?"

"I was visiting the hospital. Then I saw how Brok was holding you and the look on your face. Your face was horrified. So I kicked into action."

"Who were you visiting?"

"I wanted to see Scott, but I was told he was not there. I left and ran into you. Why do you ask?"

"I can't help but think that Scott is somehow influencing us to meet."

"I feel the same way. I mean does anything happen by chance, or is there a motivation factor behind us meeting?"

Sarah smiled at him and said, "Well, I guess I have a new friend, and his name is Graham Michaels."

"Since you said that, I am here for you. When you want to talk, I will listen. If you want to learn more about Scott, I have stories for you. I will be your friend for however long you need."

"Thank you, Graham. I will take you up on that."

"Your son—what is his name?"

"Scott Leonard Harman II."

Graham smiles. "Nice name."

"Yeah, he looks exactly like him too. It is hard to look at him and not see Scott staring back at me."

"That has to be hard. I would like to meet the little guy."

"If you come in with me, you can meet him."

"Okay, I will!"

Graham and Sarah make their way up to the day care center. "Now see if you can spot him."

Graham scans the children while they stand at the doorway. She watches his eyes; and when they got big, she smiles. "Wow, he does look like his father. Now I really see how hard it is for you. My heart aches for you."

"Thank you, Graham." Sarah walked in and picked up Scott and brought him to meet Graham. "Scott, this is your daddy's friend Graham. This is little Scott."

"It is nice to meet, you little man."

"You know my daddy?"

"Yes, I do."

"Cool, then we can be friends too."

"You are a very smart boy."

"Oh yes, I have been told that."

"And you have your daddy's wit."

"Mommy, what is *wit*?"

"You are smart like your daddy."

Sarah puts Scott down, and he goes back to what he was doing. Graham and Sarah walk back to her office. On the way back, they run into Holly. "Hi, Graham, are you here for your treatment?"

Sarah looks at him with a concerned look on her face. "Treatment?"

"Yes, I have aplastic anemia, and I am going in for a bone marrow transplant tomorrow. We caught it early enough for me to survive."

Sarah looks at him with her hand over her mouth. Then she says, "I would like to be here, if you don't mind."

"I would like that very much."

CHAPTER 6

The Second Chance

The next day Sarah is in her office waiting for the results of Graham's transplant. This again feels like déjà vu. She went through this with Scott. Holly came into Sarah's office and told Sarah that Graham is out and in recovery. "Thank you, Holly." Sarah starts on her way to Graham's room. Meanwhile, Graham wakes up. "Nurse, like last time, can you please tell me who the donor was?"

"Yes, Mr. Michaels, the donor's name is Sarah Harman." Graham smiles. She saved his life, and she did not even know it.

Sarah walks into the room, and his smile brightens. "Hi, Graham, you look good."

"I feel good. How are you?"

"I am okay." Sarah sits down next to his bed, and they talk about their lives. Graham tells her about Scott in his early years, and Sarah talks about him in his recent years.

Graham also tells her about his family. "It is just me and my brother now. Our parents died when I was fifteen, and my brother had to take care of me."

Sarah told him about her mom and brother. "When my mom died, I met Scott. He saved me that day in more ways than one."

Sarah feels good to talk openly with someone about Scott and her past. She got over the fear of her past when she opened up to Scott. The more she lets Graham in, the more she looks to him as a best friend. This is what she needs right now.

Graham seems to be studying her when he asks, "What are you thinking about, Sarah?"

"I am just thinking. The more I open up to you, the more I look to you as a best friend. I like the feeling of us growing closer as best friends."

Graham answers with a smile, "Yes, best friends."

They talked some more until Graham got tired, and he dozed off. Sarah got up and kissed her new best friend on the forehead. "Sleep well, Graham."

It is Saturday, and today will be the hardest thing Sarah has to go through. She is standing in the bedroom looking at herself in the mirror. She is wearing a black dress with little diamonds along the neckline. She never thought this day was going to come this early. He was only twenty-six, and his life is over. He had a good life. He made her life good. Today is the day she has to say her final goodbye. She is not ready for this, and she is numb. She does not think she has any more tears left to cry. She slips on her shoes and walks out to the living room. Little Scott is sitting on a chair, coloring. "Are you ready, little man?"

"Yes, Mommy!"

"Now, buddy, this may be a little too sad for you today, but remember, Mommy is here for you. Don't be scared, okay?"

"Okay, Mommy. But, Mommy, I don't want you to be sad. It will make me sad."

"I will try not to be sad today."

Sarah, Lynn, and Kevin were standing up front next to the casket. Scott's aunt Leslie was holding little Scott on her lap as people walked past and said their condolences. People from the hospital filed in and hugged. They shook hands and kissed the cheek of Sarah and her family. Patients of his came as well. Some of them told Sarah that he saved their lives. That made her smile, and she told them thank you. When the last person comes through, she feels weak. Then she noticed that Graham was not here. Just when the service was about to begin, in walked Sergeant Michaels and Graham. "I made it. I am sorry I am late."

"It's okay. At least you are here now." Graham walks over to his friend's casket and says his goodbyes. He takes his seat.

The pastor starts his service. "Sarah and Scott, please make your way up." Sarah knows what comes next. She did it with her mom and brother. Sarah picks up Scott and says to Scott with tears in her eyes, "Do you want to help Mommy tuck Daddy in?"

"Yes, Mommy."

Sarah and Scott both took the blanket and then pulled the blanket up over Scott's face. Sarah whispers, "Goodbye, my love. Until we meet again." She could not hold her tears any longer, and the sobs came out. Little Scott wrapped his arms around his mommy and held on to her tightly. She drops to the floor, holding him in her arms; and they cried together. There was no dry eye in the place. Graham stands up and lifts Sarah up and guides her to her chair all while holding on to Scott. The funeral director finished and closed the lid. The pastor spoke, and Sarah regained her composure.

As the pastor finished his speech, he gave an opportunity for people to speak about Scott and how he touched their lives. Two of his patients stood up and made their way to the mic. "We are two of Scott's patients, and if he had not stepped in when he did, we would not be here today. He fought to get us what we needed to survive. We had leukemia also, and he found us a donor. He inspired us to live and fight. Thank you, Mrs. Harman, for sharing your husband with us all. He saved lives, and he touched all hearts that he saved."

Graham stood up and walked to the mic. "I have known Scott for a while now. We were friends in high school. One night, I was driving home, and Scott was behind me, and out of nowhere, a car hit mine, and I spun out of control. Scott pulled me out of the car while it burned around us. My injury was in my abdomen, and it destroyed my kidneys. Scott was a match for me, and he freely gave me one of his. He risked his life to pull me out of the car, and he saved my life by giving me a part of him. A couple of days ago, I met his wife, and she gave me something also. She saved my life as well. I received a bone marrow donation, and it came from her. I can't help but think if Scott had never met her, I would not be standing here today. I am truly grateful to have Scoot and his wife in my life." Sarah looked at Graham with gratitude and surprise. In that moment, she realized that Scott did, in fact, send Graham into her life. Another part of him lives on in Graham. Her fondness for Graham grew even more in her heart.

Others stood up to speak, and Sarah listened contentedly. She was overwhelmed by how many people Scott touched. At the end of the service, Sarah watched as Graham, Sergeant Michaels, Dr. Stevens, and five other men carried the casket out to the waiting vehicle, which was an ambulance. They loaded it into the back. Sarah and Scott rode in the back with the casket as they made their way to the cemetery. Everyone said their final goodbyes by placing flowers on the casket. Sarah, Scott, Lynn, Kevin, and Graham stayed behind to watch the casket get lowered into the ground. Sarah walked slowly back to her dad's car. "Dad, if you don't mind taking Scott to the hospital where the wake is being held, I would like to talk to Graham."

"Okay, darling, I will meet you there."

"Thank you, Dad!"

"So when where you going to tell me how Scott saved your life?"

"I wanted to wait until today so that I could honor Scott."

"When were you going to tell me they used my marrow to save you?"

"Again, I waited to honor Scott. Are you okay with that?"

"Yes, I am. I am glad that my marrow is working for someone. It also comforts me that a part of Scott is in you. Ever since you said what you said at the service, I cannot help but think that Scott sent you to protect me. I feel that he will do anything to keep his family safe."

"I think he did also."

"Graham, thank you for being here for us."

"Sure, that is what best friends are for."

CHAPTER 7

Life Goes on

A year has gone by, and life for Sarah has been good. Scott's estate was finalized, and Sarah realized that Scott had more than she thought he had. Scott made sure that she and Scott were set for life no matter if Sarah remarried. Scott made sure that there were clauses added for Sarah's husband if she does remarry. Graham has gotten closer to Sarah. He loves Scott. That boy lights up his life. Graham is seriously thinking about asking Sarah out on a date. He is not sure if she is ready. It has been a year since Scott passed away. Is she ready to be loved again? Graham wants to love her. Graham wants to spend the rest of his life with her.

Here goes nothing. Graham pulls into Sarah's parking lot, and he heads upstairs. She opens the door; and before the door has a chance to close behind him, he captures her mouth with his. He has her in a sweeping-off-your-feet kiss, and she is kissing him back. He released her and said, "I have been wanting to do that for a long time."

Her eyes looked stunned, and she answered him back by kissing him again. They released again, and she said, "So have I." Then she stepped back in horror and said, "Should we be doing this? I mean it feels right but—" She starts to pace. "Oh, what the hell," and she goes back to kissing him again.

It's the eve of Scott's first death anniversary, and she is kissing a man. She is thinking to herself, *Is this right? It's been a year, and I don't want to be alone anymore. Graham has been great this year. He has helped me with Scott whenever he could. He has done odds and ends around my home. Now he is standing here kissing me. It feels good and right.*

She has not had a man touch her like this since Scott. She misses this, and she wants this. She gives into her thoughts and lets Graham in. She wraps her arms around Graham, and he does the same to her. They don't let go of each other for a while until Sarah breaks and comes up for air. Graham asks her, "Are you okay with this?"

She looks up at him; and with a smile, she says, "Yes!"

"Are you ready for this kind of relationship? I don't want to push you or make you feel uncomfortable. I want you in my life closer than we have been." Before he could finish saying any more, he looks at her in a way that will expose his innermost thoughts and says, "Sarah, I am in love with you. I can't live without you knowing this any longer."

Her eyes are wide with surprise, and she can't take her eyes off his. She sees sincerity in them. She sees a love that she has not seen for a long time. "Graham, I think I am in love with you also." He takes her into his arms and kisses her again.

They release each other again and move to take a seat on the couch. She puts her head on his shoulder. She says to Graham, "It is time for me to love again. It is what Scott would have wanted for me. He told me in the last message he ever said to me. I am ready to honor his wishes and let someone love me again. I am happy it is you, Graham. I don't want to be alone anymore." He takes Sarah onto his lap and holds her. Sarah can't believe that Graham feels the same way she does. She then says to him with a smile on her face, "You are bold. How did you know I would react the way I did?"

"I did not know. I just went for it. I feel it was better to show you how I feel instead of telling you. Actions speak louder, you know."

"Yes, they surely do."

"So can I call you my girlfriend and I am your boyfriend?"

"I don't know," she said that as straight-faced as possible. Then she smiled again. "Yes, I guess we should, huh! Hello, boyfriend!"

Graham smiled. "Hello, girlfriend!"

Scott comes out of his room. "What are you doing up, sir?"

"I heard Graham's voice and wanted to say hi."

Graham stands up and picks up Scott and asks him, "Is it all right with you that I came around more often and see you and Mommy?"

"Yes, it is all right. You can move in too. I know you love Mommy."

Graham's face lights up at his confession. "Do you know what you are? A very smart little man."

"I have been told that a lot."

They laugh, and Sarah said to him, "Buddy, let me put you back into bed."

"No, I want Graham to do it please."

"Okay, he can do it, but I will be at the door watching."

"Okay, Mommy. I love you."

"I love you too. Good night, buddy!"

"Good night, Mommy!"

Scott gave Graham something to think about. *What if I did move in with them? What if I asked her to marry me? Is she ready for this? Does Scott really love me that much that he wants to see me more?* Sarah could tell Graham was deep in thought.

She said to him, breaking him out of his thoughts, "I know what Scott said to you has you thinking."

"Yes, it does, but I don't want you to feel obligated to let him have his wish."

"Graham, do you still have a place to live?"

"No, they are kicking us all out by the end of the month, which is in two weeks. I have been looking but no luck at all."

"You could move in here. I would like to see you more often. I have a whole other bedroom you can occupy."

"Are you sure? I am barely home anyway. I am always here."

"Yes, I am sure."

"Okay, I will move in this weekend."

They sat down on the couch, and Sarah curled up in Graham's arms, and they watched a movie together. The next thing Graham knows, Sarah is asleep. He lets her sleep right where she is. He loves watching her sleep. He dozes off himself. An hour later, he was woken up by Sarah. She was saying, "No, please no! No, not Graham! Please don't take him from me." Her breath starts to increase, her body tenses, and she is dripping with sweat. Graham wraps his arms around her tighter and tells her, "Sarah, I am here. I am not going anywhere. I am not leaving you." He says the phrases over and over until he can feel her relax, and she wakes up. "Sarah, are you okay?"

"Yes, I am okay now!"

"How long have you been having nightmares?"

"Since Scott died."

"Oh, man, Sarah, why did you not tell me?"

"Because I did not want you to worry. That one was mild compared to the other ones I have been having."

"What have they been about?"

"The times Brok had me. I used to get them before Scott and I were married, but they disappeared when Scott and I were married. Now they are back."

"And tonight, what was that one about?"

"Brok tried to take you away from me."

"I am here now. I won't go anywhere."

Sarah smiled and fell back to sleep, snuggled in Graham's arms. He was afraid to let go of her. Her nightmares might return, but she slept soundly for the rest of the night.

It is moving-in day for Graham. This is new for him. He has never lived with a girlfriend before. But he never really had a serious girlfriend before either. He has dated and not gone past kissing. Graham is a little nervous. Memories of Graham's past are creeping back into his mind. Sarah might save him from his past. Is he ready to open up to her? Will he have the strength to open up to her? Sarah, Kevin, and Sergeant Michaels help Graham move in. Sarah is worried about Lynn. She has not seen or spoken to Lynn in weeks. Losing her son has hit her hard. Every chance Sarah got, she would go and check on her. Sarah would also let her spend as much time with her grandson as she could. It brightens her mood when she sees him. The older he gets, the more he looks like his dad. Sarah calls her mother-in-law, "Hi, Lynn, I just want to check on you. How are you doing?"

"Hi, Sarah, I am okay. How are you and little Scott?"

"He is doing fine. I want to ask you a question, and I want you to be honest with me."

"Anything, dear."

"Are you okay with me moving on with Graham? I love Scott, but I know he would want me to move on."

"Oh, sweetheart, I am happy you are moving on, and yes, it is what Scott would want for you. No matter what, you will always be my daughter. I would want you to be happy and cared for. I love Graham, and he is right for you. Just like Scott was."

"Thank you, Lynn. I agree with you. I will always be your daughter." They talk for a few minutes more. Sarah tells her about Graham moving in. Lynn gives her the "you are always saving people" quote and that she is proud of Sarah.

They finish the day out with a small celebration, and Graham is all moved in. It is weird for Sarah to have a man in her home now. She just got used to not having a man here, and now Graham is here. She feels safe now. She feels happy, and she feels like she is honoring Scott. Sarah is staring out the window at the city life below, and she starts to cry. She is ready to let Scott go; she is ready to move on. The three years she got to spend with Scott she will cherish for the rest of her life, but that chapter has come to a close. She is letting go; she is setting him free to rest in peace. She takes a look at her son, and she realizes that Scott will always be a part of her life, but she is letting go of the absence of Scott.

Graham notices Sarah with tears streaming down her cheeks, and he rushes to be by her side. "What's wrong? Talk to me!"

"I have let Scott go. I am ready to move on with you."

Graham wraps her in his arms and lets her cry. Her tears are a mixture of sadness, happiness, and the tension that she has been holding. Graham could feel her relax, and the tension disappears. Sarah closes her eyes and whispers, "Goodbye, Scott. I love you!" Then she wraps her arms around Graham as to say she is giving her whole being to Graham. As her crying subsides, she starts to smile and says to Graham, "I am happy you are here. I feel safe now, and I feel loved again. Thank you for bringing this feeling back to me."

"Anything for you."

Sarah looks deep into Graham's eyes and says, "Graham, I love you!"

Graham gasps and says, "I love you back." They kiss, and then they stare out the window together.

When Sarah and Graham rejoin the group in the living room, Sergeant Michaels gets a call on his cell phone. "Yes, understand. No, that is not good. Really! Okay, keep me posted."

Graham looks at his brother as Sergeant Michaels stares at Sarah. Sarah knows that look from Sergeant Michaels, and it is not good. He hangs up his phone and says to Sarah, "He is out on bail, and he is pleading not guilty. He wants to go after Graham for assault."

Sarah says in shock, "You have got to be kidding me!" She starts to pace. "When is he ever going to leave me alone?" Now, more than ever, she is happy that Graham has moved in. Sergeant Michaels starts his calls to get Sarah and Graham more security. Sargent Michaels knows his brother can handle himself, but he knows his brother will be traveling soon. He also knows if anything were to happen to Sarah, Graham will kill him. Graham also decides to stay local for now until Brok is out of the picture for good. He will go to and from work with Sarah as a security bonus. Graham is appreciative that his brother is taking extra precaution to keep Sarah and Scott safe. This is what he has always done when they were younger.

CHAPTER 8

The Struggle and the Triumph

A month has gone by, and Sarah is on edge. She is looking over her shoulder; and with two other people traveling with her, Scott and Graham, it makes her more nervous. Paul and Chris have joined their everyday routine. She had to add another wing to their home for Paul and Chris to stay. They do their jobs well, but Sarah can't wait until this is all over. She likes the fact that they are there, but do they have to be so serious all the time? Then again, Sarah knows that their safety are in Paul and Chris's hands, and they have to be serious.

Brok's lawyer has contacted Sarah a couple of times already, and he hounds her for the truth that he wants to hear, not what actually happened. Sarah sticks to the same thing over and over. Sarah knows that she would have to face him in court soon. Brok is defiantly fighting tooth and nail to stay out of jail. Sergeant Michaels came to Sarah's office with some devastating news. "Sarah, the assault that Brok did back in high school will not be tried at this time. He has already served time for that. Brok is also claiming that Scott is his child. Supposedly, he has proof of this fact."

"I don't care about high school, and this shit with Scott being his is bullshit. Scott looks like his rightful dad, and that is Scott. You can see Scott looking back at us every time little Scott looks at us. He looks nothing like Brok."

"Yes, I know that, we know that, but does Brok know that?"

"I don't think that he has ever seen Scott to know that he is not his."

After Sergeant Michaels leave, Sarah opens her email to get some work done. She opens the first email without really looking at it.

> Oh, I see you have increased security. What are you afraid of? I won't hurt you. I love you. You are mine, and I don't care if that oversized man of yours does not like it.
>
> > Yours forever,
> > Brok! 😊

Sarah started breathing heavily, and Graham looked at her. She had panic in her eyes. Graham walked over to her and read what had her scared. His eyes are big, and he says, "That is it. I want to take you and Scott away from here until Brok is safely behind bars."

"Graham, I can't go anywhere. They are going to need me in court. I have to be here for work. I can't uproot Scott's life because of this jerk. We can't let him win by scaring us."

"I will feel better if you and Scott are safe, and right now, that is not here."

"Graham, I can't just pick up and go." Sarah can tell that he is irritated, but she can't run scared. He is not thinking right, and he is letting fear control his feelings. Graham sits back down and goes back to what he was doing with a scared, angry look on his face. Graham gets up from his seat. "I have to use the bathroom."

Sarah asks him before he leaves, "Are you mad at me?"

"Yes, but I love you." Then he walks out the door. Two minutes later, Sarah hears two gunshots, and then her door flies open. In walks Brok. "You are coming with me if you want your son to live."

Sarah jumps up and says, "You are not touching my son." Brok closes the gap and takes hold of Sarah and leads her out into the hallway with a gun to her head. She looks down and sees Christ and Paul not moving. Tears stream down her face. She is looking for Graham, and her heart sinks when she does not see him as Brok takes her out of the hospital. He takes her and puts her in the familiar van and ties her up. He drives to a secluded place in the woods.

He takes her out of the van and puts her in the house that is there. He carefully places her in a chair and strips her and reties her to the chair. Brok pulls out his phone and video calls Graham. Sarah's eyes are wide and scared. Graham picks up immediately. "Hello, Mr. Graham, I have your woman." He flips the screen to her. "But for her to be free from me, you must die."

Graham heard Sarah say, "No, Graham, don't leave me."

Graham stares at the screen and says, "Give me a couple of minutes, and you will have your wish."

"No, Graham, please, no!" Sarah pleads with him.

"You can video chat me when you are ready." Brok hangs up and looks at Sarah. "If I can't be with you, no one else can."

Graham video calls back within a half hour. Brok is sitting on Sarah's lap, and she can see Graham. Graham's heart sinks when he sees her tears and her naked body. Graham also had Sergeant Michaels and Dr. Stevens in the room. "Sarah, I love you! Thank you for the best life ever. I am doing this for you. I want you to be free."

"Graham, please don't do this. I love you! I don't want you to go."

"Sarah, I have to do this. I need you to survive." Graham gives Dr. Stevens a nod, and he slowly plunges a needle into Graham's arm. Sarah is sobbing and saying, "Graham, please no! I love you. I love you. I love you!" Then they hear the heart monitor flatline, and Sarah sobs harder.

Brok then says, "Sergeant Michaels, here is the address. Come and get us." Brok hangs up the phone.

Sarah is sobbing so hard. "What did I ever do to you to do this to me? What do you want from me?"

"I want you to suffer the way you made me suffer. I want you to feel my pain. You gave me yourself in high school. Then you took it away from me."

"I never wanted you in high school. You hurt me, and you keep hurting me. Now get away from me and leave me alone."

It did not take long for Sergeant Michaels to get there, and he came barging into the house and saw Brok still on Sarah. Sergeant Michaels says while pointing a gun at Brok, "Get off her now!" Brok gets off Sarah and sinks to his knees. Sarah could tell that Sergeant Michaels is stricken with grief. The look on his face makes her sob harder. Sergeant Michael is kneeing on Brok's back, and he hits him in the face. "That is for my brother. Now you will pay for this for the rest of your life and rot in jail." Sergeant Michaels handcuffs him and hands him over to the officer. He then takes off his jacket and drapes it over Sarah. He leans down and unties her. Once she is free, she wraps her arms around Graham's brother. The EMTs are allowed in, and they wrap a blanket around her, and Sergeant Michael lifts her up and carries her to the ambulance. She is crying so hard, and she won't let go of Sergeant Michaels.

When they get to the hospital, her tears have subsided and she lets go of Sergeant Michaels. The first words out are "How are Paul and Chris?"

"They are doing okay." She sighed in relief.

On the way to a room, Nurse Holly is asking her questions. "Did he hurt you? Are you ok?"

"No, he did not hurt me, but I am not okay mentally." They opened the door to a room, and Sarah saw Graham's body lying there. Tears started again. "He died for me!" She stands up from the wheelchair and walks over to the bed he was lying in and crawled in the bed with him.

His body was lifeless, and the monitor still had a flatline. Dr. Stevens then put a needle into his arm. Then a few seconds ticked by, and the monitor started to beep. Graham takes a huge deep breath in, and his eyes flutter open. Immediately, he wraps Sarah in his arms. She is sobbing hard, and she wraps her arms around him in response. "Graham, I thought you were gone."

"I know. I am sorry I had to do that. I had to get you back, and that was the only way to do it."

"I love you, Graham. Do you know that? Don't ever do that to me again. I can't take it anymore."

"I know. I am sorry, but I am here now, and I will do anything for you."

Sarah smiled, "You will do anything for me?"

"Yes, you are now my life, and I can't live without you."

"Then will you marry me?"

"Sarah, I want to ask you. Please, yes, I will be your husband."

She smiled at the look of surprise on his face, and she kissed him. "Did he hurt you? Are you okay?"

Graham says as he is looking her over. "No, he did not hurt me, and I am okay now!"

The next thing Sarah hears is the voice of her son. "Mommy!" Sarah slowly sits up and opens her arms so that Scott can leap into them.

"Hey, buddy, are you okay?"

"Yes, Mommy, I am. Why are you wrapped in a blanket? Mommy, are you okay?"

"Yes, buddy, I am good now."

Nurse Holly speaks up, realizing that Sarah is still naked under the blankets. "I will go get you some scrubs."

"Okay, thank you, Holly." Sarah returns her attention back to little Scott and says, "Hey, buddy, can I ask you a question?" He nodded. "How do you feel if Graham is your daddy?"

"But, Mom, I have a daddy." "You do have a daddy, but do you want another daddy?"

"Yes, is Graham going to be my other daddy?"

"Yes, he is."

He lets out a big "Yay!" Sarah and Graham smile, and Sarah brings Scott between the both of them and hugs them both at the same time. Holly found something unique for Sarah to wear. She found some of Scott's scrubs. They had his name on them, and she brought them to Sarah, and Sarah got dressed. Sarah was smiling at the name on the scrubs, and she wore them with pride.

Sarah, Scott, and Graham head home; and Sarah is so tired from the day's events. "Scott, it is bedtime. Head to your room, and I will be there in a couple of minutes."

"No, Mommy, I want Graham to do it."

"Okay, but come here first so that I can give you a kiss."

"Okay, Mommy, I love you. Good night!"

"Good night, my sweet boy. I love you!"

Scott heads to his room with Graham in tow. Sarah is feeling a little jealous. She smiles and thinks to herself, *I have been replaced.* Sarah is smiling when Graham returns. "He is out already. What are you smiling about?"

"I have been replaced. I think he loves you more than me."

Graham smiles. "No, he does not. He told me that he wanted me to tuck him in because you looked tired. He wants you to rest for our wedding day tomorrow."

"He thinks we are getting married tomorrow?"

"Yes, he does. I told him it won't be tomorrow but a couple of weeks from now."

"What did he say after that?"

"He said okay, but you should still get some rest."

"I love that kid! He is just as smart as his daddy."

"I can tell. Oh, and before I forget—" He takes something shiny out of his pocket and slips it on her finger. She looks down at it. It is a princess-cut diamond with two smaller princess-cut diamonds on either side of the solitaire. "Marry me, Sarah!"

"Yes!" They hold each other on the couch and fall asleep in each other's arms.

Just like Graham told Scott, the wedding was a couple of weeks away. The day is upon them now. Graham is nervous, and he is pacing. His brother/best man walks in and asks, "Dude, what is the matter?"

"I did not tell her yet!"

"Tell her what?"

"I did not tell her about my past."

"Really, you did not tell her? What are you waiting for?"

"With the things that she went through, I did not want to rehash the images for her."

"She will see that damage that was done to you later today."

"I know. What do I do? Do I go tell her now and hope to God that it does not scare her away?"

"No, wait until after the wedding. She won't be scared of you."

"Okay, I will wait, but if she runs screaming, I am blaming you."

Kevin comes in to check on Graham. "Just making sure you are here and standing up my daughter on her wedding day."

"No, sir, I will never do that to her."

"You better not! Treat her right. She is yours now." "Sir, I am sorry you have to do this twice. If I could, I would trade places with Scott no matter how much I love her. Seeing the sadness in her face when Scott died, I don't ever want to see that again."

"I know, Graham. I am very honored to have you in her life now. You healed her heart and allowed her to move on. I am proud of both of you." Graham hugged his father-in-law to-be. "Oh, and one more thing, call me Kevin. None of that sir thing."

"Okay, Kevin."

"See you shortly at the altar. Remember, no running."

"Ok, sir—I mean Kevin!"

It was time for the Michaels brothers to head to the altar. Graham can't wait to see her. He spent the last couple of nights at his brother's house to make this moment more special for him and Sarah. He has not seen her at all for the past couple of days, and the anticipation is killing him. The doors in the back of the church open; and in walks Lynn, Sarah's maid of honor. Just as the music starts with the wedding canon, Holly and her family, along with Dr. Stevens and his family, stood up; and Sarah was at the end, standing with her dad and little Scott, waiting for her cue to start to walk. She is here, and she is beautiful. The thoughts are running through Graham's head. Graham was stunned when tears came running down his cheeks. She is so beautiful. His eyes are locked on hers, and she is finally standing near him, and he can smell her sweet perfume and bask in the glow of her beauty. Her father again places a kiss on her cheek and puts her hand in Graham's.

Those past few days of spending apart from her were excruciating but worth it. From this moment on, there will be no more spending time apart or alone. They say their vows, Scott hands them their rings, and the pastor pronounces them husband and wife. "You may kiss your bride." Graham slowly and passionately takes Sarah into his arms and kisses her. Everyone is cheering and clapping. Lynn has tears in her eyes, but they are not tears of sorrow but tears of happiness. Before Sarah walks to the back of the church with her husband, Sarah turns to Lynn, "Are you okay?"

"Yes, I am okay. Now quit worrying about me and celebrate your husband."

They all had an intimate dinner and celebrated the Michaels. Sarah stands up and gets everyone's attention. "This has been a rough four years for me, but I have enjoyed most of it. Today I want to honor Scott because. If it were not for him, Graham would not be here today, and neither would little Scott. I want to honor him today because he gave me some of the best years of my life. I will never forget Scott for all the sacrifices he made for his family and his patients. The final sacrifice he made was to leave his family and trust them into the hands of another man. He had to let me know that he wanted me to move on and love again. His heart was broken when he said those words. I could not have gotten through the heartache of losing Scott, my mom, and brother if it weren't for each and every one of you. Graham, thank you for bringing happiness back to me. Thank you for allowing me to love so deeply again. You are a good father to Scott, and he needs that." As she closes her speech, tears were streaming down her face. Graham reaches up and places his hand into hers and strokes her hand with his thumb. "I could not have asked for better people in my life." Then she sits down, and

Graham wraps her in his arms. Everyone raises a glass and then drinks.

Graham stands up and honors his wife. "I am grateful for this beautiful woman next to me. I met a man long time ago, and he gave me a life to live. His heart was into saving people, and his passion was passed onto his wife. He had to leave behind his heart and his memory. His wife saved people in his memory, and he lives on in his family. The role of protecting his family now is passed to me. I am honored to live in his memory and protect his family. I am standing here today because I was saved by Scott and Sarah. By loving you, Sarah, and being your husband, it allows me to honor Scott, the one who brought us together. Sarah, I wish I could take the place of Scott, but I will do my very best to make sure you are loved. I will do my very best to protect you and little Scott as you are my family now." Graham sat down, and Sarah wrapped her arms around Graham.

They say their goodbyes and head out for their honeymoon. Graham is taking her to California and then surprising her and going to Hawaii. They finally get to the hotel, and Graham looks nervous. The conversation he had with his brother was replaying in his head. "Graham, what is it? Are you okay?"

"Sarah, I have to tell you something. I should have told you before tonight, but with everything going on, I could not find the courage." He stands up and starts pulling his clothes off. She starts to see scars and burn marks all over his body. She stops dead in her tracks as she looks at the marks. Sarah then walks over to him and touches him. She traces some of the marks, and he winces a little, but he does not pull away. "Graham, who did this to you?"

"A babysitter did this to me. She used me as her anger and sexual relief because her husband did the same to her. I understand if you want to leave."

"Graham, why would you say that?"

"I am ugly."

Sarah wraps her arms around him. "I am not going anywhere. I married you for who you are as a person, not what you look like. If you showed me this before today, I would have still stayed. I love you, Graham. Nothing will ever change that."

He leans in and kisses her. Then he picks her up and places her on the bed, and they give themselves to each other. Their hearts race in unison. In that moment, Sarah feels more loved than ever in the past year. She knows now that this is right, and she belongs here with Graham.

Graham seems to still be embarrassed with his body, and Sarah looks at him. "Graham, you are sexy, handsome, and all mine. Please don't be embarrassed of what you look like."

"Thank you, sweetheart! I may need reminded sometimes of that."

"Like I said before, I love you no matter what happens or what you look like." From that moment, Graham knew that Sarah is his forever. He is grateful to have her but also sad how she became his. He is also grateful for Scott and how he sacrificed his time to help others. Sarah fell asleep in his arms as his thoughts kept him from falling asleep. He got to stare at her. She looks peaceful, and he gets to stare at her for the rest of her life. He pulls her in closer, and he feels that he does not have to hide anymore. He looks at her closely also and notices some scars but not nearly as much as he has. He recalls her ordeal; and in a way, they have the same past. At that moment, he feels safe and knows that he will not have to go through any of that again.

AFTERWORD

Sarah and Graham get back from their honeymoon in time for Brok's hearing. Even though he gave himself up, he still pleaded not guilty. His lawyer is trying to keep him free. They concluded that there will be a trial, and Sarah will have to testify. When they said her name, Brok looked up and found her with his eyes. She motioned to her left with her head, and his eyes focused on Graham. Brok's face glossed over with the look of horror, and he all of a sudden lashed out. "He is supposed to be dead! He is supposed to be dead! He is supposed to be dead!" Brok kept repeating it over and over. Brok's psychotic break gets him landed in a mental institution and not capable to testify. The judge is forced to cancel the trial and close Brok's case. Brok will never leave the institution, and he will serve his time in the institution.

This time, Sarah can breathe a sigh of relief, knowing that she will never see Brok again. They ship him overseas to one of the best mental institutions money can buy. His parents are going with him. A couple of weeks go by; and Sarah receives a letter from his parents, apologizing for all the wrong he did. Sarah wrote back with two words, "Thank you!"

Graham adopted Scott as his child, but he decided to keep his last name Harman just to honor Scott. He just adds Michaels at the end of the name. Scott is now five, and he is practicing his name for school: Scott Leonard Harman Michaels II. He knows how to spell and write his name. He knows his alphabet and how to spell most words. He writes neatly for a five-year-old.

Scott has gotten in the habit of talking to his dad before, bed and he is quick to say that Graham is taking care of him the way Scott did. Little Scott remembers his dad and everything they did together. He recalls some memories when he talks to Scott. He knows Scott won't answer back, but Sarah loves to hear him talk. His voice is starting to sound like Scott. The more he grows, the more she sees Scott. She has pieces of him with her; but when she thinks about him, she does not feel the pain she felt when he first died. She feels joy and happiness. His life touched hers, and she is grateful for that life.

Scott finally slides into his new bed, and Sarah walks over to him. "Hi, Mommy!"

"Hi, little man! Are you ready to sleep?"

"Yes, I am."

"Before you close your eyes, I want to tell you something."

"Yes, Mommy!"

"You are going to be a big brother!"

"How?" Sarah giggled a bit and thinks to herself, *Okay, how am I going to answer this one?* "I have a baby growing inside of me."

"Like me! Yay! I want a sister as pretty as you, Mommy!"

"You want a sister!" Sarah said in shock. "Usually, it is I want a brother with boys."

"Yes, I want a sister so that I can protect her like Graham protects you."

"You are a very smart boy. You know, I want a girl also."

"Yay, Mommy! When is she coming?"

"She will be here in about nine months." Scott gives her a mad look. "What is that for?"

"I don't want to wait that long. Why can't she come now?"

"I don't want to wait that long either, but that is the way it has to be."

"Okay, Mommy," he says as he gives her a sad look.

"Okay, little man, time to go to sleep. I will see you in the morning." Sarah kisses him good night and turns out the light. Graham does not know yet that he is going to be a dad. Sarah has a special surprise for him when he comes home. He has been on assignment for the past couple of days, and she is excited to see him.

She has everything set up and ready when he came through the door. The plates were set on the table, and dinner was covered. There is a gift lying on Graham's plate. As soon as he sees it, his eyes light up. "Hi, beautiful!"

"Hi, handsome! Come sit and eat. How was your time?"

"It was great, but I would have had a better time if you and Scott were with me. It is good to come home to you."

"I have missed you. I am glad you are back and safe."

Graham sits down at his seat at the table and looks at the gift. "What's this?" He picks it up and shakes it.

"It is your welcome-home present. Open it!" Sarah says with a smile.

Graham rips open the paper and opens the box. In it is a sonogram picture. Graham's face lights up when he figures out what he is looking at. "Does this mean we are—" he trails off as tears of joy start to fall.

"Yes, we are!" Sarah said, smiling widely

Graham immediately stands up and shouts at the top of his lungs, "Yes!" He is jumping, and tears are running down his face. "I am going to be a dad again." He says this over and over. He then lifts

Sarah out of her seat and spins her. He whispers in her ear, "Thank you, thank you, thank you!"

Nine months later, Sarah gives birth to a beautiful baby girl, and they name her Lynn Graham Michaels.

Two weeks after that, Scott's present comes in the mail. Sarah then remembered what Scott's lawyer said about the husband clause in Scott's will. She puts a hand over her mouth, and she slowly sits down when she realizes the name that the present belongs to. In Scott's handwriting, it says, "This investment of two million dollars goes to Graham Michaels. I believe in your work, and I am giving you your photography company." Scott included an address, and Sarah realized it is the company that Graham works for. Sarah is wiping tears when Graham walks in. "Baby, what's wrong?"

She can't speak, and she hands him the paper she has in her hand. Graham gasps. "I own a company!"

Sarah is confused. "How did he know this would happen? How did he know we would end up together? How did he do this? How did he know that Graham will be the one?" Sarah says these questions out loud, realizing that Graham heard all of them.

"I don't know!" Sarah feels that Scott planned all this. Then she looked at Graham. "How did you know to come to the hospital that day for your treatment?"

"I have always gone there for treatment. I always talk to Scott because he is the one who treated me." Sarah is brainstorming now.

Then the thought came. "No, he didn't. Please say he did not do this on purpose." She remembered that his lawyer came in a couple of times and saw them talking while she was giving bone marrow. Scott knew Graham's blood type. It was the same as his because of the kidney. Another thought popped in. "The video showing that Scott knew he was not going to survive this. He set all this up before he died. He knew I just gave bone marrow, and he knew Graham needed it. He sacrificed his life for Graham. He gave me someone to love again." Sobs started to come, and she belted out what she was thinking. Graham wrapped his arms around her. "Who would have thought that Scott would still influence our lives in a way to make sure we are happy?"

THE LOVE THAT SAVED ME

INTRODUCTION

My family and I just moved into the neighborhood. My first day of eleventh grade will be in a new school. I am an only child; and my parents, Rick, and Susan, own one of the biggest businesses on the East Coast. I am Jamie Austin, and I am a daddy's girl. I did not realize that fact until we were in a car accident a couple of years ago. My dad was badly injured when another car slammed into us after running a red light. Despite his injuries, he climbed out of the car to pull me out just before it burst into flames. My dad saved my life, and I stopped taking my dad for granted. Since then, I have grown closer to my parents.

Before all that happened, I was a problem child, and I let the money get to me. I let my status define who I was. I had friends who only liked me for what I had. After the accident, things changed; and I realized that I did not like that part of my life. My mom and dad worked hard for what they have, and they show me it is not all about the money. They show me that we can have a simple life and still enjoy some of the finer things. They also show me that they are not defined by their money either. I went from having a spoiled-rich-girl attitude to being a person who does not let her parents' money define her. I want to be treated like a normal person and not someone with money. I don't like it when people know I have money. Now it is time to go to school. Hopefully, It won't get judged like a rich girl like so many other people did in my old school.

CHAPTER 1

The Discovery

The first time Jamie stepped through the door was the first time she saw him. He had short brown hair with a chiseled jawline. He had one dimple when he smiled. His skin looks like it has been kissed by the sun. He makes her heart skip a beat. He was looking straight at Jamie. His look was a little shy, but he smiled a little when he saw Jamie. Jamie decided to walk as close to him as possible. She watched him in the corner of my eyes, and he followed her with his. Just before she was out of his sight, he stopped her. "Excuse me, what is your name?"

"My name is Jamie Austin. What is yours?"

"I am Seth Anderson. It is nice to meet you. Can I walk you to class?"

"Yes, sure, that will be nice. So, Seth, where are you from? Wait, are you an Anderson Group boy?"

"Yes, I am. Does that matter to you?"

"No, it does not." He also said the name of the neighborhood he lived in, answering her previous question. She noticed it was the same name of the neighborhood that she just moved into. "Really, I live on Front Street in that neighborhood."

"That's funny. I live on Front Street also at house number 9."

"Wow, we are neighbors then. I live in 7."

"I was wondering who was moving into the house next door. Is it just you, or do you have siblings?"

"I am the only child. How about you? Do you have siblings?"

"No, it is just me, my mom, and my stepdad. Wait, are you an Austin Group daughter?"

"Yes, I am. But please don't tell anyone. I don't want anyone to treat me any differently."

"Your secret is safe with me. Can we hang out after school today?"

"Yes, we can. I would love to get to know you better."

The bell rang, and they said their goodbyes. Seth could not believe a hot girl like Jamie talked to him. She has beautiful long brown hair. Her skin is fair, and she is tall with long legs. She has a sporty-looking body. It looks like she plays some kind of game or physical activity in her life. He can get lost in her beautiful brown eyes. He can't wait until school ends to find out more about her.

Jamie cannot believe that a hot guy just talked to her. *He is clearly into you, Jamie,* she thought to herself.

The day seems to go by slowly. At lunch, Jamie realized that Seth had the same lunch period as she did, and she saw him with his friends. They lock eyes, and he stops midsentence and walks over to Jamie. "Do you want to join me for lunch?"

She looks at him and then at his friends. They all have dumbfounded looks on their faces. "Sure, if your friends don't mind."

"Don't worry about them. They do what I say." She looked at him funny, and he laughed. "Just kidding." They walk over to the table and introduces them to her. "Jamie, this is Dan, Blane, and Jessica. Guys, this is Jamie."

"It is nice to meet the three of you." Jessica looks a little jealous but welcomes Jamie to sit down and join them.

Jamie's mom meets her outside after school and drives her home. "Hello, darling, how was your day?"

"It was good. I meet someone, and he lives right next door." Jamie is not afraid to talk to her parents. She is free to tell them anything, and she loves that feeling. They have taught her that no matter what happens, they will get through it together.

"Nice, what is his name, and is he cute?"

"Mom, really!"

"What?"

"Yes, he is cute, and his name is Seth. When we get home, we will be out back getting to know each other."

"Okay, thank you for letting me know. Should I be keeping my eye on you?"

"Oh, Mom, what am I going to do with you?"

When Jamie got home, she sat in one of the chairs by the pool. Moments later, Seth showed up and sat down on the chair next to her. Jamie asked, "So what do you want to talk about?"

"What brings you to this neck of the woods?"

"They wanted to be closer to their office, and it is a bigger house."

Then Seth asked her, "Is there anything you want to tell me about yourself?"

"Like I said at school, I am an only child and a daddy's girl. My dad and I got into an accident a couple of years ago, and he saved my life. My parents and I are close. I can tell them anything. What about you and your parents?"

"My mom and I are close because it has been just us until she met and married my stepdad. My stepdad, Jack, is okay. I am not close to him. They just got married last year. I don't think he likes me very much, and he just tolerates me because of my mom." They talked some more until Jamie's mom said, "Dinnertime." Seth told her he will look forward to seeing her at school.

Seth is liking the relationship that is developing between him and Jamie. He feels that he could love her. But he has a deep secret that might keep him from her. Seth is scared to tell someone because of the threat he hears. He is not sure if he will ever tell anyone. He got into the house, and just his stepdad was there. "Where have you been, boy?"

"Next door. I met Jamie today. They are the new neighbors."

"You know our rules. You were supposed to be in this house after school." Seth knew what was coming next, and he was not going to like it.

The next day, Seth and Jamie came out of the house at the same time. "Hey, Seth, do you want a ride?" Seth is a little worried that Jamie will pick up on what he is really feeling. He is hiding his pain from yesterday. He hides it behind his smile.

"Yes, sure." Seth walked over, and Jamie noticed something off but shook it off when she saw his smile.

"Dad, this is Seth, our neighbor."

"Hello, Seth, I am Mr. Austin. It is nice to meet you."

"Likewise, Mr. Austin." Jamie sat in the back with him. Her dad could tell there is love forming just by looking in the rearview mirror. He is smiling a little at the thought that his daughter may have found love. They pull up to the school, and Jamie thanks her dad and gives him his kiss on the cheek. Jamie and Seth walked into the school together.

On their way in, there were a couple of boys known to bully people, and they were bullying Seth. Seth froze when they came close. They started in on him. "Hey, why don't you leave him alone before I do something to you to embarrass you? Why do you pick on people? Grow up."

One of the boys stepped to Jamie and said, "Bring it, little girl."

Jamie stepped to the boy and laid one punch. Then she and Seth walked away. Jamie was smiling when she looked back and saw the boy lying on the ground, holding his eye. "You did not have to do that for me."

"I did what I had to."

"I don't want anyone to have to defend me."

"Listen up, Seth Anderson. You are now my friend, and I am the type of person who will defend my friends as I see fit. Do you understand?"

Seth laughed. "Yes, ma'am!" They walked to homeroom together. They had some of the same classes together; and the more time they spent together, the closer they seemed.

They would spend time together after school and on weekends. They helped each other with schoolwork and chores. Jamie even met his parents. His mom, Shelly, is the sweetest person. But she owns the competition of Jamie's parents' business. Shelly does not hold that against the kids. Seth's stepdad is a truck driver. Jamie did not quite feel comfortable around his stepdad. He was a little off; and even though he was nice; she saw something dark about him. His stepdad being a truck driver is good for Seth because he is gone for most of the week. But when he is home, Seth hides whenever he can.

Jamie would notice often that Seth would withdraw when dealing with bullies. Seth's reaction would make her wonder what was really going on with him. Jamie decided to ask him about it, "Seth, is there something going on with you?"

"I am good. Why do you ask?"

"You freeze when people pick on you. You look scared when someone approaches you negatively. Listen, Seth, if you are going through stuff, please talk to me. I am here for you. We have known each other for about a month now. You can trust me."

Seth feels connected with Jamie that he has never felt before. "Jamie, I know I can trust you. I know you are here for me. I am not ready to talk about it. But what I want to talk about is us."

Jamie looked at him with wanting eyes. "What do you mean us?"

"I want to know if you would go out with me."

Jamie's heart skipped a beat, and her expression turned into surprise. "Seth, I would love to go out with you."

Seth walks over to her and grabs her hands to pull her in to kiss her. Jamie's eyes widen and then closes, and she kisses him back. His soft lips against hers is taking her breath away. Jamie is thinking to herself, *Wow, is this what a first kiss feels like?* Jamie moves her hands from his and goes to hug him, but he pulls away. He wants so much to hug her and feel her arms around him, but he can't bear the pain that it will cause him. Jamie looks at him with a baffled look.

Seth seems to read her mind and says, "I can't be hugged right now. I hurt my back earlier, and it still hurts when touched." Seth thinks to himself, *That covers me for now, but what about the next time she wants to hug me? How am I going to stop her?*

"I am sorry, Seth. Do you want me to look at it or help you in any way?"

Seth holds his hands up and says, "No, I will be okay." Seth grabs her hands again and leans in to kiss her again. She closes her eyes and surrenders her mouth to him. In between kisses, he says to her, "I love kissing you."

"So do, I Seth," she says breathless.

The bell rings breaking into their warring tongues, and off they go to their next class.

As soon as Jamie and Seth got into Susan's car, Jamie told her mom the news. "Mom, please meet my boyfriend, Seth."

"We've already—wait, boyfriend?"

"Yes, Seth asked me out, and I said yes."

"Congratulations, you two look good together."

"Thanks, Mom."

When they got home, Seth was supposed to stay and study with Jamie, but he saw his stepdad's truck and decided to go home first. "I will be right back. I have to tell him I will be here studying." Seth ran over and did not come back until his mom came home two hours later. Seth did not look good when he came into Jamie's house. Jamie's heart started pounding as they went to her desk in her room. She is figuring out what is going on, and she needs to get it out of Seth before something bad happens. Jamie went to put her arms around Seth, but he jerked away and winced in pain. Jamie was shocked as she asked, "Seth, what is happening to you? Please talk to me."

"I am sorry I did that. I just don't want anyone touching me anymore."

"Seth, you need to tell me what is wrong. I won't be able to help you if you keep hiding stuff from me."

As tears started to fall down Seth's cheeks, he finally opened up to Jamie and pulled his shirt off. Jamie could see many cigarette marks. New ones and old ones. She could also see bruises all over his back and chest. There were cuts visible on his stomach and back as well. Jamie gasps and starts to cry, "Seth, you need to report this right now before he kills you. Can I get my parents? They can help you."

"You can't tell anyone. He will kill me and my mom if I tell anyone."

"I am not going to stand by and watch someone hurt you." Jamie stands up and says, "I am going over there and teach him a lesson."

Seth grabs and stops her, "No, please don't go over there. Instead, go get your parents." Seth will do anything to stop her from going over there because he will hurt her, and Seth will not be able to live with himself if anyone hurts Jamie.

Jamie runs to get her parents. With tears in her eyes, she says, "Mom, Dad, please come quick. We have a problem." Her parents follow her to her room and see Seth. Susan gasps. "Seth, what is happening to you?"

"My stepdad takes his anger out on me, and he touches me inappropriately. My mom does not know anything about this."

Rick speaks up and says, "You are not going home tonight. You are staying in the guestroom. We need to let your mom know what is going on."

"No, please, he will kill her if she found out."

Jamie asks, "Does he do the same thing to your mom?"

"No, he absolutely loves my mom, and he does not hurt her. But he threatened to start if I say anything."

Jamie looked at him with a desperate look on her face. "You will die if you don't let us help, and that will kill your mom, so please let us help you. I am not ready to lose you."

Her words pulled at his heart, and he said okay. His heart is pounding, and he can't concentrate. He did not want to bring Jamie into his mess. *She is right. I can't let him keep doing this to me. He will kill me, but what will he do to my mom?* Seth's thoughts are haunting him as he waits for his mom.

Ten minutes later, his mom was at Jamie's house; and as she heard what was going on, she was getting angrier by the minute. "Seth, you stay here. I will deal with this and him."

"Mom, please don't tell him you know. He threatened me that he will kill you if you knew."

"Son, don't worry about me. I will be okay. I need to stop you from being hurt more. You are my only son, and you are my life. If anyone hurts you, they will regret they did." Shelly leaves; and twenty minutes later, they hear tires screeching and sees Jack's truck peel out of their driveway.

Rick went to check on Shelly. Rick came back and took Susan to another room. "She is not there. I also saw blood. I called 911 when I was over there. They are on their way. Now the hard part is to tell Seth. I know he is going to blame himself for this. He needs us more than ever."

Rick and Susan went to Jamie's room and saw that they were doing homework. "Seth, we have to talk to you. I just went to check on your mom, and she is gone. She may have been taken by your stepfather."

"No, I should not have told you. It is my fault." Seth started to run out of the room, but Susan stopped him. "Seth, the police will find her. She will be okay. You are safe, and she will take comfort in knowing that."

Jamie walked up to Seth and laid her hand on his shoulder. "Seth, I am here for you." For the first time this all happened, he wrapped his arms around Jamie and started to cry. "Thank you!"

The police asked questions and got more information from Jamie's family and Seth. They also made sure that Jamie's parents were okay to take Seth in until his mom is found. Rick answered, "Yes, we are okay."

After the police left, Susan and Rick had to have a conversation with Jamie and Seth. Rick walked into Jamie's room again and said, "We now have to set some ground rules. You two are not allowed in each other's rooms with the doors closed. While looking at Seth, Rick says, "If you are going through something, we are here to hear you and help you."

"Thank you, Mr. and Mrs. Austin. I am sorry about earlier. I know you are keeping me safe."

"You are welcome, Seth," Susan Said.

Rick went over to Seth's house and got as much clothes as he could. He did not want Seth over here until they have the place cleaned up. He also talked to Susan about helping Shelly with her company so that Seth is taken care of.

The next day, Rick went to talk to Shelly's employees and explained what is happening. Shelly's personal assistant filled him in on what they have been doing as a company. He also reassured them that he was not there to take over but to help run the day-to-day activities. This company is his competition, but he does not want it to fail because of the terrible events happening to the Anderson family.

CHAPTER 2

The Support

A couple of months went by. There were still no leads on where Shelly went. Seth is about to go through his first Thanksgiving and birthday without his mother. To make matters worse, he has been getting death threats. Rick was running Shelly's company, and he came up with a way that his company and Shelly's company could survive without feeling the competition.

Susan decided to get Jamie and Seth away from this place for a while. They went to Florida, and Jamie's life is about to change hopefully. They went out to dinner the first night they were there. They went to celebrate Seth's birthday. Seth has a couple of emotions going through his mind. He feels sad that his mom is not there. He feels nervous because he is about to do something that he hopes will turn out good. He also feels happiness because he is with a girl who completes him and saves his life. It was time.

Seth stood up and got the attention of the table and basically the whole restaurant. "Jamie, I am eighteen today, and we are only in eleventh grade. Some may say that at our age, there is no way we know anything about love. But I want to prove them wrong. I have found my soulmate. Today I want to say for the first time that I love you and please do me the honor of being my wife."

Jamie froze and stared at the ring Seth was holding. Then she looked at her parents. They were holding hands, smiling, wanting on their faces. Then she looked back at Seth and with tears in her eyes replied, "Yes, Seth, I love you and will love to be your wife."

Everyone cheered, and her parents had tears of joy running down their faces. Rick cleared his throat. "Jamie, since you said yes, here is what is going to happen. You can get married anytime you want, but you are going to live in our house until you graduate. Meanwhile, both of you are going to learn the business and work alongside your mom and me at both companies. Do you like the idea?"

Jamie answered, "That was what I was planning on asking you. I want to work with you at the company and learn everything I can about it because I am heir to the company. Yes, I agree to your idea."

Seth answered with a smile, "Yes, sounds awesome."

Rick mentioned one more thing, "Seth, I do have one more condition. You can't officially marry her until she is eighteen." Seth's smile disappeared, but then he remembered she would be turning eighteen in two weeks. "Okay, on her eighteenth birthday, we will get married!"

Susan then says, "Well, we have a wedding to plan."

They left Florida after a week of being away. They came home to a mess. Someone broke in and destroyed their home. Then they saw a threatening letter stuck to Jamie's bedroom door with a knife. "From this day forward, if you run with my stepchild, you will lose yours." Seth got angry and started to pace. "No one is taking my girl from me. No one!" Again, the police was called, and they took down the information and took some evidence. Sergeant William Taylor came in a couple of minutes later with some news. He pulled Rick out of earshot of the family. "Rick, we may have found Seth's mom. It does not look good. We have officers in the area canvassing it now."

An hour later, Sergeant Taylor came back with news. Seth was in his room unpacking what he could. Rick came to the door with Jamie in tow. "Seth, they found your mom."

"Okay, can we see her now?"

Rick's heart started to pound, and his next words were hard to say. "She did not make it." Seth collapsed onto the bed with sobs. Jamie ran to his side and cried with him. She wrapped him in her arms and held him tight. Seth fell asleep in Jamie's arms, and her parents let her stay there just for the night. Susan could not help but feel guilty. They had Seth tell his mom, and now she is gone. Susan and Rick talked in their bedroom about the new situation. Susan looked at her husband. "What do we do for him?"

"The only thing we can, and that is to be here for him."

Then she said, "I don't know if he still wants to go through with the wedding."

"We will ask him tomorrow."

Seth wakes up next to Jamie the next morning, and he watches her sleep. He could not help but smile at the sight next to him. He can't wait until he gets to do it forever starting in two weeks. Seth's heart sinks. His mom won't be there. But she is safe now and not hurting anymore. He will honor her by marrying the love of his life. He will never let anyone hurt her. He left her to sleep and went to talk to her parents. Susan was making breakfast. "How are you feeling, Seth?"

"I am okay. I still want to go through with the wedding and honor my mom along with Jamie."

"Okay, we will help you do that."

The two weeks seem to go by slowly. Seth and Jamie did what they needed for their wedding. Even though Jamie would be eighteen on their wedding day, she still needed her parents' permission for the marriage license; and they gladly gave it to her. Susan and Jamie went shopping for her dress, and Susan cried happy tears the whole time. Rick took Seth for their tuxes. Seth seems to be looking at Rick in a whole new light. Seth sees him as a positive father figure, and he is now comfortable with Rick. Rick asks Seth, "Jack is your stepdad, right?"

"Yes, he is."

"What happened to your real dad?"

"He was killed in the war. I had just turned four when he was deployed, and a month later, his chopper went down in the Atlantic."

Rick's heart sank. "Oh, Seth, I am sorry. From hereon out, I consider you a son. You can come to me for anything—and I mean anything."

"Thank you, Rick. I will take you up on your offer."

"If you don't mind me asking, how long has your stepdad been hurting you?"

"He has been doing it since he married my mom last year."

"Seth, I will not let that happen to you anymore if I have anything to do with it." Rick laid his hand on Seth's shoulder so that he could look him straight in the eye.

"Thank you, Rick."

"Call me dad!"

"Dad!" Seth smiles at that idea.

Two weeks later, the day is here. Susan is helping Jamie. "You look beautiful, sweetheart. I can't believe this day is here, and I am so proud of you. I love you."

"I love you too, Mom. Thank you for all this. I can't believe that I found the love of my life on my first time out."

"Are you ready, my darling?"

"Yes, I am, Mom! Let's go!"

They walk out to meet her dad. Her dad is staring at her with tears in his eyes. "You will always be my little girl. I am happy that I was chosen to be your dad. I am proud of you."

"Thank you, Daddy! I love you!"

Susan goes first because she is her daughter's maid of honor. The wedding was attended by just the four of them. Both of Jamie's parents were only children as well, and all four of her grandparents are gone. Seth does not know where his mother's father is. The next thing Seth sees is Jamie walking down the aisle with her dad. He has tears running down his cheeks when she stops just a foot from him. Rick placed his daughter's hand in Seth's hand and said, "I give you her hand. Protect her and cherish for as long as you live."

"Yes, sir, I will."

Before Rick left her side, he kissed her on the forehead and then walked over to the side of Seth. Seth started his vows, "I, Seth Anderson, promise to protect you. I vow to honor you and love you through all our trials, all our pain, and all our sickness. I vow to honor you and love you through all our happiness and all our time together. You are my family now, Jamie, and I will never let you go." He then slipped the ring on her finger.

"I, Jamie Austin, promise to protect you. I vow to honor you and love you through all our trials, all our pain, and all our sickness. I vow to honor you and love you through all our happiness and all our time together. You are my life, Seth, and I will never let you go." She slipped his ring on his finger.

The pastor says, "I now pronounce you man and wife. You may kiss your bride."

Seth laid a sweet, loving kiss on his wife's lips, and it left her wanting more. After the ceremony, they went out to dinner where they could dance and celebrate. Rick and Susan surprised their daughter and their new son with a honeymoon in Florida during Christmas break, which is in two weeks. Meanwhile, they spent one night in a hotel room.

Jamie was so nervous; this is her first time, and she is afraid that she will mess it up. Seth was terrified he had images from his past flashing through his mind; he did not want to feel the pain he had felt before. He wants to give himself to his wife, but fear is holding him back. When he saw his wife standing in front of him for the first time with no clothes on, he froze. He started to shake, and he could not move a muscle. Flashes of his stepdad come fast before his eyes. Jamie sensed that something was wrong with him. She saw the pain in his eyes, and she crossed the room. "Seth, it's okay. I am here for you. If you don't want to do this now, we don't have to."

She held him in her arms for a while until his shaking stopped. "I am sorry, Jamie. I am not used to this. I am scared to death."

"It's okay, Seth. I love you, and that's all that matters. Let me go through what you are going through with you. Let me hold you."

Without words, Seth picked up his wife and placed her on the bed. He let her take him. He let her in, and he gave himself to her. It was beautiful. He felt complete and safe. He is looking forward to the rest of his life. He sees it now in her eyes. He knows that Jamie will hold him for the rest of his life. He falls asleep watching her sleep peacefully in his arms.

That night, he had a nightmare. Jack is standing over him; and with a gleam in his eye, he bends down to whisper in his ear, "I will take her from you." Then he could see Jamie tied up and in the back of Jack's truck with a frightened look on her face. Seth starts to run after her, and he is not moving, and she gets farther away from him. "No, no, no, not Jamie!"

Jamie shakes him awake and says, "Seth baby, I am here. I am here." She is holding him, and he wraps his arms around her, realizing that he was dreaming.

"Jamie, I am sorry."

"Don't be, Seth. I am here for you. What did you dream? Talk to me, please. Let me in." Seth told her his dream, and she wrapped him tighter in her arms. "I am here. I am not going anywhere," Jamie reassured him. He responded by kissing her, and they made love once more.

Jamie was walking out to the car with her purse as Seth was checking out. Seth looked out at Jamie smiling, and she took his breath away. Seth looked down for a second and then back up at Jamie, and she was gone. Seth ran out the door just in time to see her being whisked away by someone. He could only recognize him as being Jack. Seth ran as quickly as he could toward where he saw Jack. When he got there, the only thing left behind was her purse. His worst nightmare has come true. He should not have let her go out there alone. His heart is pounding helplessly; and he is shaking, trying to free his phone from his pocket. He called Sergeant Taylor. He then made the most heart-wrenching call he could ever make. "Rick, he took her. She is gone. I tried to go after her, but she was too far away. I promised to protect her, but I was not close enough. I am sorry. I am so sorry!"

"Seth, where are you?"

"I am at the hotel, and Sergeant Taylor is here."

"Stay there. We are on our way." Five minutes later, Susan and Rick were there. Susan wrapped her arms around Seth; and with tears in her eyes, she said, "We will find her. We will find her."

Shelly's lawyer calls Seth, "Hello, Seth, I am your mom's lawyer Douglas Scott. I want to set up a meeting with you about your mom's estate."

"Now is not a good time. My wife is missing, and my world is upside down."

"I am sorry, but we need to go over this as soon as possible."

"Okay, please see me at the house of my parents-in-law, which is Seventh Front Street. Next door to my house."

"I will see you in twenty minutes."

Seth hung up the phone. Seth says out loud, "I can't believe I have to do this now of all days."

"Seth, what is it?" Rick asks Seth.

"My mom's lawyer wants to meet with me now. I told him I can't do this now. But he insists on it. It needs to be now."

"It's okay, Seth. We will go see what he wants to tell you."

"Dad, will you be with me please? I don't think I can do this without you."

It felt good for Rick to hear Seth call him dad for the first time, and Rick took gratitude in that. "Yes, of course, Seth." They head home to wait for Mr. Scott.

Mr. Scott finally arrived, and he was invited into the living room. "Seth, I came here to let you know that your mom left everything to you. You are the new owner of the company and of the house next door. I just need your signature, and I will hand over all the information and the keys that I have."

Rick then asked, "Can I see the form before Seth signs it please?"

"Yes, sure, here it is."

Mr. Scott handed over the form, and Rick looked it over. It is a summary of the information being handed over to Seth. "It looks good, Seth. You can go ahead and sign it."

After the lawyer left, Seth and Rick looked over all the paperwork and realized that Seth just became a millionaire. There is five million dollars in a bank account with Seth's name on it. That is not including the company. The company is worth another five million. The house is already paid for, and the taxes on the house are paid up to ten years. Seth looked at Rick and said, "Dad, please help me invest this and manage all this. I want to make sure that Jamie and I are going to be okay in the future. Right now, I just want to find her."

"Yes, I will help you with all this."

It has been a couple of days since Seth's world collapsed. Christmas is just days away. Seth could tell that Jamie's absence is wearing on her parents. Seth has not been sleeping much. His nightmares are getting worse. He is dreaming that Jamie is dead; and Jack is standing over him, getting ready to do whatever he wanted to him. Each night, the nightmares change; but in each one, Jamie is dead and Seth can't get to her in time. He awakes several times during the night. Where is she? What is he doing to her? Is she still here with us? Each time he wakes up, he yarns to hold her. Seth says out loud, "Oh, Jamie, hang on to us please. Stay here with me. I will find you." There has been hits here and there when Jack has been spotted. When police have gotten there, they were always too late. Seth thought to himself, *Is she ever going to be home?*

CHAPTER 3

Heartbrake

A year had gone by, and Seth had to go through his senior year without Jamie by his side. It was supposed to be the best year of their lives, and she is not here to share it with him. Sergeant Taylor has not given up. Seth graduated with honors, and he was the valedictorian. He honored Jamie during his speech. He got a standing ovation. Seth also spent the year learning the business under the watchful eye of Rick and Susan. They have been strong during this whole thing. They have been holding on to hope that she will be home. It has been a tough year for each one of them. Sergeant Taylor would get a lead, and he would dash off in hopes to find her, but she would just slip through his fingers. Sergeant Taylor is figuring out that there has to be a mole somewhere in the office. He can't figure out why they seem to leave before he gets there. Seth is doing all he could to not give up on his wife. He goes throughout his day to honor Jamie. He knew he had to stay strong for her.

Seth had to take a break, and he decided to take a walk. He wanted to clear his head and get some air. He walked for an hour, and he was walking by an old neighborhood. It did not look like anyone lived in any of the houses he saw. One of the houses stands out to him.

He noticed someone has been using the driveway lately. It has fresh tire tracks. He was curious, and he slowly made his way inside the house. He saw that someone has been using it to live in. He then saw something familiar. It was one of Jack's shirts that he saw him wear almost all the time. His heart started to race at the thought that she might be here. He ran up the steps and looked in every room. She has to be here. She is here, but where? He ran back downstairs and found the basement door. It has a padlock on it. Seth quickly looked for something to pry it open but found nothing. He kicked at the door a couple of times. His adrenaline spiked, and the door flow open. He fell back and hit his back on something sharp. But he did not care. He had to get downstairs.

He was downstairs in a second. It was dark, and he could only see one ray of light; and in that light, he saw a body. A body that is not moving. He moved to her; she did not move. His heart is racing, and he can't catch his breath. He is wincing in pain as he breathes, but he does not care. He had to see if she is alive. "Jamie, please wake up. I am here. Please stay with me. Don't leave me." Seth felt for a pulse, and Jamie had one. It was faint, but she was still here with him.

Seth picked her up and winced. He carried her upstairs only to freeze when he saw him. Seth set her down and stepped to him. Jack then punched Seth in the face. Seth fell back but was up again. Seth had so much anger and pain that when he punched Jack back, he fell back and hit his head on the table behind him. Seth picked up Jamie and headed out the door. Seth pulled out his phone and called Sergeant Taylor. "I found her. She is alive." Seth told Sergeant Taylor the address, and he sent the cavalry. Seth then called their parents. "She is alive, and I have found her. Please meet me at the hospital."

Five minutes later, police and an ambulance showed up. The EMTs immediately started working on Jamie. Seth showed where he laid Jack out, but Jack was gone by the time they got back into the house. Seth joined the ambulance just before they pulled out. Seth heard them say she is in a coma, and she might have a fighting chance. Then she went into cardiac arrest. Seth started to shout, "Jamie, please stay with me. You are safe now. Don't leave us!" They shocked her three times and got her back. Seth held on to her hand until they got to the hospital. They wheeled her into an emergency room and told Seth to wait outside in the waiting room. Five minutes later, Rick and Susan were there. Susan threw her arms around Seth and was repeating thank you. Seth winced in pain, and he remembered that he was hurt. Then Seth went down. He collapsed, and Susan shouted, "Help!" Nurses and doctors came running. They rushed him to X-ray when they see a basketball-sized bruise on his back.

Seth's injury was bad. He had internal bleeding and bruised his muscles. They got it under control, and he will be okay. They wheeled Seth into Jamie's room, and they waited for Jamie to be wheeled in. An hour later Jamie was finally wheeled into the room. Her mom started to cry when she saw her for the first time. She had bruises and cuts on her face. Susan kissed her daughter on the forehead and said, "Hello, beautiful, you are safe now. You can wake up whenever you are ready."

Rick was there also, and he did not say anything; but with tear-filled eyes, he kissed his daughter on the forehead. The doctor came in and let them know what has happened to Jamie. "She has some head trauma, and she also had some internal bleeding in the abdomen and uterus. There was a lot of scarring in the uterus. She was dehydrated and depleted of nutrients. We have started her on fluids along with some nutrients. We also stopped the internal bleeding and gave her medicine to stop the swelling around her brain. She is in a coma, and we will check on her once every half hour. She is stable but not out of the woods. The next couple of hours will be touch and go." Seth and her parents looked at each other and then looked at Jamie. Hope was in their eyes, and Seth climbed out of his bed and into Jamie's. "Jamie, I am here now. You are so beautiful. Please I want to see your beautiful eyes. You need to come back to me. Hang on to me. I am here, my beautiful wife." Seth slowly put her into his arms, and tears came down his face. He held on to her for dear life. He never wants to let go.

Two weeks go by, and there is still no change in Jamie's condition. Seth has not left her side since she got there. Susan and Rick pop in and out every other day. Seth takes to reading to Jamie. He hopes by hearing his voice she will wake up. He also talks to her, "Baby, I know you can hear me, and I know you are waiting for the perfect moment to wake up. I am not leaving you. When you are ready, I would like to see those beautiful brown eyes of yours and your sweet smile." He kisses her on the forehead.

Another week goes by, and Seth is pacing in her room. He is nervous that she won't wake up. He walked back over to her bedside. He laid his head on her bed and dozed off. His face is facing hers. The next thing he feels is a hand on his head. He shoots up and sees her looking at him. She smiles with a breathing tube in her mouth. Seth's smile is brighter than the sun when he sees her eyes and her smile. He has dreamed of this day for a long time. He kisses her on the forehead and says, "I am going to get the doctor."

She grabs him and looks at the button on the bed. "Okay, I will stay here and use the button. I am not going to leave you." Seth pushes the button, and the nurse's voice comes across the speaker. "She is awake. We need the doctor in here."

"Okay, I will send him in right away." Moments later, the doctor comes in and starts to instruct her on taking the tube out. He takes it out and she coughs and gags. As she did, her parents walked in, and the next thing heard was her mom saying, "Hello, beautiful girl."

"Hello, Mom, I missed you."

"I missed you also, darling."

Her dad came over and said, "Welcome home, darling," and he kissed her on the forehead. She looked over at Seth and said, "Hello, husband!"

"Hello, wife! How are you feeling?"

"I am feeling okay now. But I do have one question. Why am I here?"

Seth looked at her and said, "You don't know what happened?"

"No, I don't. Please tell me." Seth took a deep breath and told her everything. He did not lie; he did not sugarcoat anything. While he was telling her, he was holding her. She cried and held on to Seth as tight as she can. "How long have I been away from you?"

"For a little over a year."

She gasped and cried some more. She also asked, "Did they catch him?"

"No, he is still out there."

A week later, Jamie was released and was able to go home finally. Jamie was still weak, and Seth picked her up out of the chair and placed her into the car. They left the hospital. When they arrived home, Seth picks up his wife and carried her into the house. Seth helped Jamie get settled into bed so that she could rest. "Jamie, we have some things to talk about. But I want you to rest."

"Please, lay it on me. I am not tired."

"Okay, are you sure?"

"Yes, please, I want to hear everything."

"When you disappeared, my mom's lawyer came to visit me, and well, she left me with everything. We now own her company and the house next door. The taxes on the house are paid for ten years. Your dad helped me invest some of the money my mom left us. We were able to turn five million into ten million. We were also able to increase the company's worth from five million to ten million. So we are both nineteen years old and multimillionaires."

Jamie's eyes got big. "Wow, that is impressive. What are we going to do with all the money?"

"We are going to keep investing it and live the way we want." Seth asked, "When do you want to move next door? I wanted to wait for you before I moved over there."

"You waited for me?"

"Yes, I also wanted to stay close to your parents through all this."

Jamie asked, "If we do move over there, and he is still out there, he might come after us. Can we run a company from, say, Florida or somewhere else?"

"That was my next question. We can keep the house but move somewhere until he is caught. Do you want to go somewhere?"

"I think that is the best thing for us right now. We can move to Florida until he is caught."

Seth and Jamie told the news to her parents and their plan on how they will help with both companies. Susan reassured her daughter, "It is a great idea. I will sleep better knowing that you are safe and not around for him to catch you again." Their parents gave them their blessing. They will miss them, but they know they will be safe.

CHAPTER 4

Life as We Know It

They are now in their new house in Florida. They are working remotely with their parents. They check in with Sergeant Taylor on occasion to see if they found him. There are no updates yet. Seth and Jamie have an update themselves for their parents. Jamie was on portal with her mom and said, "Mom, I have some news. You and dad are going to be grandparents."

"Really! That is wonderful news. I am so excited. I can't wait to meet my grandchild."

The days went on. Both Jamie and Seth worked hard; and while Jamie was working, she was also taking classes online. She did not get a chance to graduate and be a senior. Seth showed her the graduation ceremony that she did miss, and she cried during his speech. "Today I stand in front of you as your valedictorian. It is bittersweet for me. A lot happened to me over the past year. I went through the happiest day of my life. The best woman became my wife, but she is not by my side. As we celebrate our success, I challenge you to enjoy it. I also challenge you to have fun with the next steps you take. I challenge you to be spontaneous and try new things before you make important decisions. Take the one you love on an adventure. Fall in love with them over and over. Take advantage of the time you have and the next chapters in your life. My next chapter is for me to find her, so she will be by my side again. Meantime, have fun, stay safe, and take risks all before you settle down to the life you want. I made the best decision of my life when I turned eighteen. Now all I have to do is wait until the love of my life comes home so that we could go on adventures and live our lives together. I can't wait to enjoy my life with the love of my life. I am a happy man because my life is complete when Jamie Austin walked down the aisle to be my wife. I challenge you to find the love of your life and hold on to them as tight as you can. I challenge you to deeply love and to allow to be loved deeply. Never let go when you do find them. Congratulations, my fellow classmates. Now go have fun."

"Seth, that was beautiful. Thank you for sharing this."

Jamie sometimes suffered from blackouts because of her head injury. Seth knew when she would blackout. Hey eyes would glaze over, and he would hold on to her as she went through it. She would panic just before she came to. She would even drop to the floor if Seth was not fast enough. The doctors tell them that it will pass as the brain heals. They closely monitor her health and the baby's health. Slowly, Jamie's blackouts disappeared.

The way that Jamie loves Seth is amazing. She showed him how to love. She showed him it is okay to be vulnerable and open. It is okay to let someone in, especially when that someone loves you back. Jamie reached into Seth's darkness and pulled him out to safety. She saved him. He was able to save her back. He reached into her darkness and found her. Seth's life is changing for the better, and now he is looking forward to being the best dad he can be. He is happy that Jamie is the one giving him the opportunity.

Jamie and Seth shop for the baby. They have fun putting the nursery together. They sneak in a couple hours of fun themselves. The days are normal, and they are enjoying the work they get to do together. They had one fight. Seth would stay up at all hours of the night just to do work. Jamie was worried that he was not getting enough sleep. She yelled at him one day, and he yelled back. "Then fine, don't complain that you are tired." She stomped off to bed. Seth could not bring himself to admit that he was scared to go to sleep sometimes because of the nightmares he had while she was gone. He can't tell her about them. He does not want to bring back those memories at all. He is also afraid that if he closes his eyes she won't be there when he wakes up. One day Jamie had enough and decided to stay awake with him. "Jamie, go to sleep. You are six and a half months pregnant, and you need your rest."

"I am not going until either you tell me why you don't go to sleep with me, or you go to sleep with me."

"Jamie, please, I don't want to talk about it."

"Seth, we are going to talk about it because you look terrible. Are you getting any sleep?"

"I sleep."

"No, you don't. I wake up in the middle of the night and find you working away in this office. Then in the morning, you are dozing in your chair. That is not sleep. What is going on with you? I need you, Seth. I don't need a sleep-deprived husband with no energy to help with this baby."

Seth locked eyes with her and said, "You are right. I can't go to sleep because of fear. I am afraid to go to sleep and wake up to you not being here. I am also experiencing the nightmares again, but they are worse, and they got that way when you were gone."

Jamie looked at him with a pained look, and she lifted her hand to his face. "I am not going anywhere. I have been here every morning. I am here now. Have I gone anywhere since? Your nightmares—I will scare them away for you if you just let me."

Seth did not say anything; and he moved his head into her hand, closing his eyes, relishing in her touch. Then took her hand. They went up to their bedroom, and Jamie wrapped her arms around her husband. She watched him fall asleep. He stayed wrapped in her arms until morning and woke rested.

As the day got closer, their parents came down, so they did not miss the birth. Jamie can't believe that she has another life growing inside her. She can't wait to meet the little one. She will see the little one in less than three weeks. Then she feels an unfamiliar feeling and then sharp pains. She doubles over in pain, and she calls after Seth. "Seth, something is wrong. I need help." Seth rushes to help her, and he picks her up and takes her to the car. He starts the car and puts it in gear. They make it to the hospital in less than ten minutes. Seth runs to the passenger door and picks her up and takes her inside as she starts to yell out in pain. "Please, I need help! My wife is pregnant, and she is in a lot of pain."

The nurse pulls a bed over, and Seth places her on it. The nurses rush her to an exam room and start collecting information. "Jamie needs an emergency C-section. She is bleeding, and we have to save these babies."

Did Seth hear it correctly? Did they just say *babies*? The nurse updated Seth. "Your wife has preeclampsia, and she is bleeding internally. We have to take her for the C-section now."

"Did I hear you say *babies*?"

"Yes, she has two. Did you know she was pregnant with two?"

"No, we didn't. I guess the other one was hiding."

They wheeled her in and started preparing her for surgery. Seth had time to call the parents before he was able to go in.

Jamie lost consciousness, and Seth watched helplessly as they worked to save all lives. They got to the first baby, and they pulled her out. It was a beautiful sound when she cried. They cleaned her off and placed her in Seth's arms. Seth could not believe he has his daughter in his arms. She is beautiful just like her mother. "Hi, baby girl, you take your daddy's heart away with you." Then he heard another cry and saw them pull out his son. He handed his daughter to a nurse, and he got to hold his son. "Hi, baby boy, you definitely have your daddy's looks."

The next thing that Seth hears is a deafening sound. His wife is crashing, and he can't breathe. "Jamie, please stay with me. Stay with us." They worked to get the bleeding stopped and bring her back. Seth cried out and dropped to the floor, "Please, Jamie, stay here with me!" It took them a couple of minutes, but Jamie came back. She heard him, and she fought to stay with him. Seth went out to the hallway and broke down. Susan saw him, and she thought Jamie had died. She broke down; but when Seth saw Susan, he said, "She is fighting to stay with us. She is still here." Susan hugged her son-in-law. "Mom, they are beautiful."

"What do you mean *they*?"

"We have twins, one boy and one girl." Susan gasps with excitement.

They wheeled Jamie into the room. She is still sleeping. Seth could not wait until she woke up. He wants to see the joy on her face when she sees the babies. The one thing she does not know is that she has two. They can use both names they picked out. Nathan Alan Anderson and Nichole Amy Anderson are the names they picked just in case the baby is a boy or a girl. But since they have both, they got to use both. They also wheeled both babies into the room. Susan and Rick saw them for the first time since they were born.

Two days later, Jamie opened her eyes and saw Seth holding their daughter, and she smiled. He looked over at her and realized she was looking at him. "Hey, beautiful."

"Hey, sexy. You look pretty good holding that baby. Where did she come from?" she said with a smile on her face, knowing the answer to her question already.

"She was made by a beautiful woman and a very proud man. Mom, meet your daughter, Nichole Amy."

He placed Nichole in her mom's arms; and as Jamie stared down at Nichole, Seth picked up Nathan. "One more thing, Mom, meet your son, Nathan Alan."

Jamie's face lit up as bright as the sun, and she said, "We have two babies?"

"Yes, we do." Jamie adjusted Nichole in her arms so that she could hold both at the same time. Her smile could be seen from the waiting room; and as Susan came into the room, she saw the most beautiful sight a mom could ever have. She just had to capture the moment on camera.

In two days that Jamie was sleeping, Seth was able to get a second one of everything for the babies. They brought the babies home. They were enjoying their moments with their little family. But the joyous moments take a turn for the worst.

The family was outside enjoying the fresh air. Seth and Jamie were just about to sit down in the grass when a gunshot rang out. Seth's instinct kicked in, and he grabbed Jamie and turned his back in the direction of the gunshot. Seconds later, Seth feels a sharp pain in his back, and his legs go limp. Seth cries out in pain while Jamie is struggling to see where the shot came from, and she sees movement.

Her momma-bear instincts kick in, and she times it to where the figure is caught off guard. She makes her move and tackles the figure to the ground. It is Jack, and she has him where she can grab the gun and hold it on him. "Don't you dare move, or I will blow your brains out. You are done hurting me and my family." She grabs her cell phone and calls 911. She waited with the gun pointed on Jack until the police got there, but she was looking at Seth the whole time, and he was not moving. "Seth, please say something. Let me know you are still here with me."

He moved his head and said, "Jamie, where are you?"

"I am okay. Just hang tight and stay with me."

Moments later, the police and ambulance showed up. The police restrained Jack. The police officer could not help but laugh. He was taken down by a woman. The EMTs worked on Seth, and Jamie gathered up her babies. She checked them over, and they are okay. The police was talking to Jamie as the EMTs loaded Seth into the ambulance. "Listen, I need to follow my husband to the hospital. Can I answer questions there please?"

They are in the hospital, waiting to hear about Seth's condition. Jamie was filling the officer in on Jack. The doctor came to Jamie to let her know about Seth. "The bullet went through his spine, and he is paralyzed from the waist down. Unfortunately, it is permanent."

Jamie's heart sank at the news. "Can I see him?"

"Yes, he will be back down in a few minutes."

Jamie waited in his room with the babies. They finally wheeled him into the room, and he was sleeping. A half hour later, he wakes up and sees her crying. "Baby, what's the matter?"

"Seth, you are paralyzed for the rest of your life." Seth froze and could not say anything. He seems to be analyzing the situation in his head. He looks at Jamie and says, "We will get through this together if you want to stay with me."

"Seth, what are you talking about if I want to stay with you? I am in this all the way. Through sickness and health remember?"

"Okay, good because I can't do this without you."

CHAPTER 5

The Aftermath

Before Seth could come home, they had to redo the whole house. They made it wheelchair accessible. They also did the same thing to the house next door to their parents' house. Now that Jack is behind bars, they can finally go home. They are going to use the Florida home as a vacation home. Before Seth left the hospital, he had to talk to Jamie. "Jamie, I would like to know if you are okay with two kids?"

"I am. Why do you ask?"

"I am asking now because I don't work anymore. I wanted to make sure that if we want more kids, we have the means to do so. I have some stored for us just in case."

"Do you want more kids?" Jamie asked Seth.

"I would like to have more kids only if you want more kids."

Jamie eased herself onto Seth's lap and wrapped her arms around his neck. "Seth, it is good that you did that for us, and I love you for that. Let's just take it one day at a time and just be us. If we want more kids, then we will cross the bridge when we get there."

Seth smiled. "Okay, sounds good." He kisses her on the nose and then the lips.

Seth finally got to go home. He is liking the new look of the house and the hard work that Jamie put into the house just for him. Jamie watches Seth get accustomed to his new surroundings. Jamie could not hold it together anymore, and she broke down. She dropped to the floor. "Oh, baby, what's wrong?"

"I thought I lost you when he shot you. You were not moving, and I could not be by your side. I never want to go through that again."

"I am here, and I will not go anywhere. Our love will keep me here for a long time."

She craws onto his lap and wraps her arms around him. Her cries subsided as she the man that she loves very much held her. She heard one of the babies cry, and she reluctantly got up from the warm lap she was sitting on. Seth followed behind her. He watched as she took their son in her arms and comforted him. She looks so beautiful holding their child. Jamie looks up and sees Seth staring at her, and she walks over and places Nathan in his arms. Jamie went and got Nathan a bottle. Jamie handed it to Seth. Seth loves the connection he gets with his boy. Nathan is looking up at his dad, and Seth is smiling from ear to ear. Seth's heart is soaring high, and Jamie loves the sight.

Then Nichole cries, and Jamie picks her up. Jamie gets a bottle for her and rejoins her men in the room. She sits next to Seth and feeds their daughter. They switch the kids; Seth holds Nichole, and Jamie holds Nathan. They change their diapers, and then they sit and rock them back to sleep. Once they were out, they placed them back in their cribs and snuck out of their room.

Jamie asks Seth, "Do you want to wait a couple of weeks before we move home, or do you want to go right away?"

"We can wait to move in a couple of weeks. I am in no hurry to leave here."

"Okay, we will wait."

They spend the rest of the day just being with each other and enjoying their life together. Jamie is reminiscing over her life for the past months. Now she feels content, and she is loving these moments. This could not have happened if it were not for the love she and Seth shared. They saved each other, and she got to be with him for the rest of her life.

They close up the Florida house and head back home. For the first time, Seth will see the house after his mom died. He has not been in it since the day he learned about his mom. As they got closer to the house, Seth's heart started to race. He was not sure he could do this; but as they pulled into the driveway, Seth noticed it was different. It got a paint job, and the landscape was different. There was a ramp in the front and a wheelchair-accessible vehicle in the driveway. Jamie lit up and said, "Surprise."

Seth's heart seems to be calmer now. "You did all this for me?"

"Yes, Seth, I did not want you to come home to the memories. I changed as much of the house as I could. I added ramps, and your old room is the nursery, and I changed the master's bedroom."

Seth leaned over and kissed his wife's lips sweetly, "Thank you!"

At that point, Susan and Rick came running over with a welcome-home sign in their hands and a look of joy on their faces. Susan gave her daughter the biggest hug ever with tears in her eyes. "Yes, my baby is finally home." Then she snatched Nathan out of the car and carried him into the house. Then she came running and snatched Nichole out of the car and carried her into the house while Jamie was helping Seth out of the car.

As Susan was attending to her grandchildren, Seth and Jamie were looking at the new vehicle in their driveway. It was an SUV with the driver's seat that slides out of the way so that both Jamie and Seth can drive it. The gas-and-brake pedal was on the steering wheel.

When Seth would place his fingers at a certain spot, the vehicle would move forward. Then there was another spot for the brake. The kids' car seats were already loaded in the back. Jamie just had to strap them into the seat of the vehicle. There was a ramp that came out when the seat was pushed back so that Seth could get in and position himself to drive. Then there were clamps to hold his wheelchair in place while the vehicle was moving. Seth could not wait to take it for a spin. Jamie ran into the house and asked her parents if they would watch the kids, and they went out with Seth driving the new vehicle. They had fun cruising around the neighborhood. Some of their neighbors were out and waved to Jamie and Seth as they passed. Jamie could tell that Seth is loving this. He has his freedom, and this was the best investment that Jamie could have made. He can be the man that he wants to be, and that is all that matters to Jamie. They get back to the house, and Rick is cooking steaks on the grill. They spend the rest of the night in the company of their parents.

A couple of weeks later, Jamie and Seth were summonsed to Jack's hearing. He is pleading not guilty to all the charges. The judge decides to hear what Jamie and Seth have to say. Jamie could not hear Seth's testimony, but Seth was there for Jamie's. She explained that she could remember being taken from the hotel and by who, but she does not remember anything after that. "Do you see the man in this room who took you?" the judge asked Jamie.

"Yes, he is sitting right there." She pointed to Jack.

Jamie's and Seth's doctors were next to testify on the injuries they both endured. As they were testifying, a woman with big sunglasses on walked in and sat down directly behind Jack, and she touched his shoulder. He turned and put his hand on hers. Jamie got the attention of Seth and whispered, "Do you know that woman?"

"No, I have never seen her before."

After the doctor's testimony, Sergeant Taylor gave his. When the judge heard all the testimonies, he said, "Jack, please rise. I am finding you guilty and sentence you to twenty-five to life in prison with no hopes of parole," and he pounded his gavel.

Jamie and Seth heard screaming and crying as the woman collapsed in anguish. That's when Jamie realized that she was also pregnant. That's when she looked up at Jamie and Seth; and in a tear-stained voice she said, "You will pay for this!" She points to Jamie. She stands up and storms out of the courtroom. Jamie looked at Sergeant Taylor; and with a nod, he said, "I am on it." He rushes after her.

By the time Sergeant Taylor reached the hallway, she was gone. She dropped her visitor's pass on the floor with her picture on it. Sergeant Taylor picks it up and goes to visitor check-in station and the combs through the surveillance cameras and spots her. Sergeant Taylor takes it from there and starts the search.

Meanwhile, Jamie is pushing Seth in the hallway and talking. "Did you know he had a girlfriend?"

"No, I did not. He must have been going out with her while out on the road."

They got to the car and made it home. They filled Rick and Susan in on the situation, and soon enough, there were police officers guarding both houses. Then the news stations are reporting the events of the courtroom and the woman's outburst. The next thing Jamie heard was the reporter saying that Jack's wife, Tawney, is on the run from police and any information will be greatly appreciated.

Sergeant Taylor realized who Tawney is. She is his secretary, and she knew everything they did. He now knows how Jack kept one step ahead of them. She now knows how to stay hidden and toy with them. Then Sergeant Taylor got an idea. She is pregnant; so he emailed every nurse, doctor, and delivery person he can think of a description and picture of Tawney.

A couple of weeks go by, and there is no sign of Tawney. Jamie can't help but to look over her shoulder every time she is out with her family. Seth wanted to get out of the house but did not want to risk it. Jamie decided to just be outside in the backyard. The backyard is fenced in with trees lining the perimeter. Jamie put the kids in their swing and was pushing them when out of the corner of her eye she sees movement. Seth realizes that it is a not-so-pregnant Tawney. Seth yells, "Jamie, she is here!" Seth is struggling to get to Jamie, but he can't.

Jamie instinctively stepped between Tawney and the kids, and she stepped to Tawney. "What are you doing here, Tawney? You are not going to hurt any one of my family."

"Oh, I am!" Tawney pulled out a gun and Jamie launched herself at Tawney, wrestling her to the ground. Jamie grabbed the gun, and it went off. Seth watched in horror as the women did not move.

Finally, there is movement; and it is not Jamie. Tawney is trying to move Jamie off her. Meanwhile, Seth just hung up with 911. Tawney is standing up and looking for the gun. Just as Tawney spots it, the officers are on her. Seth is yelling Jamie's name, and she is not moving. He falls out of his chair and crawls to his unmoving wife. He gets to her and rolls her over and notices the bullet went into her head. "Jamie, no! please stay with me. Please don't die on me." Seth's breathing increased, and he checked to see if she is breathing. Yes, she still is breathing. He put his head on her chest and heard her heartbeat. "Fight, baby, stay with us. We need you!"

The EMTs finally arrived and took over. Sergeant Taylor helped Seth back into his chair. Seth can't catch his breath. He is staring at Jamie as the EMTs work on her. By that time, Rick and Susan came running over and grabbed the kids out of the swing and joined Seth watching as they worked. She flatlined, and Susan cried out Jamie's name. The EMTs said, "We got her back. Let's move." They rushed her to the ambulance and left. Rick placed the kids in the car and helped Seth into their car and drove to the hospital.

Rick, Susan, Seth, and the kids rushed into the emergency room. "My daughter Jamie Anderson please," Rick said out of breath.

"Please wait right here, sir. I will find out the information for you."

Rick is pacing while Seth and Susan are trying to calm the kids down. The emergency room receptionist returned and asked them to follow her to a more private waiting room. Rick went back to pacing until the doctor walked in. "Doctor, please tell me my daughter is okay."

"I have some news, and it is good. The bullet just lodged itself against her frontal lobe. It did not do much damage, but there is a chance she may not remember things, or her memory might be gone. We have her stable, and we will have to wait to see when she wakes up. She is out of the woods."

Seth spoke up, "Can we see her please?"

"Yes, we will be putting her in a room shortly. It will be 307."

"Thank you, Doctor." Seth shook his hand. Susan sighed, relieved, as they walked to the room where her daughter would be.

Fifteen minutes later, they wheeled Jamie in. She is sleeping and looks horrible. Her face is all black and blue, and her eyes look like they are swollen shut. Three hours later, she started to wake up. Jamie whimpered as she began to stir. She opened her eyes as much as she could, and Seth saw her eyes were blank. She has no recognition of those in the room with her. Seth's heart fell to the floor. Her first words were "Who are you? Where am I?"

Seth held her hand and said, "We are your family, and you are in the hospital."

Jamie begins to panic. "Who am I? Why am I here?"

Seth calmly tells her, "Your name is Jamie, and you are safe. Please let us help you."

She looked from him to her parents, not recognizing them. "I am sorry I don't know you."

"It's okay. We know. We will not leave you alone here, though. You may not remember but we do love you." Seth's heart broke. The woman in front of him is alive, but she is not his wife right now at least. He knows he is not leaving her side no matter what she says.

Seth explained to Jamie what happened to her. Jamie is silent. She feels lost. Jamie can't figure out why she would forget the most important people in her life, or she thinks they are. She has a life that she can't remember, and now she has to trust the people in the room, and they are strangers to her. What hurts the most is that she is a mother, and she does not remember being one. Jamie started to cry, and Seth held her hand tighter. "How can I forget the life I have? How can I forget you and the kids? I don't know any of you, and I am sorry."

Susan said, "It is okay, baby. It will come back. Your memory will come back. If it does not, you will create your life over again with our help." Susan wrapped her daughter in her arms. Jamie just cried. Seth wished he could do the same. He wanted so much to crawl into bed with her, but he did not want to scare her. When Jamie's tears subsided and her mom released her, she looked at Seth. "I am guessing you are my husband."

"Yes, I am!" Jamie opened her arms and asked him to come to them. Rick helped his son-in-law into the bed with his daughter. Then she asked for the kids. She wants to hold her family, willing herself to remember the people she is supposed to love.

A couple weeks later, Jamie was released, and her mind was still blank. Jamie feels weird walking into a house that is supposed to be hers but feels foreign to her. Seth was a little nervous. He is not sure if he should give Jamie a tour or just let her figure it out on her own. Seth was watching her expression as she surveyed her surroundings. "Do you want me to help you, Jamie?"

"No, I am okay. How did you end up in that chair?"

Seth smiled and said, "You waited until we got home to ask me that."

"Yes, I just thought of the question," Jamie said with a guilty look on her face.

"I ended up in this chair because I came between you and the bullet from my stepfather." He told her the reason why Tawney did what she did. She looked at him with dread. Then she looked at him with love, and he recognized that look. For a split second, he saw the love that he missed.

Seth watches her walk around the house. She looks at the pictures on the wall and smiles. She then walked into the kitchen and looked through all the drawers and cupboards. She then goes upstairs and investigates the rooms. She walks through the kids' room and then to her room. She stops at a picture of her and Seth. Tears started to fall as she tried to remember her life. It is all overwhelming for her. Seth joined her in the bedroom and saw the tears. She immediately wiped them when Seth entered. "Jamie, please don't cry. It will all be okay."

"I know. It is just all overwhelming. I am trying to remember. There is a heavy blanket on my memories. It is too heavy for me to lift it."

"I will help you lift it. Anything you need, I am here."

"Thank you, Seth. I will take you up on that offer."

"Do you want to help me put the kids to bed? Hoping to jog your memory."

"Yes, that will be great." Jamie walked over to Seth and took his hand, and they went together to the kids.

Jamie is finally in her bed since the shooting happened. It feels a little weird. What is making her feel better is knowing that Seth is there. In a way, she feels comfortable, but she also does not know him. She falls asleep feeling the love that Seth has for her but not being able to reciprocate that love. She also feels that he is holding back his full love for her, and she thinks it is because he does not want to scare her. As soon as Jamie drifts off to sleep, a dream starts. It is more like a nightmare. She sees Jack, and she is dreaming about what he did to her while he had her. She starts shouting no in her sleep, and it jars Seth awake. Her body is rigid with fear, and she is shaking.

Seth wraps his arms around her and starts to whisper, "Jamie, I love you. Find a way to come back to us." He repeats it over and over. He begins to feel her relax. Then she is smiling, and she wakes up looking straight into Seth's eyes. There, in the brown eyes staring back at him, he recognizes a familiar woman. She knows him, and she reaches up to pull his face down to hers just to kiss him. Seth is recognizing his wife, and he knows she is back. The next thing Seth hears is "Hello, handsome, I have missed you."

He responded, "Hello, beautiful, you don't know how much I have longed to hear you say that."

Seth begins to cry, and Jamie wraps her arms around him. "Your love brought me back to you. I can't believe I was lost. You found me, and I am here now. I remember everything. I remember our life. Seth, I love you too."

That made his tears come harder, and they cried together. Seth and Jamie are whole again. It can't get any better than this. Seth has Jamie back, and he is holding her like he has never done before.

AFTERWORD

Tawney went to jail, and she got fifteen to thirty years for attempted murder. Tawney has to live the rest of her life without her baby because of what she did in the name of love. Her baby was adopted right away, and it is not open. The only other family member was Jack, and he is in jail for life.

Jamie has recovered nicely with no other side effects like before. She is happy that she is not missing her life. She is happy that Seth is not being hurt anymore, and he lives. He is the best father only because his mom instilled in him the way his father was before he died. Jamie loves the look on Seth's face when he is interacting with his daughter and son. He melts her heart. She will be able to watch this for the rest of her life, and she is grateful.

Jamie remembers what Jack did to her when he had her. Jamie has some of the same scars as Seth does. She does not want to tell Seth what she went through. It might bring back bad memories for Seth. She decided to tell him only if he asks. Meanwhile, it is nice to put it all in the past so that she can enjoy her life and her family.

A BEST FRIEND'S LOVE

INTRODUCTION

Well, where do I start? I am Dawn, and I am about to make a decision that will determine the rest of my life. First, let me fill you in on a little history. I am now twenty-three years old and a college graduate. I am about to work for a business that controls most of the other businesses in the area. I will be the business consultant that finds and reports struggling businesses. The company then works to help them or take over. To top it all off, my best friend Jason is my boss. We have been best friends since grade school, and we have saved each other from time to time.

All throughout school, he and I were teased, me for being a white nerd who had her head in the books of anything business and him for being a black nerd who had his head in the same kind of books like me. But the only difference is that once they saw what Jason looked like, they backed away quickly. No one messed with him or me for that matter. Jason is a kickboxer, and he was on the wrestling team at our high school. He is all muscle, and he is six feet two inches. He has short braids at the top of his head, and they are pulled back in a tie, and the sides of his head are shaved. His eyes are the deepest shade of brown. Any girl will get lost in his eyes if they stare long enough. His smile is intoxicating and addictive.

Yes, I do have a crush on him, but I like him as my best friend. We share everything: our deepest secrets, our thoughts, and our feelings.

I don't want to lose that part of our relationship. I never acted on my feelings for him because of that reason. I don't even know if he had the same feelings for me. But I do have a boyfriend. He is also Jason's best friend. Jake does not mind my and Jason's relationship. All three of us hang out together whenever we can. Jake is in Jason's kickboxing class, as well as his wrestling team. Jake is a white version of Jason but without the braids. Jake's dark-brown hair is feathered back and split on the left side. They get along so well. They treat each other like brothers. They are both only children in their family.

I have a sister Anna, and she is seven years younger than I am. My parents were divorced at one point and then found the love that they lost and were remarried and had her. She is a spunky sixteen-year-old and is so full of life. When she came into my life, I did not like her because she took my parents from me. My mom sensed that, and she made it a point to let me help her care for my sister. Now I look at her as my best friend and my sister. Before I went off to college, we were inseparable. When I was in college, I made it a point to keep her in the loop on whatever I did. We are closer than ever before.

Jason's parents had passed away. Jason's mom died during childbirth, and his dad died ten years ago because of cancer. Jake's parents took Jason in until he was eighteen, and he went off to college with me and Jake. We all stayed local, and Jake still lived at home while Jason and I lived in the dorms. But he was over at our dorm building all the time when he was not home studying.

Then Jake changed for the worse, and he snapped.

CHAPTER 1

The Changes

Dawn started noticing changes in Jake's attitude. Dawn suggested to Jake, "Come, let's hang with Jason today."

"No, I don't want you hanging with Jason anymore."

"Why? Did something happen? What is going on with you? You are not acting like yourself."

Jake yelled at Dawn, "There is nothing wrong! Now leave me alone."

"Will you please tell me what is wrong? Why can't we hang out with Jason?"

"You are mine, Dawn, and I don't want to share you with him anymore."

This took Dawn by surprise, and she said, "You can't tell me who I can and cannot hang out with, Jake. I am going to see Jason. He is my best friend as well as yours."

Jake's face was now red, and he slapped Dawn across the face. "No, you will stay here." Dawn's eyes got big, and she grabbed her jacket and ran out the door before Jake could stop her. She ran as fast as she could and locked herself in the apartment. She is right now thinking, *Thank god, Jake does not have a key to my apartment.* She runs to her bathroom mirror and sees a bruise forming under her right eye. "Crap, he hit me so hard. Jason will definitely see this and ask. What do I tell him?" Dawn is scared to tell Jason. What will he do to his best friend? Will this be the last time she is hit by Jake? She gets some ice from the freezer and sits in her living room for a while, willing the black-and-blue mark to disappear.

The next morning, it is worse. Today she is meeting Jason for lunch to talk business. Dawn knows she does not have enough makeup to cover it up. She has to come up with a story. Jason knows Dawn is not clumsy. She cannot tell him she fell. *Oh yes, I know what I can tell him.* Dawn finished getting ready for work. Meanwhile, Jake was calling her on the phone. She ignored him. If he is going to be possessive, then she does not want any part of it. He was never possessive until now. Dawn left for work.

When she arrived at work, Jake was there waiting for her. His face turned to shock when he saw what he did. "Oh, Dawn, I am sorry. I did not mean to hurt you like that. I did not mean what I said. I was not myself last night. I hope you forgive me."

At that point, Jason walked up to them. "Sorry for what, Jake?"

Then Jason saw the bruise on Dawn's face. Jason's jaw tensed, and he looked at Jake. "Don't ever touch her again. You will regret it."

Jake looked shocked that his best friend would threaten him like that. "I am sorry, Jason."

"Why did you hit her?"

Dawn could not speak, and Jake stumbled over the next sentence. "I . . . got . . . jealous!" Jason looked at Jake with a face that Dawn had never seen before. The look was of disappointment, shock, and anger toward his best friend. Then Jason took Dawn's hand and led her away from Jake. "Dawn, I am not done talking to you yet," Jake protested.

Jason turns and says, "You are now." When Dawn and Jason were out of earshot of Jake, he asked, "Is this the first time?"

"Yes!"

"You will tell me if he has hit you before?"

"Yes! But this is the first time. I promise."

"I know this is hard for me to say, but please don't see him anymore. He does not need to hurt you. I will not stand for it no matter who he is to me."

"Jason, he is my boyfriend. Something is going on with him, and I need to figure out what."

Jason's face turned to anger again. "No, you let me handle him. I don't want to see you like this again."

Dawn looked at him as if she understood, but she did not like it. "Okay, but please don't hurt him and let me know how he is."

"As long as you cut him loose. If he did this to you now, he won't stop unless he gets some serious help."

"Okay, Jason, I will."

"Good, now let's get to work. We are late."

"Yes, boss!" she said with a little smile.

This is a decision Dawn has to make. Does she cut Jake loose? It is seven years of relationship down the tubes. She loves Jake, but now she is scared of him. He has never hit her or even raised his voice before. They argued but never with raised voices. Dawn decided to let Jake go. She is going to step aside and let Jason handle him. She does not want to be hit again. Dawn picked up her cell phone and dialed Jake's phone number, and he picked it up on the second ring. "Hi, baby, I am really sorry about everything. Please forgive me."

"Jake, I do forgive you, but I can't be hit again. I don't think we can be together anymore. Something has gotten into you, and Jason wants to help you hereon out. I am stepping out of the way, so you can get the help you need."

"You are leaving me?"

"For now, please get the help you need. I can't let you hurt me again."

"I understand, Dawn! Goodbye for now."

Dawn could hear the pain in his voice, and it wrecked her heart. As she hung up, she started to cry. She knows it is for the best, but it does not make it feel any better. Jason peeked his head in to see if she was ready for their lunch meeting. Then he realized she was crying. "Dawn, what's wrong?"

"I just ended it with Jake. He did not take it well. Please help him, Jason. Don't let him go through this alone."

"I will be there for him and you."

"Thank you."

Jason let her cry some more on his shoulder. Then they left for the lunch meeting.

They went to their usual restaurant and was in the middle of work when Jake showed up. "Dawn, I am sorry. I can't let you go. I am desperate to keep you. I need you." He dropped to one knee and said, "I can't live without you. Please be my wife, and I promise never to hurt you." Jason looked at him and then to her. Jason shakes his no ever so slightly.

Dawn's eyes darted back and forth between Jason and Jake. Then she closed her eyes and said with a heavy heart, "Jake, I can't. I need you to get help first. Then I will consider marrying you."

Then she dashed off to the restroom. "Dude, what were you thinking? You hit her the night before then expect her to say yes to you the next day? It does not work that way." Jason gave him a business card of the man who helped him get through his parents' death. "I have made you an appointment for later this afternoon. I will see you there. I agree with Dawn. Please let's get you some help."

Jake took the card angrily and said, "I will think about it." He walks out of the restaurant.

Dawn comes back twenty minutes later. It looks like she was crying again. "How is he, Jason? What did he do after I left?"

"I gave him a card and told him to meet me at the office of the man who helped me after my parents' death. Jake said he will think about being there."

"Thank you, Jason, for reaching out to him. I am hoping he takes you up on your offer."

"I do too. At least I know he is not going to hurt you again."

"I am finally listening to you for a change."

"Yes, I was hoping you would. What made up your mind besides me?"

"My fear that developed last night."

"Okay, please don't go near him by yourself. Understood?"

"Yes, boss!"

Jason met Jake at the office of his doctor. Dr. Mark Holms meets them at the door and invites them in. "Hello, Jason, thank you for coming tonight and bring Jake. What is happening, Jake?"

Jake looks at Jason and then back at Dr. Holms. Jake looked shocked, and he did not want to speak. "I don't have anything going on with me. I don't know what Jason has told you."

"Jake, you have something going on with you. I am your best friend. I don't want to see what I saw on Dawn again. Talk to us."

"No, I don't have anything going except for Dawn throwing away seven years of our relationship. You are looking at me like I did something wrong."

Dr. Holms speaks up, "What is Jason accusing you of doing?"

"I had a weak moment and hit my girlfriend last night, and now she does not want to be around me anymore."

"Why did you hit her?" Dr. Holms asks.

Jake is contemplating answering the question and looking at Jason. Jason speaks up as if reading Jake's mind. "You did not want her around me. Look, you have nothing to worry about. We are best friends, and that's it."

Jake looked mad. "Yes, I did not want her around you, and now you have her all to yourself. I bet that you will be pursuing her now that I am out of the way." Jake stood up and walked out. "You know what, I am done with this, and, Jason, I am done with you."

"Jake, wait you don't mean that. We are here to help." Jake was gone as Jason tried to go after him. Jason returned to Dr. Holms's office and asked, "What do we do now?"

"Keep giving him your support and letting him know you are there for him."

"Okay, I will try. Thank you, Dr. Holms."

Jason walked out to the sidewalk and called Dawn. "He has definitely got something going on with him. He blew up at us just now, and he is not happy. He does not want the help."

"Jason, thank you for trying. What did Dr. Holms say about him?"

"He told me to keep supporting him and letting him know that I am here for him."

"Jason, I don't want you to get hurt. Please be careful."

"I will be careful, Dawn. Don't let him in if he comes knocking."

"Okay, I am turning in now. I am tired. Good night, Jason. See you tomorrow."

"Good night, Dawn. Sleep well."

As soon as Dawn hung up with Jason, her heart sank. Jake does not want help. She can't stop thinking about Jake and how angry he got with her. She dozes off to sleep, thinking about him. It's 2:00 a.m., and she hears a pounding on the door. She gets up and runs to her door and looks through the peephole. It's Jake, and he looks drunk. "Dawn, I know you are in there." He is slurring his words. Definitely drunk. "Please open the door. I need you. I can't do this without you." She runs to her bedroom and grabs her phone and calls Jason. The next thing she hears is a crash and footsteps to her bedroom. She hears Jason on the other end of the line. "Who are you on the phone with? You are mine."

Jason could hear her struggle and the slaps. "Jake, please stop hurting me," comes loud over the phone. Jason is throwing on some clothes and while still on the phone runs to his car. He is at Dawn's apartment in less than ten minutes. Jason does not hear Dawn's cry her voice anymore as he climbs the steps three at a time. By the time Jason gets into Dawn's apartment, Jake is gone, but Dawn is a bloody mess on the floor. Jason moves her to see if she is breathing. She is unconscious and not responding to his touch at all. Jason quickly dials 911. Jason holds her until the EMTs get there.

The EMTs load Dawn into the ambulance. Jason is answering questions based on what he heard. Then Jason jumps into his car and follows the ambulance to the hospital. He was thinking the whole time on the way to the hospital, *I should have been there with her. She should not have been by herself.* Jason is kicking himself for not being there. When Jason got to the hospital, they would not let him know any information unless he told them he was her fiancée. "Okay, sir, the doctor will be with you shortly," the nurse told him. Jason is pacing as he calls her family.

An hour later, the doctor finally comes out and updates Dawn's family. "Hello, Jason, I am Dr. Carter. I am the doctor looking over your fiancée." Dawn's mom looked at him funny. "She has sustained blunt-force trauma to her head, and she has some brain swelling and some major head trauma. Some of her ribs are broken, and she is in a coma. Her back has sustained some trauma also. She is in the ICU, and we will monitor her throughout the night and day. She is hanging on, but it has been touch and go. We lost her twice but was able to bring her back. If you would excuse me, I have to go back and check on her."

"Thank you, Doctor. Can we see her?"

"You can, but you would have to stay in the observation room. We can't let anyone in at this time." The doctor had them escorted to the room where they could look at Dawn. Jason's heart sank when he laid eyes on Dawn's mangled face. Then his face turned to rage when he thought about who did this to her. Jason wants to be by her side, but there is glass between them. He wants her to know that he was there for her. Then again, he is thinking why he let her be home alone. He did not think that his best friend will be capable of such a horrible act. Jason stepped into the hallway out of earshot of Dawn's parents and sister. He called Jake. Jake answered the phone. "You are not to come anywhere near me or Dawn ever again. Do you understand me? You are not going to hurt her ever again. You better hope I don't catch you on the street."

"Dude, what are you talking about? What happened to Dawn?"

Jake's question throw Jason off, but he could tell Jake is drunk. He is slurring his words. "You know what you did. You are going to pay for it."

"Jason, please tell me what happened to Dawn. I have no idea what you are talking about."

"Don't give me that shit! I am not playing, Jake. Don't ever come near me again. We are not friends anymore. You better hope Dawn does not die." Jason hangs up. He does not want to hear any more lies.

For the next twenty-four hours, Jason watched Dawn sleep from behind the glass. He paced for most of the hours. The rest of the hours, he stared at her. Her face is swollen and unrecognizable. There were cuts and bruises all over her face. Her beautiful face is covered in anger and pain. Jason could not hold his pain in anymore, and he sinks to his knees with tears running down his face. Dawn's mom, Lydia, drops to her knees and wraps her arms around Jason. All he can say was "I should have been there for her."

"Jason, this is not your fault. She will be okay. She will pull through this." Jason hugged Lydia back. Anna had been frozen since they went into the room. Their dad, Chris, wrapped his daughter in his arms and felt her shaking. "She is going to be okay." Anna did not move or make a sound. She just stared at her sister and shook.

Lydia remembered something. "Jason, so are you going to tell me why the doctor said you are her fiancé?"

Jason looked at Lydia with a little smile. "They weren't going to let me see her unless I was related to her or her husband or husband-to-be. I am sorry. I lied."

"It's okay. I would have said you were family. To tell you the truth, I am hoping that one day it will be true."

Jason smiled a little, hopeful for the future. "If she survives this, it will be true. I will do anything for her. I think I love her."

"Well, Jason, her dad is right there. Ask him to take her hand in marriage. I bet he will say yes."

Jason's face lights up, and his grin is brighter than the sun. "That is a tempting thought. But I don't know if she likes me that way."

"Oh, Jason, she does. Don't ever tell her that you have seen what I am about to show you." Lydia pulls out her phone and plays a video for him. In the video, Dawn is talking to Lydia, and Lydia is asking Dawn questions. "But, Mom, what if he does not like me?"

"Dawn, he will love you."

"How do you know?" "It is in his eyes and the way he looks at you."

"I really love him, but I don't know how to tell him. I love how he takes care of me. I love the way we connect in certain ways. But I don't want to ruin our relationship. He is my best friend, and I am scared that he does not feel the same way."

"Dawn, he does feel the same way. I know he does. If he asks your dad and me, we will give him our blessing because you two belong together." Before the video stops, Dawn's face was a beautiful shade of hope, and he could see his future in her eyes. "Jason, what are you waiting for?" Jason looks at her father and then back to her mother. She gestures toward him. Chris looks over at Lydia and Jason. Jason's eyes met Chris's. Jason could see in the corner of his eye that Lydia motioned to Chris that Jason wants to ask something.

Chris looks at Jason and says, "Yes, you can. I will be honored to have you as my son-in-law." Jason's mouth drops open in surprise. Jason is flying high right now, and the only way this will be even better is when Dawn wakes up and pulls through this.

CHAPTER 2

The Waiting to See

One month has gone by, and Dawn is slowly healing, but she is still in a coma. Her face is looking better but still a little swollen. According to her doctor, she still has brain activity, and the swelling on her brain has gone down as well. Since she has made progress, her family can be in the same room, and Jason has not let go of her hand for the past two weeks except to go to the bathroom. Jason is anxious and can't wait for her to wake up. He has had dreams of her waking up and jumping into his arms. He would also dream of her yes answer to his proposal. Lydia and Chris come back and forth between their home and the hospital and bring Jason clean clothes and things to eat. No matter how hard they try, they can't tear him away from Dawn.

"Dawn, the day is coming you will wake up and tell me that you love me. I know that you hear me. I know you are fighting to be here with us. I am here, and I am not going anywhere. Come back to me please, Dawn. I love you, and I can't wait to tell you that. I can't wait until I can ask you to be my wife. We have known each other for almost twenty years, and I know now that I want you to be mine forever. Please wake up so that I can hear your answer."

Jason is looking down at her fingers, and they begin to move. His eyes flick up to hers, and she is smiling, and her eyes are on his. She nods. He lights up, and again, his smile is brighter than the sun. She points to the ring finger on her left hand and nods. He plants a kiss on her forehead. "I will kiss you better once that tube is out." She nods again. She smiles. It is weak, but it is still beautiful. Jason pushes the button to call the nurse without taking his eyes off Dawn.

"Hi, Jason, what do you need?" "She is awake."

"Oh, yay, I will send the doctor in."

Then Jason called her parents again without taking his eyes off Dawn's eyes. "She is awake." Jason heard a loud yes through the phone, and then Lydia says, "We will be right there."

Two minutes later, the doctor took the tube out of Dawn's throat. She coughs and winces. But then she pulled Jason with as much strength as she could, planted a kiss on Jason's lips, and held them there until she ran out of breath. She then whispers, "Yes, I want to be your wife."

"You heard me." He looks deep into her eyes, and he says with tears in his eyes, "I love you."

She whispers, "I love you."

Thirty minutes later, Dawn's family walks into her room. Lydia immediately starts to cry tears of joy. She wraps her arms around her daughter. She was followed by Chris and Anna. "I am so happy to see you awake, baby girl," her dad tells her. He places a kiss on her forehead.

Dawn whispers, "I am happy to see you."

Lydia looks over at Jason who has moved to give room for her family. Lydia motioned to Jason with her head; and with a huge smile, he nodded. Lydia gasps in surprise. "I hear congratulations are in order. My first baby is getting married." Dawn's cheeks are red now, and she looks at her mom in surprise. "Yes, baby girl, while you were sleeping, we talked," Lydia assured her daughter. All Dawn could do was smile. Dawn spent the rest of the day awake, whispering to her family.

When Jason and Dawn were finally alone that night, Jason asked, "How are you feeling?"

"I am hurting, but I am good."

"You are hurting where, and how long have you been hurting?"

"I have been hurting all day, but it is tolerable."

"Why didn't you tell me? I could have gotten the nurse."

"I just wanted it to be us. I missed all of you."

"Do you want something now for the pain?"

"Yes, please. I don't think I can sleep without it." Jason pushes the button for the nurse.

"How can I help you, Jason and Dawn?"

"Can we get some painkillers for Dawn please?"

"On the way."

"Thank you."

Dawn whispered, "How long have I been here?"

"For a month now."

"Have you been here the whole time?"

"Yes, I could not leave you."

Then she asked, "What about work?"

"They told me to take as long as we need and to take care of you. They have us both covered until we return."

"Okay, that's a relief."

"Oh, before I forget." Jason takes a box out of his pocket and opens it. "This was my mother's ring. When your fingers are not so swollen, I will slip it on your finger."

Dawn's eyes got big, and she smiled. "Okay!" It is a princess-cut solitaire with a gold band holding it in place. At that time, the nurse came in with the relief Dawn needed. Ten minutes after that, she drifted off to sleep. Jason climbed up in bed with her and wrapped her in his arms and fell asleep also.

Jake was watching them as they drifted off to sleep. He said to himself, *I knew it. Jason was after my girl. Now he is going to pay for it. My best friend and my girlfriend are getting married. She is mine. She will never be yours, Jason. For as long as I live, she will never be yours. All the wondrous things I can do to them now. I can't wait to start. Sleep well for now, Jason. I am coming for you soon.*

Dawn jolts awake, feeling Jason wraps around what seems like every inch of her. She could not help but think to herself this beautiful man loves her. I can't believe he has been secretly loving her all this time. Now she can't wait for her life to start. Then she asked herself, *Wait, how did I get here? Why am I in the hospital?* Jason wakes up and sees Dawn deep in thought. He brings her out of her head with his "Good morning, beautiful."

"Good morning, husband-to-be."

"What were you thinking about just now?"

"I was just thinking, how did I get here?"

Jason takes a deep breath and says one word, "Jake."

"No, he could not have done this to me."

"Yes, he did. He broke your ribs, injured your back, and damaged your brain. He almost killed you. You died on us twice."

Dawn was silent, taking in what Jason just said. It is hard to believe. "I was in love with him for seven years, and now you are telling me he did this to me. Why?"

"He said he did not want us to be friends, and he can't live without you."

"But he wanted to kill me?" Dawn is in shock. Her breathing starts to pick up, and her head is spinning. She passes out. Jason got up quick and ran to get the nurse. "Help, she just passed out."

Nurses came running in and checked on Dawn. She is still out cold. They start to pack her wires and tubes for transport. "Wait, what is happening to her? Where are you taking her?"

"Jason, we need to take her to radiology to find out what happened. We will have her back soon."

Five minutes after they wheeled Dawn out of the room, Lydia arrived. "Where did they take her? What happened?" Jason filled her in, and she put her head in her hands. Dawn is wheeled back in an hour later.

"Doctor what is going on with her?" Jason asked.

"She has a tumor that developed as a result of her brain injury. It is operable. We will set her up for surgery later today. We need to prepare for it, though. It is in a place that may or may not be easy to get to. We will keep you posted. Meanwhile, we have her sedated because if she wakes, it may get worse." The doctor leaves to prepare.

Jason starts to pace as Lydia calls her husband. Jason's heart is racing. Then he goes over beside Dawn. "Now, my beautiful wife-to-be, please don't leave me. I just finally allowed myself to love you and let you know that I do. You fight through this please. I love you, my beautiful girl! I will be right here waiting for you."

Two hours later, they wheel Dawn out and take her for surgery. Her family holds their breath. The surgery takes five hours to complete. Jason paces the whole time, only stopping to stare out the window a couple of times. Jason is worried and mad that she has to go through this because of what Jake did to her. The wait is excruciating. It is now going into hour four. Jason settles to staring out the window, watching the people hustle and bustle seven floors down. He eyes a couple older than he is. He is helping her limp into the hospital. He dreams of him and Dawn that way. He pictures them growing old together and sitting on a porch swing holding each other. Then he saw a young man with flowers, and that gave him an idea. Jason called down to the hospital gift shop and ordered five big bouquets and had them delivered to Dawn's room. Fifteen minutes later, the five bouquets arrived, and they were beautiful.

An hour and a half later, Dawn was wheeled back in, and she had a bandage around her head, but she still looked beautiful. The doctor came in two minutes afterward to update the family. "She will be asleep for a while. The surgery took longer than expected. She is stable, and most of the tumor has been removed. We have to wait until she wakes up to see the side effects from the surgery. She may have a couple but not much. We will check her vitals every half hour." Jason nods with his eyes fixed on Dawn. Now a whole new set of worry sets in, and Jason waits for Dawn to wake up.

Two days go by, and Dawn is still sleeping. She has not woken yet from her surgery. Jason's stomach is in knots, and he has not eaten for a day. He is up, pacing every now and then. Jason sits down next to Dawn and lays his head on her chest and listens to her beating heart. It seems to calm him; and within minutes, he is asleep. Three hours later, he wakes to hands on his head and eyes peering down at him. "Hello, my beautiful fiancée."

She says softly, "Hello, my handsome husband-to-be."

Then he sits straight up and pinches himself. "Ow, okay, it is not a dream, and you are really awake. How long have you been awake?"

"For about an hour now. I have been watching you sleep. You looked peaceful. I did not want to wake you." He just stared at her, soaking it all in. He smiled and thought he couldn't wait to wake up next to her for the rest of his life. His eyes were just sweeping over her face, creating a memory. He loves her smile, her eyes, and those lips. The next thing he knows, he is kissing those lips, loving every minute of their contact.

He broke and said, "Thank you for fighting to stay here. I was worried that I was going to lose you before we had a chance to love each other. Thank you for agreeing to be mine for the rest of my life. I have loved you for a long time. I could not act on my feelings because of Jake, and I did not want to ruin what we had. But now I can't hold back anymore."

Dawn smiled and responded to him with a kiss that shocked him. He felt the kiss go down to his toes and back again. Dawn also said, "I feel the same way toward you. I am happy you picked me to spend the rest of your life with."

He kissed her hand and buried his face on it. The love he holds for Dawn is swelling his heart, and it will only grow bigger.

CHAPTER 3

Protection and Love

Four weeks after her surgery, Dawn was able to return to work but slowly, so she decided to take half days at the office and work from home the rest of the time. Jason decided to move in with Dawn to help her get back to her life. She is the one with the two-bedroom apartment. Jason loves the fact that he gets to see her more often now. He is finally able to get back to work and move on with his life. Dawn is out of the woods and has healed nicely. He is loving his life now and can't wait for the words "I now pronounce you man and wife." They decided to have the wedding a month from now, and they are having fun planning it. Then Jake's mom calls Jason, "Is it true did Jake really hurt Dawn?"

"Yes, he did."

"Oh god, how is she doing?"

"She is good now, but it was bad. He did a number on her head and back."

"I am sorry, Jason. I don't know what has gotten into Jake, but he is bad now also. He won't come back to the house, and I have no idea where he is. I don't know what to do anymore."

Jason then said, "I tried to get help when he first hurt Dawn. He responded by blowing up at me and the doctor I talked to about my parents' death. He walked out, got drunk, and attacked her. I want to let you know that Dawn and I are getting married."

"Oh, Jason, that is good news. I am happy for you."

"Please don't tell Jake. He said part of the reason he is acting this way was because he is jealous of my and Dawn's relationship. The relationship did not develop into what it is now until she was in the hospital. This relationship did not start while Dawn and Jake were going out."

"It's okay, Jason. You don't have to explain to me. Do you have any idea where Jake will go?"

"I am sorry. I don't. I am sorry to say this, but I can't be friends with him the way he is now. If I have to do something to stop him from hurting Dawn or anyone else."

"I understand. If you see him or talk to him, please do what you must but tell him to come home. Bye for now, Jason."

"Goodbye and please take care of yourself."

Jason almost forgot about Jake, and he couldn't see him, let alone talk to him. How can he do something like that to Dawn? How can he hurt anyone that he loves? What made him snap? It is hard for Jason to not be there for his best friend, but his best friend is not the guy he was. He is someone totally different. Jason is now torn between Jake the best friend and now Jake the bad man. He has no idea what Jake is now capable of or what he will do when he finds out about him and Dawn. Jason is hoping that the police finds Jake before he does something else.

When Jason got home, there were candles lit everywhere and light music playing. Dawn is standing next to a made table with their dinner on it. She is wearing a black dress that highlights her curves.

She has heels on that accentuate her legs. Jason stops dead in his tracks and says, "You are so beautiful."

"Thank you, darling!"

"I can't wait until our wedding night. The way you look tonight—it blows my mind. I can't believe you are going to be my wife in three weeks. I am a man in love and a proud man."

As he is speaking those words, he is walking closer and closer to Dawn. When he got to her, he placed a kiss on her lips that made her feel his love for her. He was lost in her kiss back, and he could lose himself forever in her love for him. He gets to kiss her forever. They ate dinner, staring at each other and just loving the moment. It would have been different if she succumbed to her injuries. When dinner was over, Jason helped Dawn clean up, and he led her to her door and kissed her good night before he went to his door. "See you in the morning, sweetheart."

She smiles and says, "See you in the morning, baby."

The three weeks go by so slowly. The days just seem to drag on and get longer. The one good thing was they were able to get things done for the wedding. The one bad thing is Jason does not have his best friend with him through this exciting time. In a way, he feels guilty because his bride was his best friend's girl. Now, because he hurt her, he is not here. Jason is also worried about Jake and scared that he is just around the corner, ready to strike. He finds himself looking over his shoulder every time he is out. He definitely will not let Dawn go out alone.

Jason dropped Dawn off at home after working her last half-day shift. She was not thinking, and she went to the mailbox to retrieve her mail. She heard a sound behind her, and she turned. It's Jake. She screams, and her body tenses, and she freezes. "Oh, Dawn, I am not going to hurt you this time, but I just want to say congratulations on your engagement. Tell your fiancé to watch his back."

"Don't you dare go after him, Jake. Stay away from both of us."

"But I love you, Dawn, and Jason will pay for taking you from me."

"No, stay away from us. You need to get help. I don't know what happened to you to make you angry like this, but this is not you. You are a loving, caring person. Please get help."

Jake hung his head at her words, and pain crossed his face. "My dad began to beat me and my mom. He started with me and then went to my mom."

"Oh, Jake, please get the help you need before you hurt anyone else." Dawn's heart felt pity for him, and she wanted to hug him, but the pain of what he did to her stopped her.

"If I get the help I need, will you come back to me?"

Dawn was caught off guard with that question, and she shook her head no. She could see the anger back in his face, and he turned and walked away. Dawn sighed relief, but she knew he would go after Jason, and she couldn't let that happen.

Her heart is racing when she is back in her apartment. She dialed Jason and was scared of what she was about to tell him. "Dawn, what's wrong?"

"He was here, and he knows about us. He will come after you." Her voice was shaky, and he could hear her fear.

"Dawn, how did he get inside?"

"I went out to get our mail. I am sorry. I was not thinking."

"Did he hurt you?"

"No, he said he did not want to hurt me, but he wanted to hurt you for taking me from you."

"Please, don't go outside again. I can't lose you."

She heard his anger in his voice. "Jason, please don't be mad at me. I am okay."

"Dawn, you are okay now, but next time, you might not be so lucky. I am thankful that you will be here all day starting tomorrow so that I can keep a better eye on you. I need you to be safe."

"I am sorry, and I will stay in the apartment. I promise."

"Okay, you better!"

"Yes, sir!"

"I love you, Dawn. Don't ever forget that."

"I love you too, sir."

They hang up from each other. Then she realized that she knew why Jake snapped and forgot to tell Jason. She will let him know tonight when he gets home.

Dawn had dinner ready when Jason got home, and they sat down. Before they started to eat, Jason ran his fingers along Dawn's face with love and relief in his eyes. "I will never get tired of looking at this face."

Dawn smiled. "The same goes for you." She is touching his face. "I now know why Jake is acting the way he is."

"Did he tell you today?"

"Yes, his dad has started beating him and his mom."

"Oh no! I have always thought that there was something off with his dad."

"Jason, our wedding is less than two weeks away, and Jake is coming after you. What do we do?"

Jason replies, "I don't know what we are going to do. Nothing is going to stop me from marrying you."

The wedding day has finally arrived. Dawn stayed at her parents' house the night before, and Jason was worried about her. He can't wait until he sees her walking down the aisle.

Then his world goes black.

Dawn is excited and can't wait until she sees Jason. There is a note on Jason's dressing room door. "I will come out when she is at the end of the aisle. I would like to walk up when Dawn walks up." "Dawn, it is time," her mom tells her. They are met by her dad. Anna and Lydia go up first. Then, when Dawn and Chris are at the end of the aisle, Dawn hears gasps, and her mom say, "You are not Jason. Where is Jason? What did you do to him, Jake?"

Dawn's eyes are wide with fury. She runs up the aisle and slaps Jake. He returns the slap with a punch and knocks Dawn to the floor. He bends down and says, "I am sorry, dear!"

He tries to help Dawn up, but she pushes him away. "Why are you here, Jake? Where is my husband?"

"Your husband is right here. You have to marry me if you want to see your precious Jason alive." Jake shows her a video of Jason tied to a chair with his head down and blood on his face.

Dawn starts to cry. She stands and slaps Jake again. "You are insane. I am not going to marry you until you release Jason."

Jake begins to laugh, and he says, "That's where you are wrong." He pushes a button on his phone, and Jason cries out in pain.

"Okay, STOP!" Dawn cries out. Jake pushes another button on his phone and hands it to Dawn.

"Tell him goodbye."

Dawn grabs his phone. "Jason, I love you!" She sees his head move up, and he looks into the camera.

"Dawn, don't do this. Don't marry him just to save me. Let me go."

"Jason, I can't do that. I will never let you go. I am doing this for you so that you can live. Please live for me."

"Dawn, please don't! I love you."

"Jason, I have to do this. You are going to live for me."

Jake grabs the phone and says, "Enough," and he motions to the door to have the judge brought out. Jake hangs up the video chat. The judge starts, and Dawn is doing all she could not to cry out in pain. When it came time to say, I do, she cried and whispered, "I do!" Jake places the ring on her finger.

The judge says, "I now pronounce you man and wife. You may kiss the bride." She does not kiss him back. Instead, she spit out when Jake touched her lips with his.

Jake leads Dawn down the aisle and out the door where there is a waiting car. "Jake, where are we going? Please let Jason go. I am your wife now. Please let him go."

"Not until we make it official and after the honeymoon." Jake takes Dawn to a beautiful hotel. He orders room service, and he sets the ground rules for their situation. "You have to give yourself to me for Jason to live. If you run, he will die. If you resist me, he will die. Do you understand?"

"Jake, Jason was your best friend. Why are you doing this to him?"

"Because he took the only thing that mattered to me away, and that was you. Now that I got you back and you are my wife, you are mine."

Dawn tenses, and she knows what comes next. She starts to shake. She does not want to do this with Jake. She starts to cry, "Jake, I don't want to do this."

"Oh, Dawn, but you have to." Jake starts to kiss her, and she is rigid. She does not kiss him back. He starts undressing her, and she does not move to help him. Her body is tense, and she does not touch him. With her eyes closed, she lets him in. She is crying, but she keeps her mouth closed. She does not give him anything he needs. She can't believe that Jake is capable of something like this. The thought of Jason came across her mind, and it made her cry harder. Her thoughts stayed on Jason, and her eyes remained closed.

An hour later, Dawn is lying in the bed. Tears still stream down her cheeks. Jake is asleep next to her. She sneaks out of the bed and finds his phone. She tries the password she knows. It worked! She dials the number and pushes the video button. There, in the darkness, she sees Jason. "Jason, are you still with me?"

"Dawn, where are you? Are you okay?"

"I am okay."

Jason finally looked up at the screen, and he saw her bloodshot eyes. Her lip was cut from the punch earlier. "Did he hurt you?"

"No, but he did something else to me. I wanted it to be you! It should have been you."

"I know. I will be by your side. Hold on to us, baby. We will get through this."

"I want to touch you right now. I want to feel your arms around me. I can't wait until we can be together." She just gets the words out when she gets hit and falls to the floor again. Anger and rage hit her, and she jumps to her feet. "Look, Jake, you are going to have to stop hitting me," and with all her might, she punches him back. He is thrown to the floor, and his nose starts to bleed. "You are going to release Jason now, or I will run as fast as I can to get away from you."

"If I release him, what will you do?"

"I will stay here with you." Dawn heard Jason. "Please, Dawn, run. I can't live knowing that you sacrificed your happiness so that I can live."

"I can't run and let you die. Jason, I love you. You are going to live, and so will I. My happiness will be with you always."

Dawn then made Jake give the order to release Jason because she knew someone was helping him. She watched the video, and the mystery person untied Jason, and she watched as he left his captivity. That was the last time she saw Jason. She and Jake disappeared. Her heart was broken, but she knew she saved Jason's life. Now she has to pretend to love her life now.

CHAPTER 4

Find Away Out

TWO YEARS LATER

Dawn has lived in fear of Jake. Any false move and he might hit her. But he has not hit her since the wedding. She still longs for her old life. The life she almost had with Jason. She does not know where he is and how he is doing. Jake keeps Dawn locked from running because he threatens to kill Jason if she does. She is a housewife, and her husband keeps close tabs on her while he is at work. She has to check in every hour. The one thing he does not know is that she has been getting birth control shots because there is no way she is giving him a baby. She is not giving him the satisfaction. She still gives him herself, but she does not touch him, and she avoids at all costs kissing him. She does not tell him that she loves him. She is holding on to the hope that she will see Jason again. Jake gets mad sometimes and wonders why she is not pregnant yet.

Jason is desperate to find Dawn and has not given up since that day. He can't move on with his life until he knows Dawn is safe. Her picture is everywhere on missing-person posters. He lives his life numb, and he is closer than ever with her family. He spends every dinner with them. They treat him like he is their son. They hold out hope that Dawn will be home soon. Jason decided to take Dawn's story to the news station. He hopes she is watching.

The night of her story broadcast, Jake was on a business trip. Dawn was flipping through the channels on the TV. She froze on the news station that had her picture on it. The show just started, and then his face popped up on TV. Jason is on TV, wanting her back. He looks bad, and she can see his love for her. Katie, the anchor, was the one asking him the questions.

Katie: How long has it been since she disappeared?

Jason: It has been two long years.

Katie: What do you think she is doing?

Jason: I hope she is well and doing whatever she can to come home.

Katie: If she is watching, is there a message you want to tell her?

Jason: Yes, there is. Dawn, I hope you are watching. No matter what he has threatened you with, please come home. Do what you can to come home. We will face him together. I love you, and I want you back in my arms.

He has tears coming down his cheeks as he says those words. She has to come up with something that will get her home. Jake made sure they lived far away from her family. She is at least twenty hours or more away from them. She has no vehicle to take her home. She does not know if she has collected enough money to take her home. Before the news went to commercial, Dawn pauses the TV on Jason; and she drops to her knees in front of the TV and cries like she never cried before. She was glad that Jake is not home, and he left that day. He won't be back until Friday. He does monitor her phone; and when he calls, he video chats her so that he knows where she is. She is afraid to call her family. Jake knows every call she makes, but he does not know what she is saying to the people on the other end.

She decides to risk calling her mom. "Mom, it's me, Dawn."

She hears a gasp and a cry. "Hold on, dear. I will put you on speaker."

Dawn then says, "I want to come home."

The next voice she hears is a sweet one, and she starts to cry. "Dawn, I love you. I am coming to get you. Where are you?"

She tells him the address. "He won't be home until Friday. Jason, I saw the broadcast. It was so good to hear your voice. I love you."

"I will be there tomorrow," Jason says, and she can hear him getting his keys."

Then she heard her dad say, "I am coming with you."

For the first time in two years, Dawn feels hope. "I have to go now. I will see you tomorrow." Dawn hangs up. Then the video rings, and she pushes answer. "Hello, wife. What are you doing?"

"I was just getting ready to go to bed. How was your day today?"

"It was good and productive. But I miss you."

"I bet."

"What is wrong with you?"

"I am good, just tired."

"Well, sweetheart, go to bed. Get some rest. I will see you on Friday."

"Okay, looking forward to it."

"I love you." She responds with what she always says, "Okay, yes! Good night. Sleep tight, dear."

"Good night, sweetheart." She hangs up, and she sighs a relief. He did not mention the phone call before his. She can't wait until tomorrow. She will see Jason and her dad. She sleeps well knowing she will be going home tomorrow.

The next morning, Dawn gets up refreshed and ready to see her favorite men. She looks around the house, and she determines there is really nothing she wants. She packs a couple of clothes, and she leaves her wedding ring on the counter. She kept the engagement ring. That one is from Jason. She did get a couple of phone calls from Jake, and she pretended to be cleaning the house. Ten hours after she wakes up, a car pulls into her driveway; and she is out the door before the car doors are open. The doors open, and out step Jason and her father. She runs and jumps into Jason's arms and lands kisses all over his face. Then she releases Jason and wraps her arms around her dad. Dawn made sure that her cell phone is on the counter with her wallet and wedding ring. She has her bag, and she is in the car before they can say hello, and they pull out of the driveway. Dawn and Jason are in the backseat as her dad drives.

Jason has his arms wrapped around her, and he is never letting go. She feels good in his arms. He can't believe she is here with him. Dawn curls up and falls asleep. Jason also falls asleep, curled around Dawn. Chris loves the scene in the backseat. They are finally together, and it is finally perfect.

On their way home, they stop at a couple of places to take breaks. At one point, Jason got a phone call from Jake. "Where is my wife?"

"Jake, I have no idea. You are the one who took her from us. Where is she, Jake? What did you do to her?"

"She is gone. She left me."

Jason smiled and said, "She is out there somewhere by herself, and you have no idea where she is. Jake, she is your responsibility, and you are not protecting her." Jake did not like that answer and hung up.

Dawn smiles and says while looking from Jason's eyes to his lips and back again, "I am your responsibility now," and she plants a kiss on his lips. "You got that, right?" They get back on the road. Jason is driving, and Dawn sleeps peacefully in the backseat.

They finally pull into the driveway, and it is a new house. Dawn wakes and asks, "Where are we, Jason?"

"This is a new house for us, Dawn. If Jake does come after us, he will not find us."

"This is nice."

"Come, let me show you the security that we will have." Jason gives her a tour of the new house. As he showed her their bedroom, her mom and sister were hiding in it. In unison, they yelled, "Surprise!" Dawn is overwhelmed, and she starts to cry, and she runs to hug her mom and sister. "I thought I would never see you guys again."

Lydia holds both of her daughters tightly and says, "I am never letting either one of you go."

Jason walked over to Dawn and asked, "Are you tired any?"

"No, why?"

"Are you ready to be my wife?"

"Yes, but can we?"

"Yes, we can but not through the state yet until we cut ties with Jake. But we can be husband and wife through the church for now."

"Okay, let's do this."

They walk downstairs, and in the living room was a pastor ready to perform a wedding ceremony. Moments later, they were husband and wife. Just before Jason kissed her, he said, "Finally!"

CHAPTER 5

The Escape

Jason and Dawn left the country for a while. They decided to stay away for two months so that they could be far away from Jake. They explored England and Ireland. They met some interesting people there. While overseas, Dawn filed for annulment. If she files for divorce, he will not sign them, and she will never be fully Jason's. Their lawyers feels she has a strong case against Jake. She cannot wait to be rid of that man for good.

When the first night with Jason has finally arrived. The memories of what Jake did to her still haunts her. Dawn is shaking, so Jason wraps his arms around her. "We don't have to do this tonight. We have the rest of our lives to be together."

She starts to cry; and in between sobs, she says, "I want to do this with you, but Jake ruined me. It was supposed to be with you."

"It's okay. All I want to do is hold you here in my arms. I have been deprived of you for two years, and now that you are here, this is all I want right now. We will do the other stuff later."

She cries in his arms, and she lets out all the anger and pain of the past two years. She is finally in the arms she wants to be in, and she can't even give herself to Jason. Not yet anyway. She just lets him hold her, and she loves him even more that he is willing to wait longer until she ready. She is emotionally drained when her tears subside. She can't keep her eyes open anymore and falls asleep in Jason's arms.

For the first time, her nightmares did not happen. She slept through the whole night. She did not wake up in cold sweats. She wakes up refreshed and finds that Jason is watching her. Without words, she leans up and kisses him. In that kiss, she says that she wants him. She lets him in so tenderly and sweetly. It is so beautiful. In those moments, she is showing Jason that she trusts, honors, and loves him. She is finally where she belongs, and she is loving every minute of it. Jason had so many emotions running through his mind that he started to cry. Dawn can't remember the last time he actually cried like this. "Jason, are you okay?"

"I am. It is just that I have missed you, and I have been longing for this for so long. Now that you are here, I feel complete. This is beautiful. You are beautiful, and I love you, Dawn."

"I love you too. I am finally where I belong." They both hold each other for a long time, and they both fall asleep.

A week after Dawn sent the annulment papers, the lawyers call with great news. "Hello, Dawn, we have great news for you. Because of the forced nature of your marriage to Jake, the judge granted your annulment, and you are no longer married to Jake."

Dawn jumped up and down for joy. Then she said, "Jason and I will sign and date our marriage license and send it over to you for processing. Please have the pastor sign it also. Thank you so much for the news." After hanging up the phone, she ran to go find Jason. He was in the ocean, and she came running out to meet him. The minute she was in his arms, she kissed him. "We are official. Come, let's sign our marriage license." Jason jumps out of the water and follows his wife inside. They sign the license and seal it in an envelope and send it off. They send it classified, and they have a number to track it. They hugged each other, and they celebrated in the bedroom. Two days later, they receive conformation that the lawyers got their license, and they breathed a sigh of relief. Four days after that, they received the signed and dated license back. Dawn's smile is so bright that it blinds Jason, but his smile matches hers. Dawn puts the license in a frame just to commemorate the moment.

Jason and Dawn decides to stay one more month in Ireland. They love the scenery. It is so beautiful there. The people of Ireland are friendly, and they love their neighbors. They are a family of five with triplets, two daughters and one son. They connect with work and do work remotely with videoconferencing. The house they are renting is actually for sale. "Dawn, do you like this house?"

"Yes, I do."

"Do you want to buy it?"

"Can we afford it?"

"Yes, we can."

He shows her the bank account, and her eyes were big. "How did we get all that?"

"We worked hard for it. I have been saving even more than ever before."

Dawn looks at Jason, then looks around, and says, "Okay, let's make an offer. This can be a home away from home."

Jason says with a smile on his face, "Okay." He makes a call, and now they wait for the results, which will hopefully be there by afternoon.

The next day was when they got the results of their offer back. The owners accepted the offer, and they would settle on the house in two weeks. That afternoon, Jason got a phone call, and it is Jake. "Where is she, Jason? Is she with you?"

Meanwhile, Jason motions to Dawn to stay quiet. "Jake, I don't know where she is. I am not in the country anymore."

"You are lying, and you know where she is. She left me. She annulled our marriage."

"Good, you don't deserve her. You hurt her and forced her into something she did not want."

"I deserve her, and she will be mine. I will find her, and if I do and she is with you, you will die."

"Jake, you will seriously kill me? We were best friends. You are insane to think that she will ever go back to you."

"My supposedly best friend took my girl, and now I have no best friend and no girl."

"Jake, this is the last thing I am ever going to say to you. You ruined your relationship with Dawn when you put her in the hospital. You beat her to death. She did die, and luckily for you, the doctors brought her back because you got to spend two years with her. Now you lost her because she does not want to be with you. Her family has not seen her, and she is lost to them now. If I knew where she was, I would never tell you because you are never going to hurt her again." Jason hung up on Jake satisfied.

Dawn stared at him with shock. Then she walked over to Jason and kissed him. She then said, "You are sexy when you are defending me." He looks at her with a smile.

Two weeks later, they go and sign the papers and officially own the house. They made it home and sat down in their new living room. They were dozing off in each other's arms. The front door all of a sudden slammed open, and Jake stepped in. He took one look at the two of them on the couch and started to laugh. "I knew you were here. I knew you were lying. I now know that if I can't have you, no one else will." Jake lifts the gun and points it at them. On instinct,

Dawn stood up and quickly moved between Jake and Jason as Jake pulled the trigger. Dawn falls to the floor, and so does Jake. Jason looked up at his neighbor James and then moved to Dawn's side. Dawn is struggling to breathe. Jason is holding her in his arms while James is calling for help. Jason looked at Jake, and he was knocked out cold. Then Jason is focused on Dawn. "Please stay with me. You need to fight. Hang on." James came back with towels and held the towels on Dawn's wound. Dawn stops breathing. "Dawn, please no." Jason has tears running down his face, and he helps James begin CPR. While they were working together, Jason is asking James, "How did you know we were in trouble?"

"I saw him coming with a gun, and I knew I had to act fast. I am sorry I could not get here before he did this."

"You did your best, and I thank you for this."

The paramedics finally showed up, and they took over. Jason has Dawn's blood all over him as he watched the paramedics work on Dawn. He is paralyzed with dread, and all he can do is stand there useless.

Jason watched as they padded Dawn five times. They were just about to give up when the heart monitor started to beep. The paramedics rush Dawn to the ambulance. James offers to drive Jason to the hospital, and he takes the offer. They follow the ambulance; and on the way to the hospital, Jason calls her parents. Lydia starts to cry, and she puts Chris on the phone. Jason repeats the message. "Thank you, Jason. Please call us and keep us updated."

"I will definitely." Jason hangs up the phone. They finally make it to the hospital in time to see the paramedics working on Dawn again, and Jason's heart sinks. They get her back, and they rush her inside. Jason and James run after them. A nurse leads them into a waiting room. Jason is pacing, and James calls his wife to let her know that he is okay. He also lets her know that he will stay with Jason just to support him.

Jason is trying to figure out how Jake found them. Then he thought of the mystery person who let him go when Jake had him. The mystery person might have helped Jake track them down. Was it because Jake kept calling him? Did Jason lead him right to Dawn and now she is paying for it? James saw the look of confusion in Jason's face, and then the look of anger came next. "Jason, what is going on inside your head?"

"It is my fault. I lead him right to her. They tracked her here using my cell phone. Now she will die because of me."

"Jason, you don't know that for sure. Dawn will survive. Hold on to her. Don't let her go."

An hour later, the doctor came in and updated Jason on what was going on. "It was touch and go for a while, but she is holding on. The bullet grazed her lung and came within half an inch of her heart. She will be in her room shortly. I will have a nurse escort you. In the meantime, you have an officer here wanting to talk to both of you." Jason nodded, and the officer walked in. Both Jason and James recounted the event of the day. Then the nurse escorted Jason and James to Dawn's room. James stayed long enough for Jason to get settled. "Jason, whatever you need, please give me a call, and I will bring it to you."

Jason gave his house keys to James. "I will hold you to that. Thank you, James, for your support. I will keep you updated on her condition."

"Okay, thank you."

Jason turned his attention to Dawn and held her hand in his. He let tears run down his face, and he said, "Why did you do that for me? It should be me lying here, not you. I love you, Dawn. Continue to fight please. Stay here with me." Jason watches Dawn sleep, and he falls asleep with his head on her arm.

A couple of days has gone by, and still, there's no change in Dawn's condition. Both James and his wife, Amy, have been checking in on Jason. They bring him whatever he needs, and they sit with Dawn while Jason is in the shower. Dawn is slowly healing, and she hangs on. Jason is in the shower, and James is sitting with Dawn. She starts to open her eyes, and she looks at James. He realizes she is looking at him, and he says, "I will go get Jason."

James slowly peeks into the bathroom and tells Jason the good news. Jason rushed to finish putting on his shirt, and he was out by her bedside. She opened her eyes again and smiled. "Hello, beautiful!"

She whispers, "Hello, handsome."

James smiles and excuses himself from the room and calls Amy to update her. Jason stares at Dawn and says, "I thought I was going to lose you."

"I was not going to go anywhere," she whispers.

"How are you, darling?"

"I am a little sore and stiff but good."

Jason started to move her limbs and massage life back into her hands, arms, legs, and feet. He let her fall back to sleep, and he curled up next to her and fell asleep himself.

CHAPTER 6

The Stress of Not Knowing and The Results

Two weeks later, Jason and Dawn are both home. Dawn is under strict orders to take it easy. They are also updated on Jake. He was sent back to America to face trial. Dawn can't travel, and Jason has to go back to America to testify at Jake's trial. Amy and James agree to help Dawn in Jason's absence. Jason says his goodbyes and hops on the plane. Jake does not know that Dawn survived his gunshot. He is not counting on her testimony that Jason will bring to the trial via video chat.

The day of the trial has arrived. Jason is sitting in the courtroom with Dawn's parents, waiting for it to start. Everyone starts to file in, and the trial starts. The lawyers gives their opening statements. Then their first witness is Jason. The lawyers ask their questions, and Jason answers. Then they call Dawn, and Jason turns on his phone and calls her on video. Jake's face said it all. He was shocked that Dawn was still alive. Jason faced the phone to the courtroom. Dawn gave her chilling testimony. She started with the time he almost killed her and then his forced wedding while threatening Jason. Then her more recent event. The lawyers asked their questions and then dismissed Jason. Jason kept Dawn on the phone during the rest of the trial. It was Jake's turn to say why he did what he did. The lawyers asked him questions. They then asked him what he did to track down Dawn. A couple more witnesses testified, and the judge went to his chambers to go over all the testimony and evidence.

After an hour of going over the information, the judge comes back to the courtroom. The bailiff asked Jake to rise. The judge began to speak, "After careful consideration, I have no choice but to find Jake guilty of the crimes he's being accused of. Jake, you are sentenced to a life in prison with no chances of parole." Jason saw relief on Dawn's face. Then she started to cry. Jason could see the pain on her face as she let it all go. Jason saw all her emotions go through her face, and he could see Amy wrap her arms around Dawn. "Baby, I will be home soon. I love you."

"I know. I will see you when you get home. I love you," she says that in between her sobs.

Before Jason hangs up the phone, he says, "Amy, thank you for being there for her."

"You are welcome, Jason. Please stay safe."

"I plan on it. I will be on a plane later today. Can you have James pick me up at 3:00 p.m. tomorrow?"

"Sure, no problem."

"Again, thank you both for all your help. You guys are great neighbors."

Amy says, "Right back at you."

Jason hangs up the phone. Jason discusses their plans on coming home with Dawn's parents. Lydia says to Jason, "Listen, son, stay there as long as you want to. There is no rush to come home. Dawn seems happy over there, and that is the way we want to see her. Plus, we now have a great vacation spot to go to."

Jason smiles and says, "Okay." Jason said his goodbyes and got ready to go to the airport.

A couple hours later, Jason is on a plane headed home. He can't wait until he is home and Dawn is in his arms again. He had a layover in Canada before his final stretch to Ireland. During that time, he got a call from his boss. "Hi, Jason, glad I caught you. I have something to ask you."

"Hi, Bob, what's up?"

"The company is thinking about opening up a hub in Ireland since you and Dawn are already there. We were wondering if you could head it up and become its CEO with Dawn as your right-hand woman. Are you planning on staying there on a more permanent basis, or are you coming home soon?"

"You have perfect timing, Bob. I have decided to live in Ireland. I just have not told Dawn about the idea yet. But I would love to head up the project in Ireland."

"All right, I will send you all the information of what we are looking for, and your next task will be to find us a location to build."

"Okay, Bob I am looking forward to it. We will talk soon. They are calling my flight."

"Okay!"

Jason hangs up the phone and sends a quick text to Dawn, "Just wanted to say I will be home soon. They are calling my flight. Got some news for you. I love and miss you! XOX."

She sends one back to him, "Okay, looking forward to you and the news. I love and miss you too! XOX."

Jason turns off his phone with a smile. Jason boards the plane and settles down for a nap. Jason wakes to the stewardess saying, "Sir, we are about to land. Just wanted to let you know."

"Thank you." Jason sits up and prepares for their descent onto the runway. It was a soft landing; and before Jason knew it, they were at the terminal, and out of the plane he went. He saw James right away. "James, how would you like us as your neighbors for now on?"

"Oh yes, that will be great. We don't have to see the house empty anymore."

Jason looked at James and said, "I think this is a start to a beautiful friendship. Best friends even."

James smiled and said, "I think you are right."

When Jason and James walked through the door, Jason's first task was to scoop Dawn up into his arms and hug her as tight as he could. She wrapped her arms around Jason and then said, "Okay, Jason, I can't breathe."

He released her and said, "Oh, I am sorry. I have missed you so much."

She replied with a smile, "So what is the news you have for me?"

"Our company is planning on building a hub here in Ireland, and we are elected to head up the project. The first task is to find a location to start building."

James spoke up, "I know of the perfect place."

Jason replied, "Can you take us to see it?"

"Yes, we can go right now."

James, Jason, and Dawn pile into James's car; and he takes them to an empty lot with a for-sale sign on it. Jason looks at the lot and then looks at Dawn. "This is a huge lot. Do you think it will be big enough for what we want?"

"Yes, it looks good." Jason calls Bob. Jason gives him the information.

"Jason, you work fast."

"I had help from a great friend."

"I will get this approved by the board, and I will get back to you on the next tasks."

Not even a week later, Bob calls back with the approval, and they start making plans to buy the lot. The next day, the land is theirs, and the groundbreaking ceremony is scheduled for next week. But Dawn has better news. She plans to tell the news over dinner and in the presence of their best friends, Amy and James. She gets everything prepared and anticipates a very great outcome.

The table is set, and everyone gathers around it. Amy and James's kids are giggling at the faces Jason is making just to make them laugh. Jason's plate is covered by a brown envelope. Jason looks at Dawn. "What is this?"

"Open it and find out."

He picks up the envelope and opens it while looking at Dawn. Then he focuses on what he is holding. "Are you serious?"

Dawn smiles. "Yes."

Jason has tears of joy coming down his cheeks. "I am going to be a father!" He studies the sonogram. He just can't believe his eyes. Then he realizes there is more than one in the picture. "Wait, there are three!"

Dawn smiles again. Then she looks at Amy and James, "We would like you two to be their godparents."

Amy replies while grabbing James's hand, "We will be honored to accept."

Jason is still speechless, staring at the picture. He then drops it and stands up. He immediately lifts Dawn up into his arms and whirls her around in excitement. That moment, Jason realizes his dream has come true. Even though he lost a best friend and his heart ached for Jake, he could not have asked for a better life now because of that loss. He has the love of his best friend Dawn as his wife. He also gained two more best friends in Amy and James. He looks forward to watching his kids play with their kids. Life can't get any better than this.

AFTERWORD

Eight months go by, and work on the building is almost complete. Dawn is ready to explode and can't wait to meet her three little monsters; and at the moment, they are active. They seem to be cage fighting in there. Then she feels an unfamiliar pain in her abdomen. She doubles over in pain. "Jason, I think they are coming." Jason comes running and sees his wife on the floor. He helps her to her feet and retrieves the hospital bag. In one swift motion, they are in the car, heading to the hospital. At least, this time, Dawn is awake; and hopefully, it ends in happiness. Jason calls Amy and James from the car.

They get to the hospital, and Dawn is breathing heavy and is in a lot of pain. She is trying not to scream. She is holding her tongue and lets her pain come out through her hold on Jason's hands. Her ob-gyn takes one look at her and says, "Oh yes, they are coming." They rush her to a delivery room, and Jason is in tow.

After twenty minutes of pushing, Dawn has her first child. It is a boy. They named him Joseph. Twenty minutes later, another boy comes into the world. His name is Joshua. Just when Dawn is gasping for breath and running dangerously low on energy, the third and final child is born, and it is a girl. They named her Jasmine. Dawn takes one look at her three children, smiles, and falls asleep. She is so exhausted that she can't stay awake any longer. Jason lets her sleep and checks on his kids. They all look healthy, and they have their ten toes and ten fingers. All three are crying, and Jason picks up each one in turn. Dawn's ob-gyn says to Jason, "They are perfect and healthy." Jason smiles as his heart beats a totally different beat.

Dawn wakes five hours later to the sight of Jason feeding one of the kids. "Wow, what a beautiful sight. How are they?"

"They are perfect. How are you?"

"I am good now. I am ready to see my kids."

Jason hands her Joshua, and she finishes his feeding. Jason then picks up Jasmine, and he checks her over. She is content in his arms. Then Joseph starts to cry; and at that moment, surprise guests walk in: Lydia, Chris, and Anna. Dawn is so happy to see her family all together. Another thing that makes this day special is when their new best friends are there sharing in their joy. Lydia immediately picks up Joseph, and he quiets down. Then Anna walks over to her sister's bed and peeks at her nephew in her sister's arms. Dawn hands him over to Anna, and tears of joy comes down her face. The moment is so beautiful it causes Chris to break down for the first time in a long time. This could not have been possible if Jason never made the news report that brought his daughter home. He is grateful for his new son-in-law and proud to be a part of this beautiful family. This is the life now, and he could not ask for more.

A SURPRISE LOVE

CHAPTER 1

The New Life

She is an unpublished writer just starting out. She just moved into a new apartment. She is a single woman, and she likes to catch up with some of her favorite people on social media. She has her best friends on Facebook. Her last family member had just passed away a couple of months ago. Her uncle has been her guardian since she was ten. Her parents had left her on his doorstep and never looked back. She is now twenty, and she moved about twelve hours away from her best friends to afford a decent place to live. She is living on the money her uncle left her, and she is counting on her first book to be published so that she can live comfortably. She has invested some of the money he left her so that she is safe for now. She sent her first book out to publishers, and she is waiting for someone to pick it up. She loves to write crime stories with a love story behind it.

She is feeling kind of lonely right now. She decided to create a profile, and she started following her favorite TV shows and movies on Instagram. A message popped up, asking for her to accept a conversation. Her eyes opened wide when she saw the name. The name is an actor on some of her favorite movies and shows. Tori asked herself, *Could this be happening to me? I am just a simple writer.* She is

319

staring at her computer screen, the pointer hovering over the Accept button. *Why not? What can it hurt?* She clicks Accept, and the word *hello* comes up. He is an actor who is so sweet, and the way he honors his costars is amazing. Now he wants to have a conversation with her. He has gorgeous eyes, and his smile is intoxicating. He looks handsome with a little scruff on his jawline and around his mouth. His body is finely sculpted, and she loves how he shares his talent. He is great at his job, and his passion shows on screen. At the moment, he is single. Not dating anyone, not even one of his costars. Tori is one of those girls who want to get to know people as who they are, not what they do. He is famous, and he is exciting to talk to, but she is hoping to get to know the person he is. His name is Ryan, and he is reaching out to her.

She does not normally do this, and she is not sure if he is who he says he is. She is hoping he is who he says he is. She proceeds with caution. She writes back to him, "Hello!"

He writes, "What is your name?"

She responds, "It is Tori."

Ryan: It is nice to meet you. That is a pretty name. What do you do for a living?

Tori: Thank you. It is nice to meet you. I am a writer. I have not published anything yet, though.

Ryan: Interesting.

They converse back and forth. She is loving where this is going. They talk for two hours. She is answering questions, and she is asking questions. She starts to yawn. The only problem with their conversation is she is three hours ahead of him. She lives on the East Coast, and he lives on the West Coast.

Tori: Its getting late here, and I should go to bed. I will talk to you tomorrow. Sleep well, my friend. I really don't want to end this conversation.

Ryan: Neither do I, but you need to get some sleep, and I look forward to talking with you tomorrow.

Tori's heart is leaping for joy. Can this be possible? Is this really him? She falls asleep dreaming of him. She wakes smiling at the thought of possibly falling in love with her new pen pal. But what if it is someone impersonating him? She wants so much for it to be him. She retrieves her phone and sees a message from him.

Ryan: Good morning, Tori.

She smiles and types a message back.

Tori: Good morning, Ryan. How are you today?

She waits five minutes, and then a reply pops up.

Ryan: I am good now. How are you?

Tori: I am good also.

Ryan: What is on your agenda today?

Tori: I will be working on a book today.

Ryan: Okay, can I ask you if you are single or married?

Tori: Yes, and the answer is I am single.

Ryan: That's good to know.

Tori: Why is that good to know?

Ryan: It gives us freedom to get closer to each other.

Tori smiles at the thought of getting closer.

Tori: Oh, really, you want to get closer?

Ryan: Yes, I want to know everything about you.

Tori: Why me?

Ryan: You are true, and you seem to be genuine.

Tori: You got that from our conversation yesterday?

Ryan: Yes, I did. This is all new to me, and it is exciting. Will it be too much to ask for a picture of you?

Tori smiles at the thought of sending him a picture, but she is nervous. What if he does not like what he sees? Will the picture end their relationship?

Tori: I would like to, but will it end our relationship if you don't like what I look like?

Ryan: No matter what you look like, it will not change my mind about you.

Tori: Okay, here it comes, but if I send you a picture, you have to send me one in return but a now selfie, not any picture from the Internet. I want one of my own not seen by anyone else but me. She opens her camera app on her phone, and she takes one with her eyes closed, looking down and smiling. She sends it off to him.

Ryan: Wow, so beautiful.

Tori's cheeks blush, and she is feeling admiration for this man.

Then a picture of him pops up on her screen. It is a selfie of him with a grin that will light up a room. His blue eyes are gleaming in her direction. Her heart skips a beat as she gazes into his eyes. She sees love and caring in his eyes.

Tori: Thank you. You look amazing in the picture.

Ryan: Thank you. You will be the only one to see this picture.

Tori: I feel honored.

Ryan: As you know, I am in California shooting a movie right now. But it is almost done. I was thinking I could come and visit you. I would like to meet you.

Tori's heart skips another beat as she thinks of seeing him in person.

Tori: I would like that very much.

Ryan: Are there private airports around you?

Tori: Yes, there is. We have two in the area. I can give you my
       number and have your people call me, and I can give them
       direction.

She types out her number and sends it.

Ryan: Thank you. I will give this to my manager. They are calling
       me to set. I have to go. We will talk later.

Tori: Go have fun. Be epic!

Ryan: Just for you, I will.

She signs off, and she is smiling from ear to ear. Her day is bright
and inspiring. She still can't believe a hot actor wants to talk to her.
She spends the next five hours writing away at her laptop. The ideas
and words are just flowing out of her. She has found her inspiration.
Tori took her already-typed ten-chapter book and made it into thirty-
chapter book. She then got a phone call.
   "Hello!"
   "Hello, Miss Tori, I am Ryan's manager Justin. He tells me
that you know of airports we can land at that won't draw to much
attention."
   "Yes, the bigger one of the two is called Chester County Airport."
   "Thank you, Ms. Tori. Ryan is asking if we contact you in time,
could you meet him at the airport, and does your vehicle have tinted
windows?"
   "Yes, my windows are tinted, and I own an Audi Q5."
   "That is good. He has two more weeks of filming left. I will
contact you with more details."
   "Okay, I look forward to it. Thank you, Justin."

"You are welcome, Ms. Tori. One more thing: please don't tell anyone."

Tori hung up the phone. She cannot contain her excitement. She looks around at her apartment. It is clean and organized. She then goes down to her car, and she makes sure it is spotless. She returns to her apartment, and now she sits down at her computer, and she realizes there is a message from Ryan. She opens it. She sees a play triangle, and she touches it, and it plays the video. Ryan is walking to his trailer as he makes the video. "Hello, Tori I feel this is better communication at this moment. I hear you have talked to Justin. I look forward to meeting you in two weeks. I hope these two weeks go fast. For now, we can get closer as we talk for the next two weeks."

Tori is excited, and she just can't believe it. Tori sees the video icon, and she touches it. The phone starts to ring, and his face comes up on the screen. "Hello, beautiful. It is nice to see you in person."

All Tori could do was smile and blush. Then she was able to say, "Hello, it is nice to see you in person." Tori's smile is so bright, and she can't hold it in.

Ryan says, "You are killing me with that smile of yours. I can look at it all day."

Tori smiles even bigger. "Can you now?" Then she says, "I can't believe this is real. You are talking to me through video, and I still can't believe it."

He says, "I know the feeling. I have never done this before. I am intrigued." She felt an instant connection with Ryan, but does he feel the same way? He confirms it in his next words. "Do you feel that? It feels like we have known each other for years." Tori smiles again, and Ryan says, "There you go again, killing me!"

He smiles right back at her, and she says, "You have an intoxicating smile, and I can stare all day at that." They talk for another two hours, and she tells him about her past and how her uncle raised her. Her uncle taught her how to love and care for people. Her parents just tolerated her and did not do much parenting as she grew. She is so happy that they left her with her uncle. Her uncle is her dad's brother. Her uncle rescued her from a dark future, and to that, she is grateful.

Ryan says, "Well, they are calling me for my next scenes. I will call you again when they are done."

"Okay, I look forward to it. Again, be epic."

Ryan smiles and says, "You make me epic."

With a smile, she disconnects the call, and she just melts into her couch. She then goes over to her laptop and starts to type a new book idea. The words were just flowing out; and before she knew it she had seven chapters written before her phone rang again. It is two in the morning for her, and it is eleven his time. Tori touches Answer, and Ryan's face comes up on the screen. Ryan smiles when he sees her. "Hello, beautiful."

Tori smiles. "Hello, handsome."

"I am sorry I did not realize what time it was over there. Were you sleeping?"

"No, I was actually writing. I have been writing since we hung up earlier."

"Wow, I can't wait to read what you wrote."

"I would love to share it with you. You just have to wait until you are here to read my first book."

"Oh, you are going to make me wait."

Tori smiles. "Yes, I am. Before I forget, I don't know where you are staying when you are here, but I have a second bedroom if you don't want to draw attention to yourself."

"I may take you up on the offer. It would be nice not to have to dodge the cameras."

"Just in case, I will prepare the bedroom for you."

"Okay, sounds good."

They talk more about their history and what they like and dislike. Tori loves to hear all about the person Ryan is, not what he can do. She enjoys getting to know him as a human instead of a man in the spotlight. "Tori, what are you thinking about right now?" He read her face.

"I was just thinking about how I love getting to know you as the person you are and not what you can do. I am not the type of person who screams and swoons over meeting a famous person. I will be excited to meet you, but I will not go crazy when I do."

Ryan smiles and then says, "Well, that makes one of us. I may go all crazy when I meet you or weak in the knees."

Tori laughs and then yawns as she walks to her bedroom. "I should let you go so that you can go to sleep," Ryan says to Tori.

Tori says, "No, not yet. I want to talk to you more."

"Okay, we can talk until you fall asleep."

Tori tells Ryan to hold on as she steps out of view long enough to change for bed. She then slips under the covers, and they talk until she falls asleep.

The next morning Tori wakes, and she sees Ryan asleep still on the phone, and she watches him sleep. He has a little smile playing on his lips, and his slow steady breathing is so sweet. He stirs, and his eyes flutter open, and he looks straight at Tori. "Wow, you look beautiful in the morning. This is a first for me. I have never slept with anyone before."

"Are you serious?"

"Yes, I am. In my personal life, I have never woke up next to a woman."

Tori teases him a little. "But you did not physically wake up next to me. You kept the video running."

"Yes, but it was great watching you sleep. You looked so sweet when you are asleep."

Tori smiles, and they talk some more. They even make and eat breakfast together while on video chat.

For the next couple of days, Tori and Ryan were inseparable when he was not doing scenes. The minute their eyes fluttered open in the mornings, they either were on video already or message each other. The days seem to go by slowly. But Ryan gets some good news. They wrap up the movie ahead of schedule, and he is finished filming. He rings her video chat, and she answers, "Tori, I have good news for you."

"You do? Please tell!"

"The movie is a wrap, and I can see you tomorrow."

He saw her face light up with excitement. "Are you serious, or are you just messing with me?"

"I am serious. I will land at 1:00 p.m. tomorrow at the airport you told my manager about, and I will use your second bedroom so that the cameras don't spot me. Do you have a private entrance to your apartment?"

"Yes, that is why I suggested that you stay here so that no one mobs you when they see you."

"Okay, sounds like a plan. I have to go do some interviews. I look forward to tomorrow." With a sweet smile, he signs off.

Tori's heart is filled with excitement. Then worry sets in. What if he does not like what he sees in person? What if something happens to him between now and then? Tori never felt this way toward anyone. Each time they talk, she feels the connection go deeper. She looks around her apartment. Everything looks immaculate. She has been cleaning since the call from his manager. Then she runs to the bedroom and makes sure that is ready for him to sleep in. The next thought is definitely a fan thought, *Oh my god, Ryan will be here in this room under the same roof as me. No, I don't want to think of him as an actor. He is a person first.* Tori is definitely prepared for Ryan's visit. The butterflies are flying high in her stomach, and the only way she knows how to settle them is by writing. She sits down and starts to type, and the words are flowing out, and her imagination is running and controlling her. Her biggest inspiration is Ryan.

CHAPTER 2

The Disbelief and the Butterflies

It is twelve thirty, and she is at the airport with the security guard waiting for Ryan's plane to land. The butterflies in her stomach are raging war on her. She stands there with a grin that can probably be seen from his window right now. Even though he is thirty minutes from touchdown, her uncle has taught her if you are not early, you are late. Tori made sure she was not going to miss this plane landing. She loves to fly, and sometimes she watches the planes land and take off to clear her head. She has not been flying since her uncle took her up in a plane a year before he died. The feel of soaring high above everything is an amazing feeling. She misses it so much, and she misses her uncle.

It's five minutes to touchdown. Her heart is in her throat, pounding away. She can't believe this is really happening. A man flying all this way just to meet her is hard to believe. Then again, she feels like she has known him for years, and a best friend is about to be there with her. She spots the plane making its way to the runway. Her heart pounds even harder, and she stands straighter. She can hear the pilot in the walkie of the security guard. He is asking for clearance to land, and the control tower gives him the okay. Tori's eyes stay glued to the approaching plane. The landing gear is coming down. Tori holds her breath as the wheels descend and touch the ground. Then she lets it go once the plane slows to taxi to her location on the tarmac. The plane comes to a stop just a few feet from her. The door starts to open, and the first person out the door is Ryan. He is almost running to her; and without words, he captures her lips and devours her tongue. She kisses him back; she takes every inch of his mouth with hers. She is paralyzed, and she can't move as she lets the kiss wash over her. She is lost, and she does not want it to end. He releases her, and she waits a couple of seconds before she opens her eyes. Looking back at her are the most beautiful eyes she has ever seen, his eyes liking what he sees. She sees her future in them. She never wants to close her eyes again. Ryan steps back and says, "Wow, I have been wanting to do that for a long time." Tori is speechless for a moment, taking him in as he stands in front of her. Ryan laughs. "I guess I took your breath away."

Tori nods and says, "You took more than that away. I had butterflies, and now they are gone. I also had worries, and now I have no idea what I was worried about."

"I am glad I could help you." Ryan stepped back and looked at Tori from eyes to feet and back up again. "You are so beautiful. Where have you been all my life?" "I have been here waiting for you."

Ryan smiled and wrapped Tori in his arms. Then he said, "I am guessing by this action you know what I want to ask you."

"Yes, you want me to be your girlfriend."

Ryan smiled again. "You will honor me if you are."

Tori looked into his eyes, and she responded with a longing, wanting kiss. She let him know that she wanted him in her life. Then she confirmed it with a yes.

Tori asked Ryan, "What do you want to do while you are here, and how long are you here for? How are we going to do this relationship?" All her worries are slowly coming back. Tori never had thought that she would ever find love like this. Then the thought that rocked her a little is the fact that she would have to share Ryan with the world. But he was the world's before he was hers. Ryan looked over at her, and he could tell she was deep in thought. "What are you thinking about?"

"I was just thinking that this is all new to me. I have to get used to sharing you with your fans."

"When you get published, I would have to share you with your fans as well." He grabbed her hand and said, "We will get through this together."

Tori smiled, reassured. "How do you know I will get published?"

Ryan fished a card out of his pocket. "Because this publisher wants to read your work." As Tori pulled into the parking lot of her building, she took the card from his hand; and with eyes of surprise, she looked at it. "I have the time now to spend with you however long I want. When the movie is finished, I want to take you to the premiere. When it comes time, I want to show you off to the world as my girlfriend." Ryan lifted Tori's hand to kiss it. Then he said, "When do you want to meet with this publisher?"

"As soon as possible."

"I will set up a meeting for you. I would like to spend a little time with you before we go see your publisher."

Tori smiled. "Okay, I would like that very much. Are you hungry? I have lunch ready upstairs."

"Yes, I am starving."

"Okay, follow me." Tori leads Ryan to her private entrance. They walk inside. Tori's heart flipped a little. She can't believe that Ryan is actually in her apartment. Her dining room table was set for two, and she went to her fridge and pulled out hoagies. "These are a popular sandwich around here. This is why I asked what you liked."

"Those look good." They chowed down on the food and talked some more. Ryan asked, "What movies of mine did you watch?"

"All of them!"

"Which one did you like the most?"

She says the name of the movie, and he says, "I have to agree with you on that one. I loved doing that role."

She answered back, "I loved the love story in that movie. The connection on the screen was so beautiful. I was hoping you were together in real life, but then again, if you were, you would not be here right now."

"That was the best love story I ever did. The story was well written, and I was honored to do that role. I did think about dating my costar, but we work better as friends, and I did not want to jeopardize our friendship."

"I saw your passion in your performance. I cried like a baby when I was watching it."

"Thank you for the support. Do you want to watch it together?"

Tori said, "Why? So you can watch me cry again?"

Ryan laughed. "No, so I can watch your expression while you watch it."

"Okay, we can watch it." They settle on the couch and start to watch the movie. Tori snuggles up against Ryan. She can't help but look at him occasionally. She can't believe she is watching a movie with a man who is in the movie. She sees his face on the screen and then next to her. It is an amazing feeling.

They finish watching the movie, and the look on Tori's face is priceless to Ryan. Of course, Tori cried again. Ryan was smirking a little. "I am not going to watch any more movies with you if you laugh at me," she said with a smile.

"I am sorry. You are so cute when you cry over a movie."

"Okay, you are forgiven this time. Next time, you are warned."

"Yes, ma'am," Ryan said with a mischievous grin.

They talk some more, and Tori tells him about her parents before they left her behind. "My parents were the type of people who loved to party, and they partied with friends every night. They were drunk and high all the time. They tolerated me and ignored me. My uncle gave me what I needed when they didn't. That is why they left me at his doorstep. He is the reason I can love someone. I am grateful for my uncle. He saved my life."

"Wow, Tori, that is a great story. I am glad he did that for you." Ryan tells her more about his family. "I come from a small family, and both of my parents sacrificed to get me where I wanted to go. They dreamed my dream with me. I repaid the sacrifice when I made my break in the first movie. They are so proud that I am what I have always wanted to be."

"I love your story more. I would love to meet your parents."

"I would love for you to meet my parents also. We will go soon. I love the fact that you want to meet my family."

Then Tori asked, "Do you have any other family here?"

"No, just me and my parents."

Tori switches the TV back to cable and sees a *Watching the Stars* show. The host says, "We just downloaded some footage from a little town in Pennsylvania when our Ryan was spotted kissing an unknown girl. They were lip-locked and very comfortable. We will keep watch."

Tori's mouth drops open, and she is shocked. Ryan hangs his head. "I am sorry, Tori. If I knew someone was watching, I would have waited until we were here before I kissed you."

"Ryan, it is okay. If I want this, I have to get used to being in the spotlight with you. I have to get used to your adoring fans and women throwing themselves at you."

"You should not have to get used to anything. I am sorry you have to. But I want this relationship to work."

"Ryan, I am willing to do whatever it takes to be with you. I think I am ready to live your life with you."

Ryan looked at Tori with a loving, surprised look on his face. He can't believe Tori is really saying that. "Are you sure of what you just said?"

"Yes, Ryan, I want to be with you. I have the kind of career I can pick up and take with me. I want to be by your side always."

"You will really sacrifice your life for me?"

"Yes, I have nothing holding me here. I have everything to lose if I don't go with you." Tori then looked into Ryan's eyes; and with passion in her voice, she speaks the three words that she thought she never would speak again, "I love you!"

Ryan seems to stop breathing; but in one look, he replies, "Tori, I have never been so sure about what I am about to ask until now. My heart is leaping for joy. I have never felt this way before. You fill my heart with love and honor. I would not be complete until you agree to be my wife. Please take my hand and be my wife. I can no longer live without you by my side."

Tori looked down for a second and back up at Ryan; and with a smile that lit up his whole world, she said, "Yes!"

Ryan captures Tori's lips with his; passion and love course through the kiss. Ryan released Tori and ran to his bag. He digs out a small box. Tori arcs to see what he has in his hand. Then she freezes when she sees the box. "You had this planned!" Ryan smiled and dropped to one knee.

He opened the box and presented the ring to Tori. It is gold with three princess-cut diamonds on it. The middle diamond is two carats, and the two on either side are one carat each. Tori picks it up out of the box and places it on her ring finger. She says out loud, "I can't believe this is happening, and I have an idea. Are you okay with inviting the world to the wedding? I want the world to know that a wonderful man has captured my heart."

"Okay, sounds good, but before we get married, I want to get you published and read your writing."

Tori smiled. "It just so happened that I have the only copy." She retrieves the copy of her first book and hands it to him.

"Yay, I will take that." He opens to the first page and starts reading. Meanwhile, she is typing away on her laptop, working on the second book. As he reads, she can hear his gasps and laughter. He even had tears running down his cheeks. Ryan was so lost to Tori's book that he did not realize that she put dinner in front of him. Ryan just started chapter 20 when he looked up from the book. He took a deep breath and inhaled the smell of the food on his plate. "Wow, that smells really great." He looks at the food. "Steak! How did you know?"

"I found out in one of your interviews. When I saw your first movie, I wanted to find out more about you, so I googled you."

Ryan smiled. "I like the fact that you know me more than I thought you did. Now I will have the rest of my life to fall more and more in love with you."

Tori looks at him and asks, "Why did you pick me of all people to talk to?"

"It was because of this smile," and he shows her the picture that made him fall in love with her. In her picture, she had a sweet smile, and it made Tori look content.

Tori then said, "That was when I realized that my uncle saved my life. In that moment, I thought to myself that my life could not get any better than you popped up in my messages. Now my life can't get any better than this."

Ryan helps Tori clean up, and he is a gentleman and takes her to her bedroom door. He places a sweet longing kiss on her lips that leave her wanting more, but she will have to wait for the rest when the second ring is on her finger. Ryan watches as she goes into her room and closes the door behind her. Tori plops down into her bed in total bliss. She falls asleep, and she dreams. Tori's dream started out with images of Ryan. Then her dream turned into a nightmare. She started to shout out no, and little screams came out. Ryan was by her side, holding her in his arms. Her body begins to relax, and she opens her eyes. She realizes that he was there, and she wraps her arms around him. She whispers, "Please stay here with me. Don't leave," and she lifts the covers to let him slide in. He wraps her in his arms, and she falls back to sleep again. She sleeps for the rest of the night, feeling safe in his arms.

She awakes in the morning with the rays of sunlight streaming on her face. She can't move. Ryan has her so wrapped that if she moves she will wake him up. She can see him sleep, and she watches him sleep. He is so sweet when he sleeps. She can't believe she will be Mrs. Ryan Cooper. Ryan's eyes open slowly, and he realizes she is looking at him. "Good morning, handsome."

"Good morning, my sweet, beautiful woman."

Ryan then says, "I want to take you out to breakfast. Any good places around here?"

"Yes, there is one right up the road."

Ryan and Tori quickly got ready, and out the door they went. They come face-to-face with cameras. Ryan stops and sighs with a grin on his face. He gives the people gathered what they want.

CHAPTER 3

Happiness

Ryan dips Tori and gives her a kiss on her lips. Then he says, "I would like to introduce you all to my fiancée, Tori Clark. Tori and I are going to pick fifty lucky fans to join us at our wedding celebration. Details will come shortly." Ryan guided Tori to her car, and they left the people and cameras behind, all with stunned looks on their faces. Tori and Ryan walked into the diner, and some heads turned. Then the look on their faces were of awe and shock. Whispers and smiles lit people's faces. Then the news report comes on TV. It shows what happened moments ago for Tori and Ryan. The patrons at the diner started to clap and cheer. Tori's face is a bright red with the light of the sun all over it. They hear congratulations and yays! Once the roar of the patrons calm down, Ryan says, "Thank you, all."

Tori is thankful that the person waiting on them is a man. She did not want to have to watch the one hundred shades of red flash across a woman's face. They place their order, and they sat in peace as they talked. They do notice a couple of glances in their direction, and Ryan decides to ask their waiter for a pen and pad, and he signs autographs for everyone in the diner. Just before their meal arrives, Ryan stands up and says, "We are also in the presence of an author in the making. Please look for her first book coming soon. Tori Clark is her name, and she is an amazing writer." The patrons clap and cheer. Tori and Ryan also hear some, "We will look forward to reading the book." Their food finally arrives, and Ryan hands their waiter the autograph slips. "Please give these to everyone in here. Don't forget to keep one for yourself."

The waiter's eyes light up and says, "Thank you so much, Ryan. I will give these to everyone." Ryan watches as people's faces light up when the waiter places one on each table. Tori and Ryan ate; and as some patrons left, they thanked Ryan for the autograph.

"Tori, what is your plan after breakfast?"

"I will like to meet the publisher that you know."

"Okay, we can go today. We are just six hours away by drive, but an hour away by plane. Which would you like travel by?"

"I love to fly, so I pick by plane."

Ryan smiles and says, "Okay!" They finish their meal and pay for it, and they head out to the car. Ryan tells Tori to head up to the airport where she picked him up at yesterday, and off they go. They get to the airfield, and Ryan tells the pilot their destination, and the pilot makes the plans, and they get the go ahead. They take off, and Tori is at the window looking down. Her face is bright, and Ryan loves the look on Tori's face. He studies every expression she makes. The happiness on her face is mesmerizing. Ryan can stare at that face for the rest of his life. Every minute he spends with Tori, the more he falls in love with her.

Ryan moves over to Tori, and he takes her into his arms and kisses her. His kiss tells her that she is the one for him. She can feel his passion, his wanting, and his love for her. They kiss until the pilot turns on the seatbelt sign, and the plane is preparing to land. The kiss left Tori wanting more, and she is staring at Ryan biting her lip with need in her eyes. Ryan does not take his eyes off her.

The plane lands and taxies to a private part of the airport. Tori and Ryan climb into a waiting car, and off they go to the publishing company. Ryan can't wait until Tori is his wife, and he stops before they walk into the building. "Tori, I am thinking after we talk to the publisher, we could get married. I can't live another day until I make you officially mine. I can't wait to officially be yours. What do you say let's get our marriage license and get married while we are here? I know of a place where we can do it."

Tori is in shock, and she is thinking about his question. With a brightness, longing, and love, Tori says, "Okay, let's do it."

Then Ryan saw a face from Tori that he was not expecting. Pain and worry flashed across her face. Then tears started to flow, and she started to shake. "Tori, what is it? Tell me please."

"My nightmare last night reminded me about something that I have forgotten. I am nervous. I want to give myself to you tonight once we are husband and wife, but my past might prevent me from doing that."

The pain in Tori's face is heart-wrenching to Ryan. He asked her, "what happened to you that has you scared?"

She calmed down a little to tell Ryan, "Remember when I told you that my parents would have parties every night? Well, their friends helped themselves to a little more than just drugs and alcohol."

Ryan's eyes were in a state of shock, and he wrapped his arms around her. "Oh, Tori, how old were you when it started?"

"I was nine, and it lasted until my parents dropped me off at my uncle's at ten years old. My parents had no idea. You are the only one who knows what happened."

Ryan looked deep into Tori's eyes and said, "I will wait until you are ready. All I want is your love and promise to be mine for the rest of your life. We have the rest of our lives for the other stuff."

Tori sank more into Ryan, and she felt his love for her. She felt even safer now. Ryan let Tori finish letting out the pain of her past. Ryan is heartbroken that someone would do that to this precious woman in his arms. He holds her, and he is rubbing her back. "I will never let anyone hurt you like that again. I promise to protect you. I will die so that you will live."

After about an hour, Ryan and Tori are in the lobby of the publishers. Tori is now nervous for a whole different reason. She is fidgeting with the hem of her shirt when the administrator comes and says, "The publisher is ready to see you. Come follow me."

They go into the office of Tia Taylor. "Ryan, it is nice to see you again." She shakes his hand. "This is the famous Tori you have been bragging about. She is beautiful. Do you have the book with you?"

Tori hands over a flash drive, and Tia plugs it into her computer. She reads the description and then the first chapter of the book. Her eyes go from shock to love in an instant. "Ryan, you are right. This is good. Here is where we go for now. We are going to work through this book together. We are going to edit it and make sure we have all the errors corrected. Then we are going to print it and create a buzz about it. Are you planning on staying in New York for a while, or should we set up a video conference?"

Ryan answered that question, "Can we do both, Tia? Because my new movie premieres will start soon, and I want to show off my girl to the world."

"Yes, we can do both."

Tori is wide-eyed and just soaking it all in. She can't believe her dream is coming true right before her eyes. She is lost in thought back at the words "Ryan, you are right. This is good."

Ryan and Tia were discussing a living arrangement when Tori snapped back to reality. "Ryan, we have a temporary apartment for the both of you. It is for when authors come from afar and needs a place to stay. It has everything you need. Here is the address, Ryan, and, Tori, welcome to Taylor's Publishing."

Tia holds out her hand to shake and hands Tori a sign-on bonus. "Tori, one more thing. Is there a dedication you want me to add to this book?"

"Yes, there is. This one is dedicated to my uncle. He saved my life."

"Okay, I will add that to the book. Now, if you two don't mind, I will have my assistant show you out so that I can finish reading this book. I can't wait to get back to it."

Tori is reeling from what just happened as Ryan guided her. By the time they are in the car, Tori says as she focuses on Ryan, "I am an author!"

"Yes, you are, and now you will become a wife."

"This day is amazing. I get to share this with an amazing man. You brought this to me. You made my dreams come true all because you love me."

Ryan lifts his hand to her face and runs it along her cheek and then places it under her chin. He looks Tori straight in the eyes; and with a tender voice, he says, "You are beautiful, and you deserve everything you get today. I love you, Tori, and I will never stop loving you. You are my life now, and I will never let you go."

The next thing Tori realizes is that they are at a wedding chapel; and she is picking out a dress and rings and signing a marriage license. Tori is walking down the aisle an hour later, and she is carrying a picture of her uncle in her hand along with a single rose that Ryan gave her. She can't believe this is happening. Is this a dream? She pinches herself. "Ow, no it is not." Tori is staring at Ryan. He is grinning from ear to ear with tears coming down his cheeks. Other people signing up to get married are realizing who they are seeing get married.

Tori could hear people say, "Oh my god, that is Ryan Cooper. We are witnessing his wedding." People are pulling out cameras and taking pictures. All Ryan could do was focus on the most beautiful sight he ever saw. Tori reached his side and took his hand. The officiant started their vows. "Do you, Ryan Cooper, take Tori Clark to be your wife to have and to hold for richer or poorer, in sickness and in health for as long as you both shall live?"

With a smile, Ryan says, "I do!" He could hear cheers coming from the crowd that has formed. "Do you, Tori Clark, take Ryan Cooper to be your husband to have and to hold for richer or poorer, in sickness and in health for as long as you both shall live?"

With the sweetest smile, Tori says, "I do." They put rings on each other's fingers, and more cheers rang through.

"I now pronounce you man and wife. You may kiss your bride." Ryan pauses just for a second to let the words sink in, and then he captures Tori's lips with his. He kissed her just like he did when he got off the plane. She felt his love, passion, and devotion to her in his kiss. Her husband is now Ryan Cooper. She is standing here in the present and still can't believe this is real.

Tori and Ryan are bombarded by cameras and people outside of the chapel. Ryan stops and says, "Okay, yes, this beautiful woman is my wife, and we are pleased to announce that we are on the doorsteps of a couple of good things. One, Mrs. Tori Cooper is now an author. Please look for her book coming out soon. Two, we are inviting fifty of our fans to a celebration party that will happen after our honeymoon. Look for the information on Instagram. Thank you for your attention, and now, if you don't mind, I have a wife to celebrate." Ryan guides Tori to the waiting car and opens the door to let her in, then walks around to the other side, and gets in after waving to the cameras.

While in the car, Ryan checked the post on the invite for the celebration. The rules are if someone wants to participate, someone has to write a short paragraph on their love of their life. There are already one hundred paragraphs. Tori and Ryan are having fun reading them. They arrive at the house that Tia set up for them and make themselves comfortable. They start to make out on the couch, and Tori could not stop Ryan's touch. She decided right then and there that she was going to let her husband in. She let go of the past and allowed her husband to help her come out of the past. She led him back to the bedroom, and he asked her, "Are you sure?"

She answered him by placing his hand over her heart and said, "Yes, I am. I can't keep living in the past and allow myself to give my husband what he deserves. Please take me."

Ryan eases Tori unto the bed, and they create something beautiful.

Tori wakes up to Ryan wrapped so tightly around her, and she can't move. Even if she could move, she did not want to. She felt comfortable in Ryan's arms. She felt complete, and she felt like she was home for the first time since her uncle died. Tori is breathing in Ryan's scent of love, and she will remember this for the rest of her life. Tori watches him sleep. He looked so peaceful, and she realized that she did not have any dreams that sent her in cold sweats and breathlessness. She feels free from her past. Ryan saved her, and she would be forever grateful. She can't believe that the man sleeping next to her is her husband and her dreams are coming true. Tori is staring at her husband and deep in thought when Ryan started to stir. "Good morning, my beautiful wife."

"Good morning, my handsome husband."

"Tori, I love this, waking up to your beautiful face. I love how you are the first thing I get to see in the mornings now."

All Tori could do is smile as she let his words sink in. "Oh, there you go again with that killer smile. I can look at it all day."

"I love that I get to wake up to you every day. I was just thinking about how much you have saved my life. You saved me from my past and my nightmares. I am forever grateful. I will love you always."

Ryan wrapped tighter around Tori. Every muscle of her husband she feels. Every inch of him is touching her. She could stay like this forever. Then her phone rings. It is Tia, and Tori sighs before climbing out of bed to answer the phone. "Hello, Tia, what's up?"

"Hello, Tori, I have good news for you. I finished your book, and it does not need much changing. We could talk them over today, then get started on the cover, and start promoting it. What do you say?"

"Hang on."

Tori told Ryan, and he said, "Yes, we can do that."

"Okay, we will be there shortly."

"Thank you, Tori. See you soon."

Tori's heart is pounding with excitement, and she is jumping up and down. She then found Ryan's lips with hers, and she placed a thankful, loving kiss on his lips. "This is all because of you that this is happening."

"You are so welcome, Mrs. Cooper."

Tori and Ryan make their way to Tia's office, and they sit down and start discussing the book. Ryan was able to finish the last ten chapters of her book as they worked through the changes. Ryan loves the ending, and he loves the fact that it came from Tori. He also loves watching Tori at work. He sees her passion and joy in her face. He is so proud of her and proud that she is his wife. "Tori, great job today, and we are finished. The next question, are you dedicating this book to anyone?"

"Yes, I am dedicating it to my uncle. 'In loving memory of Dr. Richard Clark. You saved my life.'"

"That sounds great. Did I hear you are working on the next book?"

"Yes, I have twenty chapters written already. I may have ten more left to write."

"Wow, that is amazing. Do you have it with you?"

"Yes," and Tori hands Tia the flash drive with that book on it.

"When you are finished writing the chapters, you can send them through email, and I can add them to the flash drive. Are you dedicating this book to anyone?"

Tori looks at Ryan and says, "Yes, my husband, Ryan Cooper. His love saved me."

"Wow, that is good also. If you would excuse me, I have a new book to read." Tia plugged in the flash drive to her laptop and opened the drive. Tia was settling in to read when Tori and Ryan walked out. Once in the lobby of the building, Tori wrapped Ryan in a hug. "Thank you so much for my dream came true."

"Anything for you. I love your face when your dreams come true. It is beautiful." Tori smiles and kisses him. "Now, Mrs. Cooper, are you ready to go on our honeymoon?"

"Yes, Mr. Cooper, I am."

CHAPTER 4

The New Feeling of Love

Tori and Ryan escape the cameras as they board their plane to their honeymoon. They are going to Hawaii for two weeks. While on the plane, they decided to pick the fifty lucky people; and as a bonus, they decided to also allow those fifty people to bring the person they wrote about. The love stories they read were inspiring and touched their hearts. Some stories were simple; others were detailed. Once they landed, Ryan emailed all the winners to his manager. Justin emailed back, "The press wants a statement about your nuptials, and also, your parents wanted to know when you were going to tell them about their new daughter."

Ryan writes back, "You can make a statement that I, Ryan Cooper, is in love with his bride. Will love Tori Cooper for the rest of his life. For my parents, we will visit soon." Ryan then turns off his phone so that there are no interruptions. He wants to make sure that he devotes all his attention on the love of his life.

The two weeks go in blissful love and are the best in Tori's life. They come home refreshed and more in love with each other. Ryan surprised Tori by having her two best friends Rebecca and Stacy flown to his parents' house to celebrate their marriage. Rebecca was jumping for joy when she saw Tori. "Oh my god, Tori, why did you not tell us that Ryan was the one you married? He is sexier in person. How in the world did you hook up with Ryan Cooper?"

Tori pulled her phone out and said, "This smile is what made him fall in love with me. The minute he saw this smile was the minute he wanted to marry me. He messaged me on Instagram."

"Wow, Tori what a love story." Rebecca pulled out her phone and said, "I need to get on Instagram and find me a husband."

Ryan's mom loves Tori, and she welcomes Tori into the family with open arms. Ryan's mom, Gloria, says, "Ryan, you never told me just how beautiful your wife is. I have to admit that Ryan is happier now that he has you in his life."

"Thank you, Mrs. Cooper."

"Nonsense with that Mrs. Cooper to you. I am mom. My husband, David, is dad." Tori had tears running down her face because of the love from Ryan's parents. Gloria hugged Tori. "What is wrong?"

Tori wiped her tears and cleared her throat before she spoke, "I wish my parents were like you."

"Oh dear, please tell me."

Tori filled Gloria in on what she went through at a young age. When Tori was done, she saw passion and love in Gloria's face, and she saw the love a mother could only hold. Tori's heart is hooked. Tori never felt the love of a mother or a father. She is overwhelmed with the love of a mother. Ryan and Tori headed up to bed as 1:00 a.m. neared. Ryan turns to Tori as they enter the room. Out of the blue, Ryan asks Tori, "I was thinking, where would you like to live? We could live here in California and keep your apartment for a place to go. We could sell your apartment, or we could live at your apartment."

"I will live wherever you are. We don't need to keep my apartment. There is really nothing holding me there."

"I am glad you said that because I have a surprise for you tomorrow."

She smiled and said, "I am looking forward to it." Tori snuggles up alongside Ryan and falls asleep smiling. She slept through the night without nightmares.

The next morning, Ryan wakes to bacon, eggs, and French toast, his favorite breakfast combination. Tori is there with a big smile on her face staring at him. His heart is smiling with her. "Wow, a guy can get used to this."

Tori said with a smirk, "Now keep in mind this will not be an everyday thing, so don't get used to it. I will expect scrambled eggs, ham, and French toast on occasion also."

"Oh really?" Ryan got out of the bed and wrapped Tori in a bear hug and started tickling her. He had her where she could not move from his strong arms, and all she could do was wiggle and giggle. When she did escape, she stepped away from him, challenging him in a chase. They bounded from each other in an all-out tickle war that ended with both of them out of breath on the floor. Then they both started to laugh as Ryan helped Tori to her feet. They ate breakfast as they enjoyed each other's company.

Later that day, Ryan is taking Tori to her surprise. They pulled into a long driveway with trees lining either side of it. There is a gate and a wall attached to the gate that lines the property. Ryan typed in some numbers into the box, and the gate started to open. Tori's eyes filled with wonder as she saw the house beyond the gate. The house seems to go on for miles. "Ryan, is this what I think it is? This is too much house."

"It looks intimidating on the outside, but once you get inside, it feels intimate and feels like home."

"Did you buy this, or is this yours already?"

"This is home to me already, and you living here with me makes it complete." Ryan parked the car and gave Tori a tour.

It has everything that is needed for entertainment and then some. It has tennis courts and basketball courts outside, along with a very large pool with tables around it. It has a mini kitchen outside with a grill that puts an oven to shame. Inside the house, it has a movie theater, an inside pool, a game room, a library, and a gym. It has seven bedrooms, a living room, a den, and an eat-in kitchen big enough to fit the family in and then some. Tori is in awe of the house; she can't believe that this is all hers now.

Ryan turns to Tori. "What do you think?"

Tori is still trying to soak it all in as she says, "It is a great place, and I am going to like it here." She gives a reassuring kiss. Then she says, "I am going to like it here because you are here with me."

Ryan smiles and kisses his wife with satisfaction and honor. Ryan sends people for Tori's things from her apartment so that they can get ready for the celebration.

CHAPTER 5

Claiming The Groom

Celebration day was upon them, and Tori is putting on a wedding dress. It is a simple white dress with beads for the straps of the dress, and it fits her figure perfectly. Tori is wearing her hair up partially with long brown curls dangling between her shoulder blades. There are little diamonds scattered among her curls. Tori's beautiful blue eyes shine with happiness as she thinks about her life now. Tori is a petite person with slender but muscular legs.

Ryan is wearing a black suit jacket and pants and a light-purple shirt, which he knows is one of Tori's favorite colors. His purple shirt is partially unbuttoned with no tie. Tori and Ryan meet in the hallway after not seeing each other all morning. With signed photos of the two of them on their wedding day, they enter the ballroom. They greet each one of the winners and hand them a picture. After they greet everyone, they do their first dance. Then they invite others to join them on the dance floor. Once an hour of dancing went by, dinner was served.

Everyone takes their seat. Ryan stood up and was about to give a toast to his wife when a shot rang out. Ryan instinctively jumps in front of Tori as another shot rings out. Then a woman's voice shouting came from the shooter, "Ryan is mine, and no one can have him."

Ryan is now lying across Tori's lap with two gunshot wounds. "Ryan, don't leave me. Please stay here with me. I love you. Don't you leave me."

Ryan reaches up to put his hand on Tori's cheek and whispers, "I love you, Tori." Ryan went unconscious, and Tori could see his wounds. One is in his head, and the other is in his chest. Tori had tears running down her face, and she held on to her husband as tight as she could while trying to stop the bleeding.

Meanwhile, she heard the sobs of the woman who pulled the trigger, "The bullets were meant for her, not him. Why did he get in the way? Ryan, I love you. Please survive. I am sorry, Ryan."

The paramedics were there, and the police took over for the security guards. Tori gave room for the paramedics, and she was covered in Ryan's blood. His mom wrapped her into her arms and cried with her. They watched in horror as they worked on Ryan. At this point, Ryan had stopped breathing, and they were trying to bring him back. Tori's voice is all they hear, "Ryan, please don't leave me. Stay with me."

His heart started beating again, and she dropped to her knees. The paramedics rushed him to the ambulance and then to the hospital. David drove his family to the hospital. Tori did not want to go into the hospital to hear the words he is gone. Her heart is hammering in her chest. They went in, and Tori prepared herself to hear those words. She is pacing in the waiting room. Her white dress is red, but she does not care. Ryan has to survive this. They did not get enough time together. The thoughts going through Tori's mind was overwhelming, and she felt faint. She goes down, and David catches her before she hits the floor. Gloria runs to grab a nurse to help Tori.

An hour later, Tori came back into the waiting room in a wheelchair with smiling tears. The first words out of Tori's mouth were "I am pregnant." Gloria went over and hugged Tori and cried both happy and sad tears. Tori needs to tell Ryan he is going to be a father. She wants so much to sit by his side and whisper in his ear. She needs him to hear her to hang on to her. They wait another two hours to find out how Ryan is doing.

Dr. Kelley came in, and he looked like he had been battling just to keep Ryan alive. "Ryan is hanging in there, and he is still with us. The bullet in his head missed all the vital parts. The bullet in his chest went right into his lungs. We did lose him a couple of times. He is holding on. He has the will to live. He is stable and will be able to have visitors in just a couple of minutes." Dr. Kelley gave them his room number and left them to go do his rounds. Tori stood up from the chair and put her arm around Gloria as they made their way to Ryan's room.

A couple of minutes after they got into his room, they wheeled him in. Tori instantly went to his side. "Hey, handsome, I am here for you. I do have one thing to tell you, but you have to hang on for me. We are pregnant, and you need to be here for your child. Hang on to us, baby. I am not going anywhere."

After about an hour of sitting in the quiet, Gloria turns on the TV. It is tuned in to the news station. The anchor comes on and says, "We just learned that Ryan Cooper was shot today. He was shot by a possessive fan who posed as a caterer. Her intended target was Tori Cooper, Ryan's wife. The fan is now behind bars, and Ryan is fighting for his life in the hospital. We will have more on this story as we get it."

Tori started to cry because she would have been like this if Ryan did not do what he did. He was shot instead of her, and it made her feel guilty. Gloria went over to Tori and said, "You did not do this to him, and he is fighting to stay here with us. He will make it. He will pull through. We need to get you out of this dress. I will send someone to get you some clean clothes." Gloria calls Ryan's manager to update him on his condition and get clothes for Tori.

Tori turns to Ryan. "Why did you do that for me? It is supposed to be me here, not you. I love you, Ryan. Thank you for saving my life. Now let me save yours. Hold on to me." She wraps her fingers into his, and she lays her head down onto his arm. She was asleep when her clean clothes arrived, and her mother-in-law woke her up so that she could take a shower and change.

Tori took off her dress and held it up in front of her. She can't believe that with all the blood on the dress, Ryan is still hanging on. She folds the dress and puts it in the bag that the hospital supplied. She quickly takes a shower and resumes her place by Ryan's side. Tori also realizes that her computer is in the room, and she picks it up and starts writing.

An hour later, a nurse comes in with a cot for Tori, and she gives bad news to Ryan's parents. "Unfortunately, we can only allow one person to spend the night with Ryan."

Gloria says, "We understand." She looks at Tori. "Call us the minute anything changes." Then she leans down and kisses Tori on the forehead, and David does the same and reminds her that they are only a phone call away. Gloria and David kisses their son and tell him to hang on and not to go anywhere.

Tori sighs and stares at Ryan, wishing him to wake up. He looks peaceful as he sleeps. She writes some more for another hour. Her eyes are getting heavy, and her head starts to bob. She closes her computer and curls in beside Ryan, and she falls asleep. She dreams his eyes open, and he wraps her in his arms. She stays asleep and dreams of her life with Ryan by her side. She dreams of their child playing with Ryan and Ryan scooping up their child and wrapping their child in his arms.

Tori wakes with a smile on her face. Then her smile grew bigger when she saw eyes staring at her. Ryan is awake and staring at her with the biggest smile on his face. Tori runs a hand along his check and jawline. "Hi, handsome."

He smiles again, and he slowly moved his hand to her cheek and then down to her stomach, and his smile got brighter. "You were listening." He nodded. "You know you are going to be a father?" He nodded. Tori places his hand on her heart, and she says, "You are the only one who makes my heartbeat. If you died on me, my heart would have died with you. You are my world now, and I am glad you are still in it. Please continue to fight." Ryan nodded. Then he motioned to get the tube out of his throat. Tori pushed the call button, and a nurse answered. "Ryan is awake."

"Okay, we will be right in."

Moments later, Tori was standing and on the phone with Ryan's parents as the Dr. Kelley removed the breathing tube. Ryan coughed and winced a little. Dr. Kelley asked if Ryan felt any pain, and Ryan whispered yes. He also pointed to his head. Dr. Kelley checks his wounds and orders a change in bandages. He also places an order for some painkillers. Dr. Kelley and the nurses leave to prepare tests for Ryan.

Ryan whispers to Tori, "Tori, baby, why am I here?"

Tori grabs his hand and says, "You were shot with the bullets that were intended for me. A possessive fan did not like the fact that you picked me to be your wife."

He whispered, "I will do it again if it means you are safe. I would rather be here than watching you in pain."

"I thank you for saving my life. I am proud to be your wife and the mother of your child."

Gloria and David walk in at that moment. Gloria makes a beeline to her son and wraps her arms around him. "Baby, please don't ever scare us like that again. We almost lost you."

"I know, and I am fighting to stay here."

"That you are, son."

Nurses came in and prepared Ryan to take him for some tests. Tori gave him a kiss on his lips and said, "I will be here waiting for you."

Tori is pacing again. She is nervous about the tests results of her husband when Justin calls her. "Hello, Mrs. Cooper, this is Justin. The press is demanding an update on Ryan. Can I give them one?"

"Justin please call a press conference outside the hospital. I will give them one."

"Yes, ma'am!"

Thirty minutes later, Tori finds herself stepping up to the microphones on a podium. "Hello, for those who do not know me, I am Mrs. Ryan Cooper. I am pleased to announce that my husband has pulled through. They are running some tests as we speak. He is expected to survive. He was shot once in his head and once in his chest. The bullet in his head missed all vital parts of his brain. The bullet that went into his chest hit his lungs, and it is a miracle that he survived that one. He saved my life, and I will be forever by his side. I am always going to be Mrs. Ryan Cooper. I just want to make this clear that he picked me to be by his side. I am proud of his true and loyal fans, and I know he sends his love. I ask if there are other fans out there who want my husband to be theirs to let him be mine. At this time, I thank you, everyone, for your love and thoughts as my husband works to heal and recover."

The reporters started in on their questions, but Tori stepped away from the microphone. The police sergeant stepped up and simply said, "There is an ongoing investigation, and we can't discuss the details of the case at this time. Thank you for coming out and enjoy the rest of your day."

Some of Ryan's fans were inside the hospital, and a representative of the group walked up to Tori as she made her way to the elevator. "Hello, Mrs. Cooper, I was elected by the group of fans over there to speak to you for a moment. We appreciate you coming down here to let us know how he is doing. We also appreciate what you said at the press conference. We wanted to let you know that we started a Facebook page where fans can leave congratulations and well-wishes to Ryan, to you, and his parents. She gives her the page name and asks her to look at it. "If you need anything please reach out."

"Thank you so much for your love and support." Tori pulls out her phone and looks up the Facebook page. Her heart is now filled with love for Ryan's fans. Tori looks up at Rachel and says, "This is beautiful. I will share this with Ryan. He will love it." Tori excuses herself and goes back to Ryan's room.

When she gets back, Ryan is there, and he whispers, "Well done, baby!"

Tori smiles, and she sits on his bed. "I have something to show you." She hands him her phone with the page still up on it.

He reads the description of the page "Our Hero Ryan Cooper," "This page is made to give him well-wishes. Leave a message for him here." Ryan starts to read the messages one by one. So far, there are just over one hundred messages and all of them positive. One message just came in; and it read, "Ryan, your wife is great. You are perfect together. Hold on to her. Let her know that we appreciate her giving us an update on your condition. We pray that you stay with us and you heal fast." Ryan smiled, and he decided to type out a message on the page. "Hello, everyone, this is the actual Ryan Cooper, and my wife showed me this Facebook page. Thank you for the love, support, well-wishes, and prayers for me. I have great fans, and I appreciate all of you. Please continue to send your messages. I will read them." Ryan continues to read the messages that come in. Tori is enjoying the smiles she sees on Ryan. She opens her laptop and types out some more of her story.

It was nine at night, and Ryan had fallen asleep reading all the messages. Dr. Kelley walks in with Ryan's test results. "Hello, Mrs. Cooper, we have Ryan's test results here. He has some swelling in his head, but it is going down slowly. His lungs sound clear, and his wound is starting to heal. He is a lucky man. He is now out of the woods."

"Thank you, Dr. Kelley."

He leaves the room, and Tori is alone with Ryan. She stares at him as he sleeps. She now has her joy back in her heart, and she knows her life is complete. She picks up her laptop again and finishes the last chapters of her book. She also writes a dedication, "This book is dedicated to my loving, husband Ryan Cooper. He saved my life as well, and I will be forever grateful." She sends off her finished work to Tia, her publisher. She falls asleep watching Ryan sleep. Her feet are propped up on his bed, and her head is laid back on the chair.

Tori woke with someone massaging her feet. Ryan is sitting up in bed and working on her feet. "I love your feet. I could do this all day." Tori closed her eyes in complete relaxation. Her worry for her husband melts away. Her fear of losing him is gone. The sight of Ryan actually awake and taking care of her is an amazing.

Tori was enjoying this moment, and it could not get any better until some of Ryan's costars walked in. Tori has a fan moment. One of her favorite actresses is there next to Ryan. She starred with him in one of her favorite movies. It was the one that they watched together. "Hello, Tori, welcome to the family. Thank you for putting a smile on this man's face. I have never seen him this happy before."

Tori is awestruck for a moment that Jessie is standing in front of her. "Tori, this is my best friend, Jessie. Jessie, this is my beautiful wife, Tori."

Tori finally found the words that had run from her and said, "It is a pleasure meeting you."

Jessie replied, "Actually, the pleasure is all mine. Anyone who can capture his heart like you did is a hero to me. I am honored to meet you."

Ryan smiles and says, "She loves our movie. She did tell me that she was rooting for us to be together in real life."

Jessie smiles and says, "I was thinking about it, but I like him better as my best friend even though he does have a good-kisser quality. I am happy just to be his best friend. Now, Ryan, I have to tell you, if you hurt my new best friend Tori here, I am going to have to hurt you."

"Yes, ma'am, but don't worry, I will never hurt Tori."

"Okay, good, well, I better get going. I have work to do. I am glad I get to meet you, Tori, and we will keep in touch. I would not mind having you as a cast member with me." Jessie takes Tori's cell phone and adds her phone number to it and then calls her cell phone with it to take Tori's cell phone. Jessie then leans over and gives Ryan a kiss on the forehead. "Behave yourself, sir. Listen to your doctors and wife."

"Yes, ma'am!"

She walks out. For the rest of the day, different costars came and went. Tori is just beside herself trying hard not to act like a fan. When the parade of people stopped, Tori turned to her husband and said, "I have finished my second book and sent the remaining chapters to Tia."

Ryan holds out his hands for her laptop and his wife. Tori curled up next to him as he read the dedication. His breath catches in his throat. "I love the dedication, and I love you." Ryan gets comfortable with Tori by his side, and he starts reading her book. It is about how they met. She adds to the story different things that did not actually happen, but they make the story interesting. The one good thing that Ryan learned in acting is he can speed read and understand everything he reads.

Tori is asleep next to him when he is finished with her book. All he can say is "Wow, what a story." His next thought was *This will make a great movie.* He calls his favorite producer Dan even though it is four in the morning. Ryan knew he would be up.

"Hey, Ryan, what's up?"

"I have a story for you. I can see this being a movie, and we can star in it."

"Who is *we*, and what is the story that has you excited?"

"As you probably know by now, I have a wife now, and boy, can she write. She has written a fantastic story that I can see it being made into a movie. I am sending it over to you right now. I would like to star in it alongside a new costar of mine. The beautiful, intelligent, and talented Tori Cooper. Can you make that happen?"

Dan replied, saying, "I just got the book, and just reading the first line, I can tell it is amazing. I can make this work. I will finish reading this book. Then I would like a meeting with you and Tori to turn this into a movie. Later, for now, I have a book to read." Dan hangs up the phone. Ryan wraps even more of Tori into his arms. He can't believe that this is his life now. He has a beautiful wife by his side that he would do anything for. Now he can't wait to costar next to her in a movie that she wrote.

CHAPTER 6

New Experiences

A couple of weeks go by, and Ryan has been released from the hospital just in time to be at his movie premiere. Ryan has been waiting for this night for a long time. Now he gets to go with someone that he loves by his side. Tori will get the red-carpet treatment; but is she ready for the flashing lights of the cameras, the screams of the fans, and the split attention that Ryan has to give his fans? Ryan is reassured by Tori that she is okay with it all, and she looks forward to watching her husband being adored by his fans. After all, his fans along with Tori and his family helped him through his recovery. Ryan has a plan to surprise Tori with the new movie announcement. He is not sure how much she has heard during his conversation with Dan. The two has been communicating ever since the 4:00 a.m. phone call. Ryan knows that the movie will happen, and he is excited to let her know about it. Tia is also in and promises to help with the editing needs of the script. He is also going to let the world know he will be a proud father. Tori knows about that part, and she is excited to tell everyone.

Tori is trying on her first designer dress, and she is not used to the attention. The array of dresses at her fingertips is a dream that she never thought would be fulfilled. Yet here she is at this moment being treated like a princess. She picks a form-fitting silver dress with a V-neck and spaghetti straps. It also has small diamonds along the neckline and sparkle throughout the dress. The dress falls to the floor with a small train dragging behind Tori as she walks. Tori also slips on a pair of strappy high-heeled sandals. Her hair is pulled up into a messy bun. It has curls exploding from the bun and diamonds sitting throughout the bun.

When Tori was done, she slowly walked down the stairs to the waiting arms of Ryan. He is dressed in a tux that melts Tori's heart. His hair is feathered back, and his beard and mustache are light on his face just the way that Tori loves. A couple of weeks ago, Tori thought this might never happen, but Ryan was here still. He is by her side, and they are going to watch his new movie together. She is excited and can't wait to see her husband shine.

They climbed into the SUV limo, and off they went. They wound their way to the premiere, and Tori saw faces outside of the vehicle. They are faces of wonder as the limo passes by. Finally, it pulls up to the red carpet. Tori's heart started to hammer in her chest as Ryan asked, "Are you ready for this?"

Tori nervously nodded. Ryan stepped out of the limo first, and the roar of the crowd further amplified. Ryan stops at the door and offers his hand to Tori. She grabs it, and he helps her stand to her feet. The crowd roars with excitement. Ryan never lets go of the hand he holds. But he stops to give autographs and chats with the entertainment reporters. Just before they go inside, the organizer of the premiere hands Ryan a microphone. "Good evening, ladies and gentlemen." The crowd goes quiet as Ryan starts to speak. "We will be starting production on a new movie written by my very beautiful and very talented wife, Tori Cooper." He is staring at Tori as he speaks.

Tori looked at Ryan with a huge smile. She is blown away at how much Ryan loves her and the way he looks at her in public is amazing. "We also have one more thing to tell you. We are having our first child. My wife is pregnant, and I don't have the words to tell you just how much love I feel right now."

The crowd burst out into a cheer, and Ryan signs some more autographs before going inside the theater. "Tori, I also have one more thing to tell you. We are going to star in our movie. You will be my leading lady as I am your leading man. How do you feel in becoming a costar to me?"

Tori looked at him in amazement. She never thought of herself in front of the camera. "I have never thought of myself as a movie star." Tori sighed and said, "Let's do it." She has always wanted to experience new things. She is used to telling stories, and now she gets to be a part of one of her stories with the man she loves.

They find their seats, and the premiere director steps to the microphone. "Hello and welcome to the premiere party of a fantastic movie, starring so many awesome people. Without further ado, I would like to call a wife of one of our stars to the microphone to say a few words about one of those stars now."

Tori gets up out of her seat and walks to the microphone; and Ryan's face is in awe, shock, and surprise. "Hello, ladies and gentlemen. I am Tori Cooper, and I am here to honor my leading man. A couple of weeks ago, we almost lost him, and if he had not have acted when he did, I probably would not be here today. This brave man faced death for me in my place, and for that, I am forever grateful. Tonight, I present my husband with the Bravery Award for his quick thinking in saving my life in all ways than one. I give you Ryan Cooper."

Ryan, still in shock, stands to his feet and walks to Tori's side and accepts the award with tears in his eyes. He grabs her, dips her, and kisses her so passionately that everyone in the theater seems to melt. They hear oohs and aahs as Ryan rights himself and Tori again. He steps to the microphone and says, "Thank you. This is truly an honor. I am blown away that my wife did not mention any of this. I am blessed to have a wife like Tori. She will forever be my wife no matter what happens. Now all I want to do is sit back and watch this movie with all of you, possibly make out with my hot wife in the process."

Tori's face turned one hundred shades of red as they took their seats. When they sat down, Tori stole a nice long kiss from Ryan. The movie started. Tori's eyes were glued to the screen all the while rubbing Ryan's leg. She occasionally looks at Ryan again. She can't believe she is watching a movie with the man who is starring in it.

When the credits rolled on the screen, Tori was crying. Ryan looked at her and smiled. "You still look so cute when you cry for a movie."

"That was a beautiful movie, very moving, and the love story in it is so beautiful. The way you brought the character to life was amazing. I could feel the pain, the love, and care for your costar's character in the movie. It is powerful, and I loved every minute of it. If you, your costars, and the movie don't get any rewards for this, there will be something wrong with them."

Ryan laughed. "I guess that is Tori, for you loved it."

"Yes, it is."

By the time the credits were over, there was a standing ovation. The cast stand up and took a bow. Tori watches in amazement just how much Ryan is loved. She is so proud to be a part of his life.

Ryan looks at Tori, and he sees pride in her eyes as she looks at him. The look in her eyes warms his heart. The love in his heart grows stronger for Tori. She makes him smile, and he feels honored to be her husband.

Tori and Ryan make their way to the limo, and off they go home. Tori cuddles up next to Ryan. She is enjoying his arms wrapped around her. She feels every muscle in his arms, and she is comfortable. She dozes off and dreams of their life together. When they get home, Ryan carries his wife up to the bedroom. She is still sound asleep, and he takes her dress off and dresses her in her PJs. He lies down next to her and falls asleep watching her sleep.

Ryan wakes up to fingers tickling his chest and then running up and down his hair on his chest. He smiles and says, "A guy can get used to waking up like this." Without words Tori shows him just how much Ryan completes her and just how much she loves him. She runs her hands all over his body. Then they give each other to themselves. Tori dozed off afterward, and Ryan made his way to the kitchen. With a great wakeup from Tori, Ryan decides to make breakfast for her. He brings it to her in bed. They ate together in bed, and they discussed what they were going to do for the rest of the day.

They decided to go for walks and for a picnic. They wanted to spend as much time together as they could. They wanted to do normal couple things. They also went bowling, played mini-golf, and went roller skating. Ryan even taught her how to play regular golf. He helped her with her swing, and she beat him in one of their games that they played. The more they play, the better Tori got. Ryan created a golfing monster.

Tori is a natural and now has a golfing partner and competition. Whenever they get a chance, they go golfing. When they are not golfing, they are getting ready for baby Cooper. They don't want to know the sex of the baby until birth. In between golf and baby, Ryan is doing interviews about his new movie. They are also working on Tori's movie based on her book. Tori is working with Tim, an experienced screenwriter; and she is loving his passion to keeping the movie truthful to her book. It took them a week to write the script. Then it was time to pick the rest of the cast.

As the time came close, Tori became nervous. She was never in a movie before. Now she gets to experience what comes natural to Ryan. The one good thing that Tori has is Ryan by her side. They run lines together, and he gives her pointers. "Tori, just talk to me. Pretend there isn't anyone else in the room. Pretend there are no cameras in the room. When it comes time for the cameras to start rolling, always remember these, and you will be okay." Ryan could tell that Tori was comfortable with the lines she has. After all, she did write it.

They found a perfect location for filming in the beautiful Chester County, Pennsylvania. There have been other films raving about the locations of Chester County. Tori and Ryan decided to check it out. They fell in love with most of the locations they had seen. They set up shop at an empty parking lot and transformed it into a set and marked other locations to be filmed. There is a huge deadline on Tori's part because of the growing baby bump. She did write that her character will be pregnant, but the movie does not start that way. But they had time for to film Tori before she was showing.

Filming is underway, and Ryan is loving every minute of it. He is proud of Tori. The nervousness that she felt is gone, and she is a natural at this. He is loving every scene with her. Their chemistry is off the charts. Since they are already married in real life, Ryan can get away with so many things. He does not hold back. He lets his passion, love, and care show. They match each other in every scene.

Where his strength is, it covers for Tori's weakness; and where Tori's strength is, it covers for Ryan's weakness.

The rest of the cast members are having fun as well. Each part is important in the storytelling. Jessie is one of their cast members, and she loves to watch the interaction between Ryan and Tori. To her, it is inspiration, and it gives her the motivation she needs to do her lines.

It was finally time for Tori to do the pregnant parts of her story. She loved every minute of it. Toward the end of the film, they found a pregnant woman willing to give birth on camera. She was Tori's body double when it came time to give birth. At this point in the filming process, Tori was only two months pregnant. The authenticity of that scene gave the movie an intimate feel. It just so happens that the baby born is a girl, and Tori was able to use her name for a girl if she was having a girl. The name will be Melissa Elizabeth Faith, and that is what they named the girl born on camera.

A security guard came up to Tori after they wrapped up for the day. "Mrs. Cooper, we have two people claiming to be your parents at the gate. Should I let them in?"

"No, I will come to the gate."

Ryan said, "I will come with you."

Tori and Ryan made their way to the gate; and sure enough, the couple standing there were indeed her parents. They looked a little worse for wear, and they had tattered clothes. It looks like they have not bathed in days let alone months. "What are you doing here? You let me go a long time ago."

"Darling, we are asking for your help. We are homeless, and we have not had anything to eat for a week now. We saw you on TV, and congratulations on your marriage. We are wondering if you would help us."

Tori looked at Ryan with pain in her eyes. "Let me talk to my husband. Stay right there."

Tori and Ryan both turned their backs so that their conversation could be a little private. "I can't believe this. They come crawling back after leaving me and allowing those things to happen to me. They want my help. I don't know what to do, Ryan. I have not seen them, and now they want something from me."

Ryan hugs her and says, "If you want to help them, I know how we can help. They, after all, are your parents and the reason you are on this earth."

"What do you have in mind just in case I do want to help them?"

"We are not going to give them money, but we can set them up in an apartment and make sure they have food and clothes."

"I like that idea, but can we give them an ultimatum? If they are clean, sober, and not party anymore, we will help with the rent and food until they are on their feet. Once the have steady jobs and working hard to keep the apartment, we will hand control over to them."

"That sounds like a plan."

Tori and Ryan turned around and walked to her parents. Tori sighs and says, "Mr. and Mrs. Clark, this is how it is going to work. Ryan and I will set you up in an apartment. We will help you get food and clothes. We will pay your rent until you get jobs and up on your feet. There is one condition: you are not to party. No drugs, no alcohol, or you will be kicked out and you will have no place to live. Do we have a deal?"

"Yes, darling, your dad and I are clean and sober now. We have not had parties, drugs, or alcohol in two years. We have been homeless since then also. We lost everything because of what we did. We even lost the best part of us, and that was you."

"Let me make some thing clear. You are not my parents. You never were, and the only reason we are doing this for you is because you are the reason I am here on this earth. You also left me with someone who has been taking care of me since I was born. You have that going for you. I swear, don't mess this up, or I will never forgive you. We have to close up our trailer stay here, and we will take you to a hotel until we can find you an apartment."

Tori and Ryan walked back to their trailer. Ryan says to Tori, "I am proud of you for doing this. I am also proud that you are cautious with them. Are you okay with this?"

"No, but I will be once I see them trying to improve their life."

Once in the car with Tori and Ryan, her parents asked about her uncle. "He is gone now. He died of cancer seven months ago." She saw a glimpse of pain in her dad's face. Her heart felt the same, but she did not let them know that the pain of losing her uncle was so much greater then losing them. When they reached the hotel, her mom tried to hug Tori; but because of what she smelled like, it made Tori get sick. That is when her mom realizes that Tori is pregnant. "Oh, I am sorry, dear. You are overly sensitive because of your pregnancy. Congratulations, darling. How far along are you?"

"I am two months, and I am battling morning sickness all the time."

"I was sick with you all the time also."

Tori looked annoyed at the fact that her mom is trying to bond with her. "Look, you may have given birth to me, but it does not give you the right to try to bond with me. You gave up that right when you and Dad allowed your friends to have their way with me because you were too stoned to care. Remember, I am only doing this for you because you allowed me to live with my uncle. He is the one who deserves the credit of mom and dad. He is the reason I am a wife, and I am able to allow someone into my life. He is the reason I can love Ryan. Don't darling me or try to bond with me now. You should have thought of that before you picked drugs and alcohol over me."

The look of pain in her mother's eyes was both satisfying and painful. Tori could tell that they did not know the people they partied with would do that to their child. "Tori, how come you never told us about what happened to you?"

"I did tell you, but you never remembered." Tori started to shake at the memories this stirred in her. Ryan was by her side when he realized that. Tears started to fall, and she looked away because she did not want to let her parents see her cry or the pain in her face.

Ryan then said, "Please wait in the car. I will check them into the hotel."

"Okay, thank you." Tori climbed back into the car and watched them go inside. Then she let the tears flow. Tori cannot believe that her parents had found her and now is affecting her life like this.

Meanwhile, when Ryan and Tori's parents were out of eye shot of Tori, Ryan pulled them aside and said. "If she is hurt from this, you will never see her, and you will never see your grandchild. Do I make myself clear?"

"Yes, Ryan, you do. Please forgive us for what we did in the past."

"It is not me you need forgiveness from. It is Tori. But I do forgive you now for hurting her earlier."

"Ryan, we don't want that life anymore, and we want Tori back in our lives. We will do anything to have her back. We have missed ten years of her life. We don't want to miss any more. Please help us get her back."

"I can't make promises, and I can't make Tori love you again. I support my wife in any decision she makes. You have to prove to her that you have changed and willing to put everything aside just to be her parents."

Ryan checks them into a room and gives the hotel an advance that will cover the room for two weeks. Then he gave the hotel money for any room service they would get. He also gave them strict orders not to let them make any unnecessary charges. Ryan turned to her parents and asked for them to write down their sizes and told them he would have someone drop off clean clothes for them. He handed them their room key. "I will drop by to check on you. I suggest that you start looking for jobs while you are here. I will also let Tori come to you when she is ready. Meanwhile, you will see me more often than her."

"Thank you, Ryan. Tori made the right decision when she found you. I am glad she has you in her life now."

"Thank you, ma'am."

Ryan went back out to the car and found Tori getting sick again. Her face is pale, and she does not look very good. "Oh no, Tori, I am sorry for leaving you alone for long like this." Ryan's heart sank.

"I will be okay."

"Let me get you home so that you can rest."

"Okay, thank you."

Ryan started the car and pulled into the street.

"Pull over please!" Tori quickly opened her door and got sick again. Ryan held her hair back. When she was done, she said, "Okay, now we can go." Tori leaned forward and put her head on the dashboard, which gave Ryan the opportunity to rub her back as he drove. They made it back to their temporary home while filming without any more sickness. Tori hopes that this sickness ends before tomorrow. She has a big day of filming to do. Ryan carries her in the house and up to bed. He put a trash can next to her side of the bed on the floor. He also got her some water. He grabbed something small for himself to eat. Then he went in to comfort Tori as she slept. She was lying on her side, and Ryan rubbed her back. Tori started to shake, and her body tensed up. Ryan could tell that her nightmare is back. He wrapped Tori in his arms and whispered to her, "Tori, it is Ryan. You are safe. I am right here, baby. Hold on to us."

As Tori heard Ryan's voice, she relaxed, and her shaking stopped. "That's my girl. You are safe and here with me." Tori stirred a little, then woke up quickly, and got sick in the trash can. Tori took a sip of water, then curled up in Ryan's arms, and fell back to sleep. She slept soundly for the rest of the night. Ryan hates seeing her like this, but he is glad he is here for her. He falls asleep happy that a beautiful woman is asleep next to him.

The next morning, Tori woke up to the alarm clock, and she felt for Ryan, but he was up already. She hears water running, and she gets up out of bed and in the direction of the water. Tori was a little groggy from the night before; but when she entered the bathroom, she heard, "Good morning, beautiful. Come take a bath with me." She smiles and wraps her arms around Ryan. She rests her head on his shoulder as he begins to undress her. She lifts her head momentarily as he lifts her shirt over her head. "How are you feeling this morning?"

"I feel better," she mumbled in his shoulder. Once they were undressed, Ryan helped Tori into the tub. Then he got in behind her, and he went to work on her back massage with her soap. Ryan then shampooed Tori's hair.

Tori loved every moment with Ryan. She is closing her eyes and enjoying his hands. "Ryan, you sure know how to make a girl feel special. I love you so much."

"I love you, Tori. You make me feel special just for being my wife." They finish their bath and get ready for the day of filming.

They make their way over to the filming site and start filming. These are exciting scenes for Tori and Ryan. They are also coming to the end of filming. The experience has been so amazing for Tori. She gets to see firsthand how Ryan feels when he is a different character and being able to bring a character to life. She really does not want this experience to end. They wrap up the final scenes of the movie. Tori feels a sense of accomplishment as she looks at the smile on Ryan's face. "Is this how it feels when you finish a film?"

"Yes, it does, but the best part about this time is I get to go home with my leading actress."

Tori laughed. "Well, in that case, I the fan get to go home with the leading movie star."

Ryan got serious. "I hope you don't mind that we stop and check on people. I want to make sure they are living up to your expectations. I also have a question for you. Since we are headed back to California soon, do we keep them here or find them a place in California so that I can keep an eye on them?"

Tori thought about what he asked. "I feel better if they come with us to California. I don't mind if you check on them. I will wait in the car. I am not ready to see them again."

Ryan stops and goes into the hotel and stops at the front desk. "How is our guest in room 507?"

"They have been quiet, sir. We still have plenty of money for room service."

"Okay, sounds good. I am going up to check on them."

"Okay, sir, do you want me to phone them and let them know you are on your way up?"

"No, it is better if I surprise them." Ryan goes over to the elevators and pushes the button. The doors open, and in he goes. The next thing, he is standing at their door, knocking. Tori's dad opens the door and invites Ryan in. "Wow, you both look amazing. How are you doing?"

Tori's mom answers and says, "We are good now, and we feel like normal. We have been looking for jobs and basically hanging out here. Where is Tori? Is she coming up?"

"She is in the car. She is not ready to see you again. You have to give her some time. Our movie has wrapped up, and we will be going home soon. Please look for jobs around this address. This is going to be your new home. Tori wants you to come with us to California." Ryan hands them the address. It is an apartment that Ryan owns. "You will be flying to California tomorrow in my jet. You will go before us so that Tori does not see you before she is ready. My manager Justin will pick you up and take you to this apartment. Are you okay with all this?"

"Yes, we are okay with whatever you have for us."

"Okay, I will have a car come pick you up tomorrow around 4:00 p.m. When I get back, I will check on you."

"Okay, sounds good. We will see you then. Ryan, why are you helping us?"

"Because without you, I would not have the love of my life. Your daughter is the best thing that ever happened to me. I would not trade her for anything."

CHAPTER 7

The Thrill of Telling a Story

Ryan made sure that Tori's parents got to their plane okay, and he asked his manager to give him a call when they land. Tori is still flying high on the experience of movie making, and she cannot wait until she gets to see it all together on the big screen. Ryan was getting calls for interviews, but a very important phone call came in. Ryan has been nominated for best actor for the movie he did before his and Tori's. "Mr. Ryan, are you planning on attending the award show, and how many are attending with you?"

"Yes, I will be there in person, and I will be bring one with me."

"Okay, we will mark you down as attending with a plus one."

"Thank you." Ryan looks at Tori with a smile that lights up the room.

"What, baby? You look so happy."

"I am nominated for best actor."

"That is amazing. When do we go and accept your award?"

"I was nominated does not mean I will get it."

"Baby, I have confidence that you will get it because you were amazing in that movie. There is something wrong with them if you don't win this."

"Thank you, Mrs. Cooper, but I already have the best award ever, and she is carrying my child. But the award ceremony is in two weeks, and I told them two are coming. Will you do me the honor of escorting me to the ceremony?"

"Mr. Cooper, I will be honored to."

"I was hoping you would say that because if you said no, I would have to find one of my other fans on Instagram."

"Oh no, you do not. Why would I give up an opportunity to go out with the hottest man in the world?"

"I don't know but good answer."

"Very funny, sir." Ryan had his arms around Tori when he felt something at his belly.

"Oh, what's that, baby?"

Ryan bends down to talk to his child. He could feel the baby reacting to his voice, and it was a good feeling. "Really, yes, I have to agree with you, baby. Your mommy is beautiful. Yes, I can't wait to meet you too. Daddy loves you too, baby."

Tori is overwhelmed by emotion and love. Tears of joy combined with love are flowing down her face. She can't wait until she gets to meet her little bundle of joy. She also can't wait to see Ryan interact with the baby.

Ryan and Tori's first interview about their movie was the next day. Tori is nervous. She never did an interview before. Ryan gave her some pointers. He also reassured her that he would be there next to her. He tells her about what kind of questions they will ask. "If you think about the answers now, you won't have to think about them then. Let's try a few questions."

"Okay."

"Tori, how did it feel starring in your first movie?"

"It was an experience that I will never forget. Being able to see what my husband goes through as he brings a character to life is amazing. I never have thought I would ever do something like that. It gives me a whole new respect for those people who do it every day. The dedication they put into the making of the movie and the sacrifice they give have a whole new meaning for me."

"Wow, what a good answer. They might even ask on how you got inspired to write the story."

"That is an easy answer. I was inspired by the way I met my husband. He reached out to me because of a simple smile he saw on my face. He turned out to be genuine and everything I needed."

"I think you will nail any interview you go through."

"It is easy answering to you. You won't judge me if I say the wrong thing."

"They won't judge you either. They are only asking questions for our fans. They want to get to know you better now that you are a new face to the business."

"Okay, I will take your word for it."

The next day, Ryan and Tori are getting ready of the interview. Tori's heart is pounding out of her chest. What is keeping her grounded is Ryan, and he won't leave her. The recording of the show started, and Tori heard the introduction. Lisa says, "They are fresh from filming their first movie together. She is a new face, and we have known him for years. Please welcome my next guests, Tori and Ryan Cooper."

Tori holds Ryan's hand, and he holds it up to kiss her hand as they enter the studio. The audience is cheering, and Tori's face lights up. Ryan and Tori shake hands with Lisa. They sit down, and the first thing out of Lisa's mouth was "So, Tori, how does it feel being in your first-ever movie?" Tori gave the same answer that she gave Ryan in their preparation. Ryan looked on with pride as she answered the question.

Lisa then asked, "How does it feel starring next to the hottest man in Hollywood, according to this week's magazine?" She pulls out the magazine and hands it to Ryan. His eyes got big; this is a surprise to him.

Tori answered her question, "They are right. He is the hottest man, and he is all mine." He was voted as this year's hottest man alive.

Lisa then asked, "Ryan, what was it like doing this kind of love story?"

"It was a great experience. This movie came from the mind of my wife, and I feel honored that I was a part of this film. Helping to bring her book to life is a reward all in itself. It is a great story line, and I enjoyed my role."

Lisa then said, "We heard a rumor that your relationship started with a smile. Can you settle that rumor?"

Ryan smiled. "In fact, it did. I saw this smile." He pulled up the picture on his phone and showed Lisa. "After seeing this smile, I knew I wanted to meet the person behind it. I did something that I was not sure would work in my favor. I reached out to her through Instagram, and here we are now. She is the best thing that ever happened to me, and I am happy with my life now."

Lisa then got more serious. "Ryan, a couple of months ago, you were almost not with us. How did you survive a gunshot to the head and to the chest?"

"I was just lucky or a man in love. I could feel Tori next to me, and her strength and her love kept me here. In a way, she saved me, and she made me want to stay here."

Lisa seems to have tears in her eyes hearing that. "Wow, Ryan, that is powerful. Did you ever find out what happened to the woman who tried to take Tori?"

"She pleaded guilty for assault with a deadly weapon but not guilty for attempted murder. She feels guilty for shooting me, but she is mad that I got in the way of Tori being hurt."

"Do you ever think if she gets out she would come back?"

"In the back of my mind, the thought is there, but I hope she stays away."

Lisa answers, "Yes I hope so also. Let's move onto my next question. Tori, if the opportunity arises, would you star in another movie?"

"I would like to try other roles. I also would like to keep writing."

"Is this movie based on your first book?"

"No, it is actually my second book that the movie is based on. My first book will be out in two more weeks."

"Tori, since you are a newcomer, tell us more about yourself."

"I am twenty years old, and my uncle took care of me since I was ten years old. I love to write, and now I love to bring stories to life on the big screen."

"When you said your uncle raised you, what happened to your parents?"

"They abandoned me at his doorstep. Quite frankly, he has been taking care of me all my life. My parents weren't exactly model parents."

"I am guessing that your uncle raising you was the best thing for you."

"Yes, it has been the best. Despite what I went through, my uncle showed me how to love someone. At that point, I did know how much of an impact my uncle had in my life until I met Ryan. My uncle is the reason I fell totally in love with Ryan."

"How did you know Ryan was right for you if you only met him on Instagram?"

"I did not know he was right until I stepped out of my comfort zone and video called him. He answered, and from that point on, I knew he was right."

"Wow, Tori, this is good stuff, but that is all the time we have for today. Tori and Ryan, thank you talking with us today." Lisa turns to the camera and says, "I am Lisa, and you heard it here!"

Someone out of eyeshot said, "And we are out. Good job, people. That is a wrap."

Lisa turns to Ryan and Tori and says, "I have to admit that is one of the best interviews I have ever conducted. Thank you for coming and chatting with me. I have enjoyed myself. Tori, I can't wait to read your books and see your movie."

"I can't wait to share them with the world. Thank you for inviting us come and chat."

"We will have to do it again next time. You two have a great rest of your day."

Ryan and Tori made their way to the car. "That was fun," Tori says with a smile.

Ryan asks, "Are you ready for more interviews?"

"Yes, I am."

Throughout the day, they go to five more interviews and talk about the movie and Tori's books. One person realized that Tori was pregnant and asked how the baby was doing and asked when Ryan found out about the baby. Tori simply said, "While he was sleeping." Tori is getting worn out, and she falls asleep in the car before their last interview. Ryan lets her sleep for a half hour longer when they get to their destination. Ryan wakes her; and after the makeup crew gets rid of Tori's dark circles around her eyes, they do the interview.

They finish the interview, and Tori says, "I love doing this, but are we done for the day? I can't keep my eyes open anymore."

"We are done for the day." Ryan just gets the words out when Tori runs to the bathroom. Ryan waits outside, pacing. Tori finally comes out white as a ghost.

"Tori, you don't look so good. Let me get you home." Ryan quickly drives home and gets Tori up to bed. Tori is shaking, and it seems like she has cold sweats. Every time she drinks water, she gets sick. Ryan is worried for her. He lies down next to her and rubs her back as she falls asleep.

For two weeks, Tori has been sick. Ryan brought Tori into the hospital the morning after this sickness started. The doctors and nurses are doing their best to help Tori keep things down. They have to deliver nutrients intravenously into Tori's body. Tori is weak, and she sleeps most of the time. The doctors can't figure out what is going on with her. The baby's vital signs are all normal. Ryan is hoping that in three days Tori improves. His award ceremony is in three days. He does not want to go without Tori, and he does not want to leave her side. He whispers, "I give you my strength. Hold on to us. I love you, baby."

He squeezes her hand a little, and she stirs. "I love you too, sexy."

The next day Tori starts to improve, and she is gaining her strength back. The nutrients are helping. She is getting color back, and she is looking like his Tori again. The doctors check on her and are loving the improvement, so they send her home. She has just enough time to get ready for the ceremony. The doctor did give Tori instructions not to push too hard. She needs to stick to the clear-fluid and broths diet. She is actually holding everything down now. She gets a phone call, and she answers it while getting her nails done. "Hello, Mrs. Cooper, This is the awards director. Can Ryan hear me?"

"No, he is not around me right now."

"Good. Don't tell him what I am about to ask you. We just had one of our actresses drop out, and we were wondering if you would take her place in presenting the award for best male actor in a movie. Since your husband is nominated in that category, if he wins, you can present him with his award."

"That sounds perfect. I will do it." He tells her the details of the plan and says that she will be presenting with Vincent. Tori will read the winner while they are going to announce the nominees alternately.

"Thank you. That sounds good. I am looking forward to the opportunity."

"You are very welcome, Mrs. Cooper." He hangs up the phone.

She is now excited and can't wait for her surprise tomorrow. She loves surprises, and she loves surprising Ryan. She walks into the kitchen with the big grin on her face. "Tori, what are you up to now?"

"Nothing. I am just excited about tomorrow."

Tori's hair is done up, and her dress is on, and she is ready for a new experience. She loves award shows. She loves cheering on her favorite actor or actress as they are recognized. She never had thought she would be a part of one of them. She is wearing a light-purple dress with a scooping neckline and a slit going all the way up to midthigh. She is wearing diamond-studded strappy heels. She also has a single diamond necklace and earrings. The dress also shows off her baby bump well. When Ryan sees her, his mouth drops open. Then he smiles. Ryan is wearing a black tux with a tie that matches Tori's dress. His buttons are diamonds along with his cufflinks.

The limo has arrived, and off they go. "Tori, have you ever seen the red carpet at the award shows?"

"Yes, I would watch the pre-show entrance of the stars. Yes, I saw you a couple of times as you entered but never with anyone on your arm until now."

"Good, you know what to expect then. As for me, I was just waiting for the perfect person to go with me. I have found her."

The limo pulled up, and there were lights everywhere. Fans were screaming and cheering as other stars were walking the carpet, stopping shortly to talk. The limo door opens, and Ryan steps out and again, stopping to hold the hand of his date and the love of his life. Fans cheer louder and start calling Ryan's name. Ryan waves in their direction. Then Tori hears something that she is not used to hearing: her name being called. She waves at the fans also with bright eyes and a smile that lights the red carpet brighter. Ryan and Tori make their way slowly inside, stopping to talk to others. "Hey, look, Ryan, there is Jessie."

Ryan and Tori both wave to Jessie. Jessie smiles and waves back.

Ryan and Tori are now inside the building, and they are mingling with other stars. Tori is giddy and excited. She feels like a fan at this present time. Almost all her favorite movie stars are here. Ryan stops to talk to one of her favorites, and she has no words. She just can't believe she is standing so close to him. Finally, she finds the words to say, "I am so sorry. I am such a fan. All this is overwhelming but exciting."

"I know the feeling. I was in your shoes also when I started. It will pass and become more natural to you."

"Thank you for the advice."

They mingle some more, and the lights blink for everyone to take their seats.

Tori and Ryan find their seats, and they are sitting next to Jessie. The ceremony starts with music, and the host stepped out and did a comedian act. Tori realized that this is done live, and that makes her nervous a little. They sit through more bands and artists. They also sit through fifteen awards. The next band up is her cue. She excuses herself to go to the bathroom. Ryan is now nervous. What if she misses the next award? It is the one that he has been waiting for. Tori can tell, and she thinks to herself, *Don't worry, baby, I won't miss this part for the world.* The band is done, and the announcer speaks, "She is a newcomer to our profession and making a huge splash. He is our experienced hottie. Please welcome to the stage, Tori Cooper and Vincent Hadley."

"So, Tori, is there anyone exciting in this category that you would like to see win?"

"Yes, of course, there is a couple. But it is hard to choose just one. They are all good at what they do."

"If you have to pick, which one would you pick?"

"I am connected to one of them, and I think we share a last name, but yet I can't possibly play favorites. Let's say the names of these men before we get stuff thrown at us."

"Okay, okay, okay, let's go." Vincent says the first name, and Tori says the second name. Then Vincent said the third name, which left the best for last for Tori to say, "My personal favorite Ryan Cooper."

They showed his face, and Tori looked up to see his grin from ear to ear, and it matched hers. Tori opens the envelope. Her heart starts pounding with excitement, and she has to say the name without jumping up and down. "And the winner is my sexy man Ryan Cooper!"

Ryan is in a state of shock when he makes his way up, but it does not stop him from this next act. He grabs hold of Tori, dips her, and kisses her on the lips. Then he righted her, and she handed him his award. Tori went to step back, but Ryan held her in place next to him as he stepped to the microphone. "Wow, I am blown away. I was certain that one of the other men in this category would get this. I did not expect it. Then to have the most beautiful woman give it to me tops this off right." He rattles off a bunch of names, and then he looks at Tori. "I thank you for your belief in me and your support. I could not have done this without you. During the making of this movie is when I met you. You inspired me to do the best I could. I am sharing this with you."

Ryan hands Tori the award back and walks with her backstage. When they got backstage, Ryan wrapped Tori in a bear hug and held her there for a little while. "That was a nice surprise. I thought for sure you were going to miss it. Then they announced your name, and I was, like, 'What is going on?' Now I know. Thank you for your words. You make this man very happy. How did you become a presenter?"

"They called me yesterday and said that an actress dropped out, and they asked me because you were one of the nominated in the category, and I said yes."

"That is really awesome. Thank you so much for your support and your love."

"You are welcome, sweetheart. We should take our seats because the next awards are for best actress and for movie of the year."

"Yes, let's go."

They make their way back to their seats, and they are just starting the announcement. "That is a pretty hard act to follow. That Ryan dude sure knows how to sweep a woman off her feet."

"Yes, I agree with you. I would have loved to have been Tori in that moment."

"Let's give it a try."

The handsome announcer does the same thing to his beautiful co-announcer. Fortunately, they are both single and could do that. "Was that good for you?"

"Yes, that was good for me. Before we make out, let's announce the nominees and the winner."

Ryan and Tori both were laughing. The announcers rattled off some names and then announced Jessie's name. "The best actress winner is Jessie." Jessie smiles and makes her way up to the microphone. Jessie thanks her people and her costar Ryan.

"This is the last award of the night. This has been fun. Our next award is for movie of the year. Throughout the night, we have seen video clips of each one of the movies nominated." One of the movies nominated is Ryan's movie. "And the winner is—" He says Ryan's movie title, and everyone stands in ovation. Ryan stands up and walks with his costars to the microphone. After giving Tori a kiss, of course. The director and producer stand at the microphone, thanking everyone they can think of. The announcer steps to the microphone again and says, "Thank you, everyone, for coming out now. Let the after party begin." Ryan found Tori, and he led her to the after party. They didn't stay for very long because Ryan did not want to overwhelm Tori. He did not want to see her go through two more weeks of sickness again.

CHAPTER 8

The Excitement

Tori made it through the awards night without being sick. She is also getting ready for her book to hit the shelves tomorrow. Tori is scheduled for a signing in Exton at a local bookstore tomorrow. This will give her opportunity to practice writing her name as Tori Cooper, not Tori Clark. She is getting excited. She can't wait to see her book in print, her words on the pages of the book. Ryan is worried that if he is there, it might take the spotlight off Tori. Tori wants him by her side. It will give him an opportunity to meet some of his fans also.

Tori is feeling a little frisky, and she can't take her eyes off Ryan. She is flirting with him, and one thing leads to another. They make love like never before. Tori loves being in Ryan's embrace. This is where she feels the most comfortable. She will never tire being in Ryan's arms. She will never give them up for anything. After they were done having fun, Tori asked Ryan a question, "Ryan, how do the love scenes on-screen affect your life? I am worried that the next movie I am in it won't be with you, and it will feel like I will be cheating on you."

"Tori, when I am in character, it is that character who does love scenes. In a way, we are two different people. We are the character that we play, and we are who we were born as. If we are not playing in the same movie together and you have to do love scenes, pretend he is me and play the character. I know that if I have a love scene to get through, I will be thinking about you the whole time."

"That's good advice. Well, to solve my nerve problem, I want to be in more movies with you."

"Don't worry, we will play in more movies together."

"Okay, I will take your word for it."

Tori fell asleep while in Ryan's arms. She dreamed a good dream. It was about Ryan. They sat on a swing with gray hair and watching their kids play and run with their grandkids. Tori woke the next morning refreshed and ready to face the world.

Today is a good day for her. Tori bounces out of bed, kissing Ryan on her way out to the bathroom. She takes a shower and dresses as Ryan is about to hop in the shower. Tori is downstairs making coffee when Ryan is done his shower. "Someone has energy this morning. Is someone excited for her book signing?"

"Yes, how can you tell?"

"I love seeing you like this. We should have to have fun more often." Tori laughed and handed Ryan his coffee. "What time does your signing start?"

"We have about an hour, and we are only ten minutes away."

Tori and Ryan are on their way to the bookstore. Tori is so excited. When they get to the store, there was a line outside the door already. The manager of the store helped her go in through the back so that she was not mobbed by those standing in line. "Is that line for me?"

"Yes, it is. The line started forming about an hour ago."

Tia was there waiting for Tori. "Did you see the line? Yes, they are all here for you."

Tori turns to Ryan. She says, "I know people will ask for your autograph also. Let's give them both, yours and mine."

"Okay, let's do it."

Tori and Ryan both walk out to the table. They heard whispers and then clapping. Ryan and Tori get to work signing, talking, and getting pictures taken with their fans. Each person who came to the table treated Tori and Ryan the same. When they would give Tori attention, they would give the same to Ryan. They signed until there were no more people standing in line. Tori might have signed three hundred books today, and she enjoyed every minute of it. Then she realized she had to use the bathroom. "Ryan, I will be right back. I have to go to the bathroom."

"Okay, sweetheart, hurry back because I miss you already."

"Okay, I will try. I love you."

"I love you."

Tori goes to the bathroom, but she does not return. Ryan realizes that it is taking too long for Tori to return. Ryan goes to the women's room and knocks on the door. "Tori, are you in there?" He cautiously opens the door. He walks in, and he checks every stall. There is no one in there. But Ryan finds Tori's cell phone on the floor. Ryan started to freak out. Ryan unlocks Tori's phone and reads what is on it. "If you want Tori back, you have to give me back my wife."

Ryan is panicking, and he runs out to the main floor. "Tia, he took Tori."

"Who?"

"I don't know. He left this message for me."

"We need to call the police." Tia makes the call, and within minutes, the police is there. They are looking at surveillance video and checking if there were any witnesses. Sure enough, they spot Tori being escorted out the back door with a hand over her mouth and a gun to her head.

Ryan is now pacing. He is helpless, and he is mad. He is thinking to himself he should have gone with her. Now her and the baby's lives hang. *I can't lose her. It will destroy me. What wife is he talking about anyway? The message is so vague.* He calls his parents, and then he calls hers. He knows they are not on speaking terms, but they have a right to know. Then Ryan spots the news, "We have breaking news out of Exton, Pennsylvania, right now. Tori Cooper is missing. She is the wife of Ryan Cooper. If anyone has information on her whereabouts, please contact the police department right away. Tori is two and a half months pregnant as well. Her and her unborn child's lives hang in the balance."

Meanwhile, the man who has Tori has her tied to a chair. He slaps her in the face twice. "That is for getting my wife arrested." Then he slaps her again, "That is for making her plead guilty for assault with a deadly weapon." Tori is quiet, and she takes the hits as long as he does not hit her stomach. He hits her one more time. "That is for marrying her crush. She went off the deep end when she found out you married him."

Tori finally spoke, "Please, sir, I am pregnant, and I am going to throw up." Just as the words came out, so did whatever she ate that morning. The man got so mad at what she just did and hit her in the stomach. The pain went through her body like lightning. "Please do not hit me in the stomach. Please stop. No more!" Tears were streaming down Tori's cheeks, and Tori got sick again. He hit her in the legs this time because Tori managed to pick up her legs just as his fist came in contact. "Is it Ryan's baby?"

"Yes, it is Ryan's baby."

"That baby belongs to my wife and Ryan. But since it is in you—" He hits her twice more before he finishes his sentence, and she protects herself the best she can with her legs. When the man is done with his assault on Tori, he walks away. Tori looked around for the first time, and she had no idea where she was. She can feel her face start to swell, and she can taste blood in her mouth. But the reassuring sign is that she can feel the baby moving in her stomach. "Baby, hang in here with Mommy. Stay with Mommy."

Ryan is at the police station. He wants to be close if they find her. Then he figured out what woman the man was talking about. The woman who shot Ryan is sitting in prison right now. Ryan runs to the sergeant's office and says, "I know the woman the man is talking about. The woman who shot me. We need to get her released. I will be damned if I lose my wife over this." Then Ryan's phone rings with an unknown number. "Hello!"

"Ryan, buddy, so listen up. I have your wife, and it feels good to finally hit something."

"You hurt my wife, you will pay for it."

"Oh, Ryan, too late, but she is strong. As long as my wife is released, we will make a trade. Call this number when you have her, and I will set up a meeting point. Oh, and by the way—" Ryan heard a slap in the background and Tori's whimper in pain. "Don't lay any more hands on my wife, and you will have yours as soon as we get her transferred to this police station. Get working on it now, or you will never see your wife and your unborn child again."

Just before the line went dead, Ryan heard more hitting of Tori. Ryan's heart breaks. "Baby, please hang on to us. Don't leave me." Ryan's tears run down his face as he wills the words to Tori's ears.

The sergeant arranges for the woman to be moved to his custody, and Ryan pays for her plane ticket. She will be there in four hours.

There are police headed to the airport, now waiting for her arrival. He is pacing. The four hours go by slowly. He takes a couple of calls from his parents as well as hers. He fills them in on what is happening. Since Ryan paid for the plane ticket, he had the plane's information and he was able to track it.

Meanwhile, Tori gets sick again, and the man hits her. The cold sweats are happening again, and Tori starts to shake. Tori's face is so white, and the taste of blood is making her nauseous. When Tori gets sick again, there is nothing left; and she dry heaves. Her body feels heavy, and every movement she makes sends pain everywhere. But the feeling of the baby moving is the feeling she holds on to. Then in the back of her mind, she hears Ryan's voice, "Baby, please hang on to us. Don't leave me." She remembered saying those words to him when he was shot. She hangs on to those words. She closes her eyes, images of Ryan playing strong in her mind. Tears came down her cheeks, stinking every open cut on her face. Then the phone rings, and the man puts it on speaker. Tori heard Ryan's voice, "We have your wife. Where can we meet? I also want to hear Tori's voice before we agree to your meeting. Proof of life will get you your wife."

The man puts the phone up to Tori, and she whispers, "Ryan, I love you."

Then the man demanded that he hears his wife as well. Tori heard the woman's voice on the other end, and it sounded stronger than hers. "Hello, baby, thank you for rescuing me. I will see you soon."

"Ryan, if I see anyone else besides you, your wife is dead." Then the man gives Ryan an address to do the trade.

It has been sixteen hours since Tori went missing, and the police is making a plan to be there unseen. The place has a lot of places to hide. Officers leave to go get into place. So when the man leaves and gets far enough away, they will take him down. The one problem is Ryan is famous, and he might attract attention. He knows there are cameras ready to follow him, so he came up with a plan. An officer will escort him and her out of the building while in handcuffs and hoods over their heads.

It is time for them to move, and Ryan is only moments away from seeing Tori. Ryan escapes the cameras, and off they go. They get down the road away from the cameras, and they get into Ryan's car. They leave the officer behind. The woman starts to speak. Ryan stops her. "I don't want to hear what you have to say, and it is better that you say nothing." She started to speak again, and Ryan shook his head no. She did not say another word. Ryan finally pulls up to the location and sees the man's car. He is standing outside of it, and Tori is in his arms, limp. Ryan gets out of the car and walks over to the passenger side and grabs the woman. Without words, Ryan lets go of the woman and watches her run to her man. Then he drops Tori to the ground and grabs his wife and leads her to the car. He gets in, and he backs away.

Ryan runs to Tori's side. "Tori, I am here. Please wake up. Let me know you are still here with me."

Ryan heard sirens and then heard, "Pull the car over and get out with your hands up." Ryan felt relief that they are caught, but Tori is not waking up, and the paramedics are there to help Tori. She is breathing, and Ryan reminds them that she is pregnant. They load her up into the ambulance, and Ryan hands an officer his car keys as he joins Tori in the back of the ambulance. He grabs her hand and holds on to it for dear life. He looked at her face. It is white with blood all over. He looked over her body as the paramedics worked on her, and he saw bruises and hand marks on her legs and arms. Then the bruises on her stomach made his heart stop. He placed his hand on her stomach, and he stayed there. He bent down and started talking to his baby, "Baby, it's Daddy. Please move for me. Let me know you are okay." Ryan kisses Tori's belly. Then he put his ear to her stomach. Then he felt something move and then move again; and at that moment, the paramedic found two heartbeats. It was music to Ryan's ears. "The baby's heartbeat is strong, sir," the paramedic reassured Ryan.

Ryan then asked, "How is Tori doing?"

"Hers is weak but hanging on. We will know more when we get her to the hospital."

They finally get to the hospital, and they rush Tori to an emergency room. There were reporters in the waiting room when Ryan arrived. He is guessing that they know now that Tori was found, and they mob him. The officers who were following the ambulance surrounded Ryan and helped him through the crowd. He does not want to talk to anyone. He just wants to be by his wife's side. Ryan gets back to the room Tori is in, and the doctor gives him the update. "She has swelling around the brain, and we are prepping her for surgery."

"Will the surgery affect the baby?"

"We will make sure your baby stays out of harm's way. I am going to make sure of it." The doctor walks with Tori as they roll her up to surgery. Ryan is left standing there with his wife's rings in his hand. They have her blood on them, and Ryan stares at them. He is picturing them on her finger. He is picturing himself putting them both on her finger. He is pacing for the next two hours. The waiting is painful.

Tori is finally wheeled back into the room, and Ryan is by her side immediately. "We were able to reduce the swelling on her brain. She survived a couple of blows to the head. She has broken ribs, and her arm is broken. She is also severely dehydrated. We have her on fluids and nutrients. Now we wait until she wakes up. She is in a coma. The baby is healthy and strong and only has minor trauma. Tori took most of the blows and did her best to protect the baby."

Ryan thanked the doctor as he left the room. "Hi, baby, you are safe now. You did good. Now wake up when you are ready. I will be here." Ryan placed his head on her chest and heard her heartbeat. He fell asleep to the sound.

Ryan woke up to his phone ringing and his manager Justin on the other end. "Hey, Ryan, how are you holding up?"

"I am okay now."

"Do you want me there to help deal with the press?"

"Yes, please."

"Okay, good, I am just outside the hospital, and they won't let me in. I am also here with your parents. Tori's parents are here also."

"Okay, I will have them allow you up." Ryan hangs up the phone and goes to the nurses' station. "Can you get me through to security?" The nurse dials a number and gives the phone to Ryan. "This is Ryan Cooper. Can you make sure that the Coopers and the Clarks along with my manager Justin get up to Tori Cooper's room? Please they are family. If Tori's best friends show up, make sure they come up also." Ryan tells them they are Rebecca and Stacy.

"Yes, Mr. Cooper, we will escort your family up now." Within the twenty minutes, Ryan's family is in the room. He fills them all in on what Tori went through and her condition. Now it is just a wait-and-see situation.

After twenty minutes of silence, Ryan turns on the TV and sees Tori's story on the news. He turns it up to hear what they have to say. Then he sees his manager at a podium, giving an official statement, and he is accompanied by Tia. "This is an unfortunate state of events, but Tori is hanging in there. The husband of the woman who shot Ryan went after Tori. They are both behind bars now and waiting for their hearing." The video cut to them being shoved into a police car, and Tori's parents gasped. Ryan turned to them and asked, "What happened? Are you okay?"

"Ryan, we have something to tell you. The woman is Tori's sister Clair. I am sorry. We did not know she was around here."

Ryan looked at them in shock. "How?"

"When Clair was seven, Tori was born, and Clair was already in foster homes. We were not good parents to either one of our girls, and we had given up when Tori was ten. We did the best thing for her and left her with her uncle so that she did not end up like Clair. By the time Clair was eighteen, she was out of control, and she did not want anything to do with us."

Ryan had no words to say. Then he thought of one thing. "Does Clair know Tori is her sister?"

"Clair knows she has a sister, but she does not know who it is."

Ryan stood up and went to the nurses' station. "Can you get the police department on the line for me?"

"Yes," and she dials the number and hands the phone to Ryan.

"This is Ryan Cooper for the sergeant please."

"Okay, let me transfer you, sir."

The next thing Ryan hears is "Hello, Ryan, what can I do for you?"

"I would like to talk to Clair, the woman who shot me. She needs to know something before she goes back to jail."

"Okay, let me transfer you to my cell phone and head down to the holding cell." He makes the transfer, "Ryan, are you still with me?"

"Yes," Ryan could hear footsteps and then the sergeant saying, "Clair, you have a phone call." He puts the phone on speaker. "Clair, this is Ryan. I wanted you to know that your sister is Tori Cooper, and I guess that makes you my sister-in-law. But from hereon out, you are not to have any contact with us until you get some major help. Don't send your husband or anyone else after us. Do we have an understanding?"

"Yes, Ryan, we do."

"Good, now get the help you need, and we will talk soon."

"Okay, Ryan, thank you." Ryan hangs up the phone. He walks back to Tori's room.

Tori's mom heard what Ryan did and she said, "Thank you."

Ryan takes his place back at Tori's side. They all continue to watch the news as more of Tori's story comes up. Ryan's focus stays on Tori. The next thing they hear is monitors beeping and a code blue sounding. Ryan's heart stops, and he shouts, "Tori, no! Stay with me, baby please. Fight! Don't leave!" Ryan watches in horror as they work to bring Tori back. After ten minutes, they bring her back. It was the longest ten minutes of Ryan's life. It was caused by one of her broken ribs putting pressure on her lung. They take her up to do a minor procedure, and she is back down before long.

It has been two days, and Ryan is in bed with Tori, half asleep. He has her wrapped in his arms, holding on to her as best he can. Right now, it is just Ryan and Tori. Everyone is out getting breakfast. Ryan could feel the baby moving, and he is smiling. He dozes off a little, and the next thing he feels is a hand moving up his arm. Ryan jumps and locks eyes with Tori. Ryan's face matches his heart. "You are the prettiest sight that I will ever see." Tori smiles and motions with her hands the I-love-you sign. "Oh, baby, I love you also." Her eyes look down at her stomach. "Our baby is strong and healthy." Tori seems to breathe a sigh of relief. Ryan then pushed the button and informed the nurse that Tori is awake. She told him that she would send the doctor in.

All Ryan could do was stare into Tori's beautiful eyes, a sight he will never get tired of seeing. Her smiling eyes stare back at him. The doctor comes in, and says, "Tori, it is time to take that not-so-comfortable tube out of your throat. When I say go, I want you to breathe out for me." Tori nods. "And go."

Tori breathes out, and she coughs and gags. The first thing she says in a whisper is "Ryan, I love you." That is all she can say. She reaches up and runs her hand over his jawline, and her eyes say it all. Ryan lowers his lips onto hers, and the kiss is so sweet that it made Ryan realize just how much he missed his wife.

"I have to tell you something before my parents come back from breakfast. Your parents are here. They have been here since you came in. Are you okay with it? I could ask them to stay outside of the room."

She slowly and quietly said, "I will be okay." At that moment, their parents came in and saw Tori awake. Gloria is excited, and Tori's parents are timid. After Tori got a hug from both Gloria and David, she looked at her parents. She hesitated for a bit, but she held out her hand for her parents. She lets them hug her, and her mom breaks out in tears. She held her daughter like she never did before. Tori has tears running down her cheeks. She never felt this way with her parents. She is finally ready to let them in and trust them.

Tori is home after another week in the hospital. She was ordered to stay off her feet and take it easy for another week. She gets a phone call from Tia, and they go over her second book. Tia also tells her that her first book is flying off the shelves. Tia told her that her first royalties will be in the mail shortly. Tori finishes the editing work with the second book, which again was not much. Tia gets to work on putting it together. Just as Tori hangs up with Tia, Ryan walks in. He has a sweet smile on his face, and he says, "Oh my gosh, you are Tori Cooper. Can I get your autograph please?"

Tori smiles and says, "Sure, who do I make it out to?"

"Your husband, Ryan Cooper."

He hands her a script and says, "Do you want to do this with me?"

She smiles and says, "Yes."

Ryan smiles and says, "The filming does not start until after the baby is born. But in the meantime, we can work on lines together."

"That sounds awesome. Let's start now."

They run through some lines. Tori is loving the script. Ryan and Tori take a break. Ryan gets this look on his face, and it is a look of worry. "Ryan, what is it?"

"I totally forgot about something I found out while you were in the hospital. I have to tell you, but I don't know how you will react."

"Ryan, just tell me."

"When the news report came up with what happened, they showed a picture of the woman who shot me. Your parents recognized her and told me she is your sister Clair." Tori looked confused and shocked. "I am sorry for just now telling you. I had forgotten until now. She was in foster care before you were born. They tried with you but decided that you deserved a better life. That's when they left you with your uncle."

Tori just stared at Ryan. She did not know what to say. "And she shot you. She almost killed you, and she is my sister. I just can't believe how she got to us. Did she know at the time you brought her to trade for me?"

"No, she did not find out until I called and told her. Then I asked that she gets help before she ever talks to you. If you ever want to talk to her."

Tori does not know what to say. She is shocked that she did not know she had a sister, let alone a sister who came after her because of her relationship with Ryan. She is finally letting her parents back into her life, but now she has a sister that tried to kill her. What does she do next?

Ryan got a call that their premiere will be next week. He can't wait to see Tori on the big screen. He also gets to show off his wife again. They are also having fun reading and learning the lines of the script. Hopefully, they get the parts when they audition. Ryan is also having fun feeling his baby move inside his wife. He has his wife, and he is living his dream, and he thinks to himself life can't get any better than this. Ryan's heart beats for Tori, and he can't imagine a life without her. He knew the minute he saw that smile that made him fall in love with her that he would marry her. He looks at his wife with pride, and he can't believe she is his. He can't wait to see what they look like together in one little person.

EPILOGUE

Tori is very close to being nine months pregnant, and the growing excitement is making Tori glow. They went to their movie premiere, and they got a standing ovation. Tori did her best work in the movie. With the way that she played her role, no one would ever think that it was her first. Ryan loved seeing her story come to life on the screen. Ryan has a feeling that she might just win an award for her performance and/or her writing. Ryan and Tori nailed their new movie roles, and they would start filming as soon as Tori is ready. Tori is writing again. She is so inspired, and her inspiration is coming from her husband. The baby's room is ready, and now they are counting the days.

Tori is sitting at her computer, and Ryan is asleep by her side. She is writing, and she can't stop. It is one in the morning, and the words are just flowing out. She was typing a sentence when a pain shot through her body. Then she felt wet. She places a hand on Ryan, and another pain shots through her body again, and she squeezes Ryan where she holds. Ryan wakes and sees the pain in Tori's face. "Baby, what's wrong?"

In a breathless voice, she says, "Yes, baby is coming." Ryan shots up and grabs the bag and throws on his shoes. Tori looks at him and laughs. He forgot something. "Ryan, you need a couple more things."

He looks down and says, "Yes, I need clothes." He throws on clothes, and out the door she goes. He starts the car and pulls it up to the front door, and he helps Tori to the car. She is breathless and blowing out air. Ryan is on the road and navigates through the streets. Ryan is at the hospital in no time. Ryan runs in and grabs a wheelchair, and the nurses at the desk are dumbfounded as they watch him. He could hear one of the nurses say, "That was Ryan Cooper." Then they see why he did what he did. "My wife is having her baby." They all start to scramble to help them. As they do, the other nurse says, "Yes, and that is his wife, Tori Cooper."

After all the pushing and pain, Tori and Ryan are blessed with a beautiful baby girl. They gave her the name of Faith Elizabeth Melissa Cooper. Tori gave the honor to Ryan to give her first name, but Tori could not choose between Elizabeth or Melissa, so she got both names for her middle name. Ryan fell instantly in love with her the moment she landed in his arms. She was crying; but the moment she knew she was in Dad's arms, she stopped and was cozy and comfortable. She looks like her mom but has Ryan's nose, and the way she smiled a little was definitely Ryan.

The family of three was soaking it all in when Ryan's cell phone vibrated. "Hello! Yes, okay, sure we can be there. Really, that is awesome. Yes, I can do that. I knew it. Okay, yes, two. Thank you, bye!" Tori looked at Ryan, and he got the biggest smile ever. "We are nominated for best actress and best actor for our movie." Tori's eye got big, and she started to get excited. "Wow, I was never nominated before. Now I know how you feel."

"The award ceremony is in two weeks, and I told them we will be there."

"Okay, that day, your parents will spend some time with their granddaughter."

For the next two weeks, Ryan and Tori connect with their daughter, and the connection grows deeper with every minute spent with her. The look of pride on Ryan's face melts Tori's heart. She definitely could not ask for a better husband and father than Ryan. Her life is complete, and Ryan's love saved her from her past. She will be forever grateful.

Ryan and Tori attended the award ceremony. Ryan surprised Tori like she did him. He did not tell her she was up for the writer award, and he was the presenter of that award. Ryan excused himself to use the restroom. The announcer says, "Our next presenters starred together in two movies. He is a proud husband and new father, and she is our America's sweetheart. Please welcome Ryan and Jessie!"

Tori smiled as he walked to the stage with his best friend. "So, Jessie, where would we be without writers?"

"Definitely not here, Ryan."

"You got that right, Jessie. This next category highlights some of our best writers. These people bring stories to us, and we bring them to life. I know these writers are some of the best." Ryan looks at Tori when he says the next sentence, "I should know. I am, in fact, married to one of them." Tori's face registered surprise, and all she could do was smile.

Jessie reads the first two nominees. Ryan reads the next one, which leaves, "And this next one is smart and sexy, my wife, Tori Cooper." Ryan opens the envelope. "The winner is"—his smile grew huge—"my beautiful wife, Tori Cooper."

She stands up still in shock and walks to the microphone. Ryan grabs her up and spins her around. Then they let hear say her speech. "Wow, I never expected this. I owe this all to my husband. He encouraged me to write the script from my book, and we would not be here if it was not for him. Thank you, Ryan, and thank you, Tia, for making this happen. Thank you to all who had a hand in the movie writing and making," she said that all the while holding on to Ryan by her side. They went and won for best actor and actress. The movie also won best movie.

Tori is so grateful for her Instagram account. She is grateful that she pushed yes to Ryan's invitation to talk. She never thought her life would turn out like this. She was not expecting to fall in love with Ryan when she pushed yes, but she is glad she did. She also sees the change in her parents, and she forgave them. She is finally feeling like a daughter. Clair has a little more work to do, but Tori is getting to know her sister. Tori is living her best life ever, and it is only the beginning.

LOVE IN
THE RAIN

CHAPTER 1

Fate Finds Them

It is just about late August, and they are having a rainy week. A woman had a dream of meeting a brilliant man. He had to be funny with a caring heart. She knew her better half is out there somewhere. She is smiling at the thought that he is trying to find her. His better half could be her. Her thoughts keep going to her past, and she hopes that it does not come back to haunt her. She is at a laundromat, finishing up the folding of her clothes. As she folds, she is relaxed. She loves to listen to the rain as it drops on the building. She closes her eyes and imagines standing out in the rain and letting the rain wash all her worries away. She is the only one in there, and he walks in dripping wet from the rain. He spots her, and instantly his face lights up. He walks up to her and asks, "Can you help me?" She turns and recognizes him. "The rental car they gave me broke down, and they can't get me another one for another couple of hours. I am going to be late for an audition."

Her heart is pounding because he is a local artist, a song writer, and she is one of his fans. She also had a crush on him back in high school. She replies to him, "Yes, let me get these clothes in the car, and then we can go."

"Let me help you with that please." He picks up her laundry basket and heads for what he assumes is her car. It is an Audi Q5, and she pushes a button on the key fob to open the trunk.

He places it in the back of her car. She follows with the smaller one and places it in the back. Ashlee stops for a second and closes her eyes and lets the rain wash down on her with a smile on her face. She is thinking that this is maybe a start of something great. She can't wait to see where this encounter takes her. He takes off his rain jacket and places it in the backseat as he gets in the car. She then slides into the driver's seat. "Where to, sir?"

"Philadelphia please!" He hands her the address. She could not stop looking at him from the corner of her eye. He is even more handsome up close. He is tall and looks great in a suit. He has deep-blue eyes that look gray in different light. She also sees some hints of green in them. His hair is dirty blond and a little long at the top of his head. He has a chiseled jawline and dimples when he smiles. He asks her, "What is your name?"

"You don't recognize me? I did go to school with you."

"Now that I think of it, you do look familiar. Ashlee, Ashlee Foster."

"It took a while, but yes, that is me."

"Well, Ashlee, I thank you for taking me to the most important audition of my life."

"I hope you get whatever you are auditioning for. I have faith in you that you will get your dream. You are a good singer."

"You have heard me sing? I was wondering if you did."

"Yes, I have heard everything you have done. I am one of your fans."

Sean looks at Ashlee with gratitude. He also has something else in his eyes, and he can't stop looking at Ashlee. She is the most beautiful woman he ever laid eyes on. She is glistening as the rain starts to dry on her. The rain seems to be his new favorite fashion. Ashlee is a petite brunette with long muscular legs. She has a gorgeous smile, and Sean could get lost in her hazel eyes. She is singing along with a song on the radio, and Sean is falling in love with her voice. "Your voice is amazing. Did you ever hear that before?"

"Yes, all the time, but I never heard from anyone but my mom and dad." They are listening to one of the local radio stations that likes to play local artists, and one of Sean's songs comes on, and Ashlee starts singing to it. She harmonizes to his song perfectly.

He is staring at her, mouth open and eyes open wide. Then he realized something, "Not only did we go to school together, but did we have classes together also?"

She stopped singing and said, "Yes, I was in just about every class of yours."

Then he realized that he had a crush on her in high school, but he is not going reveal that fact. He did not want to scare her away. She is touching his heart with her voice, and she just proved to be his vocal match. He is interested in getting to know her better.

"What have you been doing with yourself since graduation, Ashlee?"

"I have been traveling for work." There is a secret that she did not want him to know. She does not want his pity. She is not really traveling for work. She is hiding. Her passion is to help people who experienced what she has experienced. She gives voices to women who do not have one or are scared to speak out.

"What kind of work do you do?"

"I advocate for women. I give them a voice."

"Wow, that is honorable."

"There are women out there who need a voice and need help. I felt led to help them any way I can. I joined an organization that specializes in helping women."

"That is a good job."

"Thank you. I love what I do. I know firsthand what women go through sometimes."

"What do you mean you know firsthand what they go through?"

Ashlee thought to herself, *Oh no, I think I said too much.* She thinks fast and says, "I am a woman, and I have seen things happen to women."

"Okay, I would like to get to know you more. Would you like to go out with me Ashlee?"

Ashlee smiles as some of the old feelings she had are resurfacing. "I think I will like that. I do have a confession to make."

"What is your confession?" Sean smiles.

Ashlee's face turns fifty shades of red as she says, "I had a crush on you in high school. I am glad we had classes together."

Sean smiled and decided to tell her his confession. "My confession is I had a crush on you as well. I was glad I got to stare at you all the time."

Ashlee's face turned more shades of red. "So you are telling me we both had crushes and did not act on them? What is wrong with us?"

Ashlee pulled up to the destination of Sean's audition with ten minutes to spare, and all Sean could do was stare at Ashlee. Sean leaned to her side of the car. He placed his lips sweetly on hers, and she accepted his kiss. They tasted each other, and Ashlee got lost in the kiss. Her eyes are closed. She can't believe that she is finally kissing her crush. Her toes are curling, and her tongue is exploring. When Sean released her, she still felt him there, and her lips were swollen from the mind-blowing kiss. Sean looked into her eyes, "I could love you for forever." He realized he said that out loud and braced for impact waiting for Ashlee's reaction. Ashlee could see a look of shock pass across Sean's face. Her reaction was her kissing him again and then saying, "Oh, could you now? I could love you for forever also."

Sean smiled, and a look of completeness came onto his face. He said, "Come in with me please." Ashlee nodded.

They go inside, and Sean directs Ashlee to a seat where she can see him audition and not let who he is auditioning for see Ashlee. Sean steps to the mic and starts to sing. Ashlee's heart is fluttering in his voice. Hearing it in person is so much better then hearing it on the radio. She is lost in his voice, and she has tears rolling down her cheeks. It is a beautiful song, and a beautiful voice is singing it. When he was done, she heard the person say, "Wow, that was amazing. You will definitely hear from us by the end of the week."

Sean said, "Okay, I will look forward to your call."

When Sean was leaving the stage, he overheard them talking among themselves. He heard, "We still don't have a female lead yet."

Sean stops and says, "I know someone who may be just what you are looking for." Sean runs to Ashlee and says, "Come on. Now is your chance to audition. Let them hear you."

"No, I can't. I am not prepared for this."

"Come on, just sing to me please." Ashlee looked at him, still protesting, but she got up and allowed him to guide her to the stage. "You got this. Forget that they are there and sing to me."

She sighed hard and looked at him with "I am going to kill you for making me do this" look. "What is your name, miss?"

"I am Ashlee Foster, and I am sorry I was not prepared for this. Please forgive me if this is awkward in any way."

"Thank you for that heads-up. You may start when you are ready."

Ashlee started the only song she knows by heart. She knows every lyric and every note. It is one of Sean's songs. After a couple of lines, Sean joins her; and they harmonized together. When they were done, the people listening had shock and awe on their faces. All Sean saw was Ashlee. His first thought was *I am going to marry this girl.* He did not realize that they were giving them a standing ovation, and it did not even register to him what they were saying. All he thought was he found his perfect match. "We want both of you for the lead roles. You are amazing together."

"Wait, what role? Sean, what did I just sign up for?"

Sean laughed. "I am guessing you are my leading woman, and you will be next to me in a musical called *The Power of Marriage*." Ashlee looks at the director and producer of the play and then back to Sean. "Please, do this with me."

Ashlee is contemplating the offer. "Okay, I will. But you have to help me, Sean. This is the first-ever play I have ever done."

"I will be here with you every step of the way."

The director Mike handed both Sean and Ashlee a script and a practice schedule. "Welcome aboard, and I look forward to working with the both of you." They smiled and walked out to the lobby of the building. Ashlee throws her arms around Sean. "I can't believe that you did that to me. You ambushed me, but I am glad you did it. I never dreamed that I would be onstage."

"I am glad you will be next to me onstage. Let's celebrate."

Ashlee hands him her keys. "Take us to wherever you want to go."

He takes her keys, "You trust me enough to drive us?"

"Why? Should I be worried?"

Sean laughed. "No."

"Okay, let's go."

He drives them to his favorite restaurant in Philadelphia. "Sean Garison, is that you? I have not seen you in a while. How is it going?" A woman came out of nowhere and threw herself at Sean and kissed him right on the lips. Sean drew back and did not kiss her back. Ashlee looked the other way, but in a way, she was a little jealous. "Hello, Lisa, I would like to introduce you to my girlfriend. This is Ashlee. Ashlee, this is Lisa, my ex!"

Lisa stepped back and said, "I am sorry. I did not realize you were with him." Ashlee had a look of shock on her face. She was more shocked that Sean said girlfriend than she was about the kiss Lisa and Sean just shared. "It was nice seeing you again. Take care of yourself, Sean. It was nice to meet you, Ashlee."

"Likewise."

Lisa walks away, and Sean takes his seat. "Sorry about putting you on the spot like that. She would have been all over me if I did not say girlfriend."

Ashlee, still in shock, says, "That is okay. You can use me as your girlfriend anytime you want." Ashlee thought to herself, *Why did I just say that? I can't believe I am out with Sean Garison. I don't want this to end.*

Ashlee is falling for Sean more and more. Sean ordered his favorite meal for both him and Ashlee. She kind of likes when a man takes over and orders for her. It made her think of her past and how someone did that for her.

They talked about life after graduation. They have something in common. They both lost their parents in car accidents. It has been ten years for both of them. She was twenty when she got the phone call on a snowy dark night. It was a five-car accident, and the fault was an icy road. As Ashlee was describing the night her parents died, Sean heard something that sounded familiar. Sean lost his parents on a snowy night also. "Wait, you said five cars and slipped on ice? What road were they on?"

She said the road name, and Sean gasped. "My mom and dad were in the same accident as yours. I was told that a man tried to save them, but as he tried to pull a couple from their car, the car exploded, taking him with it. I heard his name as Mr. Foster. Wait, Foster—your dad."

Ashlee gasped and said, "I was told that my dad tried to save people. He was only able to save one. My mom died instantly. My dad died trying to save your parents. Oh god, Sean, we are connected in more ways than one."

Ashlee feels closer to Sean now. She is wishing she really is Sean's girlfriend. Ashlee and Sean talk some more about their life since graduation. Sean can sense that Ashlee is holding something back. "Is there something you are not telling me?"

Ashlee's heart skipped a beat when he asked that. She does not want to tell him about her past. She does not want his pity. "There is nothing more. You now know everything about me."

"Okay, but listen, if you need to talk about anything, I am here for you."

She responds, "Thank you, and the same goes for you also."

"Thank you for that, Ashlee." He looked into her eyes, and he saw his future. The look on his face is passion, and he is looking at Ashlee. "Ashlee, I want to know if you want to take a risk with me. I want to know if you want to be my girlfriend."

Ashlee's face lit up, and she saw the want in Sean's eyes. She sees herself in his future. But she is also afraid. She wants to say yes, but can she? She wants a new life. She wants to feel loved again—the real love, not the kind that a man uses when it suited him. Her next answer shocks her, and she can't believe what she is about to say. "Yes, I would love to be your girlfriend."

Sean smiles and slides in next to Ashlee. He is kissing Ashlee when their food comes out. They keep kissing until Ashlee's stomach growls. Sean laughs and says, "I better let you eat before your stomach protests some more." They both dig into their food and can't take their eyes off each other.

It has been a week since Sean stepped into Ashlee's life. When he had his rental car, he had just gotten back from a performance, and Sean realized that he lived thirty minutes away from Ashlee. It has been a week of running lines and kissing. Sean made a vow to Ashlee that he will wait until marriage to have all of her. For now, he loves when she is tucked in his arms. They spend every waking moment together. Sean saw a scene coming up, and he warned Ashlee, "Keep in mind that a scene is coming up that we have to fight. Are you ready for this?"

"Yes, I can handle it."

Sean gets into character and starts the scene. Sean starts to yell, and Ashlee freezes. She then throws her hands up in a defensive position around her face, and she begins to shake. Sean is seeing for the first time scars on her exposed arms. She also cowers in place as Sean realizes that he sees fear in her eyes. Sean is shocked at her reaction, and he is starting to figure out that someone hurt her in the past. "Ashlee, tell me what happened to you to make you react like this. Did someone hurt you?" Ashlee is still frozen, his question not really registering. She is breathing heavy, and her fear is heart-wrenching that Shawn slowly wraps his arms around her. "Ashlee, please talk to me."

Ashlee lets him hold her until she stops trembling. She hates this next part; but before they get any deeper, she needs to tell him.

She whispers, "I am married, and I am running away from my husband. He beat me when I did things wrong in his eyes. I had to dress a certain way and cook his food a certain way. If I did not fold his clothes a certain way, he would hit me. I have had broken arms, hands, ribs, and legs. I have had a bloody nose and black eyes. My lips were cut, and they would swell."

Sean sat in shock as he held her. He just can't believe that someone would hurt her the way she was hurt. "Oh my god, Ashlee, I am going to be here to protect you. I won't let anything happen to you. How did you get away from him, and how long ago did this happen?"

"I got away from him when he was at work. I took what I could and ran. I did have a neighbor's help, and I moved all the way to the East Coast to hide from him. This happened two months ago." Sean wrapped her tighter in his arms. "I know he won't let me have the divorce I want. I am stuck in a marriage I don't want. He started out so sweet and so loving. He treated me well. I felt like a queen, but the minute I said I do, and we were alone, he showed his true colors. I endured his punishment for two years."

"You will never go through that again. Oh no." Sean got a sudden thought. "If I would have acted on my feelings for you in high school, you would never have gone through that. I am sorry I did not do that."

"Sean, please don't think that way. You would not have known this would happen. Besides, I should have acted on my feelings also. I am glad you are here now. I feel safer here in your arms."

"I had an opportunity to save you from that, but you are here now. I am never letting you go. Are you going to be able to do this scene in our play? Your reaction scared me."

"Yes, I just have to keep telling myself that, one, I am not in that position anymore. Two, this is just a play, and three, I am with the person who makes me feel safe."

"You will always be safe with me. I am glad you finally trust me enough to tell me this."

"I do trust you, and I do feel safe. I am sorry I did not tell you when you asked me. I did not want to relive the past."

"I know now what happened to you. That is all that matters."

"Do you want to try this scene again?" Ashlee asked Sean.

"Yes, let's try this again." They started the scene, and the fear and the pain that Ashlee had stored up helped her through the scene. She did the scene with flying colors.

Now that Sean knows her past, she feels like a weight has been lifted off her shoulders. But she can't shake the feeling that someone is watching her. She feels hunted, and she is looking over her shoulder when she is out and about. She knows that her husband will stop at nothing to look for her. He is a bodybuilder, and he does not like to lose. He owns a couple dozen gyms, and he is well-known. No one believes that he hurts Ashlee. No one would dare go against him either. Some of the time when he hit Ashlee, it would knock her out.

Ashlee started getting weird text messages. She knows who they are coming from, so she does not reply to them. One of the messages that just came in has her scared. "Find you where, find you not. Find you there, find you here. Still looking, still watching." Now she is on edge, and she is afraid to show Sean. But she can't keep secrets from him. She gets enough courage to show him. Sean decided not to leave Ashlee alone.

A day goes by, and they have been running lines together. The more they practice together, the more confident Ashlee becomes. After practicing their lines, Sean and Ashlee were watching a movie;

and Ashlee was dozing off, wrapped in Sean's arms, which were warm and comfortable. Sean watches her sleep. Then he realized that her body started to jump. Her brow wrinkled, and then she started to groan. She was sweating. Then she started to shake. Sean wrapped her tighter. "Ashlee, it's not real. I am here, and you are safe." Sean felt her relax and stop shaking. She remained asleep, and he turned off the movie and carried her back to her bed. He laid her down and pulled up a chair next to her and watched her sleep. He did not leave, and he was glad he didn't. He heard a noise as he was startled awake. He walked to the spot where he heard the sound. Then he got hit from behind.

Sean came to and realized he was tied up with duct tape over his mouth. Then he saw the most horrifying sight. Ashlee was being restrained by the man, and he was yelling at her. "How could you do this to me? You would cheat on me with this piece of crap. You are mine, and I will never let you go." He hit her, and then he said, "I am going to make him watch me take what is mine."

Sean could see the pain in her face and tears coming down her cheeks. Sean also saw a bruise start to form and blood start run from her eye. Sean struggled to get free. The ropes are cutting into his wrists. He watched in horror as Ashlee's husband took her against her will. Sean is fighting against the rope. Then he feels the rope loosen, and he is free. Sean rips off the duct tape on his mouth and says, "Get off her." Sean leaps and knocks Zach to the floor. Sean picked up Zach, "You need to leave and never come back." Zach got loose from Sean's grip and punched Sean. They fought, and Zach ended up going out the sliding glass screen door of Ashlee's bedroom, which was two stories up. Sean went to Ashlee. She was cowering under the covers of her bed; but the minute she saw Sean, she opened her arms and allowed Sean to hug her. She cried as Sean called 911.

The police were there within five minutes. Sean helped Ashlee get dressed as she trembled. As she did, Sean saw more bruises and scars. He also saw blood on the bed. He helped her out to the living room where the officer was waiting to take their statement. Sean assumed that Zach was on his way to jail; but when the officer asked about the suspect, Sean showed him the location of where Zach fell, and he was gone. Both Sean and Ashlee were checked out by paramedics. They wrapped Sean's cuts on his wrists and checked the big knot on his head.

Sean is more worried about Ashlee. She had tears inside her, and her eyes were swollen and bleeding. Sean went into Ashlee's room and packed her bag with as many clothes as he could. Ashlee went to the hospital to get checked out, and Sean followed the ambulance to the hospital. Once there, they do a kit on Ashlee and repair her tears. When she is released from the hospital, Sean takes Ashlee to his place. She has not said anything since she talked to the officer. She sits paralyzed in the car. Sean can't read her expression. He pulls up to his house, and Ashlee sit motionless. Sean picks her up and carries her into the house. He tucks her into his bed, and he sits in the chair next to the bed and watches as she falls asleep, and he dozes off himself.

Chapter 2

Hiding in Comfort

Ashlee woke up in a new bed and barely remembering what happened the night before. There were rays of sunlight shining through the opening of the curtains. The handsome smell of Sean touches her nose. Immediately, she remembered where she was. The feeling made her feel safe. She spotted Sean. He was lying back in his chair with his feet propped up on his bed, sleeping sweetly. She does not want to wake him up. She watched him sleep. He started to open his eyes, and he smiled when he saw her eyes looking at him. Despite what she just been through, her eyes and her face are smiling. "Ashlee, you look so beautiful."

Without another word, Ashlee climbed out of bed and onto Sean's lap; and they wrapped their arms around each other. They held each other for a while. Ashlee felt safe in Sean's arms, and she was so thankful that he was there last night. She probably would not be in his arms right now if he was not there. Ashlee held Sean as tight as she can. She could not let go. Sean just held her as long as she needed it. Ashlee started to cry and shake. He held her tighter. Sean whispered, "I am here for you, and I will never leave you. Let it all go."

Some weeks go by, and Ashlee is still at Sean's place. They have not found Zach yet. She knew he is out there somewhere. He is sending her threats through text messages. From Zach: "I know you are out there somewhere, and if you are with him, he is dead. You are going to be punished." She never responded to Zach. Then she had a sickening. Maybe Zach can track her through her cell phone. She immediately turned it off and decided to get a new one with a new number. On the way to the store, Ashlee quickly asked Sean to pull over. She opened her door and got sick. The look on her face was shock when she was done. Her eyes got wide, and she said, "Oh no, no, no! Please no!" Sean was looking at her with a questioning look on his face.

Ashlee had Sean stop at a drugstore so that she could pick up a test after she got her new cell phone. When they got home, she took the test and waited the three long minutes. The results appeared in the little window, and Ashlee's heart skipped a couple beats. Then her heart started to race. Sean read that Ashlee is indeed pregnant. He vowed at that moment that he was the one who was going to help Ashlee take care of the baby. The real father is never going to know about the baby. Sean looked at Ashlee with a tender look of want and need. Sean is about to give away his heart in three words, "I love you."

Ashlee stopped dead in her tracks when those words came out. Her reply was priceless. She kissed him; and in that moment, Sean knew Ashlee loved him back. "Sean, I love you!"

"Ashlee, do something for me please."

"Yes, anything!"

"Marry me!"

Ashlee's heart skipped more beats. "Sean, I want to so much, but I can't. For as long as Zach is still on this earth, he will never let me go."

"Then we go to another country and get married, or we get a court order to let him sign the papers. We do whatever it takes to get you away from him. I never want to see you go through that again. I want so much to be yours forever."

Ashlee looked into Sean's eyes as she searched her thoughts. "Okay, yes!" Sean's smile blinded Ashlee as he scooped her up in a bear hug.

Ashlee said yes because she knew she would have a better life. Ashlee said yes because she has known Sean since high school. Ashlee said yes because she knows she loves Sean, and she can be with him for the rest of her life. She knows she will never hurt again in the arms of Sean. He will never hit her, he will never make her do anything she does not want to do, and he won't put her down. She will love him like she has never loved anyone before. Even though the baby now growing inside of her is not Sean's, he will make a great father to the baby. She can't wait to see them together.

A week went by. Ashlee and Sean went to practice for the first time. The first scene they practiced was the scene that Ashlee fell apart on when she and Sean practiced. She made it through like a professional. Ashlee enjoyed practicing, and she enjoyed working with Sean. She thought to herself, *He looks so hot while in character.* The way he sings with her is so amazing. His voice is mesmerizing, and she can't help but get lost in it. She looks at him with pride in her eyes and love in her heart. He loves the way she looks at him. He feels her love for him in every word and every note she sings. The way she looks at him melts his heart, and he falls deeper in love with her. He loves singing with her. The way they sound together takes his heart by storm. The way he looks at her during their songs is sure to melt the audience's hearts. Since Sean and Ashlee are in love for real, it makes for great chemistry onstage.

Since practice has started and the opening night is approaching, Sean and Ashlee decided to stay in the city. They work day and night at the play. They are enjoying every minute of it. They do the scenes with ease, and they heat up the stage as they do it. Ashlee and Sean also hire a lawyer to help them with Zach. He has ways to get Zach to sign the papers. She files the papers she needed to get Zach out of her life. She filed the divorce papers and a restraining order. Then she applied to have Zach served to sign the papers, or he goes to jail. Ashlee waits now for the signed papers. She is hoping to be free of Zach. She can't wait to start her life with Sean. But the opening night is just two days away.

Ashlee got a text message, "Oh, you think you could change your number and hide from me? I will find you. Just so you know, I did sign your papers, but it does not mean you are no longer mine. You will always be mine." Ashlee started to breathe heavily.

Sean was at her side when he realized what was going on. Ashlee handed him her phone, and he read the text. "How did he get your cell phone number again?" Ashlee's world began to spin, and she fainted. Sean caught her before she hit the floor. She comes to a second later, and Sean has her wrapped in his arms. "Are you okay?" Sean asks.

"I must have gotten lightheaded. I am okay now." Ashlee turned off her cell phone so that he couldn't track it. She cannot understand how he keeps finding her. She cannot focus on that right now. She has to focus on opening night and the next eight weeks, the length of the play. She also decided to give her phone to the police so that they could track him down.

Opening night is finally upon them, and Ashlee is a little nervous. She is also excited. She is staring at Sean as he gets into character. She heads back to her dressing room. She is looking forward to seeing his hard work brought to life. It amazes her that she gets to be by his side through his dream. She is also excited to share the good news with him because she got the signed divorce papers in the mail. Eight weeks from that point, they will be married. Ashlee is busy getting into character when there is a knock on her dressing room door. Ashlee opens it and sees a huge bouquet and Sean holding them with a smile. "These are for you, sweetheart. I will see you out there. I love you. Break a leg."

"These are so beautiful. I love you. Break a leg also." They kissed each other, and Sean left for the stage. Ashlee followed him a moment later.

Ashlee could hear the announcer start the show as she got into position. Her heart is racing as she gets to stare into Sean's eyes for the opening scene. The play starts with the character's wedding day. Ashlee cannot wait for it to be real. The curtain opens, and Ashlee's face lights up as she gets to say her character's vows. The play goes on without a hitch. When the play ends and they get to take a bow, it is the most amazing feeling Ashlee ever felt. The audience is giving them a standing ovation. The announcer says each name of the actors and actresses, and they step forward. When Sean stepped forward, he took Ashlee with him; and he wrapped her in his arms, dipped her, and kissed her. The applause roared louder, and Ashlee's heart fluttered loudly.

When Ashlee and Sean were leaving, reporters stormed the exit and got them on camera. They had no choice then but to stop. Ashlee did not want to be on camera, but there was nothing she could do to avoid it. She heard questions like "Are you two an item in real life?"

"That was some play. The chemistry was off the charts. Are you two really married?" They stopped, and Ashlee answered, "Yes, we are an item, and yes, we will be getting married soon."

Then she heard, "That kiss at the end—will we see more like that?"

Sean smiled and answered, "Yes, you will be because I love Ashlee Foster." They continued to ask questions, but Shawn ushered Ashlee to the car and drove off.

Ashlee is feeling the rush of everything she has just been through. The assurance from the audience of how the play went and the way people reacted to the kiss and their relationship. She is sitting at the breakfast bar reading the paper highlighting the play from last night. Sean walks into the kitchen and goes for the orange juice in the fridge. Ashlee reads the opening lines of the review, "*The Power of Marriage* is an inspiration that we all need in our life. Ashlee and Sean heat up the stage with their chemistry. Yes, you heard it right. They are a couple on and off stage. We are looking forward to seeing this couple light up stages for years to come."

Sean turns on the news and hears the anchor say something about the play. "I was a witness last night to an amazing play. *The Power of Marriage* held their opening night last night. It was inspiring, and it kept my attention. The chemistry between the two main characters is hot. If you weren't there last night, I encourage you to go and see this play. The schedule is on our website along with the address of the theater."

Sean flips to other news stations, and they are all talking about the play. Some comments were "Both Sean's and Ashlee's voices together will blow you away." The kiss was hot." "The way Sean and Ashlee bring the characters to life is amazing."

Ashlee is standing still in shock as Sean flips more news stations. Even the entertainment world in New York is talking about the hot new play coming out of Philadelphia.

Sean's phone rings, and he picks up, "Hello!"

"Hello, Sean, my name is Greg, and I am a producer out of California. I have a project that you may be interested in. Your leading lady—is there a way you can get hold of her and see if both of you can come for an audition?"

"Yes, Greg, she is actually right here with me. She is my fiancée."

"That is great. When is your next show, and when do you have a break so that we can fly you and Ashlee out here to audition?"

"We have another show tomorrow night, and we break for two days. We can come out after the show, which will end around 10:00 p.m. EST."

"Okay, we will have plane tickets waiting for you at Philadelphia Airport. We will also have hotel reservations ready for you."

"Thank you, Greg. Is there a way you could give us something to practice until we get there?"

"Yes, check your email. There should be something there for you to review. Thank you for taking my call, and I look forward to meeting you and Ashlee soon. Talk to you soon."

Before Sean had a chance to say anything more, Greg hung up. Sean now has the shocked look on his face. "We have an audition in two days, and they are flying us to California for us to audition."

Ashlee's heart started to flutter, and she heard her heart pound with excitement. Ashlee moves over to Sean and sits on his lap as he pulls up the script that was just sent to him, and they both read it together. The opening lines made Ashlee fall in love with the story that they might be able to help tell. "Sean, I am really hoping we get these roles. I am loving this script, and I can relate to the lead character." The next thing Sean gets is their ticket reservation confirmation. They have to be at the airport by midnight, and they are in first class.

The next night, the play receives another standing ovation and goes as well as it did opening night. Sean and Ashlee were inundated with business cards from agents to producers to directors. They gathered all the cards and placed them in their wallets so that they could look over them when they travel. They made it to the airport by 11:00 p.m. They were on the plane and waiting for takeoff by twelve fifteen. They landed around 3:00 a.m. California time. Greg was there with Sean's last name on a sign. "Hello, Sean and Ashlee, I am Greg. We talked on the phone. Do you have checked bags?"

"No, we don't. Just what we carried."

They walked to the car. "What do you both think of the script?" Greg asks the couple.

Ashlee speaks up first, "I love it. I can relate to the main character."

"That is good to hear. I was hoping you liked it."

Sean speaks up, "I love the story that we may get to tell."

Greg asked, "When is the play over for you?"

Sean answers the question, "We have seven weeks left with two shows each week."

"That sounds perfect. It is good timing for us." Greg gives the driver the address to the hotel where they will be staying, and off they go. They talk more about the script. Greg also gives them their audition time, which is 2:00 p.m. later that day. "Meanwhile, I would like you two to sleep so that you are refreshed for the audition. I really want you two to be a part of this movie."

Sean and Ashlee check in and get only one room. That was the last room they had. They are okay with that because they know what is important to them. They curled up together and fell asleep.

Around noon, the alarm goes off, and they begin to wake up. The face Ashlee sees when she first opens her eyes is Sean's, and she is overwhelmed by the way he looks at her. She can't wait until she can wake up like this for the rest of her life. She untangles herself from Sean and claims the shower first. She is ready to go in less than twenty minutes. Sean then hops into the shower, and he is ready in less than twenty minutes. They decided to go get a snack from the hotel lobby. There was a restaurant and bar there, and they ordered a snack. They got it and sat down outside to eat. They talked and watched for the car to pull up.

The car pulled up around one forty-five, and they recognized the driver from earlier this morning. Around 2:00 p.m., they pulled up to the audition, and into the building they went. The audition went well, and they felt they nailed it. They will find out later that day if they got the part. Meanwhile, Sean got this crazy look on his face. "Ashlee, what are we waiting for? I mean, let's get married today." Sean got down on one knee and asked again this time with a ring. "Ashlee, I can't wait any longer for you to be my wife. Please be my wife today?"

Ashlee has tears running down her face. She looked from Sean to the ring and back up to him. "Yes, let's do it today!"

Sean knows of a wedding chapel that is not too far from where they are now. They decided to walk there. They walked and enjoyed the beautiful afternoon. They arrived at the chapel, and they did not have to wait long. They got everything they needed and had to wait for at least an hour. They took that time and bought a dress and a suit. They even picked out their wedding bands. They decided to surprise each other by picking out each other's bands. Sean found one that matches her engagement ring perfectly. Her engagement ring is a one-carat diamond stud with two smaller diamonds on either side in a gold band. The wedding band has diamonds that matches the engagement ring. It is also gold. They made their selections and headed back to the chapel.

When it was their turn to take their vows, Ashlee was all smiles, and her face was bright. Her real life is about to start. They step up to the officiant, and he starts, but all they can do is to stare at each other. "Sean, you prepared your vows?"

"Yes, Ashlee, when I stepped out of the rain, my life changed. I never thought I would ever find my perfect match. I am happy that you were in that laundromat that day. I found you my perfect match. I promise to love you, protect you, and trade my life for yours. I promise to love you through all our trials together. I promise to love you through our good and bad times and never leave you. I promise to cherish you because you are the love I have been waiting for and the love of my life."

"Ashlee, what do you have prepared for Sean?"

"Sean, I spent some of my life in darkness. I knew there was a better life for me. When you stepped into my life on that rainy day, I knew I was saved from that darkness. You are my dream, and I have been waiting for you also. I promise to love you and protect you. I promise to love you through anything we go through. I promise to love you through sickness and health. I promise you are mine for the rest of our lives. You are the love of my life, and I will forever love you."

Sean placed the ring on Ashlee's finger, and she looked down at it with tears in her eyes. Then she placed Sean's ring on his finger. His ring was like hers. It had twelve little diamonds tucked into the gold band. The officiant says, "I now pronounce you husband and wife. You may kiss your bride."

Sean leaned in and placed the most tender kiss he had. In that kiss, Ashlee felt his love, honor, and respect for her. She felt her future, and she felt passion in his kiss. Then they turned and walked out higher than anything on love and devotion for each other.

They went back to the studio where they had their audition, and Sean got a call from Greg. "Hello, Sean, are you two still around so that we can talk?"

"Yes, we just got back to the studio. We will be right in."

Mr. and Mrs. Sean Garison walk into the building. "Hello, Sean, nice to see you again." They followed Greg to his office. There are two other stars in his office already. Ashlee's heart skipped a beat when she realized who they were. They are two of her favorite actors. They costarred in one of her favorite movies. They lit up the screen with their chemistry. He, Peter, is a great actor and cares for his costars. His passion for his work shows in every role he plays. She, May, loves her job and gets to play different lifestyles and brightens up the screen in every role she does. "Sean and Ashlee, do you want the good news or the bad news first?"

"There's bad news?"

"The bad news is we decided to change the movie a little bit. The good news is you two will be costarring alongside these two as best friends."

Ashlee's face lit up, and her smile lit up the room. Her heart is racing two miles a minute as excitement raced through her veins. Today cannot get any better.

As Ashlee and Sean signed their contracts, Greg noticed something different. "Wait, you two got married?"

Sean smiled. "Yes, we did. We just did it."

Peter and May both say congratulations. Peter suggested that they go out and get to know one another and celebrate. Ashlee said yes right away, and Sean followed in response.

May and Ashlee started to talk to each other. "I am guessing you know who I am by the look on your face when you walked into the office."

Ashlee responded, "Yes, I am a big fan especially when you two starred together in one of my favorite movies. If it is not too much to ask, may I have your autograph?"

"Yes, you may, but I want yours also because when we are done, people will love you."

Peter looked back and said, "I want yours also."

Ashlee smiled, "You can have mine if I get yours as well."

"Deal."

Peter looks just as good as Sean does, and she is loving her view right now. They make their way to an out-of-the-way restaurant. It is where all the stars go to get away from the paparazzi. Sean and Ashlee spend the rest of the afternoon and most of the night with their new friends, and it feels like they have been friends for a long time.

That night, when they got back to their hotel room, it was all-out desire for each other. They were finally able to explore each other. It was the most beautiful experience. They connected in ways that no one has ever done. Ashlee was so overwhelmed that she started to cry. "Ashlee, are you okay?"

"Yes, Sean, I am perfect. I have never felt this much love in my lifetime, and it is so amazing."

Sean smiled and took her again.

CHAPTER 3

What Else Does Life Have

Sean and Ashlee headed home to finish the seven weeks of their play. They are having so much fun with the characters they play. Each night, they get better and better. Greg takes Max to watch the play, and Max says to Greg, "I can't wait to see what they do with the role they will play for our movie." Meanwhile, their movie *Best Friends* is scouting out movie locations. Greg and Max, the director, decided to see what treasures Pennsylvania holds. They fell in love with a location in Chester County, Pennsylvania, and they decided to use that location. Chester County is a great location. It sits just outside of the city of Philadelphia, and it has great views of the changing of the seasons. Greg and Max find a newly built neighborhood and ask to rent out some of the new houses that have not been sold yet. They were able to get seven houses for temporary use. They were in a cul-de-sac that does not have any residents in yet. That was a perfect setting for a lot of the scenes.

Sean and Ashlee prepare for the last show of their play. Ashlee gets flowers delivered to her, and she reads the note attached, "I will be watching you." Ashlee's heart sank because she recognized the handwriting. Sean watched as Ashlee went from a pretty rosy pink to white. She hands him the message, and he gasps. "This means he is out there in the audience. I don't think I will be able to focus on what I have to do."

"Ashlee, I am by your side. Focus on me while we are out there. But I will be okay if your understudy goes out there and you safe in here."

"No, I am going to do this. It is our last show. I am going to do this for you."

Sean takes his wife's hand and leads her to her opening spot. At first, Ashlee was so nervous as the curtain started to open. She almost ran out, but she caught the eyes of Sean, and all her worries melted away. She used her fear to her advantage and gave the performance of a lifetime.

The director of the play steps to the stage and gives the finale closing. "This has been an amazing eight weeks for all of us. I just want to introduce you to our actors. First of all, this couple auditioned for the main two roles, and during their audition, we were blown away. We watched as their love grew both on and off stage. Our husband and wife, Mr. and Mrs. Sean Garison. I want to present them with this year's best actors award for their onstage performance. This play would not be as successful if we did not have all the actors you see before us."

He started naming all the actors. Ashlee caught a glimpse of movement from the corner of her eye. She looked and saw Zach standing to the right of the stage. Sean realized what Ashlee was looking at, and he pulled her closer to himself. Zach did a little bow and clapped. Then he ran his hand across his neck to signify that someone was going to die. Ashlee started to panic, and she did her final bow and left the stage. Once they got to their dressing room, Ashlee started to cry, and Sean wrapped her into his arms. "He will never leave us alone," Ashlee said in between her sobs. Sean called security and had them ready to escort them out of the building.

Sean kept looking over his shoulder as security led them out. They made it to the car safely. They were on their way home, and Sean kept looking in his mirrors as he navigated the streets. As far as he sees, there is no one following him. They pull into the driveway, and out of the car, they step. The next thing Ashlee hears is a gunshot, and Sean falls to the ground. Ashlee runs to his side. "Sean, please no! Sean, breathe. Don't leave me." Ashlee cries out, and neighbors come out of their houses. The next thing Ashlee feels is arms around her, and she is lifted to her feet and thrown into a car. Her world goes dark.

Ashlee wakes up, and her head is throbbing. She looks around and sees nothing but darkness. Her hands are tied behind her back, and she can't move. Her thoughts immediately go to Sean. Her last sight of him was when he was on the ground, not moving. Tears started flowing down her cheeks. She does not know if he is alive or dead. She starts to say out loud, "Sean, please be okay. I love you. Fight for us. I will see you again. Hang on, baby. I will be by your side as soon as I can."

The sound of footsteps interrupted her thoughts, and a familiar voice came before the light clicked on. "Now that I have you back, we can move on with our lives. Don't worry, sweetheart, I do forgive you, but you need to be punished."

Zach punched her in the face. Then he kicked her in the legs and stomach. "Zach, please don't hit me in the stomach. I am pregnant." He stopped, and he contemplated. He then punched her in the stomach. Ashlee cries out again; and before she could stop her words, she screams, "The baby is yours!"

He stops dead in his tracks, dropping his hands and rubbing her stomach. "It is about time that I have a child. We will make great parents together."

Ashlee did not say much after that. He was not worth more of her words. He hits her one more time in the face; and as he exited the room, he says, "I will see you tomorrow morning with your breakfast." He turns off the light and leaves her in the dark.

Meanwhile, the neighbors that came out of their houses rushed to Sean's aid. One of his neighbors called 911. Five minutes later, an ambulance could be heard screaming down the street along with police. The paramedics rush to Sean as the police took statements. The neighbors could hear the paramedics say, "I can't believe this man is still alive with this head wound." They load Sean into the ambulance, and they rush to the hospital. The witnesses told the police that Ashlee was taken, and they need to start a manhunt for her and her abductor. They gave the police the best description they could. Officer Josh Bradly asked, "Is there anyone we could notify in case of emergency?" Sean's closest neighbor John gives Officer Bradly the number of Mike's director from the play. Officer Bradly calls Mike and gives him the news. Mike's heart sank, and he then called Max, the movie director. Mike rushes to the hospital to be by Sean's side.

The next day, Max, Greg, Peter, and May show up to be by Sean's side. Despite Sean's injury, he is hanging in there. The bullet entered his head and lodged in a spot that was not interfering with anything vital. But it does not rule out brain damage. The damage may keep him in a coma, but there is still brain activity. The doctors are keeping a close eye on him.

It has been two days, and Ashlee is still tied. When Zach comes to the room, she asks, "Zach, please untie me. I can't feel my legs or arms. I won't leave I promise."

Zach contemplated her request, and he untied her arms and legs. She was able to stand up and shake the feeling back into her limbs. Zach took this time to undress her against her will, but she has learned not to go against him. He also had water and a sponge. He started giving her a sponge bath. Then he brushed her hair, and then he cleaned her chair. After he was done cleaning up, he left her naked and tied her hands together in front of her but left her to roam the room. He took her clothes. He has plans for her later. Ashlee's mind goes to a safe place, a place where Sean is, waiting for her. She closes her eyes, and she is with him. He is holding her, and she feels him wrapped around her. His eyes are so sweet and loving. She feels that he is fighting for their love. She feels him hanging on. She hangs on to the feeling that she will be with him soon. She is imagining Sean when Zach comes back with some food. He also brings wine. His plan is to give her a romantic dinner, and then he can have his way with her. He does just what he planned. She did not give him the satisfaction of any sound or word. He wanted her to say his name, but she stayed silent. Her body reacted to his touch and his need, but she gave him nothing else. He wanted to kiss her, but she kept turning away. After Zach was done, he left her alone to her thoughts.

Ashlee tried to go to her safe place again but could not find Sean. She can't feel him anymore. She has a feeling he has slipped away from her. She is panicking, and she is searching for him. Meanwhile, at the hospital, the nurses and doctors are running to Sean's room as his heart and breathing machines start to alarm, telling he is not well. They fight to bring him back. Peter and May watch in horror as they fight to save him.

Ashlee has tears running down her face. She is searching for her love. She can't live without him, and now she is worried that she is stuck here forever. She is holding tight to her love for Sean, and she is never letting go. "Sean, please be here with me. Don't leave me. Hold on to me and never let go. Find me. I love you so much. Feel my love for you."

It has been a month since Ashlee has been abducted. Zach comes in every day to bathe her and make love to her. Her body is weak, and she can barely move. She is asleep in the corner of the room when the door to her room flies open. She barely opens her eyes and catches a glimpse of an officer. "Ashlee Garison, I am Officer Josh Bradly, and I am here to take you out of here." Josh throws his jacket around Ashlee as he unties her hands. Josh picks her up and takes her out to the waiting ambulance. Ashlee is relieved but empty. She can't feel Sean anymore. She had lost her will to survive.

Ashlee is on her way to the hospital, but all she could think about was Sean. She knows he left her not by his will but by the hands of Zach. She can't feel Sean, and the only way to see him now is in her dreams. She is also slowly losing her will to live. She is finally with her match, her soulmate, but he was taken from her by the man she now hates. She is weak, and she can't move. She hears the paramedic say, "Take her to where her friends are waiting for her." Her thoughts went to Peter and May. Then her thoughts went to the movie. *Oh god, we will have to be replaced. I can't do it without Sean.* Ashlee drifts off to sleep. Her last thought was on Sean.

A couple of hours later, Ashlee wakes up to Peter and May sitting next to her. She stares at May, and May has the biggest smile on her face. Ashlee is too weak to move or smile. Then again, she does not want to. Tears come out of her eyes. "Ashlee, don't cry. Everything is going to be okay. You are here, and you are safe. We are here for you, and he is here for you." May moves slightly to her left, and Ashlee's eyes focus on the figure in the bed next to her.

Ashlee's eyes darted back and forth between the man in the bed and May and then to Peter. "Sean?" May nods. Ashlee mustered all he strength she could just to get up. It was a slow move. Peter helps her get untangled from the bed covers, and he picks her up. He then gently places her in the bed with Sean. "Sean, I am here, baby. Please wake up. I love you," Ashlee whispers. Ashlee moves a little to get comfortable, and she falls asleep. Her energy is wiped out. Peter and May stay in the room with them.

Ashlee sleeps soundly until morning. It is the best sleep she has gotten in a month. The baby is already active and kicking. Ashlee has not opened her eyes yet; but she is feeling a hand on her head, caressing her hair over and over. She then heard May gasp and let out a cheer. But Ashlee did not have to open her eyes to know who is touching her. "Sean." She brings her hand up to his on her head. She opened her eyes and saw the most tender, most loving eyes looking back at her. Sean still had the tube in his throat, but he was smiling down at her. Then he frowned as he saw the bruises and cuts to her face. He touches each one, and his brow creases. She kisses his hand. "I am okay. Yes, they do hurt but not as bad as my heart did when I was away from you." He smiled a little, but he still looked mad at what Zach had done.

By that time, the doctor was in the room, ready to remove the tube from Sean's throat. His first words were a whisper, "Ashlee, I have missed you, but I have heard you. You told me to fight and not to leave you. I love you."

Tears were flowing down Ashlee's cheeks. "I thought I have lost you. I could not feel you anymore. I could not live without you, and I was ready to give up."

Sean wrapped his arms around Ashlee and held her as tight as he could. They fell back to sleep together. May watched in awe as Sean and Ashlee are together again. Peter and May stayed in their room until they got hungry. They left a note for Sean and Ashlee, giving them their numbers and letting them know that the movie will be on hold until they recover. If they need anything, they can call.

It has been three weeks, and both of them are recovering well. Ashlee is gaining her strength back. Sean is healing perfectly, and the baby is healthy. Sean and Ashlee got word that they are going home tomorrow. Since the baby is four months and Ashlee has not seen the baby, her OB doctor takes her and Sean up to do an ultrasound. For the first time, Ashlee saw her baby, and Sean could not believe his eyes. Then Ashlee remembered something. Tears started to flow down Ashlee's face again. The nurse excused herself for a bit, and Ashlee said, "Sean, I had to tell Zach that this baby is his. He was hitting me in my stomach, and I had to keep this baby safe."

Sean looked at Ashlee and said, "You had to do whatever you had to protect yourself and the baby. I am proud of you for that, and I love you."

"I love you also, but remember, your name is going on the birth certificate. He is not going to have any connections to this baby."

"I agree. This baby is going to be ours."

It has been a week since they have been home, and they are running lines together. Getting ready for the movie is taking their minds off the past month. Ashlee gets nightmares at night, and Sean holds her as she trembles. Peter and May join them for dinner on most nights, and they work together on the script. The more they spend together, the more they feel like best friends. May surprised both Sean and Ashlee with a baby shower. They invited the cast members who will accompany them on the movie. Ashlee felt overwhelmed and had the time of her life there with people gathered around her. With what happened, she thought she would not have this if it was not for Sean. She watches him as he interacts with Peter and some of their other costars. She can't believe that this is really happening. Her life is on the right track, and she can't ask for anything else. She studies and stares at Sean every chance she gets. Ashlee keeps falling in love with Sean.

A couple of days go by, and Ashlee thought to herself, *I don't know what happened to Zach.* She decides to call Officer Josh. "Hello, Officer Bradly, this is Ashlee Garison. I never asked you what happened to Zach."

"Hello, Ashlee, I am sorry to tell you that he was not there when we found you, and we are on a manhunt for him."

"Why am I just finding out about this?"

"I am sorry, Ashlee. I wanted to make sure you heal before letting you know about Zach. We are keeping an eye on you and Sean because he is still out there."

"Please, Officer Bradly, keep me updated."

"I will, and please call me Josh."

"Okay, thank you, Josh."

Ashlee got off the phone and started to pace. Sean walked into the room and stopped dead as he looked at the anguish on Ashlee's face. "Ashlee, what is the matter?"

"I just got off the phone with Josh. He tells me that Zach is still out there somewhere."

Sean stopped Ashlee from pacing, and when he wrapped her in his arms, she was trembling. "Don't worry, he is not going to rip you from my arms again ever." Ashlee sank into Sean until she stopped trembling.

Three months have gone by. Sean and Ashlee are in the middle of filming with their best friends Peter and May. They are having so much fun. But in the back of Ashlee's mind is the fact that Zach still has not been found and he could be anywhere. Ashlee has learned to take her fear and use it to give her performance a boost. When they are not working on the film, Sean, Ashlee, May, and Peter all hang out with one another. When they are on break on the set, Ashlee is able to take naps. She is usually wrapped in Sean's arms when she takes naps. Sean loves watching her sleep in his arms. He lies on his back, and Ashlee has her head on his chest. One of her arms is tucked up just next to his body, and the other one is hung around his torso. Her legs are intertwined with his as she dozes off. Sean is in awe of his wife and of his life now. He never ever wants to be anywhere without the love of her. He is kind of thankful in a way that he was in a coma when she was gone. He would have been a mess. He knew he would never sleep until she was in his arms. He would have been out looking for her, and he would have not given up until he found her. He never wants to feel loss, so he will do whatever it takes to keep her by his side. No matter what, he will love her forever.

CHAPTER 4

Life Changing

Another two months have gone by, and the movie was a wrap for about two weeks now. Ashlee can't wait to see the movie when it is all put together. She also can't wait until she gets to see the baby. The baby is two days overdue but still healthy. It seems like the way Ashlee sits or sleeps is uncomfortable. The only way Ashlee gets any sleep is when she is sitting up with her head on Sean's chest. For now, they both are on their sectional sleeping. For Sean, it is the best place to be. For Ashlee, it is so comfortable that she falls asleep almost immediately. It is two in the morning, and Ashlee is in her usual spot when the pain shots up out of nowhere. She lets out a whimper, and Sean wakes up immediately. "Baby, what happened?"

"I think it is time."

Sean springs to action. He quickly grabs her and his shoes. He slides her shoes on her, and then in less than two seconds, his shoes are on. He then grabs a jacket for her and her bag. He wrapped the jacket around her; and in one swift move, he had her in his arms. He moves to the car with ease; and the next thing Ashlee knows, they are on the road. Even though Ashlee is in a lot of pain, she is smiling. "You have been practicing. You made that look so easy."

"Yes, I have. I knew I had to be prepared, and I did not want to miss anything. I was told the story of my dad when I was about to meet the world. All I can say is it was not pretty."

They make it to the hospital in record time. Sean is at Ashlee's door, picking her up in yet another swift move. He raced inside. He throws his keys to the valet and runs inside. "My wife is having a baby." The closest nurse moved a bed to his direction, and he laid Ashlee on it. Sean, Ashlee, and three nurses rush Ashlee to delivery. An hour later, Ashlee is exhausted but is holding her bundle of joy. Sean is in awe as he sees mother and daughter together. She is seven pounds five ounces and twenty-one inches long. She looks exactly like her mother. Ashlee gives the honor of naming her to Sean. "You want me to name her?"

"Yes, after all, she is our daughter."

Sean picks the names that will honor both of their mothers: Kristine Amelia Garison. His mom's first name was Kristine, and Ashlee's mom's name was Amelia.

Ashlee smiles at her daughter and says, "Daddy gave you a beautiful name."

Kristine is asleep in Ashlee's arms so content and peaceful, but she hands her off to Sean to hold. Kristine gets comfortable in his arms and is still content. She does not make a sound, and Sean makes an instant connection. Kristine's mouth goes up into a little smile only for a second. Sean caught it, and his heart melted. She may not be his flesh and blood, but he is her father, and he will cherish this child forever.

A couple of hours later, the records receptionist came into the room and asked Ashlee to sign the birth certificate if it was correct. Ashlee looks it over and notices the father's name is blank. Ashlee says to the receptionist, "This should have Sean's name on the line," and

Ashlee grabs the pen from the receptionist's hand. She writes Sean Michael Garison on the line.

"Thank you for the correction, Mrs. Garison."

"You're welcome."

Ashlee loves hearing Mrs. Garison. It has a nice ring to it. She also loves the name Kristine Amelia. It is so pretty. Ashlee is watching Sean with Kristine. He is so natural with her, and she sees the love of a father in Sean's eyes. He is over by the window of the room. He is standing near the last rays of sunlight as the sun continues its descent to the horizon. Sean is looking down at Kristine's face. Then he looks at Ashlee and then back at Kristine as she settles down to sleep again. He says out loud, "This is amazing, and you know what, your mom is amazing also."

The nurse came in to take Kristine to the nursery to allow Ashlee to get some much-needed sleep. Sean and Ashlee ate dinner. Then Sean climbed into bed with Ashlee, and they both fell asleep.

Zach is at the nursery window scanning the babies, looking for the baby of Ashlee Foster. He came across Kristine. Zach recognized Kristine because she looks like her mother. But he does see himself in her as well. She has his eyes. Then he realized the name over her head. Zach's face turns red with fire burning through his cheeks. He says out loud, "Garison, Kristine! She is supposed to be mine. Her last name is Garison!" Zach hit his fist against the wall as he walked out. The nursery nurses were startled at the sound and watched as Zach stormed off. Moments later, he passed Ashlee's room, and he stopped, and he saw Sean and Ashlee fast asleep. The sight of Sean infuriated him more. He thinks of a plan, and he leaves the hospital to put it in motion. "She is going to regret taking my child from me."

Sean is excited. He is taking his family home today. As Ashlee is getting Kristine ready for the drive home, Sean went to go put the car seat in the car and pull the car to the door. May is there helping Ashlee, and she grabs Ashlee's bag, and the nurse is rolling Ashlee and Kristine out to the waiting car of Sean. When they get to the outside door, Sean is nowhere to be found. Ashlee looks at May. "Maybe he is having trouble with the car seat."

"I will go see if he needs help. I did park right next to him." May motioned to the security officer to please watch them as she went. May rounds the corner and heads to the parking lot. She can see the vehicles from a distance, but Sean is not anywhere around the car. May rushed to the car and saw the back door open and the car seat in place. Her heart starts to race. She gets the keys and closes the door. When she closed the door, she saw fresh blood on the ground. She locks the car, and races to where she left Ashlee. She immediately asks the security officer to call the police, and Ashlee's eyes get big. Her heart starts to race also. "May, where is Sean?"

"He was not at the car, and there was blood on the ground."

Ten minutes later, May is talking to the police. They are inspecting the Audi. The officer even asked to see video surveillance. Officer Josh showed up finally and got all the information. His heart sank when he saw the video. He found Ashlee by the car. She is holding on to Kristine on the verge of tears. May is rubbing her back. "Josh, where is my husband?"

"It does not look good, Ashlee. We caught Sean being abducted by Zach. He keeps playing games with us, and he manages to slip through our fingers when we get close."

Ashlee starts to panic. She hands Kristine to May, and she starts to pace. Tears are coming down her cheeks. She just can't believe that Zach has Sean now. Ashlee stops and sinks to the ground in a heap of tears.

Meanwhile, Sean is waking up to his arms tied above his head, and he is hanging from them. He feels blood coming down his cheek. Then he feels the sharpest pain as he is struck from behind. "You took my life from me. You have my wife and my daughter. You don't deserve my life, and you will pay for stealing from me."

Sean laughs a little and says, "You don't deserve your life either."

Sean feels another blow to his back. "I have a plan for your bride. She better go for it, or you are dead. When she does not show up, you will get hurt."

Ashlee gets smart and goes to the store and buys a prepaid phone. She sets it up and calls Zach. He answers on the first ring. "Zach, what did you do with my husband? Let him go now."

"No, I am not going to do that just yet. You are going to suffer the way you made me suffer."

"When I find you, you will pay for this."

"Oh, darling, you made me suffer for over a year now. I will keep you suffering for as long as I want. I want to see your pain that you go through. Once a week, you are going to have dinner with me for a year. As long as you don't break our date, you will have your precious Sean back."

"How would I know you are not hurting Sean in the process?"

"I will give you video access of him."

"Let me see him now." She could hear Zach flipping over to video. The next thing she sees is Sean's marked body hanging by his hands. "Cut him down right now, and I will make that deal with you. But the minute Sean is hit or uncomfortable, our deal is off, and your life will be torture."

Ashlee heard Sean speak. "Ashlee, please don't do this for me. Let me go. I can't let you do this for me. Please don't let this asshole win."

Zach punched Sean for that. "Zach, don't touch him ever, or our deal is off, and you will let him go."

"We will see about that. Our first date will be this Friday at our first-ever restaurant at 7:00 p.m. You need to bring our daughter to this one. Oh, and one more thing, if I see a cop, Sean is dead."

"No, she will never see you. She will be with a babysitter. She is Sean's daughter. She may have your DNA in her, but she will never be your daughter."

"Okay, I will let that go for now. Who are you allowing to watch her?"

"It is none of your business. I will see you Friday. Now give me the code so that I can keep an eye on Sean."

Zach texted the code to her. Then she watched him cut the ropes to Sean's hands, and he dropped to the floor. Ashlee saw more bruises and cuts on his body. "Now in the video, Ashlee, you will be able to hear Sean, but, Sean, you will not hear Ashlee." Zach hangs up, and Ashlee immediately goes to the text message and instantly connects to the video feed going into Sean's room. Sean is still lying on the floor, and it breaks Ashlee's heart. Ashlee is staring at the phone, tears running down her cheeks. Sean is right there, and she can't hold him. She can't touch him or comfort him. Sean starts to talk out loud. He pleads with Ashlee to let him go, "I can't bear for him to be near you. I can't bear for him to touch you. Please, Ashlee, don't do what he wants. Take care of yourself, and please keep Kristine safe. I love you, Ashlee, and I will never let go of you, but please let me go."

Ashlee cries harder. Her heart is breaking and shattering into a million pieces on the floor. She is in her car, yelling, "Sean, I will never let you go! I love you. You will be with us soon. Please, Sean, don't let go of us."

The tears subside, and Ashlee starts the car. She heads straight to Josh's office. Josh could tell that she has been crying. "Ashlee, what's wrong?" She hands him the phone with the video feed. Josh's eyes go wide as he realizes what he is looking at. "Is there any way you could track the feed to where it is coming from?"

"Did he give you a code to log into this feed?"

"Yes." She shows him the code.

He logs onto the feed from his computer, and he taps a couple of keys and sees that the signal is bouncing all over the place. "Oh, he is good. It is going to take a while before we can trace the signal. But I think we can work with this."

"But the next thing I am going to tell you, you have to promise me that you will not show up until we find Sean and he is safe."

"Okay, I promise."

"Zach is making me go out to dinner with him once a week for a year before he will release Sean. If he sees cops, he will kill Sean. If I miss one night with him, he will hurt Sean. Right now, May and Peter are in California. I was wondering if you could go undercover as my babysitter. I am never taking Kristine with me."

"We can make some arrangements for that, and yes, I will be happy to be your undercover babysitter."

CHAPTER 5

The Torture

It has been a long eight months, and Ashlee has kept her end of the deal. She has sent food to Sean through Zach, but she has to threaten Zach to give it to him. Ashlee also had to go to their movie premiere without Sean. May and Peter helped her get through it, and the world still thinks that Sean is still missing. She has been recording every first of Kristine for Sean. Ashlee would hear the words coming out of Sean's mouth, and she would write a letter to him in response. She watches Sean every day. She falls asleep with the phone in her arms as she cries. She woke hearing him say, "Ashlee, I hope you are awake to hear this, but I had a dream last night. You are so beautiful, and you have found me. You are my knight and shining armor. I dream of the day that I get to see your beautiful face. You are what keeps me going. You are my beautiful wife, and I am holding you in my heart. I am guessing since I am still here you are doing what you need to do to keep me alive. I honor you for that, and I love you. If you have to kiss him, I understand you are doing it to keep me alive. There is a TV in here, and I saw where you had to go to the premiere without me. I love how you had a picture of me with you. I honor you for that." He has tears coming down his cheeks. Ashlee sees the love he has for her in his tears.

Josh has worked so hard on tracking the video feed. But he has not had any luck; and in between helping Ashlee with Kristine and sleep, he has been working nonstop on tracking the feed. At those times that Zach would pick up Ashlee from the house, he wanted to arrest the guy on the spot, but that will mean there will be no information on Sean. Zach is smart, and he will lawyer up before he would have a chance to talk to him. When Ashlee would return home, she was always as white as a ghost. The worry, frustration, and pain were written all over her face. Ashlee would add to the growing list of inappropriate things Zach would do to her. He would aggressively kiss her, touch her where he does not belong, and hit her when she said something wrong. Ashlee is strong, and she is fighting through this with everything she has because she loves Sean. Because she has been taking some self-defense classes with Josh as her teacher, she has fought Zach as well. When he would drop her off, Josh would see bruises and scratches on Zach. She is putting him in his place.

One afternoon, Josh is just looking at the video feed, and he is noticing Sean saying something. He turns up the volume, and he hears, "Ashlee, I hear the rain, and it reminds me of the day we met again. That was one of my best days. I will never forget that day. That is the day I fell in love with you. Your beauty, your smile, and the way you looked that day in the rain took my breath away. I will hold on to that memory for the rest of my life. I also think I figured out where I am." He is weak, and he is huddled in the corner. His voice is low. "I hear a train over there," and he points to his left. "I hear water over there," and he points to his right. "I think I am in the woods by the Brandywine River that meets the railroad crossing."

Josh pulls up locations where the river meets train tracks with buildings nearby. There are only three locations that fit that type of location. Josh's phone rings.

"Did you hear that?" is the first thing out of Ashlee's mouth.

"Yes, I did, and I have already found three locations."

"Can I come with you please?"

"Yes, but you will have to stay in the car."

"Okay. May and Peter are here now ready to watch Kristine. Can we go now?"

"Yes, I am on my way to get you." Josh hangs up and runs to his car.

Ten minutes later, he is at Ashlee's house, and Ashlee is out the door as soon as he pulls up. Ashlee's heart is pounding as she is focused on the phone in her hand. "Hang on, baby. We may have found you."

Moments later, which feels like a lifetime, Josh pulls up to the first location he found. Before Josh had a chance to stop the car, Ashlee is out the door, running up to the building. "Ashlee, stop. You are supposed to stay in the car. But I knew you were going to do this." Josh has a flashlight. It is ten at night, and there are no lights at all. It is cold, and a storm is threatening to dump water on them at any moment. Ashlee can't help but think of Sean's words about the rain as she runs around the building. It is old and falling apart. The roof is caving in, and it does not seem like anyone has been there in decades. "He is not here," Ashlee says with disappointment. "Next location please."

Josh and Ashlee get into the car and head to the second location. At the second location, it is just a skeleton of a building that was there. Ashlee is starting to panic. Josh pulls into the third and final location, and Ashlee spots a light on in a window. It seems like a single-story small dwelling. The building looks like it only has three small rooms in it. Ashlee jumps out of the car again. In a quiet voice, Josh calls after Ashlee, "Stop, Ashlee. Let me go first."

She does not stop, and she is in the door before he could stop her. Ashlee comes face-to-face with Zach, and she smiles. "I found you, and I have been wanting to do this to you after we were married." Ashlee takes all her strength, pain, and anger she has been saving, and she punches Zach dead in the face. He falls to the floor, knocked out cold. She steps over him and goes to the first of two doors. She opens it and sees it is a bathroom. Then she goes to the next door and sees it is locked. Again, she uses the same strength and kicks the door open. The room is dark, and she can't see a thing until the light from the room behind starts to flood in. There in the corner is a figure curled up. She runs to the corner, and her hands lands on his body. "Sean, it is me. I am here. Please be here with me." She has very little light, but she finds his chest. She stops long enough to feel if he is breathing. She feels his heart beating.

Then she feels him move. His hand meets hers, and in a whisper, she hears, "Ashlee."

Her heart is leaping and racing a hundred miles a minute. "Sean, you will be okay." Ashlee helps Sean to his feet. She leads Sean out to the lighted room, and she gets a better view of the condition he is in. He is still wearing the same clothes as he was wearing when he was taken. He has lost a lot of weight, and he is having trouble keeping his eyes open. He is so weak, but he holds on to Ashlee for dear life. He whispers again, "I am not letting go."

Josh had already handcuffed Zach, but he is in awe of Ashlee. She knocked him out in one punch, and she knocked down a door in one kick. Ashlee's love for Sean gave her the strength to fight. He thought to himself she would make a good cop. Josh is on the phone for an ambulance and Ashlee is holding Sean. Ashlee has tears running down her face. The ambulance pulls up, and Ashlee watches as Sean is loaded into the ambulance.

Then the monitors started to beep, and Ashlee is watching as the paramedics jump into action. "Clear!" They shock Sean and nothing. Ashlee is screaming, "Sean, please no! Don't leave me. Hold on to me." Ashlee hits the ground with uncontrollable sobs, their time together flashing before her eyes. They shocked him three more times, and they were about to call it when the heart monitor started to beat again. Ashlee heard, "We got him back. Let's move."

One of the paramedics looks at Ashlee and asks, "Do you want to ride along?"

"Yes, please." Ashlee hops into the ambulance and takes a seat by Sean's head. She is stroking his head, and whispering, "I love you, Sean. I am here with you. You are safe now. Kristine loves you also, and she misses her daddy." She places soft kisses on his forehead and continues to stroke his head.

It has been a couple of hours since they made it to the hospital. As the adrenaline wears off Ashlee, she realizes that her hand hurts, and it is swollen. She went to the nurses' station and asked if there was an available doctor to look at her hand. "Yes, I will send someone in as soon as I can." She had made the call to May and Peter to tell them the news. A couple of minutes later, a doctor came into the waiting room and looked at Ashlee's hand. He touched it, and she writhed in pain. "Oh, it is definitely broken. We have to take you up for an X-ray."

The doctor sets her hand and puts a cast on it. She has to keep it on for six weeks. Ashlee walks back into the waiting room and sees May, Peter, and Kristine. May looked at Ashlee and asked, "What happened to you?"

"I punched Zach so hard that I broke my hand and knocked him out."

"Nice job."

Ashlee holds up her hand and says, "This is well worth it."

The doctor finally comes in with the news on Sean. "He is out of the woods now, and he is stable. He is dehydrated and has not had any sustainable nutrients for eight months. He has head trauma and some internal bleeding. He is in and out of a coma right now. If you had not found him when you did, he would not be here with us now. You can go see him now."

Ashlee said, "Thank you, Doctor." Ashlee looks down at the sleeping baby in her arms. "Let's go see daddy." They all walk to Sean's room, and he is asleep. Ashlee walks over to Sean, and she kisses him on the forehead. He does not wake up. "Hi, baby, Kristine and I are here. You can wake up anytime you want." She places Kristine between his right arm and his body. She lays her head down on his chest and listens to his heartbeat. She starts to cry, and she just lets it all go. She lets go of the fear that she will lose Sean. She lets go of the eight months of being alone. She lets go of the pain that Zach put her through. She holds tight to Sean, and she can dream again of the life they are going to have. Her tears are coming in sheets, and they are making Sean's hospital gown wet.

Moments later, Ashlee feels a hand on her head, moving down onto her back and back up again and then down again. Ashlee looked up and saw the blueish-grayish eyes that she missed staring back at her. Her face lit up like a Christmas tree. With tears still running down her cheeks, she kissed Sean. "I thought I would never see you ever again."

Sean whispered, "I will never leave you unless we go together."

Those words hit Ashlee so tenderly that it made tears fall faster. She is falling in love with Sean all over again. Very slowly, Sean focused on the little girl to his right. With the last of his strength, he lifted her and placed a kiss on her forehead and placed her on his chest on her stomach with her head turned to the side. Kristine settled down and fell back to sleep. Sean watched with joy as his girls fell asleep on him. He is back where he wants to be, and he could not be happier.

A couple of weeks later, Sean, Ashlee, and Kristine were all home together. Sean is still recovering, and he is loving the time he has with his family. Sean gets a phone call from Max. "Sean, I have news for you and Ashlee. We have been nominated for best movie, best actor, best actress, best director, and best supporting actress and actor. Can you and Ashlee come for the award ceremony?"

"Yes, count us in."

"Oh, and yes we will have a babysitter for Kristine when we are at the award show. It will be my wife. She is willing to stay home to watch your little one. She misses having babies around the house. Our kids don't have kids of their own yet."

"Okay, thank you. We will take you up on the offer."

"Okay, we look forward to seeing Kristine. There will be a plane set up for you in two days. The award show will be this coming Sunday."

"Okay, we will see you soon." Sean hangs up and lets Ashlee know the news.

The Garisons are on their way to California, looking forward to being surrounded by people they only see on the screen. They are also going to surprise May and Peter with something. The minute they land at the airport, Ashlee sees May and Peter. She gets excited. She can't believe that her favorite actor and actress are their best friends. Ashlee immediately hugged May, and Peter helped Sean load their bags in the car. Sean, Ashlee, and Kristine are staying at May and Peter's place. Ashlee is filling in May on all that has happened since they last talked. "Zach is behind bars, and he was found guilty of all that he did. He keeps telling everyone that I was the one pursuing him, and he tried to plead insanity, but it did not work for him. He will be in there for the rest of his life. He also wants to fight for custody, but he can't. He is behind bars, and the lawyers just laugh at him. I made sure that he can't get his hands on Kristine."

They get settled into their room for the next week and put Kristine down for a nap. Ashlee and Sean met Peter and May in the living room of the gorgeous huge house. The house has seven bedrooms, and each bedroom has a bathroom. There is a billiards and game room downstairs. They even have an entertainment room with a movie theater. The kitchen is huge and great for entertaining. With the living room, dining room, and kitchen, it is an open concept. Whoever is in the kitchen would still feel a part of the activities in the living room.

"May and Peter, Sean and I were talking. We decided that we would be honored if you could be Kristine's godparents. You have been there for us through all our struggles, and we want to make you a part of this family."

May looks at Peter. They gave each other a nod, and Peter said, "We would be honored to be her godparents. Thank you so much for the honor. It means so much to us because we found out we can't have kids. It will be great to be able to treat Kristine as our own."

Ashlee also smiled and said, "Sean and I decided to move here also because we have another movie audition and another play deal coming up."

May let out a happy screech and hugged Ashlee. "We will be hanging out all the time now. I am so happy."

The night has come, and they drop Kristine off with Max's wife, Maggie. Her face lights up when she sees the little bundle. She takes her inside and smiles and waves as she goes. The limo with Sean, Ashlee, May, and Peter is making their way to the ceremony. The limo pulls up, and they hear the announcer, "Could this be one of the hottest couples on the big screen right now?" Sean steps out first, and the crowd erupts into cheer. Then Ashlee steps out, and the crowd goes louder. Then May and Peter step out. The crowd goes as wild as when Ashlee and Sean step out. They make their way hand in hand as they get stopped by entertainment news representatives. For Ashlee, it is an amazing feeling, but it is all overwhelming, and the only thing keeping her grounded is the hot guy standing next to her. Ashlee's face starts to turn red when she sees some of her favorite actors and actresses. May introduces Sean and Ashlee to some of them as they go in. They find their seats and settle in as the show is about to start.

The one thing Sean knows that Ashlee does not is that she is up for both supporting actress and best actress award for their movie. Sean gets to present the best actress award. The night goes on as they announce the different awards, such as best soundtrack, best foreign film, best sound effects, best set design, and best costumes. They also did best television show and talk show. The musical artists were amazing, and Ashlee got an idea. At one point, she leaned over to Sean and said, "We should do an album together."

Sean has the biggest grin on his face and says, "I was just thinking the same thing." Sean excused himself. "I will be right back. I have to use the restroom."

Ten minutes later, the host steps to the mic and says, "The next award is for best actress in a motion picture, and here to present are two costars of the movie *Best Friends* that was nominated tonight. Please welcome Sean and Peter."

They walked to the microphone with smiles, and Sean eyed Ashlee. She has the biggest smile of them all. Peter starts out serious and says, "It has been an adventure for you, Sean, this year."

"Yes, it has, and I just want to say thank you, Peter, for being there for my wife and me. I also want to thank my wife, Ashlee, for her unconditional love and her support through all this. I could not have asked for a better partner by my side than her."

"You are welcome, and anytime you need anything, let me know. Are you ready to announce the nominees?"

"Yes, let's do this." Peter starts out by announcing the first two names with May being one of them. Then Sean announces the last two names. For the fifth name, he looked directly at Ashlee and said, "And the last nominee is my beautiful wife, Ashlee Garison."

Ashlee's mouth dropped open, and then she looked at May. May was all smiles and shocked just like Ashlee. Peter opens the envelope and shows Sean. Sean lets out a loud yay. Both Peter and Sean say, "The winner is Ashlee Garison."

May stands up, but Ashlee is still sitting there, stunned. Ashlee finally stands up as May wraps her in a hug and says, "Congratulations, you deserve it." Ashlee made her way up to Sean and Peter. Sean takes her in his arms and twirls her around and then places her down by the microphone. "Wow, I never thought I would be here. I have always watched these shows and wondered how it felt to give one of these speeches. It feels intimidating. I want to say this is a surprise to me, thanks to my husband. He never told me about this." She looked over to Sean as she said it. He is beaming from ear to ear.

"Thank you to the love of my life for giving me this opportunity to act by his side. If it was not for you insisting that I audition, I would not be here. I honor the laundromat that I was standing in when he came in from the rain. I also thank all that is in my life and made this happen." She holds up her award and walks away from the mic and into Sean's arms.

The backstage manager went to Ashlee as they made their way. "Ashlee, the presenter who was supposed to present with May left on an emergency. Can you fill in for her please?"

May turned to Ashlee after reading the look on Ashlee's face and said, "You can do this, and I will be by your side the whole time."

"Okay, I will do it."

The manager hands Ashlee the script, and she sees the award is for best actor. She reads the names on it, and her face lights up when she sees Sean's name and Peter's name on the list. The host comes back to the stage and announces the next category, and it is for supporting roles of a motion picture. The host reads off the names of the female supporting-role nominees. Ashlee heard her name and May's name. "And the winner is May for her role in the movie *Best Friends*."

May walks out and accepts her award. She thanks Ashlee and Sean as well as the rest of the crew and cast members.

The host steps up to the microphone again and presents the award for best supporting role of an actor in a motion picture. "And the winner is Peter for his role in *Best Friends*."

Peter walks onstage to accept his award. He thanks the people that May forgot. "I thank the Garisons for making me a proud godfather." Cheers were going wild when he said that. He walks backstage and hugs both Sean and Ashlee.

The host steps back to the microphone and says, "Tonight is turning out to be a *Best Friends* night, and there are three more awards that they have been nominated for. This next award is for best actor in a motion picture. Please welcome to the stage two winners already, May and Ashlee."

They made their way to the microphone. May started her lines, "Ashlee, do you see who is on this list? Two of the hottest men are on this list."

"Which ones are you talking about, May? I think all of them are hot."

They both laughed, and May announced the first three men. Then Ashlee announces Peter and Sean as one of the nominees. Ashlee opens the envelope. Ashlee smiles and says, "The winner is the hottest of them all, my husband, Sean Garison."

When Sean walked to the microphone, he had tears in his eyes. "Wow, I am blown away. This is my first-ever award, and I am honored to hear my wife say my name for this award. Today means so much to me because if it was not for my wife, I would not be here with you today. She had to sacrifice her comfort and freedom to keep me alive. This is for you, my love. Thank you to all of you who helped make this movie possible. Peter and May, thank you for welcoming us with open arms." He turned around and kissed Ashlee and went backstage.

The movie went on to win for best director and best movie of the year. Ashlee and Sean go back to May and Peter's, feeling overwhelmed. Ashlee curls up next too Sean in the limo and falls asleep. Sean carries his sleeping wife up the steps and into the house. He changes her into her PJs and watches her sleep before he goes to sleep himself. The next morning, Sean wakes up to sweet eyes looking at him and frisky fingers. They are tantalizing his body, and he has no choice but allow onslaught. He repays the wonderful torture with some of his own. It was a very long time since they were able to give themselves to each other, and finally, they lose themselves in each other. Sean will never take anything for granted. He knows that he could lose this anytime. He will live life and make sure that his family knows that he loves them. That fateful day, he is forever grateful for that car breaking down. He would not have reconnected with Ashlee. It is so beautiful, and he could live like this forever.

EPILOGUE

Nine months later, it is Christmas Day, and Ashlee is in labor with their second child. She has been in labor for ten hours already. She is exhausted, but she can't wait to see her child. "Are you ready to push?"

"Yes, please!"

Sean is holding on to her hand. He knows she is tired. He gives her all his strength and helps her push. When she sits up, he puts a hand on her back and supports her. She pushes three more times, and out comes a beautiful daughter. Sean's eyes light up the minute he lays eyes on her. He now has two beautiful daughters. Ashlee looks up at him and says, "You can name her as well. If we have a son, I will name him."

Sean walks over to his daughter and looks down at her as they clean her off. He comes up with the name of Rebecca Rose. They place her in his arms, and he instantly melts. "Hello, Rebecca Rose, you are so beautiful. Come on, let's go meet your mom." Sean carries her over and places her in her mom's arms.

Ashlee and Sean were moved to a new room. Peter, May, and Kristine joined them. Kristine's face lit up when she saw her sister for the first time. At one and a half years old, Kristine is a happy bundle of energy. Sean places Kristine in the bed with Ashlee and Rebecca. Ashlee takes one arm and drapes it around Kristine, and she changes the position of Rebecca to where it looks like Kristine is holding Rebecca. Just the sight of Sean's three girls together is enough to swell a heart to three more sizes. His family feels even more complete now. He is feeling blessed, and this is the best Christmas ever.

It's been four months, and the family is adjusting to their new life in California. Ashlee and Sean are almost done with their first album. They will start their play in a couple of weeks. May and Peter got a little surprise that they aren't expecting. They are expecting their first child, and they made Sean and Ashlee the child's godparents. This is an amazing life. Ashlee dreamed of this life back in the laundromat. Because of Sean, it came true. If he had not walked into that laundromat at that moment, she would not have had the life she has now. She knew her other half was out there, and he found her. His other half is her.

Author Thanks

First of I thank God for giving me the gift of writing and allowing me to share it. I thank my husband, family, and friends for inspiration to keep going. I thank my niece Summer and her boyfriend James for agreeing to be the face of the book. I thank Tara for giving us awesome pictures. Then I thank Xlibris for making it a reality.